Sue Margolis was born into a Jewish family in Ilford, Essex. She studied politics at Nottingham University, and while a student married Jonathan Margolis, now a journalist and biographer. Their first two children were born in Yorkshire, where she also started her career as a BBC radio journalist. Sue and her family later moved to west London and, along with having a third child, she specialised in making off-beat items for Radio 4's WOMAN'S HOUR.

Sue Margolis's first novel, NEUROTICA, is also available from Headline.

Praise for Sue Margolis:

'A tremendously funny, colourful and gripping read'
Mail on Sunday

'I almost had to read this book with my eyes shut, it's so naughty . . . but so nice' *Jenni Murray*, WOMAN'S HOUR, Radio 4

'Lots of uninhibited sex, some joyous slapstick and a pleasing tally of one-liners' *Good Housekeeping*

'A saucy romp' *Independent*

'Light, frothy and fun' *Bookseller*

'Hilarious . . . great fun' *Jewish Chronicle*

'Its humour is irresistible' *Jewish Telegraph*

Also by Sue Margolis

Neurotica

Sisteria

SUE MARGOLIS

HEADLINE

First published in 1999
by HEADLINE BOOK PUBLISHING

First published in paperback in 2000
by HEADLINE BOOK PUBLISHING

10 9 8 7 6 5 4 3 2 1

ISBN 0 7472 5774 4

Typeset by
Letterpart Limited, Reigate, Surrey

Printed and bound in Great Britain by
Mackays of Chatham PLC, Chatham, Kent

HEADLINE BOOK PUBLISHING
A division of the Hodder Headline Group
338 Euston Road
London NW1 3BH
www.headline.co.uk
www.hodderheadline.com

For my children, who have brought me untold joy.
Particularly since they started leaving home.

Chapter 1

Artex, Beverley Littlestone had to admit, was a bugger. If a time came when they could afford to redecorate the bedroom, then those short, spiky stalactites hanging from the ceiling would definitely need going over with an electric sander. Or maybe it was possible to plaster over it. Alternatively they could leave the Artex alone and get a quote for a false ceiling, which could hang a few inches below the original. Might be cheaper and less messy in the long run.

Usually as Beverley lay on her back, gazing heavenwards while Melvin was humping and grinding on top of her, the Artex question would keep her occupied for the full two or three minutes it took him to come. Their sexual encounter this month was, however, taking him a minute or two longer than usual. As a result Beverley, having exhausted all the options bedroom-ceiling-wise, found herself contemplating in her mind's eye a map of the British Isles in an attempt to work out which was further west, Liverpool or Bristol. It was a quiz show question she'd heard on the radio the previous afternoon. She'd missed hearing the answer because the phone rang just as the contestant was about to reply.

Bound to be a trick question, Beverley thought, thrusting her pelvis and offering Melvin a perfunctory, but she hoped encouraging, moan. Bristol was in the West Country, virtually Devon. Most people would be bound to think it was further west than Liverpool. In which case the answer had to be Liverpool. Hadn't she read somewhere that the whole of the country tilted slightly to the left, so many places in the north were actually west of the West Country? She dug her nails into Melvin's back and thrashed her head from side to side. Unless of course it was a double bluff and the answer really was Bristol. There was nothing for it. Once she was up and dressed she'd go out to the car and check the answer in the road atlas. She was vaguely aware that Melvin's breathing had become faster and his grinding more urgent. A few more seconds and he'd be done.

It was only as he lay hot and breathless on top of her, his head buried in her breasts, that a thought, by no means unconnected with the Bristol/Liverpool conundrum, struck her.

'Oh my God.' The words left her lips before she had a chance to stop them.

'What?' Melvin asked groggily, lifting his face towards her.

'No, no. It's nothing. Really.' She was biting her bottom lip to stop herself laughing. This was one joke she daren't share with him. It would be far too hurtful. It would destroy his confidence utterly.

No, she just couldn't. It was inconceivable that she

should tell her husband that, while he had been engaged in what he liked to think of as lovemaking, she had, quite literally, been lying back and thinking of England.

'It's not me then?' Melvin asked, looking distinctly as if he didn't want to know the answer. 'Look, I know you haven't had your turn. But you know how long you take and I've got to get to work.'

'It's OK, Mel,' she said, 'I'm not angry. Honest.' Beverley had come to terms with their indifferent shagging years ago. She simply accepted that sex with Melvin was a bit like shopping at Kwiksave. Not much to get excited about, but better than nothing.

'No,' she went on, still desperately searching for something to say which would explain the Oh my God. 'It wasn't that. It's just that . . . I . . . Melvin, do you think I'm fat?'

'Christ. Not this one again,' he said, groaning and rolling off her. 'Haven't I got enough on my mind without having to cope with you constantly going on about your weight?'

'I know. I'm sorry. I just get a bit insecure, that's all.'

'Look,' he said, gently now, 'I've told you before. You're not fat. You're just . . .'

'I know. I'm just short for my weight. By rights I should measure eight foot three. Ha blinkin' ha.' She sat up, pulled a pillow from behind her back and whacked him not altogether playfully on the side of his arm.

'C'mon, Bev,' he said, ignoring the pillow and swinging his feet on to the carpet. 'You're forty-two. So, you're carrying a couple of extra pounds . . . Aren't we all?' He prodded one of his own fleshy breasts. 'Look, I

3

haven't got time for this now. I've got to get in the shower. Go on a diet if it bothers you that much.'

'But I do diet. I diet all the time. You know I do. Then my willpower flags and I start eating again. I've lost the same half-stone so many times my cellulite's got *déjà vu*. I tell you, Mel, I don't need a diet. What I need is a tape worm.'

As Beverley plodded down the stairs in her dressing gown, she couldn't help wishing that instead of belittling her anxiety about her weight, Melvin had, just for once, taken her in his arms and told her she was still as beautiful as the day they met and shouldn't even think of going on a diet. Naturally it wouldn't have made any difference to the way she felt about herself. In her mind she didn't see a pretty, exceedingly well-preserved forty-two-year-old who had simply put on a few pounds since having children. She saw a blubbery lump who one day not long from now would step on the scales and they would read: 'To be continued.'

As she walked down the hall towards the kitchen, she decided to weigh herself. It had been a couple of days since she'd got on the scales. Then she'd been ten stone one. There was always the possibility that the two Danish pastries she'd eaten the night before had hood-winked her digestive system by slipping through disguised as a pair of broccoli florets and that she'd dropped a couple of pounds.

'Yeah, right,' she said with a self-mocking half-laugh.

She found the bathroom scales in their usual place in the bottom right-hand corner of the chest freezer, hidden

4

under a jumbo bag of Iceland mini pizzas and a box of vol-au-vent cases dating back to 1995.

She kept them hidden because she was determined that her skinny, permanently-on-a-diet seventeen-year-old daughter shouldn't develop a full-blown eating disorder by discovering she had a mother who was equally obsessed by her weight.

She placed the scales on the floor and took off her dressing gown and slippers. Standing naked in the middle of her kitchen, she put one foot on the scales and winced as she registered the cold on her skin. Gingerly, she placed the other foot next to its partner. Anything under ten stone would be acceptable. An ounce over would have her seeking solace in doorstep slices of white bread and jam.

She dared to look down. Ten stone three. Ten bloody three. Panic surged through her. She was quite clearly turning into her elderly Aunty Dolly from Bournemouth, who had great fleshy underarms and a knee-length stomach. Beverley was putting on her dressing gown and imagining going into M&S and one of the nice lady assistants saying, 'And what size knickers does madam usually take? Large, extra large or Suffolk?' when she heard the sound of letters dropping on to the mat. Resolving to start a new diet that very day, she put the scales back in the deep freeze, under the pizzas and vol-au-vent cases, and flip-flopped into the hall.

It was the hand-written address on one of them, as well as the envelope being of good quality and white, not bill-brown, which caught her eye. Beverley was convinced that while the rest of Jewish north-west London received nothing but a daily trickle of dinner party thank-you notes, invitations and the occasional presentation of polite, embossed compliments from Harley Street consultants, she and Melvin were the only couple whose post was made up almost entirely of final demands, warnings and threats of imminent distraint.

Due to Melvin's lack of anything approaching business sense, the Littlestones had been hard up throughout their twenty-year marriage. The only time they made ends meet was once a month when they had sex. Unlike her husband, who lived in perpetual and abject fear of what he always referred to as the 'hate mail', Beverley was able to open bills, even red ones, without descending into a full-scale panic. She'd learned over the years that the receipt of a final demand meant they had several weeks' grace before the electricity people or whoever would 'terminate' their supply. Letters from the water company she even managed to ignore completely. What would they do if they carried out one of their six-monthly threats to sue them and cut them off from water *and* sewerage? Would they send the Littlestones' waste products back up round the U-bend in final settlement? Even the final final demands – for which the creditor always abandoned red print and went back to the cold fury of black – had stopped causing her the anxiety they once did. This was largely because she knew from experience that no matter how close to financial ruin they had come over the last two decades, there had never been a time when Melvin hadn't managed to deliver them from the brink at the last moment by pulling off some heroic act of robbing Visa to pay Mastercard.

Beverley had no desire to be hugely rich. Like most

people, she knew money didn't bring happiness. It was just that given the choice she would rather have been miserable *and* owned a dishwasher that worked, not to mention a few new bras. Most of hers had lost their underwires years ago and were offering her about as much support as Andrea Dworkin at the Miss World contest. Not that she allowed herself to get miserable. As she wandered round the supermarket, rummaging through the cut-price bins full of unwanted tins of water chestnuts and pilchards, she would always remind herself that she had her health and two beautiful, intelligent children, and that life could be so much worse. She'd even managed to save a couple of quid every month out of her housekeeping and put it in a building society. It was her rainy-day fund. Even now it didn't amount to very much. A slight drizzle would have wiped it out.

Beverley couldn't remember the last time she'd received a real letter. Her delight was almost childlike. Ignoring the bills for once and deciding to leave them on the mat for Melvin, she bent down and picked up the white envelope. She instantly recognised the handwriting.

'Good Lord,' she gasped, her excitement turning to mild shock. As she stood staring at the upward-slanting loops and swirls, she could feel her heart starting to pound with delight – but simultaneously with the unpleasant memories of five years ago. For a second, she even thought about binning the letter there and then. But curiosity soon got the better of her. After a moment's hesitation, she ripped into the envelope and unfolded the smooth, expensive paper.

★ ★ ★

Perched on one of the high kitchen stools, Beverley took a mouthful of tea and began reading the short letter for the third time. She was so engrossed that she failed to hear the quick, angry thud from the front hall of platforms on stair carpet. The thuds grew louder and finally turned into a hard, clacking sound as Natalie Littlestone's leopardskin suede boots, new from Shelly's the previous weekend, and paid for with her baby-sitting money, made contact with the ceramic kitchen tiles. The clacking was accompanied by a short burst of the hysterical shrieking Beverley had now come to accept as her daughter's sole means of communication.

'Omigod, my life is so fucking pants.' Natalie, for whom the letters PMT stood for Permanent Menstrual Tension, stomped over to the fridge, yanked open the door and then let go of the handle so that the door swung back violently on its hinges.

Beverley didn't look up from the letter.

'You break that fridge door, Natalie,' she said with studied calmness, 'and you pay for it.'

'See, you don't care about me,' Natalie wailed at full volume. 'Your daughter's life is fucking pants and you don't give a toss. You can't even be arsed to look at me.' She took the two-litre plastic bottle of milk from the fridge and slammed the door shut. 'I could have cancer and you still wouldn't care.'

Beverley tugged her dressing gown, which had started to gape slightly, across her knees and then drained her mug of tea.

'At least if you got cancer,' she said, putting down the

8

mug and turning towards her daughter, 'you wouldn't have the strength to break the fridge.'

'That's it, you hate me, don't you?' Natalie howled as she opened the bottle and brought it crashing down on to the worktop so that milk came shooting out of the top. 'Bloody hell, what kind of mother wishes cancer on her daughter?'

'Natalie, why is it that every other word which comes out of your and your brother's mouth is a swear word?'

It was a rhetorical question. Beverley knew only too well that her children's school was to blame for their constant bad language. She and Melvin couldn't begin to afford private school fees, and Melvin had refused to let them go to the Jewish Free School because although he liked the Free bit, he always felt the Jewish bit was somehow too, well, *Jewish.* So Natalie and Benny had ended up travelling from Finchley to Muswell Hill each day to a comprehensive which prided itself on a third of the kids coming from middle-class backgrounds, while conveniently glossing over the fact that two thirds didn't.

'Stop trying to change the subject,' Natalie said. 'C'mon, tell me . . . What kind of a mother wishes cancer on her daughter?'

Beverley let out a long sigh. 'For heaven's sake, Natalie,' she said, watching her daughter sploshing milk over a minute portion of Coco Pops, 'I do not hate you, and nor do I wish you to get cancer. I don't know how you could even suggest such a thing. Come on, sweetheart, I'll scramble you a couple of eggs. What you've got there won't keep you going till lunchtime.' As she spoke, she folded the single sheet of notepaper into four and slipped it underneath the wooden pepper grinder.

'It's OK, Mum. Just leave it, will you,' Natalie snapped. 'Cereal's fine.'

Beverley looked at her daughter and shrugged.

'OK,' she said, 'turn into an anorexic. See if I care.' She paused before changing emotional tack.

'Come on, Nat,' she said warmly, 'talk to me. What's happened now? When is your life not "pants"?'

Natalie didn't reply. Instead, she rammed a single spoonful of Coco Pops into her mouth, so that Beverley caught a glimpse of her shiny silver tongue stud, and grimaced.

'Please, darling, don't go all silent on me.' Beverley got off the stool, went over to her daughter and put an arm round her. She expected Natalie to push her away, but she didn't.

'I can't believe you haven't noticed,' she said miserably. 'Just look at my nose.'

Natalie had her maternal grandfather Lionel's sizeable, though by no means record-breaking, hooter. Somehow the Gold family nose had skipped a generation. Beverley had escaped it, but Natalie had inherited an instrument which was long and broad, with an ever-so-slightly bulbous end that drooped towards her top lip. With her mother's olive skin, long dark hair and huge brown eyes she had the look of an exquisite Old Testament heroine about her. Beverley and Melvin had spent many hours trying to convince their daughter that she was beautiful. Each time they thought her self-confidence was improving, some revolting toe-rag at school would destroy it by ripping the piss with a remark like 'Oh, miss, why don't you ask Natalie Littlestone that question. She always NOSE.'

Today, in order to compound Natalie's usual agony, her nose had sprouted on the side of one nostril a large angry red hillock which was about to evolve into a spot, but hadn't yet developed a head.

Beverley squinted at the spot. She was determined to play it down. The faintest acknowledgement that Natalie's nose had spawned an embryonic super-zit would guarantee that she skipped school and spent the day locked in her squalid, dirty-knicker-strewn bedroom consoling herself by playing her Verve CD at full volume.

'Natalie, for heaven's sake,' she said, 'it's just a pimple. You can hardly see it.'

'Where from? Fiji?'

Ignoring her daughter's sarcasm, Beverley picked up Natalie's half-finished bowl of cereal and took it over to the sink.

'Just put some TCP on it,' she soothed, 'and then cover it with some of my concealer. There's a tube in my make-up bag in the bathroom. It'll probably go down by tomorrow. Now then . . .' she continued as she picked up two foil parcels, 'I've given you a couple of tuna fish bagels for your school lunch, and there's a piece of Grandma's cheesecake for afterwards . . .'

'My God,' Natalie said between sobs, 'you don't get it, do you? You just don't get it. I have a throbbing boil the size of Brent Cross on my already hideously deformed nose which the entire school makes fun of, and your

11

solution isn't sympathy and the offer of a consultation with a plastic surgeon . . . no, it's blinkin' tuna fish bagels and cheesecake. Mum, when are you going to get real and stop behaving like some nineteenth-century Ukrainian Jewish peasant? Grandma's lived with us for five years and in all that time I've never seen her fuss like you.'

Beverley said nothing. It was true. But Natalie was clearly in no mood to be reminded that despite her grandmother's celebrated lack of interest in fussing and *kvetching*, she served up ample aggravation in other ways. Hardly a day went by when Queenie didn't let Beverley know how much money the husband of some old school friend or other was rumoured to be making selling software (which she assumed meant he travelled in duvets, pillows and cushions) and how much better Beverley could have done for herself than to marry Melvin.

By now Natalie had clacked off towards the door, only to collide with her father, who was on his way into the kitchen fully dressed apart from one bare foot. He was carrying a handful of socks.

Without saying a word, she barged past him.

'Morning, sweetness,' he said with good-natured sarcasm. He turned towards Beverley. 'Blimey, what's got into *her*?'

'Don't make fun, Melvin. It's serious,' Beverley explained, putting the foil parcels in the fridge. 'She's got a slight spot on the side of her nose. Honestly, her mood swings are getting intolerable. You're a pharmacist. Couldn't you bribe some bent doctor to take her ovaries out one night while she's asleep?'

'You wish,' he chuckled.

'Listen,' Beverley said, 'did you give Benny a shout?'

At some stage, which she found impossible to pinpoint precisely, their son had turned from a boisterous, eager little boy who was always up and ready for school each morning by seven thirty, to a lolloping, grunting nearly-sixteen-year-old who could sleep through the after-effects of a six-mile-wide meteorite landing next door.

'No, I didn't. For the simple reason that I've been too busy trying to sort this lot out.' He sounded fraught now as he brandished the socks at Beverley. 'Do you mind telling me why I have just found nine odd socks in my drawer? I mean, what happens in this house? Is there some sock pervert who gets a thrill from going round separating them from their partners? I tell you, Beverley, if you are incapable of managing the laundry, I'll have to take it over.'

'Melvin, I know I'm not a pretty sight in the morning, but has something Kafkaesque happened to me since we made love ten minutes ago? Have I turned into a punch ball?'

'I'm sorry, Bev, but it's just that this bloody fucking sock thing drives me insane. I mean, where *do* they go? I would just love to have the time to write a thesis on this disappearing sock conundrum.'

'Try the tumble dryer,' she said, smiling to let him know his apology had been accepted.

While Melvin pulled the entire tumble dryer contents out on to the floor and began rummaging irritably through the pile, Beverley went over to the breakfast bar and took the letter from under the pepper pot.

'By the way, this came in the post,' she said, holding the folded paper towards him.

Melvin, who was by now lining up socks along the kitchen worktop while muttering to himself about having discovered a warp in the space-time continuum into which all the world's single socks were disappearing and being teleported to the constellation Ursa Major, suddenly looked at her and turned white.

'For Chrissake, Beverley,' he pleaded irritably, 'don't ever *this* me. I don't need to be tortured with *thises*. Be specific. Who's it from? The bank? The building society? Barclaycard? Don't just stand there . . . I need to know. How much do they want?'

'Melvin, it's not a bill. Here, read it.'

Melvin was just about to snatch the letter from her when the mobile phone in his jacket pocket started ringing.

'For crying out loud. What now?' Furious, he pulled up the aerial and stabbed one of the buttons. Almost at once he raised his eyes heavenwards. It was several seconds before he got the chance to contribute more than half a sentence to the one-sided conversation.

'Alma, I know . . . Alma, please . . . please will you listen to me? I know it was very good of you to come into the shop at six o'clock this morning and start the stock-taking . . . Of course I understand how shocked a woman of your age must have been . . . No, I would not like to feel a rat brush past my ankles. It must have been horrible.' Putting the phone between his chin and shoulder, Melvin triumphantly picked up a navy ribbed sock which more or less matched the one he was wearing, and lifted his right foot. 'OK, Alma, so now you know it was only one of the toupees which had fallen off the stockroom shelf, go and make yourself a nice cup of sweet tea . . .'

Melvin was beginning to sway as he stood on one leg trying to pull on his sock. In order to stop himself falling over, he started hopping on the spot. 'OK, OK, Alma, listen. If you really think you're having angina pains, dial 999. But remember the last three times you went to casualty with a suspected heart attack, they told you it was your crumpets lying a bit heavy.'

Melvin pushed down the aerial and shoved the phone into his jacket pocket. Then, leaning against one of the kitchen cupboards, he finished putting on his sock.

Realising there were now more important matters to address than the letter, Beverley put it back under the pepper grinder and stared at her husband in disbelief.

'Toupees? You are flogging *toupees* now? Since when did a chemist's shop sell toupees? I don't get it, Melvin. There must be something I'm missing. What's wrong with toothpaste and panty liners?'

'Look, I was going to tell you,' he said, absentmindedly putting a maroon sock over a navy one so that he was now wearing two socks on one foot. 'I was reading in *The Sunday Times* Style section a few weeks ago that toupees have really taken off in New York. I just know it will only be a matter of time before they start to catch on here too. I think by getting in on the ground floor of a trend, we could be sitting on a gold mine. I mean it, this could be the end of all our money worries. I don't know how I did it, but I managed to convince old McGillicuddy at the bank to extend the overdraft on the business account by a few grand. Said I could keep it going for six months if I wanted. So now I've got ten gross best-quality micro-fibre Korean toupees in the stock-room waiting to go. I thought I'd start by seeing how they do in the shop, and if – I mean when – they take off, I'll start flogging them by mail order. They're the future, Beverley. I just know it.'

'OK, so when you say a few grand,' she said, trying to sound casual, 'what are we talking? Two? Three?'

'Five,' he blurted.

'Five,' she gasped. 'But Mel, you already owe nearly fifteen. I hope to God you know what you're doing. Sweetheart, please don't take this the wrong way, but your track record isn't exactly . . .'

'Shh,' he said, gently placing a finger over her lips and smiling. 'Trust me. It's in the bag. A few months from now everything's gonna be peachy, Bev. Absolutely peachy.'

With that he gave a decidedly doubtful Beverley a peck on the cheek and was gone. Seconds later she heard the front door slam. A few seconds after that, she heard it open again.

'Forgot my shoes,' Melvin called from the hall. She heard him charge upstairs, charge down again and leave the house for the second time.

As Beverley sat herself back down at the breakfast bar, she listened to the car pulling off the drive and shook her heard. 'Toupees,' she said out loud. 'So now it's toupees.' On the other hand, what did she know? Maybe for once in his life Melvin *had* hit on something –

found not so much a gap in the market as a bald patch.
Certainly Mr McGillicuddy thought so.

'These were on the mat. More of the usual, I see.'
Beverley looked up to see her mother coming into the
kitchen. Queenie Gold was an inch or two shorter than
she'd been in her prime and limped slightly as a result of
an only partially successful hip replacement operation.
But people meeting her for the first time were never in
any doubt that looks-wise she'd most definitely had a
prime. Even in her mid seventies she possessed a
smooth, milky complexion, and her pretty almond-
shaped eyes, which Beverley and Natalie had inherited,
were, despite their fleshy hoods, still a brilliant blue.

Queenie took the hate mail from the pocket of her
long sleeveless cardigan and handed it to her daughter.
Beverley said nothing. Clearly Melvin had either failed
to notice them on his way out or had taken fright and
ignored them on purpose. She'd open them later when
her mother wasn't looking over her shoulder.

'So,' Beverley said in an effort to deflect the lecture
she knew was coming, 'how's your hip this morning?'

'Fine. It's not my hip I'm worried about. It's you and
Melvin.' Queenie heaved herself on to the stool next to
Beverley.

'Oh, God. Here we go again,' Beverley said under her
breath. She reached across the worktop for last night's
Evening Standard and pretended to read it.

'Of course, even twenty years ago I knew Melvin
would never amount to anything,' Queenie continued,
while Beverley mouthed her mother's words from

17

inside the newspaper. 'I'll never forget the day the pair of you got married. When I saw Melvin turn up at the synagogue in jeans and that tie-dyed grandad vest covered in CND badges, I wept from the humiliation of it all. Then there was the honeymoon. You couldn't go to the Canaries like all the other young marrieds – no, my son-in-law the hippy decides you have to go on a tour of all the Cruise missile bases in Europe. I tell you, Beverley, that night you ended up in prison in Germany, I turned to your father and said, "Lionel, that boy will never amount to anything." A year later poor Daddy was dead. I tell you, Beverley, he died of a broken heart.'

'Mum,' Beverley said from behind the newspaper, 'he died because he was run over in Cranbrook Road by a 144 bus.'

'Only because you were giving him so much aggravation that it had started to interfere with his concentration . . . I don't know, Beverley, why couldn't you have married a rich doctor? Donatella Greenberg – you remember, the one in your class at school with the gums – she married a rich doctor.'

'What are you talking about? Donatella Greenberg went to Sierra Leone fifteen years ago and married a *witch*doctor.'

'Believe me, even from witchdoctoring he's making a better living than Melvin.'

At that moment Natalie came charging back into the kitchen, her school bag slung over one shoulder. Beverley put down the newspaper.

'Mum, I'm dead, dead late,' she said, ignoring her

grandmother and hopping agitatedly from one plat-formed foot to the other like a three-year-old desperate for a wee. 'Please tell me this looks OK. Do you think anyone'll notice the zit?'

Beverley looked at Natalie's face. It was covered in a thick layer of pinky-orange concealer.

'It's fine. You can't see a thing. Promise . . . By the way, Nat, you did GCSE geography. Which is further west, Bristol or Liverpool?'

'Mum, what are you going on about? I mean, like I care. Will you stop changing the subject? Now tell me honestly. Does my nose look gross? Yes or no?'

'How many more times? I've told you, it's absolutely fine. The only thing about you which looks gross is that bloody stud you've got in your tongue. Believe me, nobody will notice the zit.'

'Liverpool's further west,' Queenie broke in. Beverley turned to look at her mother.

'Don't look so surprised. I heard it on the radio yesterday on the way back from the day centre. The minibus driver was listening to some quiz show or other.'

'Ah, so it *is* a trick question, then?'

'Seems like it,' Queenie said. 'All went way over my head, I'm afraid, but apparently the entire country tilts or something.'

'I knew it. I remember reading somewhere about . . .'

'OK, fine,' Natalie said, smiling with faux jauntiness. 'Don't mind me. My emotional needs clearly come second to your interest in cartography.'

With that, Natalie flounced out.

'Listen to me, Bev,' Queenie said. 'You have to do something about that child. She's too thin. What does she look like? A nose on a string.'

'Good God, Mum, don't you ever tell *her* that.'

'As if I'd do such a thing,' Queenie said, her voice full of indignation. 'You know me, I'm the epitome of tact . . .'

'Yeah,' Beverley chuckled, gently patting the top of her mother's hand, 'the absolute epitome.' She pronounced it *epi-tome* as her mother just had.

'Right,' Queenie said, 'I suppose I'd better go upstairs and put a face on before the minibus gets here. What time is it?'

'Just after half eight.'

As the words left Beverley's lips, she suddenly remembered Benny.

'Good God, that boy must still be asleep.'

'Stay where you are,' Queenie said. 'I'll give him a shout.'

Beverley smiled gratefully at her mother and helped her off the stool.

'You know,' Queenie said, 'about the money thing – I've told you before, if things get really bad there's the money from when I sold the house just sitting in the building society doing nothing. I can always lend you a couple of thousand to tide you over.'

'That's really kind of you,' Beverley said gently, 'and don't think I'm not grateful for the offer, but we need more than just a couple of thousand, and even if I could persuade Melvin to swallow his daft pride and accept a loan from his elderly mother-in-law, I just don't know when we'd be able to pay it back . . . if we'd ever be able to pay it back.'

'Well, it's there if you need it . . .'

'OK. And Mum . . . thanks.'

Queenie nodded.

Once her mother had gone, Beverley straightened her back and began rubbing her neck. As she dug her fingers into her sore, knotted muscles, she turned her head slowly from side to side. Feeling the tension beginning to ease, she took the folded letter from under the pepper grinder and stared at it.

Naomi, her younger and only sister whom she hadn't seen or spoken to since their huge bust-up five years ago, was suddenly full of apologies and begging to see her. It seemed almost inconceivable to Beverley that Naomi, who as far as she knew had never apologised for anything – even as a child – could have changed so much. But five years was a long time. Naomi was now in her late thirties. Perhaps she'd started to mellow, decided that life was too short for feuds and genuinely wanted to patch things up. If, on the other hand, Naomi being Naomi had some selfish ulterior motive for getting in touch, she'd discover it soon enough. In the mean time, what possible harm could there be in a phone call?

Chapter 2

Naomi Gold winced as she felt the involuntary tightening of her rectal muscles round the plastic tubing. A few moments later came the not unpleasant sensation of warm water coursing through her large intestine. As the water level rose up to her navel, the pressure inside her gut increased to something close to pain. She speculated as ever whether the stainless-steel contraption beside the couch looked more like a piece of kidney dialysis apparatus or a knitting machine.

As she lay watching the first dozen or so golden nuggets of her colonic irrigate float through a clear, corrugated pipe, Summer, her San Franciscan colonic irrigator, began massaging Naomi's abdomen through the blue cotton surgical gown.

'That's real good, Naomi, just relax . . . excellent.' Summer's voice was calm and soothing. She pressed the heel of her palm down harder on Naomi's stomach and began rubbing in a circular motion.

'Ow, that fucking hurts,' Naomi said, sucking in a sharp breath through pursed lips.

'I know. Just hold on in there for a few more

moments. You have no idea how much putrefaction and stagnant build-up I can feel.'

As Summer continued her pressing and rubbing, Naomi heard the tinkle of her silver bangles. After a few moments, Summer looked up and turned her thicket of henna-ed corkscrew curls so that she was facing the corrugated pipe.

'I tell you, Naomi,' she said, her finger following the progress of one particular piece of irrigate, 'unless you start laying off caffeine and all the processed crap you put into your body, and start replacing it with whole-grains and organic produce, you are going to see this stuff really build up inside you. One autopsy report I read recently talked about a colon that was so loaded with mucoid faecal matter that it weighed forty pounds. Forty pounds, I ask you. Can you believe that?'

'That is amazing. Truly amazing,' Naomi gasped, feigning astonishment purely for the sake of politeness. In fact, Naomi had about as much interest in bowels, healthy or otherwise, as she did in anchovy futures and only ever came for a colonic when, like today, she needed to drop a few pounds fast. This evening she was due at a telly-showbiz charity do at the Lanesborough and at eight o'clock this morning her black silk size eight Rifat Ozbek had refused to do up round the middle.

'So tell me, Naomi,' Summer continued, 'how long would you say it takes you to complete a bowel move-ment? And how would you describe the smell? Would you say it's pretty much odourless, or more putrefied cooked meat with a kinda lemony top note?'

'No,' Naomi shot back, 'I'd say it's more blackcurrant and gooseberry with an understated yet well-rounded woody edge.'

Summer nodded seriously, picked up Naomi's notes, which were attached to a clipboard, and began writing.

Naomi watched Summer's earnest scribbling and couldn't help smiling as she wondered why it was that all Americans seemed to lack the gene which made human beings capable of appreciating sarcasm.

Her deliberations lasted no more than a few seconds. They were disturbed, first, by the sensation of much cooler water suddenly entering her bowel, and then by the muffled ringing of her mobile.

'Summer, be an angel, darling,' she said, 'and pass me the phone from my briefcase. I don't think I'm in quite the right position to reach down.'

Summer made no effort to pick up the phone. She simply stared at Naomi. The look on her face stopped short of a fully fledged glare. It was more of a wishy-washy, peace-loving, alternative-lifestyle, tofu version of a glare.

'Naomi, maybe you've forgotten, but we have addressed this issue before . . .' Summer's voice was as calm as ever, but it had taken on a faintly miffed quality which was the perfect accessory to her facial expression. 'I really don't think it's appropriate for you to be taking calls during a cleanse. This should be a time of tranquillity and relaxation. Your constant refusal to hear what I say is causing me to develop some quite negative feelings toward you.'

At this point the phone stopped ringing.

The nation's most beloved talk-show host and consumer champion, steadfast devotee of the underdog and eight times winner of the Pritchard and Jarvis (Debt Collection and Bailiff Service) Award for Compassionate Journalism, raised herself on to her elbows and glowered at Summer in a way that said: Lynching follows. Start trembling.

'And your fucking refusal to pick up the sodding phone, you tie-dyed, pumpkin-seed-brained moron,' she bellowed, 'has probably just caused me to develop the sack.'

Summer's eyes immediately filled with tears. What she did not appreciate, however, because she barely knew Naomi, was that on a bad day the woman's temper could reach fundamentalist Taliban proportions. By Naomi's standards, she was subjecting Summer to the tamest of tickings-off.

'For all you know, you stupid wholewheat tart,' Naomi carried on shouting, spraying the air with tiny goblets of spittle, 'that could have been Alan Yentob offering me a new series . . . or . . . or Cherie inviting me to cocktails at Number Ten.'

Naomi's rant was interrupted by the phone starting to ring again. Summer, whose tears were by now streaming down her face, bent down, snatched the phone out of Naomi's briefcase, slammed it down on the couch, and then ran out of the room sobbing. Naomi jabbed a button with a menstrual-red talon. 'Plum,' she barked in recognition. 'No, it's OK. This is a good time. Speak to me. What's the line-up looking like for this afternoon's pre-record?'

As Plum, Naomi's long-suffering PA, spoke, the features on Naomi's face started to form themselves into a gurn of prize-winning ugliness. There were two reasons for this. The first was that the woman who had agreed to come on the show and tell the story of how her three-month-old baby drowned in the bath after she left it alone while she went downstairs to watch Supermarket Sweep, and was now suing Armitage Shanks for negligence, was, according to Plum, having doubts about whether she wanted to appear after all. The second was that Naomi's colon was still filling with water. Summer had been so distraught when she left the room that she had forgotten to turn off the tap on the knitting machine. The result was that as more and more surged dam-like into her gut, Naomi had begun to experience the kind of abdominal griping pains that were usually associated with aid workers in Africa suffering from amoebic dysentery.

Whatever physical pain Naomi was in, it didn't begin to compare with the anger she was feeling towards the Armitage Shanks woman. So furious was she that her brain failed to register that her gut pain was being caused by her colon filling with water. As it continued to dilate and distend, Naomi simply gurned and groaned and took out her agony on Plum.

'What the fuck do you mean, she's refusing to appear if she has to weep on screen? What fucking use is that? How many times do I have to tell you, Plum, it's tears which make ratings. Listen to me, I don't want her unless you draw up a contract and she gives us a written undertaking to cry. Tell her we'll stick raw onion down her cleavage if it'll help. Offer her tickets for *Les Mis*. Tell her we'll arrange a night out for her with Michael Winner. Anything. Just get her, Plum.'

Naomi pressed the off button and dropped the phone on to the couch. She then let out a cry which sounded like a cross between two coyotes on the job and the death throes of a parrot. Suddenly realising that her gut was on the point of exploding, she tried to yank out the tube which had been inserted into her backside. For some reason, probably because of the searing pain coming from her bowel, her muscles were holding on to it for dear life and the thing wouldn't budge. Naomi screamed for Summer.

In a second, Summer's head appeared round the door. It was almost as if she had been waiting for Naomi's frantic call, and that she hadn't forgotten to turn off the tap but had left it running on purpose.

'Turn off the fucking tap. Turn off the tap. I'm swelling up like the sodding Michelin man here.'

Summer smiled in a way which indicated that she had in the last few minutes mastered the art of wickedness.

She moved forward and put her fingers on the water tap, but made no attempt to turn it.

'Only if you apologise for being so rude,' she grinned.

Naomi, who saw apologising as losing face, said nothing. Despite her excruciating agony, she couldn't bring herself to say she was sorry.

'Just turn it off,' she shrieked.

'Apologise.'

'No.'

'Come on, Naomi. In a few seconds, the contents of

your insides are gonna hit the ceiling like some good ol'
Dallas gusher.'

Naomi could tolerate the agony no longer.

'All right, all right. You win. I'm sorry. I'm truly
sorry for being so rude.'

With that, Summer, who was still smiling, turned off
the tap. A few moments later, Naomi experienced a
bowel evacuation so sublime that as bodily sensations
went, there was little to choose between it and the most
magnificent of orgasms.

Naomi got to the Channel 6 office in Hammersmith just
before eleven. As she stepped out of the lift, she patted
her stomach and smiled. Delivered of its stagnant build-
up, it was flatter than it had been for weeks. Then,
almost immediately, as she set off down the long corridor
towards her office, temptation struck in the form of the
glorious greasy-spoon smell which was wafting down
from the canteen upstairs. She realised she could murder a Bacon Bastard. This was a canteen special which
consisted of three or four rashers of cheap streaky
shoved between thickly buttered Sunblest.

Although she was starving and her mouth was now full
of saliva, Naomi, who, along with her fierce temper,
could, when required, summon up gargantuan quantities of self-control, was determined not to give in to her
desire for a bacon sandwich. Having just spent fifty quid
getting rid of her stomach bulge, she had no intention of
allowing it to reappear an hour later. What's more, as
someone who liked to shower three times a day, who
insisted on every cubicle in the Channel 6 Ladies' being

fitted with a bidet and who used tampons even when she didn't have a period, she was rather taken with the idea of fasting for a couple of days in order not to get dirt on her freshly irrigated bowel.

There was, however, another reason why Naomi decided against the bacon sandwich. Image. A strong, powerful woman like Naomi Gold, whose success was due in large measure to her ability to instil the fear of God into her colleagues, did not sit in the canteen stuffing her face with grease, looking like some desperate cow who'd just tunnelled out of an Overeaters Anonymous meeting.

She had always made fun of gym junkies and food faddists, but late in the day had come to the conclusion that it was important for media high-flyers to prove their physical as well as their mental strength.

The upshot was that she made sure everyone in the office knew she had joined a gym and was now working out from six until eight every morning with a personal trainer. What's more, in front of her colleagues, she was determined to give the impression that she had also embraced healthy eating. During production meetings she would sneer at people's Eccles cakes and slices of Battenberg while passing round a bowl of carrot batons accompanied by some dark green dip which looked like it had been made from puréed algae.

Her junk-eating marathons only ever happened when she was home alone. After one of her four-slices-of-Nutella-on-white-bread-followed-by-an-Indian-take-away binges, she would either live on Lucozade and water biscuits for a week or make an appointment with Summer.

★ ★ ★

Furious at having to forgo the Bacon Bastard, Naomi slammed her briefcase down on the desk and bellowed for Plum, who had an interconnecting office.

By the time Naomi had sat down, Plum – goatee beard, flares, Adidas Gazelles – was standing in front of her. Plum's real name was Jason Plumley. He came from Preston, and because he was a bit of a wuss and built like a sparrow with growth hormone deficiency, Naomi enjoyed emasculating the poor lad even further by calling him Plum. Humiliated as he was, Jason didn't have the balls to fight back. He simply blushed.

His puny frame, combined with his slightly bowed head and anxious smile, made him look like a petrified first-former up before the head.

'Right,' Naomi said, giving a single clap of her hands, 'how many cripples, cretins and inadequates have we got lined up today?'

Keeping up his smile, but saying nothing, Plum handed his boss a print-out of the list of stories they were proposing to cover in that day's show. Naomi sat back in her leather swivel chair and scanned the page. Plum watched the familiar frown form on her face as she went down the list searching for an excuse for molten abuse to start pouring from her mouth. As usual, the two-hour show was to be a mulch of consumer stories, showbiz interviews and Oprah-style talk and tears.

When Naomi had decided on the show's present mixed-bag format, none of the producers or editors thought it would be popular with the punters. In private they referred to the new structure as 'a fucking shambles' and 'a ragbag of crass and unfocused ideas'. A few of them even dared to hint at this to Naomi's face. She simply rode roughshod over them, pushed on with her plans and, when the show became a runaway success, insisted that the Channel 6 bosses sack her detractors. When the newspapers found out that a TV presenter had become so powerful that she was sacking her producers, it suited Naomi's purposes admirably; if there was previously anybody in television who didn't regard her with fear and awe, there wasn't now. As for the public, she fobbed them off with a heartrending interview in *Hello!* in which she accused the media of fabricating the entire story, possibly for anti-Semitic purposes.

Today's *Naomi!* line-up included the story of the homophobic caterer who gave all the guests at a gay 'wedding' salmonella by deliberately serving them off sushi; some D-list Hollywood starlet who was coming on to promote her controversial new range of padded clothing designed to make anorexics look curvy; and a woman, now on probation, who had been invited on to the show to tell the moving story of how, on Christmas Eve, she had bludgeoned her bully of a husband to death with a frozen turkey and then, with the help of her nine children, all of whom had learning difficulties, ate the evidence the following day.

Naomi finished going through the list. For once, the traditional abuse failed to erupt from her mouth and her frown disappeared. She looked up and gazed into the distance. The expression on her face flirted with becoming one of satisfaction, as she pictured the close-up of her holding the husband-killer's hands and urging her, with tears in her eyes and almost saint-like concern in her voice, to reveal every grizzly, blood-squirting moment of her tale. She would then turn to the nine children and bestow a beatific caress on each of their cretinous little heads.

Plum, registering his boss's rare approval, felt his pulse begin to slow down.

'OK. That doesn't look too bad,' Naomi declared, suddenly coming back to earth, 'the only thing you haven't mentioned is what's happening with the Armitage Shanks woman.'

Plum, feeling his heart rate beginning to gallop again, ran a hand over his bleached crop. He knew he must at all costs avoid doing what he inevitably did as Naomi's mercury level threatened to rise past critical – lapse in his nervousness into broad Lancashire. This happened at least once a week, and every time, without fail, Naomi would scythe him down with an exaggerated hand behind the ear and the same withering joke: 'No, no, sorry, Plum, darling,' she would cut across him when he was halfway through briefing her, 'all I'm getting is some strange noise. You'll have to run that lot past me in English this time.'

Plum's cheeks turned crimson. Finally he took a deep breath and started to speak in an overstated attempt at Home Counties English. 'The Armitage Shanks woman will be here at half past two,' he said in the slow, studiedly baritone voice, his vowels ridiculously rounded. 'And she's agreed to cry if we promise her four tickets for *Les Mis*. Said Michael Winner doesn't do a lot for her really.'

'Brilliant, fucking, fucking brilliant.' Naomi was actually brimming over with excitement. 'Well done, Plum. What I think we need to do now is find some suitable musical accompaniment for the stupid cow as she comes on. Instead of going for lunch, see if you can dig out a recording from somewhere of "Your Baby has Gorn Down the Plughole".'

'Right chew are, then, Nay-ohmi,' Plum said cheerily. Despite his accent and his uncontrollable nerves, he harboured ambitions to become a *Blue Peter* presenter and had no intention of jeopardising his career by challenging Naomi's capricious demands, or indeed her grotesque choice of music.

'OK, now I need food,' Naomi declared, bashing the top of her desk with an outstretched hand. Her joy at having snared the Armitage Shanks woman had caused all thoughts of fasting to vanish.

'Plum, be a love and go upstairs to the canteen and get me a green salad, no dressing, and some lean ham. And don't forget to take the scales. I must have precisely four ounces of salad and eight of protein. And make sure you wipe the leaves on a paper towel. Residual water buggers up the weight reading. Remember, my lettuce needs to be more than just green. It should be positively emerald, darling. If the canteen have only got that pale, limp stuff, then jump in a cab and pop up to Planet Organic.'

The moment Plum shut the door, Naomi dived into her Il Bisonte briefcase and began hunting for a Wagon Wheel. If she couldn't have bacon she would make do with chocolate. Rummaging furiously among the letters, documents and folders, all she could find were two

Clubs, a couple of Penguins and a Walnut Whip. She couldn't make up her mind between a mint-flavoured Club and the Walnut Whip. She had just decided to sod it and have both when the phone started ringing. She left it for a few seconds while she ripped into the plastic Walnut Whip wrapper with her teeth. Then, with the piece of swirly chocolate on one hand, she picked up the receiver.

'Beverley!' Naomi exclaimed, her voice meandering from falsetto to contralto between one end of her sister's name and the other. 'Darling, it really is wonderful to hear from you after all this time. So, you got my letter.'

As Beverley spoke, Naomi brought the narrow end of the Walnut Whip slowly towards her mouth, clamped her teeth around it, paused for a second or so and decapitated it.

Chapter 3

'So,' Naomi said warmly, breaking yet another awkward telephone silence, 'how are you? I mean how are you *really*? Are things still difficult – you know – money-wise?'

'Oh, you know. In the midst of life we are in debt,' Beverley said breezily.

'God, really? Is it that bad?' Naomi said, her voice full of concern.

'No. I'm exaggerating,' Beverley laughed. 'We're doing OK. Honest.' Having found out that Naomi had just bought a three-quarters-of-a-million-pound flat in Holland Park ('Complete wreck, of course. Daren't tell you what I've spent on it'), she was blowed if she was about to come across as a complete charity case.

'In fact,' she went on, 'things are really starting to look up. It's all a bit hush-hush at the moment, but Mel's just pulled off this amazing import deal with the Koreans.'

'Oh, fabulous, I'm *so* delighted,' Naomi said. 'Let's just hope it's more successful than the homeopathic-sticking-plasters-that-didn't-stick fiasco.'

'Oh, God, that was yonks ago,' Beverley said, trying to convince herself as much as her sister. 'I don't think he'd make a mistake like that again . . . Look, Nay, it was really good to get your letter. I've missed you.'

'Yeah, me too.'

'I meant to pick up the phone so many times, but there was just so much, you know, water under the bridge, and I didn't know what to . . .'

'I know. You don't have to explain. Look, Bev, I'm truly sorry for the rotten things I said. You must hate me.'

'Don't be daft,' Beverley said. 'I was angry, but I never hated you.'

'So, do you forgive me?'

Beverley didn't hesitate.

''Course I do,' she said kindly.

'Bev, I can't tell you how happy that makes me,' Naomi said, sounding close to tears. 'Listen, I'd really like us to meet. We've got so much to catch up on. Plus there's something really major I need to discuss with you.'

'Sounds ominous . . . Oh God, Nay, you're not ill or anything, are you?'

'No, no, I'm fine. It's nothing like that. Promise. Look, I don't want to talk about it over the phone. How about meeting for lunch?'

'Great. When?' Beverley reached across the worktop for her diary.

'What about one day next week. Say, Tuesday?'

'Fine.'

'Tell you what, let's go somewhere really posh. What

38

about the Ivy? You won't have heard of it, darling, but it's simply *the* place to go. It'll be my treat.'

'Oooh, brilliant,' Beverley shot back. 'I love it there.'

'No, darling, you misunderstand. I mean *the* Ivy, in Covent Garden.'

'Yes, so do I. You remember Rochelle and Mitchell, our rich friends from round the corner? He made a fortune in the deli business, she's got breast implants and a four-wheel drive with interchangeable soft tops – pink for summer, green for winter? Well, they took me and Mel to the Ivy for our last wedding anniversary.'

'They did?' Naomi said, coughing in disbelief. 'Goodness, I had no idea its fame had spread quite so . . . so far afield.'

Beverley closed her diary and smiled. Her sister was still full of herself. Still the dreadful snob she'd always been. Those bits of her would never change. On the other hand, much as Beverley had predicted, she seemed calmer, less angry and more at peace with the world than she'd ever been. There was no doubt in Beverley's mind that she genuinely and desperately wanted to be friends again. Even the suspicion that Naomi had only got in touch because she wanted something from her had begun to fade.

Beverley was also pretty sure she knew what Naomi wanted to discuss. Their mother. Naomi had spent her entire adult life hating Queenie – and not without reason. If she remembered, she sent her mother a cheap card on her birthday. When Queenie had gone into hospital for her hip operation, she'd sent a small bunch of carnations. For as long as Beverley could remember, that had been the extent of their relationship. They hadn't actually seen each other for six years. If Beverley's memory served her correctly, that had been at their mad hippy cousin Roma's welcome-to-the-world party for her first baby, at which Mad Roma had served up fried placenta on bridge rolls.

Now all that was about to change. At last Naomi was ready to make peace.

One thing the two sisters had never argued about was what a dreadful mother Queenie had been.

They always said her child-rearing methods had more in common with a sixteen-year-old unmarried mother living off benefit than a lower-middle-class Jewish mother with a husband living off a modest but adequate housekeeping allowance in Gants Hill. In a neighbourhood teeming with the kind of *kvetching*, overprotective Jewish mothers who fussed about overbites and breastfed their offspring matzo balls until they left home, Queenie's style of mothering stood out like a black pudding on Yom Kippur.

Although she never raised a hand to the girls, she neglected them emotionally and physically from the moment they were born. Family gossip had it that even when Beverley and Naomi were babies, Queenie seemed to want nothing to do with them. She would leave them in their cots to scream for hours while she lay in the bath drinking tea and reading Harold Robbins. When the crying became too much she would feed them by putting a bottle of milk – complete with floating fag ash – in the cot, propped up on a pillow.

By the time Beverley was eight and Naomi was three she thought nothing of leaving them alone in the house while she spent hours drinking coffee in Lyon's in Ilford or wandering round West's and Bodgers picking up and putting down clothes she couldn't begin to afford. When she finally got back, she would barely react when Beverley cried and said they had been scared and hungry and asked her why she had been such a long time. Queenie would simply draw on her cigarette and tell her not to be such a baby. Occasionally she would console her by reading to her – usually from Harold Robbins, minus the dirty bits.

Their father, Lionel, was an equally inadequate parent. A meek, mild-mannered man with a girlish giggle, no eyebrows to speak of, and that bulbous bit on the end of his nose, he occasionally nagged his wife about the pissy smell in the lavatory and the festering piles of washing-up, which from time to time developed maggots. But because he feared losing his beautiful Queenie, whom he worshipped and who he was sure had only married him out of pity, he was too scared of saying or doing anything which might put their marriage at risk. He never reproached his wife for her neglect of the children.

By the time she was ten, Beverley had become a second mother to Naomi. Each afternoon, she would come out of the juniors at Gearies School, collect her sister from the infants, walk her home and let them both in with the front-door key she wore on a ribbon round her neck. Then she would make tea, which usually consisted of clumsily applied Marmite on toast and baked beans.

Both girls did surprisingly well at school, although their mother never showed the remotest interest in their academic progress. In her last couple of years, Naomi in particular developed a fierce ambition. She craved the plaudits which went with adult success, because at some subconscious level she saw them as a substitute for the maternal love and attention she still needed so desperately. She used university (Sussex, English) as a stepping stone to a career. Beverley, on the other hand, went to university (Nottingham, history) in search of a husband and the care and security she hoped marriage would bring. She found this in Melvin. At the time, it didn't matter to her that, although she loved him, she wasn't 'in love' with him, that for her he was a clone of every other sweet, intellectual but never quite alpha male lad she had ever met at the Ilford Jewish Youth Club. Because she was certain Melvin adored her, would wrap her in affection and do his best to take care of her, she chose to ignore the fact that she wasn't particularly attracted to him physically.

When Beverley and Naomi's father died in the mid seventies, a light seemed to go on – as opposed to off – inside Queenie. As the years passed she seemed to positively blossom. She gave up smoking, became a doting grandmother who baked the children slightly wonky Jane Asher birthday cakes and began taking a more than perfunctory interest in the state of Beverley and Melvin's finances. As Queenie began to get in touch with her Jewish mother within, it became clear to Beverley that Lionel hadn't quite been the devoted husband he'd always appeared. Exactly what had gone on between her father and her mother she had no idea – Queenie had never once spoken ill of Lionel – but there was no doubt in her mind that he had contributed in large measure to Queenie's behaviour.

By now Beverley's attitude to her mother had softened considerably. She knew she would find it hard to forgive her for the past, but she'd stopped hating her. Occasionally, over a cup of tea, she would broach the subject of their miserable childhood. Clearly distressed, Queenie would immediately change the subject. Beverley never had the heart to press her.

Time and again, Beverley tried to share her thoughts on their parents' marriage with Naomi, but her sister, who believed Lionel had been led a dog's life by their mother, wouldn't hear a word against him. She always made it clear that as far as she was concerned their mother had been spawned by Beelzebub and deserved absolutely no compassion.

Five years ago, when Queenie began to develop severe arthritis in her left hip as well as very high blood pressure, it was Beverley who began to worry about her falling over in the bath or having a stroke. It was also Beverley, fed up with phoning her mother ten times a day to check she was still alive, who decided Queenie could no longer live on her own. One Sunday morning while Melvin was in the park playing maladroit football with his usual gang of wobbly, overweight Jewish professionals, Beverley invited Naomi over to discuss what should be done.

Things had got off to a shaky start the moment Naomi arrived. Even though she was earning a fortune in her spare time presenting corporate videos, she was still working as a local TV news reporter in Luton. Nevertheless, she swanned into the house looking down her nose like a dowager who'd taken a wrong turning and ended up in Moss Side. Clearly fearing contagion, she air-kissed Beverley on both cheeks, actually, to Beverley's astonishment, saying 'Mwah' as she did it.

'Oh, come on, Naomi,' Beverley said, laughing and giving her sister a proper hug, 'this is me. Your big sister, not one of your telly-kissy chums.' She then led Naomi into the living room, which had just been redecorated.

'Oh, so you went for pale lemon anaglypta,' Naomi said as she took in the new colour scheme. 'And ruched nets with just a blush of pink. Do I detect an ironic nod towards fondant fancy?' She lowered her voice. 'Who did you get to do it, Mr Kipling?'

'Sorry?' Beverley said, missing her sister's last remark.

'Oh, no, nothing. It doesn't matter.'

'Actually,' Beverley went on, 'we didn't give it much thought. To be quite honest, interior design isn't my and Mel's strong point.'

'Really? You'd never have guessed.'

A few minutes later, over coffee and a couple of slices of Beverley's home-made marble cake, Beverley mooted the idea of Queenie moving in.

It was a full five seconds before Naomi spoke.

'Move in? With you?' she repeated flatly, clearly astonished at the suggestion.

'Yes. Why not? I've sort of mentioned it vaguely and she seems to be up for it.'

'I don't doubt it. Three meals a day. You running round after her. Who wouldn't? You're mad, Bev. For Christ's sake, the woman fucked up both our lives. Now you want her living with you? Sharing your house? Why can't we just put her in a home? Then we wouldn't have to do much more than visit her on her birthday with a couple of giant bars of Fruit and Nut.'

'Come on, Nay, she's a bright, intelligent woman. She'd die if she had to spend all day sitting in front of the telly with a load of old people.'

'And your point is?'

'Stop it, Nay,' Beverley came back at her. 'Even you don't wish her dead.'

'No, I suppose not,' Naomi said reluctantly. 'Well, it's no skin off my nose, I suppose, if you have her come and live with you. Just don't involve me, that's all.'

'Oh, God, no,' Beverley said. 'This would be entirely our responsibility. Although it did occur to me that you might have her from time to time – for the odd weekend or few days here and there – just to give us a break.'

Naomi nearly choked on her marble cake.

'Let's get one thing straight,' she snapped. 'If you think I am having that neglectful, self-centred old bat living in my flat then you've got another think coming. Plus, it may have escaped your notice, darling, but we are not all little home bodies. Unlike you I have a career. I am up at six and don't get home till ten at night. There is no way I can look after her. What's more, I've just bought a new white sofa from Conran and I'm not having her sitting and weeing all over it.'

While Naomi brushed cake crumbs off her expensive navy trousers on to the carpet, Beverley made the point that Queenie was still perfectly continent and reiterated that it would only be a couple of times a year, but Naomi wouldn't budge.

'Great,' Beverley said. 'So I get landed.'

'No, Beverley, you haven't simply got landed,' Naomi said, about to shoot from the lip. 'You've *chosen* to get landed. There's a big difference. Do you know something, Bev, you're a fool. You're a fool for giving a damn and you're a fool because you've made nothing of your life. You married too young, you had children too young and all you've succeeded in doing is turning yourself into a sad domestic drudge, a fat semi-animated matzo pudding with nothing better to do all day than worry about whether her children are wearing vests. Now you want to martyr yourself into the bargain.'

Instead of standing up to Naomi, Beverley immediately burst into tears.

'I may not have a career,' she sobbed, 'but at least I've got a husband and children to love and who love me back. Who do you have to hug when life gets rough?'

'Easy. My Alfa Spider,' Naomi snapped, standing up to go.

At that moment, Melvin walked in. He had come home early because the game had been rained off and had been standing in the hall listening to the last minute or so of the sisters' exchange. Melvin traditionally mishandled disagreements. While he would smile inanely at being grievously insulted, he couldn't even take a dud transistor radio back to Dixons without getting so worked up that he frequently ended up threatening to punch out the lights of some blameless seventeen-year-old shop assistant. On this occasion, however, for once in his life, Melvin got it right. He simply walked over to Beverley, put his arm round her and in a very quiet, calm voice suggested that Naomi leave, carry on enjoying her life as a weather girl or whatever she was, and never show her face in his home again.

'My pleasure,' she hissed. 'And for your information, I'm a senior news reporter.'

'Yeah, right, famous throughout Luton,' sneered Melvin. A few seconds later the door slammed and she was gone.

Beverley was more proud of Melvin at that moment than she had ever been.

Today, five years on, Beverley could only think about all the time she and Naomi had wasted. 'Pair of idiots. Somebody should have bashed our heads together ages ago,' she said, taking a couple of crispbreads out of the packet and spreading them with cottage cheese. The warmth she was feeling towards her sister was suddenly overtaken by the animosity she was feeling towards her lunch. Why did going on a diet always involve eating sheets of stuff which tasted like they should come in a flat pack with an Allen key and cheese which looked like it had already been digested once? As she took a bite and grimaced, it occurred to her that Benny had eaten nothing all day. Her son had refused to go to school that morning, claiming he had silicosis.

47

'Silicosis,' she repeated with more than a hint of ridicule.

'Yeah. I've been up all night coughing,' he said weakly, falling back on his pillow, like some Victorian heroine in a swoon. 'Plus I feel tired and my legs have gone all weak.' He illustrated his point with a few seconds of highly theatrical hacking and wheezing.

'Benny, this is Finchley, not a twenties Nottinghamshire pit village. You do not have silicosis.'

She felt his forehead. Neither did he have a temperature.

'I promise you, there's nothing the matter with you other than you've been reading too much D.H. Lawrence. Come on, Benny, I'm not daft. I suspect the only reason you don't want to go to school is because you have a piece of course work due in today which you haven't finished. Well, you're going to have to face the music. You're not ill. Get up and go to school.'

'I can't, Mum. Honest, I feel dead ill. I want a second opinion.'

'OK. I'll tell you again. You're fine.'

'God,' he said indignantly, 'why won't you ever believe me? If I say I'm ill, I'm ill.' There was more melodramatic coughing.

She looked down him. Despite the bleached head, and the hairy arms sticking out of his Cradle of Filth T-shirt, to her he still looked about three. What was more, he had changed emotional tack and was now looking up at her with huge pleading eyes.

Even though she had no doubt he was swinging the lead because he hadn't done his homework, she knew she would give in eventually – on the strict understanding that Benny spent the day catching up.

While Beverley threw the second crispbread into the swing bin and began making a plate of Benny's favourite peanut butter, chocolate spread and jam sandwiches, her son lay in bed and continued to gaze at the Year Eleven school photograph.

Sixth row back, third from the left, there she sat. Lettice Allard, the love of Benny's life, his wanking muse and the reason he had refused to go to school. He had been desperate to stay at home not because he had got behind with a school assignment, but because he was exhausted, having spent the entire night trying to work out whether he stood even a remote chance of pulling this exquisite blue-eyed goddess.

Yesterday during lunch break, when a gang of them got together to smoke some weed at Lettice's house, which was just over the road from the school, he'd felt pretty sure she'd given him reason to hope. But he couldn't be certain. On the other hand there had been that long, sexy look she'd given him, not to mention the hair flick. Correction. Two hair flicks. These had to be sure signs of her unspoken desire. On the other hand, maybe he'd misread the signs and her desire was only unspoken because she didn't desire him.

Somehow, the conversation got round to circumcision. As usual, Lettice had been riding on her PC high horse. (She'd inherited her overbearing manner and politics from her mother, a Marxist aristo who had married beneath her.) She began by saying that in her opinion circumcision was the institutionalised mutilation of infants who couldn't give their permission. A lad called Neil then accused her of being the knob police. She lost her temper. He then accused her of being ratty because she was menstruating. She gave a high-pitched screech of fury.

'For your information, *Neil*,' she said, 'women don't *men*struate, they *fem*struate.' She took a deep breath and returned to the subject under discussion.

'Anyway, all I know is that when I finally decide to renounce my celibate state, there's no way I'm doing it with a bloke who doesn't own a foreskin. It's just so unnatural.'

She then turned to Benny, smiled and performed the first hair flick.

'By the way, Benny, you might be interested to know that while I was on the Web looking for stuff on female circumcision the other night, I found this group of circumcised men who are totally vexed about it, and call themselves circumcision survivors. They've even worked out ways to reclaim their foreskins.'

She went over to the leather-topped desk standing in the bay window and picked up half a dozen print-outs. She handed them to Benny.

'I thought being Jewish and all that you might find it useful . . . I mean, you must be pretty angry with your parents for having you chopped without your permission.'

Benny, hugely embarrassed by this public discussion of his penis, yet simultaneously flattered by the idea of Lettice having spent even a few seconds considering its existence, let alone its well-being, coloured up and said he'd never really thought about it.

'Well, maybe it's time you did. I mean . . .' she said, throwing him an unmistakably sexy look.

She smiled at him for what must have been a full five seconds. This was followed by the second hair flick. Blushing, Benny folded up the papers and slipped them into his jacket pocket. Was she giving him the come-on? He just couldn't be sure. But as he lay in his bed, he knew he had to do everything he could to make her his. And what was more, he had no doubt about the first step.

Benjamin Moshe Littlestone was about to renege on the covenant Abraham had made with God five thousand years ago, not to mention trample on the generosity of his ultra-orthodox Uncle Shmuley, who had flown all the way from Montreal for Benny's barmitzvah bringing with him a set of the finest kosher phylacteries from Israel.

Benny was to set about reclaiming his foreskin.

Chapter 4

Melvin pulled up at the traffic lights in his rusty 1982 VW Passat. Immediately, his mobile started to ring. He stabbed the send button and straight away wished he hadn't.

'Och, Mr Littlestone. I'm glad to have caught you. McGillicuddy here . . . from the bank.'

The words 'McGillicuddy' and 'bank' in the same sentence were usually enough to have Melvin hyperventilating into a paper bag. The man may have just agreed to extend his overdraft, but historically Mr McGillicuddy was rarely the bearer of glad tidings where Melvin was concerned.

'Ah, how are you, Mr McGillicuddy?' he said, a touch too jovially, failing to conceal the anxiety in his voice. 'How are you getting on with the hairpiece?'

The lights turned green, but Melvin didn't notice.

'Well', Mr McGillicuddy said uneasily, 'truth to tell, that's the reason I'm ringing. Of course I could be worrying about nothing. I mean, mine could be a one-off experience, but I thought I ought to inform you . . .'

Melvin wasn't about to shit a brick. He was about to

relieve himself of an entire garden wall.

By now the cars behind him were starting to hoot. A Lada pulled out and spluttered past him on his outside, the driver enjoying the rare treat of mouthing 'Wanker' as he went.

'Up yours,' Melvin yelled back, but by now the Lada had disappeared.

'I'm sorry, Mr Littlestone, I didn't quite . . .'

'Oh, goodness heavens, no,' Melvin spluttered. 'I didn't mean you, Mr McGillicuddy – some moron just cut me up, that's all.'

Melvin shoved the Passat into first. As usual, the car moved off with all the grace of an oversized mechanical rabbit with the farts.

'I see,' Mr McGillicuddy said, sounding a trifle uncertain, 'now then, where was I? Ah, yes. First of all I would like to say that being somewhat follically challenged, as they say these days, the gift of a hairpiece was most appreciated . . .'

If the old duffer didn't spit it out, Melvin was going to drive over to the bank and ram a haggis up his Scottish backside.

'And for the first couple of weeks,' McGillicuddy continued, 'everything went swimmingly. Then, last night in bed, to my horror, I discovered great clumps of hair all over the duvet and pillows. Morag got into a reet stoochie, I can tell you. She didn't thank me for making her get out her crevice tool at eleven o'clock at night. The reason I'm phoning, Mr Littlestone, is not to complain, but to drop you a word to the wise. I strongly suspect that all the hairpieces could be faulty and that you should take the matter up with your wholesaler. I do hope you haven't purchased too many of the things, because if mine is anything to go by, they really aren't of merchantable quality.'

'Heavens, no,' Melvin said, thinking of the ten gross he had in the stock-room. 'I just bought a dozen to, er, test the market, that's all. I'm sure my supplier will refund the money on any faulty ones. And let me say how sorry I am that this has happened, and I promise I'll get another hairpiece to you as soon as I can.'

'Och, don't worry yourself about me. It's you I'm more concerned about. You see, it did occur to me that you may have invested heavily in the things and been – er, diddled, shall we say? Naturally it further occurred to me that this could mean you would have insufficient monies to clear your overdraft as we agreed.'

'Thank you so much for your concern, Mr McGilli-cuddy,' Melvin said, feeling he was going to throw up at any moment. 'But let me assure you, the bank's monies are in safe hands. Everything's under control at this end. Absolutely fine, in fact. Couldn't be better. Peachy. Perfectly peachy.'

Peachy? Perfectly fucking peachy? Who was he kidding? He was finished. Washed up. Ruined. The toupees had been his final chance of a reprieve from bankruptcy, and the cunting things had let him down before he'd even got round to selling them.

'Vladimir,' Melvin growled, gripping the steering wheel so hard his knuckles turned white, 'I don't believe it. I do not fucking believe it. He knew they were faulty.

He must have known. He conned me. The Russki bastard conned me.'

The toupees were the most recent in a long line of gimmicks which had been supplied to Melvin courtesy of his former school penfriend Vladimir Chernyenko, formerly of Novosibirsk, lately of Friern Barnet.

Once a leading light in Siberian communism, Vladimir had been one of the first Russians to foresee the dawn of capitalism in the early eighties, and as if symbolically to stake his claim in the new Russia he believed was imminent, had managed somehow to import through relatives in Brooklyn an elderly – but not nearly elderly enough to be interesting – Chevvy Impala. The Chevrolet was beyond question the flashiest car in western Siberia, and when, a few months into the new Russia, Vladimir decided his future lay after all in the West, the Impala travelled with him on the boat to Harwich.

One of the first people he contacted after landing was his old British penfriend. Melvin, still hanging on to the vestiges of his left-wing student past, was instinctively drawn to Vladimir, even though with his droopy seventies moustache and big tinted specs – not to mention the ridiculous car with its long-out-of-date New York licence plates – the Russian was about as manqué as it was possible for a communist to be without actually wearing morning dress and a monocle and claiming to be one of the long-lost Romanovs. Melvin helped Vladimir set up a small flyblown import-export business over a minicab office in Hendon. The Chevvy, still untaxed and uninsured, became Vladimir's trademark. It was not surprising that within a very few months, across a considerable stretch of north-west London, Vladimir Chernyenko became known as Vlad the Impala.

Some of Vladimir's pharmaceutical import lines, like the industrial-thickness 'Big Lady' sanitary towels from Poland, and the Aussie condoms which came in Large, Jumbo and 'Brace Yourself Joyleen', had proved remarkably successful for Melvin. Others most definitely had not. Most infamous of these were the DIY ear-syringing kits from the old USSR.

Melvin paid £100 a gross for the yellowing boxes, which were wonkily stamped 'Plodexport Moskva'; he reckoned he could sell them for £4.99 each. In six months he sold four kits. What's more, he'd been forced to give refunds on three. The kit's tiny plastic bottle which was meant to hold twenty millilitres of finest Armenian olive oil to soften the wax before syringing in fact contained the Russian equivalent of WD 40.

Whenever Melvin complained about faulty merchandise, Vladimir was always full of apologies and had never hesitated to refund his money. Until now, that had never amounted to more than a couple of hundred quid. This, however, was five thousand. Even if Vlad hadn't suddenly gone bent and scarpered to the Costa del Crime with Melvin's money, there was a strong possibility that he simply didn't have it any more. In which case Melvin was bankrupt. In a matter of weeks the Littlestones would be living off Pop Tarts on some Rottweiler-strewn council estate in Park Royal.

As he became more and more convinced that he could kiss goodbye to the five thousand, Melvin started to think about topping himself. The problem was, he couldn't decide on the best way to do it. Pills were slow to take effect and there was always the dread possibility he might be brought back from the brink. As for putting a gun (even if he had the remotest idea of where to get hold of one) in his mouth, a GP mate of his had once told him that such suicides often succeed, if that was the word, only in blowing away their face and the frontal lobes of the brain without killing themselves. Such self-performed frontal lobotomies, his friend assured him, cure depression all right, and the person lives happily if uglily ever after – which wasn't quite the effect Melvin was considering.

Anyway, even if he did manage to commit suicide, his most drastic plan for a financial turnaround, the life insurance company would be bound to find some way of worming out of paying, leaving Beverley to inherit nothing but debts, which, since they had remortgaged the house last year, were now nudging a hundred grand. He simply couldn't condemn Beverley – endlessly patient, tolerant Beverley, who had stood by him for twenty years while he lurched from one financial disaster to the next – to lonely poverty. His gratitude to his wife, not to mention his pride, meant he also had to protect her from finding out about the toupee débâcle. He resolved there and then to remain alive, do everything in his power to get his money back from Vladimir and find some other way to rescue them from their pecuniary nuclear winter.

Melvin reached forward and switched on the manky old car radio. Underneath the loud crackling noises, a woman was speaking in what sounded like Serbo-Croatian. He fiddled irritably with the tuner for a few

seconds in an effort to find the six o'clock news on Radio
4. All he got was more crackling, followed by silence.
Then, from nowhere – as if to taunt him – there came an
interview with some lottery winner who was saying that
despite his seven-point-eight-million-pound win he
wasn't planning to give up his window-cleaning round.

'Tosser,' Melvin muttered, thumping the radio's front
panel, whereupon it died. 'Catch me running the shop if
I won eight million quid . . . fat chance of me winning
eight pence.'

At this point Melvin did what he always did, which
was to start thinking that his life had only turned out the
way it had because he was cursed by bad luck. He was,
he thought, the kind of bloke who would save up for a
trip to the Himalayas only to get there and find them
closed and covered in scaffolding.

Although he gained a certain amount of perverted
pleasure from blaming fate for his financial downfall, he
could only indulge the fantasy for so long. He knew full
well that bad luck had nothing to do with his predica-
ment. He had only himself to blame. His entire adult life
had been a catalogue of self-made fuck-ups, brought on
by an unlikely combination of arrogance and weakness,
not to mention sheer stupidity.

For a start, he should have stuck to his guns and
never have taken over the business from Sam, his elderly widower father, after he died in 1980. Melvin had
always made it clear that he had no intention of getting
involved in the chemist's shop, which was small and
decrepit and on precisely the wrong side of the tracks
out in Buckhurst Hill, Essex.

Sam, however, had made it equally clear that Melvin would inherit the shop one day and that he expected him to carry on running it. So determined was he that he insisted on Melvin taking science A levels and reading pharmacology at university, rather than sociology, which Melvin begged him to let him take.

From the time of the miners' strike, when he was sixteen, left-wing politics had been Melvin's passion. He was a cause and demo junkie. Hardly a weekend went by when he wasn't at an anti-apartheid rally, or noisily demanding justice for some allegedly virtuous jailbirds named by the left after some locale, be it the Streatham Six, the Forest Gate Four, or even the Torquay Two. Melvin had set his heart on backpacking round India before university, and after graduating, getting a job as an aid worker with Oxfam. Sam could see the idealism and desire burning in his son's eyes, but because he was the kind of pompous, arrogant man who strutted even when he was sitting down, he refused to acknowledge it as anything more than adolescent nonsense.

He announced that he would not pay the parental contribution to Melvin's grant unless he acquiesced. Realising he was fighting a losing battle, but not wanting to forfeit the chance to go to university, Melvin ended up studying pharmacology at Nottingham. He hated his course and scraped a third, not because he lacked ability, but because he did no work. Instead he spent most of his time standing outside the student union building dressed in his faux-lefty uniform of donkey jacket and Lenin-style blue denim cap, flogging copies of

Militant to sociology wonks and African students who were shivering away their time in Britain sustained by dreams of starting their own socialist dictatorship as soon as they got home. So committed was he to the cause that he became known as Melvin Militant.

Although he was short and had a beaky Jewish face, women, particularly non-Jewish ones, found Melvin extremely attractive. It seemed to be of no interest to them that at parties he danced like a dyspraxic baboon, or that he found it impossible to walk down the street and hold a conversation without tripping over his feet or treading on theirs. They were desperate to play Diane Keaton to his Woody Allen and couldn't keep their hands off him.

As a result, Melvin was never short of a leg-over, and spent his first couple of years at Nottingham satisfying his substantial appetite for tall, blonde *shikseh* goddesses.

Of all his goddesses, Rebecca Fludd, with her Faye Dunaway looks, not to mention her firm buttocks which were always tantalisingly outlined and divided by the back seam of her Levis, was the most divine. What was more, for a lass of twenty, her shagging abilities were extraordinarily advanced.

Once, just after they'd started going out, she turned up at his room brandishing a pair of handcuffs. 'Wotcha, Militant,' was all she said, plunging her tongue into his mouth. A few seconds later she had forced him on to the bed, unzipped his fly and was going down on him with all the skill of a seasoned hooker.

61

Their backgrounds couldn't have been less similar. Like many middle-class students, Melvin nurtured romantic notions of poverty and was gagging to identify with the class struggle. Rebecca, on the other hand, who had been brought up in a terraced house in south Leeds, felt she had lived her own class struggle long enough and couldn't wait to end it. While Melvin played at jettisoning his privileged past by selling *Militant*, nicking textbooks from the university branch of Dillons and living in a fetid little house in Dunkirk with an outside bog and intermittent hot water, Rebecca was putting her heart and soul into her business studies degree, had blagged free elocution lessons from a rich Sloaney girl on her course and was nurturing dreams of one day becoming what her parents called 'a tycoon'. Her only problem was that she hadn't the foggiest what she might become a tycoon in.

Whereas Melvin's world view was shaped by the intellectual might of Marx and Engels, Rebecca's was shaped by the capitalist might of Marks and Spencer. As a result, when they weren't handcuffing each other to Melvin's rickety iron bed frame, they were having blazing rows about whether or not the Co-op represented the apotheosis of benevolent capitalism.

In the middle of one particularly vicious post-coital bust-up which Melvin knew he'd lost the moment he suggested that the working class actually preferred margarine to butter, and Rebecca almost made herself sick with laughter, he got out of bed, pulled on his dressing gown, declared he couldn't be bothered to argue with somebody so politically retarded and disappeared downstairs into the greasy black hole that passed for a kitchen.

Ten minutes later, still smarting from defeat, Melvin walked back into the room, chewing. He was consoling himself with a bagel which was oozing cream cheese and smoked salmon.

'Militant, you fucking hypocrite,' Rebecca shouted teasingly, clocking the smoked salmon. She leapt out of bed, her large, firm breasts bouncing as she went. In a second she had snatched the bagel out of his hand, opened it and removed the cream-cheesy mass of pink gossamer slices.

'Very ideologically sound, I'm sure,' she said, waving the salmon under his nose. 'You're all the same, you middle-class lefties. You spend three or four years at university living in shit holes and pretending to identify with the proletariat, while conveniently skirting round the fact that you've got stereos in your rooms which would set a worker at the Plessey factory back two weeks' wages, and fridges full of smoked fucking salmon.'

'Look,' he said, getting defensive, 'my Jewish mother, who is convinced I am starving to death just because I live north of the Scratchwood service area, turned up armed with the contents of an entire kosher deli when she came to visit yesterday. What should I have done – thrown it away?'

As he spoke he made repeated grabs for the salmon, but Rebecca kept dodging him.

'No,' she laughed, deciding to let him off the hook, 'but you could at least have offered me some.'

'I was angry. Sorry.'

'Militant,' she said, reassembling the bagel and taking a closer look at it, 'why's this bap got a hole in the middle? I know Jews are meant to have sex through a hole in the sheet – Christ, they're not meant to eat through one as well, are they?'

Melvin laughed, took off his dressing gown and pulled her back into bed with him. While they sat cuddling and Rebecca ate the bagel which Melvin said she might as well finish, he set her straight about the anti-Semitic myth of the hole in the sheet and explained what bagels were.

'You can buy them anywhere there's a Jewish population – Manchester, Liverpool, Leeds.' He paused and thought for a moment.

'I tell you, Becca,' he said, some tiny forgotten strand of entrepreneurial Jewish DNA poking its molecular head above the parapet and forcing his lefty principles to beat a brief, temporary retreat, 'if you're looking for a business idea, why don't you start trying to flog bagels outside Jewish areas? I mean, they're a bit chewy, but basically they taste brilliant. With the right kind of advertising you could have fishermen in Polperro ditching their pasties for smoked salmon bagels in no time. I reckon there could be millions to be made from these.'

She started to laugh.

'Oh yeah, I can see it all now,' she began dismissively. 'Rebecca Fludd . . . *shikseh* bagel queen.'

'What's wrong with that?' he said.

'I've just told you – I'm not Jewish.'

He shrugged.

'So what, you're not Jewish?'

She paused for a moment to let the idea wash over her. Then she laid her head on Melvin's chest and began pulling gently at his hairs.

'You really think it wouldn't matter?'

'I've told you . . . you think Marks and Spencer were both Jewish? You could be the new Spencer. Just as long as I don't have to be Marks.'

'God, Melvin,' she said excitedly, suddenly kneeling up on the bed and pulling the off-white sheet round her. 'Do you know, I think this could just work. It's exactly the kind of idea I've been looking for. But you'd have to come in with me. I couldn't possibly do it on my own. You know everything about Jewish food, I know nothing. With your knowledge and my business degree, we could make a mint. Just think.'

In an instant Melvin came to and pulled himself back from his capitalist reverie. How on earth he had let down his Marxist guard, he had no idea.

Furious with himself, he proceeded to deliver an indignant snotty lecture, the gist of which was that he had no desire to become another slave-owning cog in the plutocratic machine, and that his allegiance remained with the urban proletariat and their struggle against the greedy capitalist might of Callaghan and his henchmen.

In the weeks that followed, she asked him again and again to give up the Oxfam aid worker idea and become her business partner once they'd both graduated. Each time she mentioned it, he got furious and presented her with another left-wing diatribe. After a while, she stopped asking. In the end she said that as their political differences kept coming between them and making them both miserable, she thought it best they stopped seeing one another. Although she turned him on like no other woman he had met, his commitment to Rebecca couldn't compete with his commitment to the class struggle.

While Melvin sat alone in his room night after night mourning the passing of their relationship, particularly the passing of the sex part, Rebecca, he discovered from mutual friends, was, alongside studying for her finals, plotting and planning her way towards becoming the world's first bagel mogul, Jewish partner or no.

It wasn't long before she had convinced Emma, her sweet but thick elocution teacher, to lend her five hundred quid and her Mini. A couple of weeks later she was making a regular Saturday-morning foray to the Redbridge Lane Bagel Bakery in Ilford, which Melvin had told her about, and which, being run by Israelis, didn't bother with such religious niceties as closing for the Sabbath. She would leave campus at four in the morning, get to the bakery just as it opened, load up the Mini with ten dozen ready-made smoked salmon bagels and then dash back up the M1 in order to reach the entrance to the Nottingham Forest ground – where she'd convinced the club to let her set up a stall – well before kick-off. If she could sell bagels to rain-soaked, beer-filled Midlands football fans, and she did, right from the start – she reckoned she could sell them anywhere.

Melvin meanwhile decided that the only way for him to get over Rebecca was to immerse himself even further in political activity. Uninterested though he was in anything remotely Jewish, he had begun to get quite disturbed by the trend towards old-fashioned anti-Semitism which was sweeping the left in the guise of anti-Israel sentiment. It was due to this phenomenon that he developed a new, if qualified, support for his kinfolk – and met and fell in love with Beverley Gold.

It happened one lunchtime in the students' union bar. Melvin, along with fifty or so other Jewish students, had turned up to disrupt an anti-Israel meeting organised by the Young Liberals. The speaker, an overweight, sweaty boy in a Harris tweed sports jacket with leather arm patches, was less than five minutes into his address, at the bit where he was suggesting that the six million Holocaust victims were a Hollywood myth sponsored by Jewish capital, when the Jews began hurling abuse and chanting, 'Nazis out.'

Beverley was standing in front of Melvin, yelling and waving her arms in fury. At some stage during her passionate display of ethnic solidarity, her fist ended up making contact with his nose, causing it to discharge a thick stream of blood which coursed down his chin and neck and ended up defacing his brand new Stuff the Jubilee T-shirt. So great did Melvin's blood loss appear that the Jews, convinced that he was experiencing some rare form of brain haemorrhage, immediately began shouting to the bar staff to dial 999. After a minute or so, a Jewish medical student in his white coat pushed his way through the hysterical crowd, which was by now completely oblivious to the speaker's calls for a boycott of Zionist capital. He took a look at Melvin's nose. 'I don't want to be a scaremonger,' he said after a few moments, with a face that was scaremongery personified, 'but are there any haemophiliacs in your family?'

Shouting through a huge wad of blood-soaked handkerchiefs and bits of old tissue, as well as against the still-ranting anti-Semite and the chanting Jews, Melvin replied, 'Not that I know of. Most of my family are Polacks.'

Finally the bleeding stopped, the meeting fizzled out, and Beverley insisted on buying Melvin a drink to apologise for almost causing him to bleed to death. By the time the drink ended four hours later, he knew he was in love. He could barely believe it was happening. He had never been attracted to Semitic-looking women, and yet Beverley, with her flawless olive skin, long chestnut hair and huge brown-black eyes which sparkled like jet, was definitely giving him the horn – and a very hard horn at that.

Nevertheless, after they made love for the first time, in Beverley's flat on Gregory Boulevard, Melvin was forced to admit that he had found himself pining for Rebecca. It wasn't that his feelings had changed towards Beverley. They hadn't. She was beautiful, intelligent, sexy. She laughed at all his jokes. What was more, because they shared a religion and a culture, he didn't have to explain himself twice an hour as he had to Rebecca, be it about holes in sheets or his profound aversion to the very idea of tripe. Beverley even came from the same part of London as him. Yet despite all that, there was something Rebecca possessed that Beverley didn't. Gentile genes. When he licked Rebecca out he was tasting forbidden fruit. It was wicked and dirty. It was a sin. Sleeping with her was the sexual equivalent of eating roast pork on Yom Kippur – only a hundred times more exciting. She nurtured the rebel, the heretic in Melvin, in a way that neither Beverley nor any other Jewish woman ever could.

Melvin and Beverley were married in the September after they graduated. Because Beverley's parents had no money, Sam Littlestone paid for the wedding, a modest affair at the Walthamstow Assembly Rooms.

Four weeks later, barely recovered from their honeymoon tour of European Cruise missile bases and the two nights they had spent locked in a German police station cell (during which Melvin had addressed the exceedingly polite and kind policeman as 'Oi, you, Goering, yer fat Nazi cunt'), they had to bury Melvin's father.

It also fell to Melvin and Beverley to sell Sam's business. After three months, however, there was not even a sniff of an offer, and Melvin realised he had no option but to take over the pharmacy, if only temporarily.

But he was unemployed and Beverley was still a student, training to be a teacher in London, so temporary swiftly became permanent. The knowledge that his father had finally got his own way filled Melvin with rage and frustration. He dealt with this by running the shop in a way he knew would have his father performing Olga Korbut acrobatics in his grave. Melvin Littlestone became Buckhurst Hill's first and only PC – pharmaceutically correct – chemist. For a start, he refused to hand out any medicines which in his opinion were likely to produce side effects. This included aspirin and paracetamol and anything containing even minute quantities of hydrocortisone. He banned all products containing food colourings. He also outlawed baby milk on the grounds that breast was best, refused to stock disposable nappies because they contained bleached fibres, and wouldn't have tampons in the shop because they caused toxic shock syndrome.

When Melvin's stock of little more than Vick, Anusol and a few dusty bottles of syrup of figs failed to draw customers, the gimmicks began.

In order to stave off bankruptcy and keep going, Melvin had descended into a cycle of paying off one credit card with another and was permanently exhausted from fending off calls from the ladies at Barclaycard.

But by the mid eighties, while he was driving from Finchley to Buckhurst Hill every day to run what he still regarded with distaste as his father's chemist shop, Rebecca had made it big in the bagel business. Very big. During one period, he was haunted on a nightly basis by snatches of *Hole in One*, a BBC 1 documentary series entirely on Rebecca. The programmes seemed to Melvin to do little more than show her hopping from helicopter to limo – from one of her company boardrooms to another.

Constantly beaming a perfectly capped Hollywood-type smile, she told the story of how, a few weeks after she'd begun selling bagels at the Nottingham Forest ground, Brian Clough had driven past in his Mercedes, wound down his window and said, 'I've heard about these, young lady. Let me try one.'

So smitten was he with what he insisted on calling beagles that soon she was supplying the pre-match lunch for the squad, ground staff and stewards. The day Forest won the European Cup, Brian Clough gave a press conference and announced that his team's success was due to himself, hard work by the players, and beagles – in that order.

'Bagels Play their Roll in Forest's Fire' was the headline in the *Guardian* the next morning, and Rebecca, the 'Brainy Bagel Babe', was even featured beaming through bagel spectacles in the *Sun*.

A year later, thanks to the publicity, orders for bagels were pouring in from nearly every football team in the country, and Rebecca, with the help of the Israeli baker she'd poached from the shop in Redbridge Lane, opened her first bagel bakery in the new Covent Garden market. She called it Tower of Bagel.

As the London bagel craze took off, lunchtime queues outside the shop stretched from the Piazza to Long Acre. Soon there were six shops in London and dozens more planned for the provinces.

American tourists who came into the London shops declared Tower of Bagel bagels far superior to any they could get back home. One of them, a young Jewish Harvard Business School graduate named Brad Weintraub, whose father owned half the Hamptons, became her business partner and later married her.

By 1990, the Ilford bagel was sweeping across the US. There was hardly a strip or mall in the country which didn't boast a Tower of Bagel. Tower of Bagel trucks plied the interstates day and night, the corporate logo of a toppling pile of cartoon bagels becoming as familiar as Walmart's. Soon, reports began to appear on the British financial pages of bankrupt, desperate American bagel bakers committing suicide because of the competition. First the owner of New York's famous Bagel Schmegel drowned himself in a hundred-gallon vat of dough. Then the Boogy Woogy Bagel Boys in San Francisco ended it all by taking sleeping pills crushed in Kahlua.

The Clintons adored Rebecca and Brad, as did Tony and Cherie. Both first ladies always insisted that their garden parties be catered by Tower of Bagel. The only dissenting voices on the planet came from Saddam Hussein, for obvious reasons, and from the Reverend Ian Paisley. Having discovered that the Pope had started to enjoy a couple of chopped herring bagels for breakfast, he declared them to be the Devil's Doughnuts and refused to cross the threshold of the newly opened five-lane drive-thru Tower of Bagel in Belfast.

The night Mme Yeltsin was shown on the nine o'clock news opening the first Tower of Bagel in Moscow, Melvin stood in front of the screen weeping tears of fury. For Christ's sake, it had been his fucking, bastard idea. He could have been a multi-millionaire by now, instead of a serial failure in a rusty VW. If only he hadn't been such an arrogant arsehole when Rebecca had asked him to become her partner. If only he'd seen the utter balls-aching uselessness of Marxism sooner. If only he hadn't been such a fool . . . If only he hadn't let her go.

As he pulled slowly on to the drive, his mind was engulfed by that final thought, by what might have been, by what *he* might have been had he stayed with Rebecca. Moreover, no matter how hard he tried, he had never forgotten or stopped aching for the molten passion he had felt for her. He had lost count of the times he had lain awake in bed next to Beverley, guilt surging through him as he remembered the night he and Rebecca had made love eleven times on the trot, and how the next day his balls ached so much he had to see the doctor at the university health centre. And how the pain had caused him to have to mosey, John Wayne style, into the surgery. And how he had never felt so happy in his life, before or since.

Chapter 5

The Morgue was filling up fast. By now the body count had risen to well over a hundred. Taut, harassed-looking attendants, unused to accommodating such large numbers, careered round the harshly lit tiled room in their long green surgical gowns, thick rubber gloves and white Wellington boots. A couple of them swabbed down recently vacated marble slabs. Some wheeled hospital trolleys. Others, laden with large porcelain kidney dishes, charged in and out of the plastic swing doors at the back.

Despite the attendants' best efforts at emergency stops, two trolleys, one with a pile of kidney dishes on board, had collided a few moments ago. The dishes had fallen to the floor and smashed, adding to the chaos and din. A large area of previously spotless white tiles was consequently now covered in kangaroo tail with garlic polenta, and green shell mussels with mooli, hijiki, chilli and rocket.

The Grim Reaper, who was stationed by the front door, greeted new arrivals.

'Hi, my name's Phil,' he boomed from the far reaches

of his black hood while at the same time extending his scythe in welcome, 'and I'll be your Angel of Death this lunchtime. Would you prefer post-mortem or non-post-mortem?'

When the Grim Reaper asked Beverley, who by now had begun to feel decidedly queasy, whether she had a reservation, she'd been tempted to say, 'Yes, at least a dozen,' and then make a dash for it before somebody in a surgical gown tried to whip out her spleen and weigh it. But instead of being rude, she simply gave him Naomi's name.

Having been told by the Grim Reaper that her sister had phoned to say she was stuck in traffic and would be a few minutes late, Beverley was shown to a marble slab in the window by an Aussie Morgue attendant called Lance. Their route took them past slabs full of intimidatingly trendy men and women, all of whom seemed to be wearing narrow oblong spectacles with thin black frames. It was only as she sat down that Beverley noticed the large badge pinned to Lance's surgical gown advertising the restaurant's Valet of the Shadow of Death parking service.

'Can I offer you a *stiff* drink while you're waiting?' Lance had asked chirpily as he handed her the black-edged menu. 'We do some absolutely *harrowing* cocktails. What about a Hemlock Wallbanger? That's similar to a Harvey Wallbanger except we add a couple of drops of squid ink. Then there's our special Black Death Die-quiri? That's Guinness garnished with floating oozing boils made from advocaat and grenadine. Or what about a Gravesend Surprise, that's . . .'

'Don't tell me . . . one shot of embalming fluid, two shots of Formalin, a swizzle stick and a black umbrella.'

Lance gave her a hurt look.

'No thanks,' she shouted firmly over the general hubbub. 'A glass of Perrier will be fine.'

'C'mon, how's about a Lethal Injection? People say it has an instant calming effect.'

'I'm sure it has, but I'd prefer fizzy water – unless of course you have a problem with that. Perhaps all the bubbles have gone flat on account of them being in mourning.'

'No, we can do fizzy water. Regular, or with lemon and lime coffins?'

Beverley took a deep calming breath.

'Regular.'

'In an urn or a glass?'

'Honestly,' she said, doing her best to hold on to her patience. 'All I want is a glass of water – no squid ink, no black grapes, no hearse-shaped ice cubes . . . just water.'

Lance finally seemed to get the message. He nodded, smiled and headed off towards the bar.

'One Watery Grave,' she heard him shout to the bartender. 'Hold the Klamati olive crucifix.'

Beverley knew precisely why Naomi had phoned her and insisted they had lunch at the Morgue. Having discovered that lower-middle-class suburbanites like Beverley and Melvin were now going to the Ivy, she would have been desperate to find somewhere even more fashionable. And she most certainly had. The Morgue wasn't just another tacky themed restaurant designed to attract tourists and the occasional cast member from *Brookside* or *Emmerdale*. The Morgue was stellar. According to B.B. Finn's restaurant report in last week's *Sunday Tribune*, not only was its post-Pacific Rim cooking 'so pulsating and animated that it defies description', but the place also had a 'momentous' mission statement. New Zealander Terry McSweeny, the Morgue's creator, whom gossip columnists always described as 'flamboyant' (and whom the *Standard* diary recently referred to waspishly as 'London's favourite Kiwi fruit'), was quoted as saying: 'Death is just so out there right now. It's Linda. It's Gianni and Diana. Inside the Morgue, taboos surrounding death disappear. I like to think we greet death here in a fun way and make it our friend, an intimate – a playmate, if you will.'

For some reason, the chattering classes had reacted to Terry McSweeny's mission statement as if it were a Socratic treatise. In the two weeks following the *Tribune* article, cabals and cliques of London's leading pseuds, poseurs and prats had flocked to the Morgue to discuss mortality over plates of gently sautéed lamb's brains. Hot on their silly heels came the girl bands and footballers.

Beverley buttered another piece of sweet, nutty bread and began looking at the menu, praying it wasn't all scallops and pork bellies and that she would find something which once had scales or a cloven foot, or chewed

the cud, and was therefore kosher. From time to time
she looked out of the window to see if there was any sign
of Naomi. There wasn't. According to Beverley's watch
she was now fifteen minutes late. For an uncharitable
moment she couldn't help thinking that this had less to
do with the traffic and more to do with her sister
playing the kind of egotistical power games favoured by
divas and Hollywood starlets. She immediately felt
guilty for thinking it, but she couldn't help it. She
blamed Melvin. Somehow, she was allowing his refusal
to accept that there was even the remotest possibility
Naomi could have changed to rub off on her. The
moment she'd told him about the letter and their phone
call he said, 'Believe me, Bev, women like Naomi don't
change. Ever. For as long as I can remember, she's
always put you down about something. What about
when we were at your cousin Rita's wedding a few
months after Benny was born? First she swans round
the place like Lady Muck, looking like she wants to
spray breath freshener in everybody's mouth. Then she
comes up to you and what was it she said? Some remark
about your hair.'

'Oh, I don't know, Mel. It was a long time ago.'

'No, come on, you remember. Women never forget
stuff like that. What was it?'

'OK,' she said reluctantly. 'It was, "I love what
you've done with your hair, Bev. You should wash it
more often." '

'See? She's evil, Bev. Let her back into your life and
I'm telling you it'll end in tears.'

If he'd said this once over the last few days, he'd said

it a hundred times. In fact he'd trailed her round the house saying it.

'Melvin,' she'd said in exasperation when he finally followed her upstairs and into the bathroom, 'I think you've made your point. Now, I'd quite like to wax my pubes in private if that's all right with you.'

'Oh, right. Sorry,' he said, turning to go. She tugged gently on his shirt sleeve.

'Mel, I just don't understand why you're getting yourself so worked up about this. I'm the one who got hurt. If I can forgive and forget, I think you should be able to do the same. Look, is there something else bothering you? Something I should know about? How are the toupees doing?'

'Fine. Absolutely fine,' he snapped back. 'Why shouldn't they be?'

'No reason,' she said, desperate not to offend him and ruin his confidence. 'No, that's brilliant. I couldn't be more pleased.'

Beverley glanced out of the window yet again. Still no Naomi. She reached into her bag and took out her compact. As she looked into the mirror and dabbed her chin with powder, she couldn't help thinking that despite the strain of being permanently broke, not to mention living with her mother and two adolescent children, she was probably looking the best she'd looked in ages. She'd blown the last seventy-five quid of her rainy-day money on a haircut – the first she'd had in months. Russell at Beyond the Fringe had persuaded her to let him put some auburn lowlights in her hair.

High on cash and four cups of Russell's complimentary cappuccino, she'd then let him go all the way with her lank shoulder-length shambles and cut it into a geometric Mary Quant bob.

Her new hairstyle, combined with the black Kenzo suit Rochelle had let her borrow, was making her feel decidedly sexy. Rochelle Softness (breast implants, four-wheel drive, interchangeable soft tops) was Beverley's best friend. She lived a few streets away. Natalie had teamed up with Allegra Softness during their first term at primary school, and the two mothers got to know each other through the girls. Although Natalie and Allegra were now at separate schools – Allegra at a private school in Hampstead – the girls remained friends.

As well as the 4x4 which her husband Mitchell always joked she needed to negotiate the treacherous terrain of Sainsbury's car park, Rochelle also owned an entire spare bedroom full of Versace and Lacroix. The suit she'd lent Beverley was the only garment she owned which didn't have gold buttons, some kind of embroidered insignia or sparkly bits on the lapels. This was because it was her funeral suit.

'Look, Beverley, I don't give a toss about this less-is-more thing they always go on about in magazines,' Rochelle had declared one afternoon over cappuccino at the Café Rouge in Hampstead, when Beverley had tentatively suggested that having her manicurist glue tiny silver dolphins on to apple-green fingernails might be going a bit too far.

'As far as I'm concerned, more is more. That's me. Terence Conran can go and drown himself in a coulis of his own urine if he doesn't like it.'

Beverley loved Rochelle; not simply because she possessed that rare ability to understand and accept herself and not give a toss what anybody else thought, but because she was, despite the flashy clothes, the house full of hideous murals and wallpaper borders illustrated with lines of pale pink bows, the most generous and least snobby person she knew. She also made no secret of having been brought up in a Peabody building in Bethnal Green.

'The only difference between us,' Rochelle had said on one occasion a couple of years ago as they sat drinking coffee in Rochelle's kitchen, 'is that this Cinderella finally got to go to the ball and you are still waiting.'

'So, does that make Mitchell Prince Charming?' Beverley asked.

'I guess so . . . if your idea of Prince Charming is a short, balding Jewish man who can never find a parking space and for whom sex has never extended beyond elementary humping because every time he attempts anything slightly imaginative he can hear the voice of his dead mother yelling, "Take that out of your mouth, Mitchell dolly, you don't know where it's been!"'

Beverley laughed so hard she sprayed Rochelle with half-chewed biscotti.

'So, come on,' Rochelle said. 'Your turn. What's Melvin like in the sack, then?'

'Oh, you know . . .' Beverley sighed.

'What do you expect after nearly twenty years? You have to work at these things. Take me and Mitchell. We always have at least two nights out a week. A romantic dinner – a little dancing. He goes Tuesdays. I go Thursdays.'

Beverley hooted.

'No, it's not that,' she said when she'd stopped laughing. 'It's always been the same.'

Rochelle was the first person she'd ever told about having married Melvin not because she fancied him, but because she was desperate to be looked after.

'The point is, I've come to love him almost like a sister loves a brother – except that we have sex once a month. He always seems to enjoy it, and he does his best to turn me on, he really does, but . . .'

'He doesn't quite baste your brisket.'

Beverley gave a weak chuckle and nodded.

Just as Beverley's thoughts were about to become truly maudlin, she looked up. Through the restaurant window, she saw a taxi pull up and Naomi get out. She was waring a beautifully cut scarlet suit with a pencil skirt. She watched her sister pay the driver. 'Oh, God,' Beverley sighed, feeling Rochelle's size twelve skirt straining over her size fourteen hips. 'She's thinner than ever.'

Beverley suddenly felt about as sexy as Flipper. What she had failed to notice, however, was Naomi's distinct tummy bulge. This had come about first because she'd spent the last three nights pigging out on giant tubs of Ben and Jerry's, and second because Summer, her colonic irrigator, was on holiday.

A few moments later, Naomi was striding out towards the table, beaming. Beverley scraped back her chair, stood up, and gave a nervous wave of her fingers. 'Bev-er-leee,' Naomi trilled, throwing her arms round her sister and hugging her. This almost knocked Beverley off balance because she'd been expecting nothing more by way of affectionate greeting than one of Naomi's customary double air kisses. 'So sorry I'm late. Traffic was murder along the Bayswater Road. Plus I couldn't get away because I had Loyd Grossman and an entire film crew at the flat doing a *Through the Keyhole*. They promised they'd be gone by twelve. At one o'clock they were still rearranging furniture. In the end I just left them to it. Bloody media intrusion.'

Beverley, inwardly chortling over the fact that it was clearly Naomi who had been intruding on the media by inviting them in the first place, hugged her back and said not to worry. As they pulled away and sat down, Naomi was quite obviously eyeing her sister's new hairstyle and the Kenzo suit.

'No more calf-length florals, then, Bev?' she said, eyebrows raised. 'One of the things I always admired about you was the way you never seemed to give a monkey's about how you looked. Such a strength. It'd be a real shame to lose it.'

'You reckon?' Beverley said, smiling. She could hardly believe it. Naomi was actually jealous of the way she looked. It was the biggest compliment she'd had in years.

'Oh, without a doubt . . . So,' Naomi went on, 'what do you think of this place? Isn't it a hoot? I came for lunch last week with Donna Karan and they put on a death fashion show – all the models were prancing around in five-hundred-pound couture shrouds. I bought one for Mum . . . dunno why. Wishful thinking, I s'pose.'

Try as she might, Beverley couldn't stop herself giggling.

'You didn't really, did you?' she said.

'Might have done,' Naomi smiled. She stopped a passing Morgue attendant and without asking Beverley what she would like to drink, ordered kir royales for them both.

While they waited for their drinks, Naomi asked after the children.

'Yeah, you know . . . fine,' Beverley said, assuming Naomi was only asking out of politeness.

'So how are they doing at school?' Naomi pressed her. 'Natalie must be, what, in the lower sixth now?'

'Yes, that's right,' Beverley said.

'Don't look so surprised. She's my niece. I haven't forgotten how old she is.'

'Sorry. I didn't mean to be rude. It's just that you never used to be interested in hearing about the kids.'

'Well, I am now,' Naomi said, smiling.

For the next few minutes, after the drinks arrived, Naomi listened intently while Beverley told her about Natalie wanting to do English at Manchester and how Benny had been predicted straight As in his GCSEs.

'You must be so proud of them, Bev,' she said gently and reached out to pat her sister's hand.

'Yeah, I am. Really proud. That's not to say they

don't give me a hard time and there aren't moments when I would happily trade in either one of them for a new washing machine.'

They laughed.

'But you must be proud of yourself, too. I mean, it can't have been easy bringing them up with so little money around.'

'No, it wasn't,' Beverley said, looking down into her kir. 'But you know me. I've always tried to stay positive . . . So, Nay, what's happening with you, aside from the amazing career, the wealth, the fabulous new flat?'

'Well, funny you should ask,' Naomi laughed, 'because I do have news.' She bent down, picked up her handbag and opened it.

'There,' she said, 'a present for you.'

'What's this?' Beverley said, taking the squat glass jar Naomi was holding in front of her. It was full of what appeared to be tomato purée.

'Look at the label,' Naomi said.

Beverley looked. A simple line portrait of Naomi smiled up at her from the side of the jar. Next to the portrait were the words *Pure Gold*.

'Isn't it wonderful, Bev?' Naomi purred. 'Aren't you pleased for me? I've got my very own cook-in sauce.'

'Wow,' Beverley said with genuine enthusiasm. 'That's amazing.'

'I knew you'd be over the moon. I mean, for somebody like you, I guess there's nothing like a bit of vicarious success and glamour. I can hardly believe it, I'm the first woman on British TV with her own range of gourmet sauces. They go on the market in three weeks.

So far there's bolognese, stroganoff, bourguignonne, coq au vin and tomates aux fines herbes. I brought you the tomato because it's kosher.'

'Gosh, thanks, Nay, that's really sweet of you.'

'My pleasure,' Naomi said. Then she leaned across the table and whispered, 'I tell you, Bev, I stand to make a fortune from this. An absolute fortune. One day I'll be richer than Anthea, Esther and that bloody Vanessa put together. Just you wait and see.'

'But you're loaded as it is,' Beverley said. 'Why do you need even more money?'

Naomi laughed and looked at her sister in mild astonishment.

'Because, my darling,' she explained, 'you can never have too much of the stuff. Never.' She took a huge glug of her drink.

For the next ten minutes Naomi gabbled on about how Maurice Saatchi had phoned her every day for a month, begging her to let him handle the advertising. This was followed by accounts of how Delia had got into a strop when she found out her proposed recipes for the cook-in sauces had been rejected in favour of those designed by the Two Fat Ladies, and how Diana Rigg had turned down an offer to play Cleopatra at the National in order to become the Pure Gold mum in the TV ads.

Although she fought to conceal it, after ten minutes Beverley's fascination was starting to flag and she was grateful when Lance arrived to take their order. Naomi announced in a distinctly holier-than-thou tone that she wouldn't bother with a starter because she was watching her weight. Feeling like some Hogarthian glutton for even considering ordering the spicy carrot, coconut and coriander soup, Beverley said she'd skip the first course too. She scanned the menu again for something vegetarian and low-fat, but there was nothing. Reluctantly she ordered plantain, chilli and polenta fritters. Naomi ordered achiote and honey-cured elk carpaccio with chorizo, pomegranates, green lentil horseradish mash and miso wasable syrup, which made Beverley feel slightly less glutton-like until her sister added: 'And I would like that without the mash, the chorizo – oh, yes – and the elk.'

For a few moments Lance stared at her, apparently lost for words. 'I'm sorry, I don't quite understand,' he said, his biro poised over his pad. 'You'd like the elk and chorizo without the elk or the chorizo.'

'Or the mash,' Naomi replied briskly. 'Just bring me the pomegranates – *al dente* of course – in the sauce.'

Then, after making sure a bewildered Lance understood precisely what was meant by *al dente*, she dismissed him and drained her glass. She paused for a second or two.

'So, how *is* Mum then?' she said finally.

'You really do care, don't you?' Beverley said.

Naomi said nothing. Instead she stared down, a look of mild embarrassment on her face, and began straightening her knife and fork, which were perfectly straight to start with.

Beverley decided not to push it, but she was in no doubt now. She'd been right all along. The important matter Naomi had brought her here to discuss *was*

Queenie. Naomi wanted to make peace. It was simply pride that was making it hard for her to get the words out.

At that moment, Lance arrived at their table, pushing one of the Morgue's hospital trolleys. They continued in silence while he placed their main courses in front of them.

'All I know,' Naomi said after Lance had trundled off to his next slab, 'is that I'd be five hundred times better a mother than she ever was.'

'Wouldn't take a lot of doing, I'll admit,' Beverley said, putting a forkful of plantain, chilli and polenta fritter into her mouth.

All of a sudden, Naomi fell silent. She was clearly building up to something. Here it comes, Beverley thought. Here it comes. But Naomi said nothing.

'C'mon, Nay,' Beverley said kindly, 'what is it? What was this amazingly important thing you wanted to discuss?'

Naomi took a deep breath.

'OK, here goes. Look, I know we've had our silly squabbles and disagreements, but I'd like to think that's all in the past now . . .'

While Naomi continued to beat round the bush, Beverley listened and took the occasional bite of food. As she chewed on the second or third of these, she suddenly sat bolt upright in her chair. She shook her head and started to frown. Naomi was far too wrapped up in what she wasn't saying to notice her sister's troubled expression. By now Beverley had stopped chewing. She glanced round to see if anybody was watching, then discreetly transferred the mouthful of food into her napkin. She was in no doubt. The polenta definitely contained something meaty. Meaty verging on porky.

'You see, Bev,' Naomi continued, still utterly unaware that her sister wasn't listening, 'there's something I would like you to do for me.' She paused for a few moments. Beverley didn't look up. By now she had spread the napkin open on her lap and was busy poking her finger around in the glistening mulch of half-chewed-up food.

'Jeez, this is hard,' Naomi went on, sounding nervous and unsure of herself for the first time in her life. 'I've been rehearsing in front of the mirror for days. Right, I'm just going to come out and say it. You see,' she went on, her voice dropping, 'I need to ask you something – something big, well, huge, actually . . . Oh God . . . Beverley, look, do you think there's any possibility . . . I mean : . . will you have my gravy?'

'Christ, how many calories do you think there are in a puddle of gravy?' Beverley said, finally looking up from the mulch and holding her flattened palm out towards Naomi. 'Does that look like a piece of crispy bacon to you? . . . For God's sake eat the gravy. You know I can't. It'll be made from meat juices. It's not kosher.'

'No, Beverley . . . you didn't hear me . . . God, the bloody racket in here . . . that's not what I said.' She paused and took a very deep breath.

'Beverley, I don't want you to have my gravy, I want you to have my *baby*.'

Chapter 6

'What?' Beverley had said, wiping the last bit of suspect pork off her hand and at the same time doing her best, but failing, to pick her jaw up off the table. 'You want me to be a surrogate mother?'

'That's pretty much the size of it,' Naomi said, running her finger round the rim of her empty champagne flute.

Neither of them spoke for a couple of seconds. 'Listen,' Naomi said eventually, 'do you want me to complain about the bacon . . .?'

'No, really,' Beverley said. The food was the last thing on her mind. 'It doesn't matter. I'd nearly finished anyway . . . But I don't understand. What's wrong? Why can't you have your own baby?'

Naomi swallowed hard, as if she were fighting back tears. She looked up at Beverley.

'I'm infertile. According to my gynaecologist, my eggs are next to useless, my tubes are blocked like the Bakerloo Line in the rush hour and my cervix is so weak that if I could get pregnant, I wouldn't be able to carry a foetus beyond the third or fourth month.'

'Oh, God, Nay,' Beverley said, reaching out and squeezing her sister's hand, 'that's awful. What can I say? I'm so, so sorry.'

'I found out a few months ago.' By now the tears were beginning to roll down her face. At that moment Lance passed by. Beverley caught his eye and ordered two more kirs.

'At first I was in shock,' Naomi went on. 'I couldn't believe it. You know . . . everything had been going great till then. I had it all. Brilliant job, stacks of money in the bank. I'd even managed to find a wonderful bloke I wanted to make babies with. We started trying – and when nothing happened after six months or so, I went to the doctor, and then . . .'

Her voice trailed off.

'So . . . so, how would it work – this surrogacy thing?' Beverley asked, her head still spinning with shock at her sister's mind-boggling request. 'I mean, what about the actual getting pregnant bit?'

'Oh, right. Well, for a start there's no actual sex involved. You'd have to be – I mean, if you agreed, that is – artificially inseminated. Tom – he's my chap – and I agreed we shouldn't involve fertility clinics just in case somebody blabbed to the press. But according to all the books and articles I've read, do-it-yourself artificial insemination is dead easy. Apparently when lesbians want to get pregnant, they put the bloke who's agreed to father the child in another room with a few dirty mags and get him to come into a jar. His sperm is then transferred into a turkey baster which is a bit like a huge eye dropper. The woman then sticks this up inside her and simply squeezes the rubber top to release the sperm. It's easy.'

'Easy,' Beverley repeated. She took a glug of her kir. 'Easy bloomin' peasy.'

'I know I could make a good mother,' Naomi said, almost pleadingly. 'I'd try to be the exact opposite of ours. I just want a chance to prove it.'

She paused and stared into Beverley's eyes.

'Please, Bev,' she pleaded, 'I know I'm asking for the moon, but please be the one to give me that chance.'

Beverley took another sip of her drink. For a moment Naomi looked like the needy, vulnerable little girl she used to collect every afternoon from Gearies School.

'Look, Nay, I have a pretty good idea what it must feel like to be told you can't have children, but you said it – what you're asking of me is absolutely huge. I mean, to carry a child – and using my egg, it would technically be my child – to give birth to it and then give it up . . . I'm just not sure I could . . .'

'But will you at least think about it?'

'Yes, I will. Promise.'

Beverley decided to change the subject in order to give herself time to think.

'So, tell me about this Tom, then,' she said. 'who is he? Someone famous?'

Naomi dabbed her under-eyes with her napkin and gave a half-smile.

'Fairly. He's Tom Jago, the drama director. You know, did that amazing production of *Blue Remembered Hills* for the BBC last summer – won all those awards.'

Beverley nodded, but was none the wiser.

'We've been together just over a year. I tell you, Bev – not only is he amazingly talented, but he's also a bit of a dish.'

'They've all been good-looking, Nay – and rich. The bit you always seem to find difficult is hanging on to them for more than three months.'

'I know. It's the job. I'm always working. How can you make a relationship work when one of you is constantly putting in fourteen-hour days?'

Beverley knew full well it was her sister's personality which put men off rather than the hours she worked, but she decided to let it go.

'Funny,' she said instead, 'I suppose I always imagined you settling down eventually, but it never occurred to me for one minute that you might want children. You've never shown the remotest interest in them. For God's sake, Nay, you bought Natalie a Prada handbag for her first birthday.'

'Oh God, didn't she like it?'

'Well, she didn't say she didn't, but then again she couldn't speak yet. She did love playing with it, though. She kept her Duplo men and bits of soggy old biscuit in it.'

'I suppose she was a bit on the young side. I'm no Maria Von Trapp, am I?' Naomi said. 'But what do you expect? I don't know how you did the mothering thing, Bev – I mean, what sort of maternal role model did we have? I've always been so scared that I'd repeat our mother's mistakes. Then, a year or so ago, things began to change. Whenever I went out, I found myself gazing into prams and getting all soppy and tearful. Did you know, Beverley, new-born babies have this heavenly smell about them?'

'Yeah, I know, that kind of delicate blend of shit and vomit,' Beverley said.

Lance arrived with their second round of kir royales.

'No,' Naomi said, picking up her glass and taking a sip, 'I mean the smell of their skin. It's so soft and pink. Look, Bev, you wouldn't breathe a word of this, would you? If the press find out they'll have a field day, but I've even been seeing a shrink. I know how hard I can be and Renate's been brilliant at forcing me to confront my feelings about Mum. I mean, getting angry in therapy is so different from getting angry with people in the office. It's just so cathartic, you wouldn't believe it.'

'Does all this mean you're ready to do some emotional bridge-building with Queenie, then?' asked Beverley. 'Originally I thought that's why you got us together. She's dying to see you. It's been ages.'

'I know. It's unforgivable of me to have left it this long. I'll give her a ring, Bev, as soon as I've got an hour or six to kill – I promise.'

Beverley laughed.

'That would be wonderful,' she said gently, taking her sister's hand again.

There was a pause while Naomi gathered her thoughts.

'Look, getting back to the surrogacy,' she said, 'you know, I wouldn't expect you to do it for nothing . . .'

'Heavens, Nay. If I agreed I wouldn't want paying. It didn't even occur to me.'

'Well, it occurred to me. Look, I've got a fair idea how

things are financially with you and Melvin, and I thought two hundred and fifty sounded about right . . .'

Without thinking, Beverley let out an uncharacteristically sardonic laugh.

'Great,' she said, 'that should just about cover the milk bill.'

'Bloody hell, how far does it go back – 1485?'

'No, June.'

'Hang on. I think we're at cross-purposes here. I mean two hundred and fifty *thousand*.'

Beverley sat blinking at her sister. It was a few seconds before she could speak.

'What, as in a quarter of a million?'

'The very same.'

'Pounds?'

'No, cocktail gherkins, you dope. Yes, of course pounds.'

Beverley knocked back the rest of her kir in one gulp.

While Beverley was on the Tube, still desperately trying to take in the enormity of what she was being asked, not to mention offered, Benny Littlestone was sitting on his bed, ripping into a pile of bubble packs and tipping their contents on to his duvet: one twenty-five-millimetre butterfly hose clip, six thirty-two-millimetre rubber washers, twelve clear plastic shower curtain rings and half a dozen inlet hose washers.

He picked up a couple of the inlet hose washers and gave a short soft laugh. Why on earth had he bought them? They had a diameter of less than half an inch. They wouldn't fit over his middle finger, let alone his penis. A thirty-two-millimetre rubber washer, being lightweight and slightly stretchy, might on the other hand be just the business. He would try it much later when his sister wasn't around and everybody was asleep.

He turned back to the print-out Lettice had given him last week from the Foreskin Reclamation Web site.

The six pages of information and instructions had been written by Dr Dwight Lafayette, founder of the San Francisco-based foreskin reclamation self-help group, Recover. Lafayette was a Christian vegan and former missionary who had spent much of his professional life converting 'primitive peoples' to Christianity. Having spent thirty years watching members of African tribes distend various body parts with the aid of weights, he had become an expert in the art, and on the plane home to the US after retiring from his post had a vision of the Almighty standing by him in the aisle commanding him to apply what he had learned about earlobes and mouths to heathen Jewish penises.

In order to carry out Dr Lafayette's instructions, Benny had on his way home from school that afternoon got off the bus two stops early and visited the Plumbing and Bathroom Accessories department at Homebase.

As a teenager who regarded himself as passably cool, Benny felt distinctly uncomfortable among all the DIY-savvy dads. He wandered bewildered and awkward past shelves full of planer blades, spigot adapters and sanding discs and headed towards a huge brightly coloured 'Plumbing and Bathroom Accessories' sign suspended from the ceiling.

Twenty paces later he came to an area thickly colonised by bent tank connections. These immediately gave way to quiet ball valves (side fed), compression nuts and anti-syphon units. Still no penis girth washers or metal rings. Then, out of the blue, next to some mahogany loo brushholders, he spotted the shower curtain rings. Finally he came upon a row of shelves brimming over with packs of different-size washers. He picked up three packs and headed towards the checkout.

There were three tills open, each operated by a man. Shit. There was no chance of him making it through without the cashier, purely by way of matey, blokish conversation, asking him what he was planning to do with all these washers. On a scale of one to ten his plumbing knowledge was about minus fifteen. He didn't stand a hope in hell of bluffing his way through such an inquisition. Such was his panic, it didn't occur to him that all he needed to do was to shrug, admit he knew nothing about plumbing and say they were for his dad. As far as Benny was concerned, he only had two choices, of which just one was viable, since he wasn't about to explain the essential role of a washer in his mission to reclaim his foreskin. He took a ten-pound note from his back pocket, about five pounds more than the cost of the washers and shower curtain rings. If the cashier asked him any technical questions, he would simply chuck the money at him, pick up his packages and make a run for it.

Just as he was about to join the queue nearest to him and fall in behind a particularly capable-looking woman in baggy fawn cords who was paying for a tumble dryer venting kit and two cans of T-Cut, a fourth till was opened by a pretty Asian woman wearing a waist-length plait and an armful of gold bangles. Benny raised his eyes heavenwards and muttered his brief but heartfelt thanks to the God he didn't believe in.

He moved swiftly towards the Asian woman's check-out, but the venting kit woman pushed in front of him and he was forced to wait while she hunted for her chequebook and filled out the cheque with the speed of a dyslexic tortoise. Then, after spending a full minute wrestling the venting kit into a Homebase brown paper bag, she realised she couldn't find her receipt. Another couple of minutes passed while she accused the cashier of failing to hand it to her. In the end she found it in her coat pocket. After mumbling a less than heartfelt apology, she stuck her nose in the air and strode off towards the automatic doors.

Benny smiled at the cashier, partly as a show of solidarity against the obnoxious venting kit woman and partly because he was confident that he had escaped any possibility of being subjected to a plumbing oral.

The woman smiled back at him and began passing the bubble packs over the electronic swipe.

'Oooh, I see someone's got a leaky gland nut then,' she said with the confidence of a person who could plumb for Europe. 'They're buggers. I had one last week. How you gonna tackle it? Are you going to remove the capstan head before you have a go at the verdigris and scale or detach the spindle completely so that you expose the waste flange?'

Benny stood blinking at the woman.

'Er, yes, probably,' he blurted out as he slammed his ten quid on the counter, picked up the bubble packs, which had by now all been swiped, and bolted towards the doors.

Having congratulated himself on what he was positive would be the excellent fit of the thirty-two-millimetre rubber washer, he began rereading Dr Lafayette's instructions, a complicated procedure involving stretching some of the loose skin on the penis, holding it in place with a ring, and then letting good old Mr Gravity do the Lord's work – with the help of some fishing weights. Benny flinched when he read about the weights; his visit to Homebase had been traumatic enough. A trip to an angling supplies shop was unthinkable. Instead of using the fishing weights recommended by Dr Lafayette, he decided to improvise. It came to him immediately. Earrings. That was it. He went on to the landing, checked he could still hear his sister tapping away on her computer and headed towards his mother's bedroom.

'Ooh, I love the cracked paint effect,' Beverley said, walking into Rochelle's kitchen and admiring her newly decorated walls.

'Yeah, I'm pleased with it,' Rochelle said. 'I was going for the distressed look. Mind you, Mitchell's not so keen. He walks in last night, grimaces and says if you ask him it doesn't look so much distressed as bloody tormented. Still, what does he know about interior design? The man sells smoked salmon for a living . . . So, how was lunch?

I'd forgotten you were seeing Naomi today. I only remembered when my taps began running with blood.'

'God, you're worse than Melvin,' Beverley said, sighing. She pulled a chair from under the table and sat down. 'Why won't either of you believe me when I say she's changed?'

''Cos she hasn't,' Rochelle said in a matter-of-fact tone as she poured boiling water into the cafetière. 'Look, hardly a week goes by when Mitchell doesn't show me something in *Private Eye* about her. Apparently she struts round the Channel 6 offices like Machiavelli in drag, sacking people who look at her in the wrong tone of voice. They've got this brilliant cartoon of her with 666 tattooed across her head.'

She brought the cafetière and two mugs over to the table.

'I know. I've seen it,' Beverley said, watching Rochelle push down the plunger. 'It's horrible. But that's just the media being jealous and malicious. Look, maybe she was like that in the past, but the woman's in therapy, for Christ's sake . . .'

'Is that what she told you? God, she's good. She's very good.' Rochelle began filling their mugs.

'You're saying she's lying?'

'OK . . . I could be wrong, but it sounds like part of some elaborate buttering-up exercise to me. She wants something from you, doesn't she? I can smell it. Come on, tell me I'm wrong.'

Beverley didn't say anything for a few moments. Then she took a deep breath.

'OK, you're right. She does want something.'

'I knew it,' Rochelle said triumphantly.

'She's asked me to have a baby for her,' Beverley said softly, '. . . to be a surrogate mother.'

Rochelle almost choked on her coffee.

'Come again.'

Beverley simply nodded.

'Blimey,' Rochelle said, clearly at a loss for words.

'That was pretty much my reaction.'

Rochelle sat thinking for a couple of moments.

'Oh, right,' she said eventually, beginning to laugh as her thoughts took shape, 'I get it. Heaven forbid La Gold should risk losing her figure getting pregnant. So she reckons she'll get good old Bev to get fat and have her stretch marks for her. I tell you, Bev, she only wants a child for spare parts in case she gets terminal one of these days.'

'God, you'd smell flowers and ask where the coffin is,' Beverley said, starting to get irritated. 'Look, I dashed over here as soon as I got back because you're my best friend, I'm shocked and confused and I needed to talk to somebody. But if you're just going to be cynical and make a joke of the whole thing, then . . .'

'Oh God, Beverley, I'm sorry,' Rochelle said. 'I didn't mean it. Honest. It's just that after everything you've told me about Naomi – about the way she's treated you and your mother – I find it hard to believe she's not out to get you in some way, that's all. Look, she's your sister. You know her better than I do. I'll take your word for it that she's undergone some kind of personality change.'

Beverley gave a half-smile.

'So,' Rochelle said, 'I take it she's been told she can't have children.'

'Yes. She's living with some film director guy and they're desperate to start a family. She's offered me two hundred and fifty thousand pounds if I agree to have a baby for her.'

'Christ, she doesn't mess about. So, what did you say?'

'I said I'd think about it.'

'And . . .'

'And nothing. I've only been thinking for three hours.'

'OK, so what are you thinking?' Rochelle stood up and fetched a plate of M&S Belgian biscuits from the worktop.

'Well, for starters, I'm thinking another pregnancy would give me about as much pleasure as an all-over body wax. I'm forty-two years old, I've already spent eighteen months of my life up the duff, undergone two excruciatingly painful labours, the second of which was so traumatic the midwife needed gas and air.' She reached out and took a biscuit. 'What's more, I now have a permanently leaking bladder, an episiotomy scar so hideous that by rights the obstetrician should be doing a five stretch, and veins in my legs which look like they once starred in a lump of Stilton. Then again, Naomi is my sister, she is desperate for a child and I can make that happen. Despite all the bad feeling there's been between us, I still care about her. I don't think a day went by during that five years when I didn't think about her and wonder how she was.'

'And there's also the question of the money,' Rochelle said.

'I know,' Beverley said, munching on her biscuit. 'All the way home on the Tube I did my best to keep the money outside the question. I mean, if I did agree to have Naomi's baby I'd want to do it for love, not simply for financial gain. But I kept coming back to it. Over and over again. Just think what Melvin and I could do with two hundred and fifty grand. We could pay off all our debts, have a holiday, buy a new car. He could set himself up in a new business – I know he could be a success, Rochelle, I just know it. You remember me telling you how Tower of Bagel was his idea all those years ago – and now that's more successful than McDonald's. It just has to be something that excites him and is light years away from dishing out Senacot and elasticated stockings to old ladies in Buckhurst Hill.'

'You think he might be up for the surrogacy deal, then?'

'Mel? I dunno. He might be tempted by the money, but then again, the thought of his wife carrying another man's child . . .'

'God, if Mitchell thought I was doing that, he'd go berserk. You know how jealous he is. The au pair had to chaperon me when I went to see *Braveheart*. Runs in the family. He gets it from his grandfather. When his grandmother was on her death bed she told him she'd been unfaithful during their marriage. He leaned over her and said, "I know. That's why I poisoned you." '

Beverley started to laugh.

'At least that's something I wouldn't have to worry

about with Mel. I mean, he may be a bit of a dope where the business is concerned, but I couldn't imagine him becoming unhinged.' She paused and took a mouthful of her coffee.

'But even if Melvin's OK with the surrogacy,' she went on, 'the fact is, Naomi's asking me to carry a baby, a baby which would be biologically mine, and then give it up. I just don't know if I'm up to that . . . and what about this Tom Jago bloke? I don't know him from Adam. He may be some hotshot film director, but that doesn't mean he'll be a good father . . . then there's you trying to convince me Naomi isn't to be trusted . . . God, I'm so confused, Rochelle.'

'So, now you agree that maybe she isn't to be trusted?'

Beverley shrugged. 'Yes. No. Who knows? What should I do, Rochelle? Tell me. What would you do?'

Rochelle stood up, walked round the table, put her arm round Beverley and kissed the top of her head.

'I don't know, Bev,' she said gently, 'I just don't know.'

Beverley decided to walk home because she wanted more time to think. She'd told the children she might be late because she was having lunch with a girlfriend and might go for a wander down Oxford Street afterwards.

As she passed the identikit detached houses with their hideous loft extensions and paved front gardens, Naomi's words kept flying round her head. 'Please, Bev, please be the one to give me that chance.'

Naomi – hard-bitten, self-sufficient Naomi – was reaching out to her in a way she had never done before.

Beverley had never stopped loving her sister, but as she walked home in the rain she found herself actually starting to like her. By now she had put her suspicions about Naomi to one side. If her sister did have some self-seeking agenda cleverly hidden, which she wouldn't discover until it was too late, for the life of her she couldn't imagine what it could be.

Surely, she thought, didn't every woman deserve the chance to become a mother? Maybe women like her and Naomi, who had been brought up without proper parental love, deserved it even more. The love of a child, like the love of a caring, tender parent, is unconditional. A child would love Naomi in a way she'd never known before, in a way that no lover or husband, however adoring, could. A tiny, dependent being would make her feel truly valued, give her a sense of self-worth that no amount of fame, money or professional accolades could provide.

Perhaps Beverley was soft. But that was hardly surprising since she'd mothered Naomi almost since she was born. She knew she still had days and days more thinking to do, but she suspected that in the end she wouldn't be able to refuse her little sister the help she was asking for.

Chapter 7

'I don't care three ha'pence how popular you have been with the public until now, m'dear,' he continued. The atmosphere at Naomi's lunchtime meeting with the newly appointed head of Channel 6 was becoming distinctly uneasy. Eric Rowe took some more Sweet Briar from the leather pouch on his desk and began tamping it down into his pipe. 'The fact of the matter is, you have overstepped the mark and gone beyond the bounds of good taste. I will brook no more of this tripe, this disgusting sensationalism.' He sounded like an avuncular vicar driven to the brink after discovering his curate with his hand up a choirboy.

'We don't want people to have to watch your gratuitous rubbish any more, to see mad women who let their babies drown in the bath or bump off their husbands with frozen turkeys, to mention just two of your recent capers. You will with immediate effect concentrate on decent, popular issues. Such as, ooh, I don't know . . . petrol prices. Now there's a topic every member of the public cares about. Then there's all the racket we get on our beaches and streets these days from those wretched gateau-blasters. And holes in the road – that's another thing . . .'

By now Naomi was hyperventilating with rage. Instead of bestowing upon her the fawning obeisance she had come to expect from all members of the Channel 6 staff, including chief executives, Eric Rowe had dared, as he had at their first meeting ten days ago, to address her like some errant researcher. As the room began to spin, Naomi dug her nails into the arms of the leather chair, partly to stop herself fainting and partly to stop herself getting up and beating Eric Rowe to within an inch of his pointless life.

While Eric wittered on about 'good clean fun' and the 'splendid' idea he'd had for a sponsored London-to-Brighton supermarket trolley race, Naomi stared at the man in utter disbelief, taking in the pipe, the check Viyella shirt, the sandwich-filled Tupperware container sitting on top of the filing cabinet. She was in no doubt. There was a definite niff of pilchard in the air.

Like most people at Channel 6, Naomi blamed Eric Rowe's appointment on Tony Blair. Eric was part of the Real People Initiative promised by the Prime Minister in a throwaway comment he had made on *Newsnight* where he was being interviewed about the first two years of the Labour government. He was getting into his stride about how he wanted government to reflect the concerns of ordinary people when he appeared to pluck the idea from the air;

'You see, I feel very strongly,' he waxed, 'that we must breathe some fresh air into such areas as public transport, the Health Service and even your own sphere, Jeremy, of broadcasting. And I'm convinced that the way forward is to bring in people who are completely fresh to these fields and to, er, put them into positions of really quite considerable power within these organisations.'

'Prime Minister,' Jeremy Paxman butted in, 'come on, you can't seriously be suggesting that you could take a . . . I don't know, a dinner lady or a farmer from the West Country and just say, here you are, here's Railtrack, or the BBC, now go off and run it.'

'Well, now you mention it, Jeremy, I think it's a terrific idea. I mean, take broadcasting . . . programmes like this are *for* dinner ladies and farmers from the West Country. So we say, let's find a farmer in the West Country and offer him the chance to . . . to stamp his input into the heart of the industry. I think people are fed up with having their thinking dictated by trendy, wealthy people from London who eat at smart restaurants and have houses in Tuscany.'

'You mean people like yourself, Prime Minister?' Jeremy Paxman shot back at him.

The Prime Minister ignored Paxman and carried on, making the policy up as he went along, an evangelical gleam in his eye. The Real People Initiative – the RPI – had been born.

Eric Rowe, who until then had farmed eight hundred acres in the Quantocks, been a stalwart of the Somerset Rotary, but lost a fortune in the BSE crisis, was one of the first real people to apply for a job under the RPI scheme. The day Eric Rowe replace Alan Yentob as the director of Channel 6, the Prime Minister and the Culture Secretary Chris Smith were there to wish him well. His official unveiling to the hundred or so reporters and photographers gathered in the lobby was performed to Jarvis Cocker singing 'Common People'.

When reporters asked him for his thoughts on the state of British television he drew deeply on his pipe and said, 'Well, boys, to tell you the truth, I rarely watch the thing, but my wife Audrey is quite keen on the nature programmes and the *Antiques Roadshow*.' With the enthusiastic backing of both the right-wing press and the government, it was no surprise that he felt able to treat even the great Naomi Gold (whom he had never even heard of before taking up his post) as nothing more than a particularly obstreperous mare.

'Eric,' Naomi said as her breathing finally returned to normal and the room stopped spinning, 'if our relationship is to be an amicable one . . . indeed if I am to remain at Channel 6, you have to get one thing absolutely straight. I will not be spoken to like some . . .'

'You see, m'dear,' he said, ignoring her and picking up a pile of papers from his desk and waving them in front of him, 'there is also the somewhat pressing matter of chitties . . .'

'Chitties,' she repeated flatly.

'Yes. Or in your case a very distinct absence of them. You see, not to put too fine a point on it, I've been getting complaints from Ee-laine, the canteen manager. As you well know, each senior member of staff is allowed to offer guests free refreshments – to wit a maximum of sixteen cups of tea and eight slices of cherry Genoa each month. The problem is that the canteen ladies have been watching you claiming your allowance without signing for it.'

Naomi could take no more.

'For fuck's sake, man,' she yelled, standing up and leaning over his desk, 'in case it has escaped your addled compost heap of a brain, you mangleworzled inbred bumpkin, *Naomi!* is the Channel 6 flagship programme. Haven't you looked at the ratings? Every sodding show you put out is losing viewers, except one. Mine. Without me this fucking station is kaput, Eric. Kaput. Do you hear me? Now, you have two choices. You either give me the respect and recognition I deserve, or I walk.'

Eric Rowe leaned back in his chair and drew on his pipe.

'The door is open,' he said softly. 'You see, I *have* looked at the ratings. In fact I have the latest ones right here.' He slid a sheet of paper across the desk towards her. She snatched it.

'As you can see,' he went on, 'they're not just slightly down on the previous month – they are considerably down.'

'It's a statistical glitch,' she snapped, 'nothing more. They'll be up again. It happens every summer when people go on holiday.'

'Maybe,' he said, 'but it's my considered opinion – as well as my wife Audrey's, I should add – that the public is beginning to come round to our way of thinking. They've had enough of this prurient rubbish and they're voting with their off buttons. I know you'd have found out about the viewing figures eventually, but I didn't want to upset you by mentioning it today because we do still value your contribution here at Channel 6. But your extreme rudeness and arrogance has left me with no option. Now then, let me give you what I think our American cousins refer to as the "bottom line". Quite simply, you either take my recommendations on board – or you leave.'

'OK, I'll leave,' she said. 'You know as well as I do that I could walk into a job at the BBC tomorrow.'

'You may . . . on the other hand, I think it's fair to say that the days of overpaid announcers like yourself are over. There's a lady traffic warden called Betty who already has a big following on Border Television and has been given her own show – on the BBC, as it happens. In fact I think it's scheduled to go out at the same time as your little programme. Do you know what they are paying her? I'll tell you what they're paying her. Two hundred a week. That's right. Just about your weekly expenses claim for taxis.'

Naomi plonked herself back on to her chair, defeat etched into her face.

'That's better,' Rowe continued. 'Now then, I suggest you go back to your office and think yourself lucky that you're still earning what you are in a profoundly changing industry.' He then brought out a matchbox from his pocket, struck a light, lowered it into the tobacco and began taking short, rapid puffs on his pipe.

'Sheep worrying,' he said finally, 'there's another major issue for you. Or senior citizens. Intrepid OAPs, battling grannies – that's the ticket. Blow me down, they're coming thick and fast now. D'you know, I can see we're going to get along . . .'

As he chuckled to himself, a stream of pipe smoke escaped from the side of his mouth and wafted towards Naomi. She coughed and waved her arm vigorously from side to side as she became trapped inside the fug.

Immediately after slamming Eric Rowe's door behind her, Naomi charged up to the canteen, barged her way to the front of the queue, and demanded a triple-decker Bacon Bastard. 'With extra Bastard,' she snapped.

The woman in the long mauve cardigan and woolly hat picked up the ringing telephone. Before she had a chance to say hello, the sobbing, hiccoughing lass on the end of the line began gabbling about her gigantic nose and how she thought no boy was ever going to fancy her and that she was certain she would remain a virgin for the rest of her life. The girl had barely got into her stride when the woman let out an elongated sigh.

'Nose, schmoze. You think you've got problems. That's nothing. Let me tell you about the aggravation I got with my grandson. He doesn't call, he doesn't visit . . . so, what's your name, darling?'

'Natalie,' the girl said through another hiccough. There was a pause. 'Hang on,' she said, sniffing, 'I thought this was meant to be a student counselling service. You're supposed to be listening to *my* problems . . .'

'No, darling, this is the Sidney and Bessie Hamburger Jewish Day Centre. I was on my way to the dining room and as I was passing by the office I heard the phone going.'

'Oh gosh, I'm so sorry. I dialled the wrong number . . .'

'No, no, darling, wait – don't hang up. My grandson – to tell you the truth, he's not such an oil painting. He's got bat ears. Listen, he's got big ears, you've got a big nose. You're a perfect match . . .'

Finally realising the line had gone dead, Millie Resnick, eighty-three years young next week, as she delighted in telling the staff at the centre several times a day, shrugged, shuffled across the office and continued on her way.

'Smells like some kind of fried fish.' The voice came from behind her. She turned round to see her friend Queenie Gold. Millie sniffed the air, nodded her agreement and waited for her chum to draw level.

'All my married life,' Queenie said as they walked down the corridor, 'I stood and fried fish . . . every Friday night without fail. On these ankles . . . you wonder why they look like tree trunks.' The need to out-Jewish-mother her friends at the day centre constantly forced Queenie to re-invent her past. 'And in forty years I never smelled anything like this. I can't put my finger on it, but something's not right. I tell you, Millie, this new catering manager they just took on, I don't like the look of him. In my view, you can never trust a man with too much hair. It's all over him, sprouting through his shirt front, out of his nose, his ears. I ask you, who ever heard of a man with a handlebar eyebrow?'

The two women reached the door – Queenie limping a little more than usual because her hip had been playing her up. They paused at the notice board to look at the hand-written lunch menu. Millie couldn't make it out because of her cataracts, so Queenie read it aloud. The shaky mix of swirly upper-and lower-case letters surrounded by incompetent felt-tip drawings of fish, shells and nets proclaimed fried fillet of plaice, chips and peas followed by fresh fruit salad.

'Fresh, my backside,' Queenie spat, as they joined the lunch queue. 'The only thing fresh about that fruit salad is the crook who opened the tin.'

The general crashing and clanking of pots and pans on the opposite side of the serving hatch was accompanied by Martin Posner, the newly installed catering-manager-cum-chef, belting out 'My Way' as he lowered baskets of battered fish into the huge stainless-steel deep fryer.

Directing the men and women in wheelchairs or with walking frames to the head of the queue was Lorraine Feld, the famously jolly fifty-something day centre manager. With her caring expression and her pale pink sweatshirt with a huge teddy bear motif, she looked like an ever-so-slightly twee hybrid of a social worker, a lower-middle-class Lady Bountiful and an angel.

Queenie and Millie sat themselves down at one of the Formica-topped tables, next to their friend Lenny Shupak. Queenie liked Lenny not simply because he was a widower – there were umpteen of those at the centre – but because he was still on the ball and he hadn't let himself go to pot. He wore his shirts with the cuffs rakishly folded back two or three turns, and droopy gold-rimmed glasses which had been vaguely trendy in the seventies and which Queenie still regarded as the height of fashion. He was also one of the few men at the day centre who didn't have a niff of stale wee about him.

Lenny had only been coming to the centre for a few months. He'd lived all his life in Leeds, and after his wife died had moved down to London to be near his daughter. Nobody ever used Lenny's proper surname. To everybody at the day centre he was always known as Lenny Leeds.

'Beef dripping,' Lenny said, filling his lungs with air and grimacing. 'I'd know that smell anywhere. Every chip shop in the north uses it for frying. People up there like the taste. But the point is, it's far cheaper than oil . . . and it sure as hell ain't kosher.'

'I knew it.' Queenie thumped the table with her palm. 'I knew it didn't smell right. The fact is, the food's been bloody awful since Posner took over. Bits of scraggy, tasteless old meat. Fruit that's either tinned or half rotten. And the only green we get is in the bread.'

'The thing is,' Lenny said, 'it's not just the food situation, there's another much more serious issue to consider.'

'Like what?' Millie asked.

He beckoned the two women closer. As he pushed his spectacles on to his head, Queenie couldn't help thinking how attractive he looked.

'Money has been going missing,' he said in a whisper, 'and jewellery too.'

'What?' the two women gasped in unison.

116

He nodded.

'Last week Ronnie Silverstone had fifty pounds disappear from his wallet. Frieda – you know, with the legs – lost the necklace her husband bought her for their golden wedding anniversary. And other people have been reporting stuff going missing.'

'Well, it's the first I've heard of it,' Millie said.

'So why hasn't somebody called the police?' Queenie asked.

'Well, when Ronnie lost the fifty quid,' Lenny started to explain, 'he went straight to Lorraine and begged her to do just that. I was there when he asked her. You should have seen her. She just stood there, her arms round Ronnie's shoulders, nodding and smiling in that caring, patronising bloody way of hers. She kept telling him it was all in his imagination, that he was a confused old man and that she'd go and make him a nice cup of tea. She just didn't want to know. She laughed – made a joke of it. I tell you, she's in league with that villain Posner. They think that just because so many of the people here have lost their marbles, we're all sitting ducks. I reckon that between them they're coining it in. For God's sake, you only have to look at the pair of them to see they're up to no good.'

Lenny jerked his head to one side. Millie and Queenie turned in their seats. Through the serving hatch they could see Lorraine standing in the kitchen, clearly deep in conversation with Martin Posner. Every so often she would take a drag on a cigarette and turn to flick ash into the sink. Then she would look towards the old people in the dining room. Once or twice she pointed to a particular person. On the last occasion she pulled Posner to her by tugging gently on the gold medallion hanging round his neck and seemed to whisper something in his ear. As she moved away they both giggled.

'You're right, Lenny,' Queenie said finally. 'They're plotting something. I just know the pair of them are up to no good. I can feel it in my stomach.'

'All I can feel in my stomach,' Millie said, 'is wind from that bloody fish.'

'What are you on about?' Queenie came back to her. 'You didn't touch it.'

'I didn't need to. With a sensitive digestive system like mine, even a smell can leave me in agony.' She let out a loud belch.

Raising her eyes heavenwards, Queenie reached into her handbag, took out a tube of Rennies and handed it to Millie.

'So, what do we do?' Queenie said to Lenny.

'What we do,' Lenny said, turning his head to check they weren't being overheard, 'is build up a case. This means keeping our cool, going softly softly and taking our time to collect hard evidence against Martin and Lorraine.'

'You mean watch them and then compile a . . . a dossier,' Queenie virtually squealed with excitement.

'Then, and only then, when we are absolutely sure of our facts, do we go to the police,' Lenny said.

'Yes,' Queenie said, 'but it would be great if we could get some publicity along the way.'

'I agree. Maybe we should get in touch with the local paper?' Lenny said.

'Ach, forget the local paper,' Queenie said, waving her hand dismissively. 'When the time comes to think about publicity, I reckon I just might be able to go one better.'

Chapter 8

The single pubic hair in the palm of his hand, Melvin
climbed onto the double bed. Manoeuvring his head in
such a way as to avoid bashing it on the candelabra-style
simulated-dripping-wax centre light which hung over the
bed, he picked up the hair with his fingers, held it up to
the light and narrowed his eyes.

It was the third time that week that Melvin had come
home from work, disappeared into the bedroom and
gone hunting for signs of his wife's infidelity.

After checking for obvious evidence, such as lowering
of the level of perfume in her one, ancient bottle of
Coco, and searching for any suspiciously new underwear, the final stage of his obsessive routine involved
pulling back the duvet and running the palm of his hand
slowly over the fitted bottom sheet in order to seek out
damp patches and foreign pubic hairs. For some reason,
he assumed that if Beverley were to be unfaithful, she
would lack the imagination and good taste to be it
anywhere other than in their bed.

It was during this last part of his search that Melvin
had, today, struck gold. Or at least, ginger. Focusing

clearly on the pubic hair, Melvin was in no doubt that when the light caught it a certain angle, he could make out traces of a colour quite foreign to him. His own pubes were dark brown, almost black. Beverley's were a shade or two lighter. Neither of them possessed a bush which was even remotely ginger. He was now certain that Beverley was having an affair.

Finding such irrefutable forensic evidence as the pube was a conundrum for Melvin; the sane, logical side of his brain knew that Beverley was utterly faithful. He was also aware that his suspicions about his wife, which he had first felt a couple of years ago, rose and fell in direct proportion to the extent that his business was haemorrhaging money. Each time a new financial disaster loomed, he became more certain than ever that she was about to leave him for someone taller, better looking and more financially ept.

The thought of her leaving terrified him. For twenty years he had lurched from crisis to crisis and Beverley, endlessly tolerant Beverley, had been his constant rock and support. He simply couldn't go on without her.

This week's bout of lunacy had been prompted by two things. First there was his quarterly game of cat and mouse with the VAT people – with him, as usual, cast firmly in the mouse role. If that wasn't bad enough, Melvin was more certain than ever that Vlad the Impala had done a bunk with the five grand toupee money.

Melvin had been trying to reach him for days, but all he got was the answer machine.

'Thees ees world global head quarters of Tip Top eemport-export consortium in association with Snappy

Styles Couture. Vladimir Rimsky-Korsakov Chernyenko
at your service. Pliz to leave message after thees.'

'Thees' was thirty seconds of Abba singing 'Money,
Money, Money'. Melvin had left umpteen panicky messages about the toupees, pleading with Vladimir to
phone him at the shop. So far he hadn't heard a word.

He got down from the bed and flicked the pube into
the air as he did so.

He began to pace. Beverley was about to leave him and
that bastard Vladimir had unquestionably done a run-
ner with his five grand. In his mind he could see himself
in a few months' time. There he was, alone and on the
street, rooting through litter bins for discarded bits of
old burger bun and muttering to himself, while in some
seedy villa in Magaluf or wherever, Vlad the Impala was
impaling the local talent, drinking Stolichnaya from a
pint glass and pissing himself with laughter at Melvin's
gullibility.

There was no doubt in Melvin's mind. God had abandoned him. To Melvin it felt like the only light at the end
of the tunnel was being shone on him from an oncoming
juggernaut driven by Mr McGillicuddy and the entire
staff of the Finchley and District Inland Revenue office.

Melvin went over to the dressing table and picked up a
can of Soft and Gentle. He spritzed both armpits. Then,
as he lifted his penis and began spraying his balls, logic
started to take over from raw emotion and fear. He'd
always known Vlad was into some dodgy deals, but he'd
never been dishonest – at least not as far as Melvin was
concerned. He might yet turn up. Maybe he was on holiday. He would simply sit tight, pray and keep phoning.

He suddenly realised he was still spraying and that his balls were now covered in snowy deodorant build-up.

'Bugger,' he said, putting the can back on the dressing table. He was so busy saying bugger and flicking off the snow that he didn't hear Beverley come into the bedroom.

'Sir's laundry,' she smiled, holding out three or four freshly ironed shirts on hangers. He looked up.

'Amazing, isn't it?' she continued casually, opening the wardrobe door. 'Twenty years we've been married and I've always thought your pubes were black. But do you know, when the window light catches them in a certain way, they've got a definite ginger tinge to them.'

'Really?' he shot back. Then he said with faux breeziness, doing his level best to give the impression that he had no idea why on earth he'd questioned her observation, 'Oh, yeah . . . I've always known that.'

Beverley finished hanging the shirts in the wardrobe.

'Listen, Mel,' she said uneasily, closing the door and turning to face him, 'I've got a really huge confession to make . . .'

Christ. Maybe it wasn't in his imagination. Perhaps Beverley really was carrying on behind his back. She'd been behaving oddly for nearly a week. He'd catch her staring into space while they were having dinner. Or he'd get to the end of telling her about something that had happened at work and she'd admit she hadn't been concentrating and ask him to repeat it.

He plonked himself down on the edge of the bed and looked at her like a puppy at the vet's awaiting the chop.

'You see,' she continued, slowly, 'these last few days

I've been keeping something back. Something really important. I know I should have discussed it with you earlier and I'm really sorry. But I just wanted to be sure in my own mind that I was making the right decision.'

'What?' he said, turning the same colour as his snow-covered testicles. 'What is it you haven't told me?'

Notepad in hand, Naomi swept into Plum's cubbyhole of an office. (When she worked late, it went without saying that Plum did too.) As she sat herself down on the corner of his desk, Plum looked up nervously from his computer and waited for her to speak.

'Right,' she announced briskly, 'I've had this absolutely stonking idea. I think I should do a two-hour special some time during the next month about women who killed their husbands' lovers.' She suspected that even she would eventually be forced to submit to Eric Rowe's 'good clean fun' directive, but their meeting had been days ago. She was over that now, and was beginning to feel defiant.

Plum picked up a biro.

'. . . killed . . . their . . . husbands' . . . lovers,' he repeated slowly, taking this down in his laborious long-hand. 'Righty-ho, Nay-ohmi.'

'Now then,' she continued, stabbing her notebook with her pen, 'what we'll need is several in-depth interviews with the killers. You know the kind of thing: "I came home from line dancing, found them in bed together and something just snapped inside me . . ."'

'. . . snapped . . . inside . . . me . . . ok . . . gotcha, Nay-ohmi.'

'Oh, and I'll want the husbands too, and the lovers . . .'

'. . . lovers . . . too . . .' He stopped writing and looked up. 'Half a mo, the lovers will be dead, won't they, Nay-ohmi? I mean, aren't they the ones who got murdered when the wives came back from line dancing?'

'Oh yes. Right,' she said, slightly flustered. 'OK, forget the lovers then . . . No, wait. On second thoughts, don't do that. No, find me a clairvoyant, a medium who can raise one of the lovers from the dead. Get her point of view. You know the kind of thing: "As the blows from the meat cleaver rained down on my body, all I could think of was how my whippet was going to manage without me." '

Plum thought for a moment.

'Does it *have* to be a whippet, Nay-ohmi?' he said slowly. 'I mean, would, say, a Scotch terrier or a miniature poodle do?'

'No, Plum,' she said, for once managing to control her temper, 'it does not have to be a sodding whippet. That was just an example.'

'Ri-chew are. I thought so. It's just that I didn't want to spend ages finding somebody only to discover I'd got the wrong breed of dog.'

'OK. So we're straight on all that now, are we?'

He nodded. 'Now,' she went on, getting off Plum's desk, 'I want that lot set up by tomorrow lunchtime latest, so that I can go into the editor's planning meeting on Thursday with everything sorted. Oh, while I remember, what luck have you had finding virgins who've been drugged and raped on a beach?'

126

'Best I've got so far is a fifty-six-year-old grand-mother who had sex in the Virgin Islands with a bloke she didn't know after downing ten pints of lager . . .'

'Plum,' Naomi snapped, leaning towards him so that her face was no more than an inch from his, 'read my lips. London is full of eager twenty-somethings desperate to get into TV who would be prepared to cut off a limb to work on this show. If you want to hang on to your job you will find me drugged and raped virgins by tomorrow morning. I don't care if you have to stay here all night. Do I make myself clear?'

'Crystal, Nay-ohmi,' Plum said with the most timid of snarls. 'Absolutely crystal . . . oh, by the way, you remember the British Association of Rose Growers were planning to name a rose after you? Well, they've done it. The new catalogue arrived this afternoon.'

'Oooh, really?' Naomi squealed. 'Show me. Show me.'

Plum handed her the open catalogue and pointed to the huge yellow rose. ' "Naomi Gold," ' she read aloud. ' "Not ideal for bedding, but fine up against a wall." '

The memory of Naomi's murderous expression, not to mention the way she flounced out, didn't make Plum's task of finding raped virgins and bludgeoned lovers any easier. It simply made it a tad more bearable.

Back in her own office, Naomi sank into her leather swivel chair and began ripping into a packet of Revels. She tipped back her head and poured at least half of the contents into her mouth. The chocolate hit came almost immediately and she felt herself start to calm down.

As she sat gently swivelling the chair from side to side

and chewing the last of the chocolates, she couldn't make up her mind whether to call it a day and go home, or phone her mother first. It had been nearly a week since she'd made her promise to call the old bat. She'd been putting it off ever since. Naomi knew the two hundred and fifty grand alone wouldn't be sufficient bait to hook her sister. She was such a soppy, sentimental cow. To stand any chance of getting her to agree to the surrogacy, she needed to convince Beverley she was ready to play happy sodding families as well.

Naomi took a deep breath. God knows she'd used up every last ounce of her emotional energy being nice to her sister. The mere thought of getting in touch with her mother and trying to play the caring, affectionate daughter turned her stomach.

She spent the next few minutes on delaying tactics. She went to the loo, did her make-up, tidied her desk. Finally, deciding there was no point in procrastinating any longer, she picked up the phone. Her fingers hovered over the buttons for a few seconds. Then she punched out Beverley's number. After eight or nine rings she breathed a sigh of relief. There was clearly nobody home. She was just about to hang up when somebody answered.

It was Queenie. Shit. She'd been hoping against hope that Beverley would pick up and say Queenie had gone down with some lurgy or other and taken to her bed.

'Oh, hi, Mum,' Naomi said with forced cheeriness. 'It's me.'

'Me who?'

'Me. Naomi. Your daughter.'

'Naomi?' she squealed down the phone, causing considerable pain to her daughter's right ear. 'Is that you? Really you? Beverley told me the two of you had got together for lunch and that you might phone. I can't believe it. Oh, sweetheart, I've missed you so much. How are you?'

'Yeah, you know, fine,' Naomi said, shifting the receiver to her other ear. 'So listen, Mum. You been watching me on the telly?'

'Of course, darling. I never miss. Naomi, I'm so proud of you. You wouldn't believe how much I show off about you at the day centre. Mind you, I would say just one thing, darling. Don't be offended, but I think maybe with your high forehead you should bring your hair more forward. And that suit you wore the other night. Admittedly it was beautiful. Must have cost a fortune. But with your pale complexion, cream is so draining.'

At that moment, Naomi's complexion was more red with a hint of purple. How her sister put up with this day in day out, she couldn't imagine.

'So listen,' Queenie went on, 'when am I going to get to see you? It's been such a long time.'

'Well, the thing is, Mum, I'm really busy in the run-up to Christmas, but I was wondering how you guys were fixed for Christmas Day. There's this gorgeous new man in my life. His name's Tom. Tom Jago. He's a famous TV drama director. I'd love you to meet him. I was wondering whether maybe the two of us could come for lunch.'

'Christmas? But that's a couple of months away. I thought maybe we could get together a bit before then.'

'Sorry, Mum. That's the best I can do,' Naomi said, looking at her nails and noticing some of the paint was chipped. She began thumbing through her Filofax to find her manicurist's number. 'But I promise faithfully, we'll have a really good talk. Beverley's right. It's time we started being a proper family again.'

'All right, darling. That would be wonderful. I'll mention it to Beverley. I'm sure she'd be only too pleased for you to come. I can't wait to see you, Naomi. I just can't wait.'

'Yeah, me too,' Naomi said flatly.

'Oh, while I remember. Look, Naomi, I was just wondering. My friend Millie at the day centre, she collects autographs . . .'

'Mum, that's no problem at all,' Naomi cut in, suddenly perking up. 'Just give me her address and I'll get my assistant to put a signed photograph in the post.'

'Oh, no, darling. It's not yours she wants. She can't stand you. No, she was wondering if you could get her Anthea Turner's.'

Naomi began winding the telephone wire round her wrist, imagining it was her mother's neck.

'OK,' she said, 'tell your friend Millie I'll see what I can do.'

'You will? That's wonderful. Millie was worried you might be offended, but I knew you wouldn't be . . . Now, tell me about this new man, darling . . . Jago, Jago. Doesn't sound like a Jewish name . . .'

Upstairs, Melvin and Beverley were still deep in conversation. By now, Melvin was sitting on the bed, running his fingers through his hair. 'A quarter of a million,' he said for the umpteenth time in the same gobsmacked, incredulous tone.

'I mean, just think what we could do with that kind of money, Bev. We could buy a new car, go on holiday, get this place done up. No more debts. No more dodgy deals with Vlad the . . .'

'What? Who?' she came back at him. 'Who have you been doing dodgy deals with? It's those bloody toupees, isn't it . . .?'

'Calm down,' he soothed. 'It's nobody. Honest. Private joke. I was just thinking out loud, that's all.'

She knew full well he was lying, but decided to let it go for the time being.

'So, come on, bottom line. What do you think about the idea?'

He picked up his dressing gown from the end of the bed.

'Oh, God, I dunno,' he said, sticking his arm through one of the sleeves. 'I mean, the money's one thing, but think what you'd have to do to earn it. Naomi is asking you to get knocked up by her boyfriend and carry a baby which would technically be yours, and then give it up . . .'

'Melvin, please don't refer to my becoming pregnant as getting "knocked up". You make the whole thing sound utterly grubby. Look, how many more times do I have to tell you – if I agree to this, I would be inseminated with a bloody syringe thing. I promise there would be no actual sex involved.'

Melvin grunted. He walked over to the window and stood with his back to her.

131

'God, you're jealous, aren't you?' she said, smiling. Despite their lack of a decent love life, it was flattering to think that Melvin should still feel like that after twenty years.

'Don't be ridiculous,' he snapped, without turning round. 'Of course I'm not.'

'It's OK, Mel. I'm glad you're a bit jealous.' She went over to him and put her arms round his waist. Finally he turned to face her.

'Look,' she said, her head leaning on his chest, 'I know it would be bloody strange to say the least – me carrying a child which wasn't yours – but it's not as if we're planning to keep it. It's not like the baby's the result of an affair and I'm asking you to be its father.'

'No, I guess not,' he said quietly, acknowledging her point at an intellectual level, but buggered if he could take it on board emotionally. After all, he'd spent most of this week secretly obsessing and driving himself virtually insane with images of Beverley carrying on behind his back. Although he accepted she wasn't about to run off with this Tom bloke – he was in love with Naomi, who was beautiful, rich and successful, not a Finchley housewife – he still found the thought of Beverley becoming pregnant by anybody other than him (even if there was no actual sex involved) utterly humiliating. Irrational as it seemed, he knew that if Beverley went ahead with the surrogacy he would be left with an overwhelming sense of betrayal.

He stroked her head. She gazed up at him, her beautiful black eyes sparkling and eager. She suddenly looked about nineteen. He began pushing her hair back behind her ears.

'You really want to do this, don't you?'

She nodded.

'She's my sister, Mel. I love her.'

'But Bev,' he said gently, 'just look at the way she's treated you.'

'Mel, let's not get into another argument about whether or not Naomi has changed. OK, I admit it. I can't be one hundred per cent certain. I know you're going to tell me I shouldn't trust her any further than I can throw her. Maybe you're right. But Mel, what sort of a woman lies about being infertile? I mean, she'd have to be pretty bloody warped. And *why* would she lie? I can't see what she'd have to gain.'

'Easy. Women like Naomi see babies as some kind of fashion accessory. And she'd rather shell out for one than risk losing her figure by getting pregnant.'

'That's what Rochelle said.'

'Christ,' he came back at her, 'Rochelle knows about this? Who else have you told? God, if you've mentioned it to Queenie it'll be all round the bloody day centre by now. Half of Finchley'll be gossiping about it.'

'Don't be daft. I haven't said a word to Mum. I only told Rochelle because I needed to bounce it off another woman, that's all.'

She moved away and began needlessly rearranging bottles and jars on the dressing table.

'Mel, you should have seen her sitting in that ridiculous restaurant,' she went on. 'There were tears pouring down her face when she told me she couldn't have babies.'

'I don't doubt it,' he said with more than a touch of

cynicism in his voice. 'And you think you're emotionally strong enough to give away a baby you've carried for nine months?'

'Believe me, Mel, I've thought about nothing else for the last few days. But yes, I think I could do it.'

'And what about the kids? I mean, you'd be giving away their half-brother or sister.'

'I know. It'll need some delicate handling, but I thought if you and I were agreed, we could talk to them together and try to make them understand why I . . . we want to go ahead with it.'

He stood close behind her now, looking over her shoulder into the dressing table mirror. They gazed at each other. He could see the pleading etched into her face.

'I'm going to need some time to think about this,' he said.

'I know,' she said gently. 'That's OK. I didn't expect you to make your mind up on the spot.' She turned round and kissed him affectionately on the cheek.

After she'd gone downstairs and he was getting dressed, Melvin found himself suddenly overwhelmed with guilt. In twenty years of marriage what had he given Beverley? Bollock all. Two kids to bring up in a shabby semi and an ever-increasing mountain of debt. Allowing her to go ahead with the surrogacy would in an odd way be his chance to make amends, to give her something she really wanted. Maybe he was underestimating his emotional strength. When the moment actually arrived, perhaps he would be able to cope with the idea of her carrying another man's child. Certainly the money would give him an incentive. He pulled on his jeans and began buttoning the fly. A quarter of a million. No more debts. No more hate mail. Security. Melvin allowed himself to wallow in the possibility, to sink deep into its embrace and feel its warmth. As he did so, the juggernaut being driven by Mr McGillicuddy and the Inland Revenue people suddenly went into reverse and began disappearing back down the tunnel.

It was only as he lay in bed that night with Beverley asleep beside him that he began to have second thoughts. Who was he trying to kid? How would he ever be able to look at Beverley or make love to her knowing that some other bloke's seed was growing inside her? His entire being was suddenly awash with revulsion. The money was beginning to be no comfort. The very opposite, in fact. *He* had wanted to be the one to get them out of financial trouble. More than anything, he'd wanted to prove to Beverley he was capable of making a decent living. He'd dreamed that one day he might even make their fortune. Now his chance was gone for ever. Beverley had got there first. Done it instead of him. The kids would see her, not him, as the family's financial saviour. If he wasn't already an inadequate saddo in their eyes, he was most definitely about to become one. Beverley would no doubt say he was raving, but the way he saw it, everything he spent from now on would be her money, not theirs. Christ, every time he bought a ticket to a football match or paid for petrol, it would feel like he was accepting a handout from his wife.

All the same, he couldn't bring himself to refuse her. He couldn't bear to watch her face crumple as he said no. All their married life he'd been saying no. No new carpets. No holiday this year. No new car. He couldn't bear the thought of saying no to this too. He would have to find another, infinitely more subtle, way of putting a stop to the surrogacy. His first line of attack would be to go and see Naomi.

Chapter 9

Naomi giggled into the kitchen phone and picked up another forkful of Aunt Bessie's Tidgy Pudd covered in Bisto.

'. . . not half as much as I'm missing you, my darling,' she purred. 'I'm just counting the hours till Friday night . . . What am I wearing? What do you want me to be wearing?'

She listened and let out another giggle.

'Crotchless? OK, Tom, they're crotchless. God, I hope there isn't somebody on the bloody hotel switchboard listening to this . . . My nipples? Huge, darling. Absolutely huge . . . No, you dope, I can't suck them. I can't get my head down that far . . . What? No, of course I'm not chewing anything. Believe me, all I want to chew is you . . . Oh yes, they're open, Tom – wide open . . . Wet? Baby, you should feel what I can feel down there. The floodgates have opened. Little Rose Bud is swollen and so, so wet. God, your breathing's got really heavy all of a sudden. I bet you're really hard. Come on, tell me how hard you are.'

While she listened, she ran another piece of ready-made

Yorkshire pudding round the plate, mopping up gravy. She put her hand over the telephone while she ate it.

'OK,' she said, trying to make her voice as deep and sexy as possible and at the same time swallow her mouthful of food, 'imagine I'm giving you a tongue bath. I'm straddling you in these crotchless pants . . . What? . . . Oh, I dunno, red with black lace . . . Right now I'm licking you all over – dead, dead slow . . . Yes, I can feel your hands squeezing my breasts . . . Yes, of course I've got the vibrator on. Can't you hear it?' She jumped up from the kitchen table and stretching the curly phone lead as far as it would go, went over to the cooker hood. As she switched on the extractor fan, she popped the last bit of Tidgy Pudd into her mouth. 'OK, now I've got Little Tommy deep in my mouth. I'm running my tongue all over you from the bottom to the top. Feels good? Ooh, I bet it does . . . Tom, honestly, you have to believe me. Why would I be eating at a time like this? Come on. Now pretend you're doing that special thing I like . . . What do you mean, what thing? You know the thing . . . with the feather and the Issy Miyake bottle.

'Oh God, yeah, I can feel it. Ooh, you've really hit the spot. Oh, now you're inside me. You're licking my hard little love buttons. And thrusting. Thrusting. Ooh, ooh, can you feel me, Tom? Can you feel how hot and wet I am for you, baby? Oh God. Oh God. Oh . . . Oh . . .'

She could hear him trying to get his breath back.

'Great?' she sighed. 'That was more than merely great, darling. That was blissful. Now then, go and get something to eat and I'll speak to you tomorrow. Yeah, love you too. Bye.'

★ ★ ★

Naomi put down the phone. Tom had been away filming in Newcastle for almost two weeks. Each evening, around this time, he would call her from his hotel room, tell her how much he was missing her and then persuade her to play their telephone sex game. Only she could never really be bothered. Even when they were in bed together she felt the same. She usually put it down to exhaustion and overwork, but if she was honest, she'd always been pretty unenthusiastic sex-wise with each of her boyfriends.

Tonight she'd felt as apathetic as usual, but added to this, she'd also been starving. In fact she'd been ravenous, on account of still being furious with the British Association of Rose Growers. But she would do anything rather than disappoint Tom or put their relationship in jeopardy, so whenever they made love she faked it. And Naomi, being Naomi, faked it quite magnificently.

Tom was the best thing that had happened to her in years. She knew she wasn't in love with him, but love was of little or no interest to her. He was handsome, talented and successful. He even coped with her bad temper. Naturally she tried not to reveal that side of herself too often, but despite her best efforts she was incapable of being pleasant for more than two or three days at a stretch. After one of her regular explosions she would burst into tears and beg forgiveness. This was always forthcoming.

Another factor Naomi considered vital to her relationship with Tom was that, with the commercials he made quietly on the side, he earned very nearly as much as she did. This meant there was no question of him only being with her for her money. All in all, she'd decided a matter of hours after being introduced to him at a party at the Soho House that Tom Jago was everything she required in a consort.

She brought the plate to her face, stuck out her tongue and began licking up remains of Bisto. Only when there wasn't a trace of brown left did she put the plate in the dishwasher. What she fancied now was something like jam roly-poly or spotted dick and custard. But after downing twelve mini Yorkshire puddings, she decided to make do with fruit. She also made a mental note to phone Summer the next morning and book a colonic. She broke off a stem from the bunch of grapes in the fruit bowl and went into the living room.

'Christ, this thing is so fucking uncomfortable,' she groaned, sprawling out on the Regency chaise-longue and holding the grapes, Greek goddess style, above her mouth. But comfort wasn't something Odd ever considered when he was designing a room.

'Form, elegance, grace. These are what matters, darling,' he'd gushed the first time they met at the flat to discuss the decorations. He'd not so much wandered as glided round the place, proclaiming, 'Barbarians. Savages,' whenever he came across an anaglypta-covered wall or a fitted wardrobe.

Finally he'd come back to the living room where she was waiting.

'Well, my darling, I won't pretend it's going to be easy, or cheap,' the celebrated Norwegian interior designer had said, adjusting the cream cashmere pashmina hanging over his shoulder and assuming the balletic second position. 'For the vestibule and bedroom I see walls bathed in fromage frais. Then for the living room, since we have this wonderful Georgian fireplace and huge French doors to work with, I think we should go a tad off piste with lots of rich purples and golds. I see cherubs, perhaps an ornamental fountain in the middle. Maybe a love seat even. Ooh, and a Grecian-style mural – a trompe-l'oeil even – on the far wall . . . Oh yes, definitely.'

Odd – nobody knew his second name – might well have interior-designed everybody from Geri Halliwell to Idi Amin, but Naomi was starting to have doubts.

'Odd, with the greatest respect,' she said (her syco-phancy knew no bounds where the rich and famous, or the 'geniuses' and 'virtuosi' employed by the rich and famous, were concerned), 'this is a home, not a – how can I put it? – a tart's boudoir.'

'Now then,' he said, slapping her playfully on the wrist, 'what have I told you about trusting me? If you don't I shall flounce, darling. Simply flounce. I did it to Ivana when she argued. Don't think I won't do the same to you.'

In the end she managed to convince him to ditch the love seat and the fountain, but he won out over the gold cherubs (two over the mantelpiece, one at each end of the walnut credenza) and the mural. The wall painting was a replica of Botticelli's *Birth of Venus*. It was exact in every way except that the Odd Venus had the face of Naomi Gold.

Odd had also got his own way over the black and white tiled floor when she'd wanted stripped boards

('Ooh, no, darling, no. Very five minutes ago'), the purple walls and the exquisite, but unyielding, Regency furniture which had cost tens of thousands. She had to admit that with lighted candelabras and huge vases of white lilies everywhere, the room had a definite grandeur about it, but if she wanted to get comfortable, like now, she had to go to bed.

While Naomi was less than keen on the way the flat had been decorated, but pretended to adore it because the entire art-showbiz-media world both sides of the Atlantic considered Odd to be a genius, Tom loathed it. Every time he walked in he said he felt like he should be prancing around in a powdered peruke and a beauty spot. One Saturday night, when they were sitting around trying to think of something to do, he suggested going to the Bastille to watch a couple of guillotinings.

Mrs Triplet, Naomi's cleaning lady, wasn't any more supportive.

'Well, at least the bedroom's nice. I like a four-poster and you can't go wrong with magnolia walls. I've got it indoors.'

'No, no, Mrs T,' Naomi said patiently, 'it's not magnolia, it's fromage frais. Cost me forty quid a litre.'

Mrs Triplet squinted for a few seconds and grunted.

'Well, if you say so, Naomi, but it looks exactly like magnolia to me.'

As Naomi finished the last of the grapes, she looked round the room. She had everything, she thought: the Holland Park address, a flat decorated by the world's most fashionable designer, a live-in lover who looked

like he should be starring in something opposite Julia
Roberts. She even had a baby planned, even though this
had less to do with maternal desire than with another,
more Machiavellian plan entirely. And yet, still, somewhere deep inside her, there was an emptiness she
couldn't quite put her finger on.

Naomi picked up the miniature bronze nude which
lived on the small table next to the chaise-longue and
began stroking her head.

'What is it?' she whispered, staring at the nude's face.
'What is it?'

But Naomi wasn't one to waste her time running
fingers over the map of her psyche in an effort to locate
and explore some far-flung emotional continent. Instead
she decided to have a bath and go to bed. She'd put the
statue back and was just getting up from the chaise-
longue when she heard the buzz of the intercom. She
looked at her watch. It was nearly nine. A puzzled frown
on her face, she made her way to the front door,
throwing the grape stalks on to the unlit fire as she went.
She pressed the intercom button.

'Yes?'

'Naomi, it's Melvin. Could I come in for a few minutes?'

'Melvin?' she said, utterly taken aback. 'What, as in
my brother-in-law Melvin?'

'Yes.'

'Christ. Right. Yes, I guess so. Come up.'

She opened the front door and waited for the lift.

'Melvin,' she said, ushering him in and trying desperately, but failing, to hide her shock. 'Gosh, this is a

surprise. The last time you spoke to me you were throwing me out of your house.' She eyed the unease on his face, and couldn't make out if it was anger or nervousness. She made no attempt to kiss him hello. He made no move towards her.

She showed him into the living room.

'Blimey,' he said looking round, 'Beverley said you were living with a bloke. She didn't tell me it was the Scarlet bloody Pimpernel.'

She ignore the comment and smiled.

'Sit down, Mel. Sit down.' She pointed to one of the hardback chairs and sat herself at one end of the chaise-longue.

She looked at him for a few seconds, taking in the battered leather bomber jacket and baggy Levis.

'So . . .' she began edgily, 'I take it Beverley has told you about our little meeting the other day?'

'Yes, she told me,' he said acidly, putting his hands into his jacket pockets. 'Told me last night.'

'And she's made up her mind?'

'Pretty much.'

'So?' Naomi said, leaning forward, her eyes wide with expectation. 'Come on . . . don't leave me in suspense, what has she decided?'

'Oh, she'll do it all right,' Melvin said, with faux casualness. 'Can't wait, in fact.'

'Bloody hell . . .' Naomi squealed with excitement, failing to notice the black expression on Melvin's face. 'You mean she's said yes? Beverley's actually said she'll do it?'

'Yup.'

'God.'

She stood up and began wandering round the room.

'Beverley's agreed,' she repeated over again. 'Jeez. I just can't believe it.' Eventually she came back to the chaise-longue and sat down. She looked at Melvin.

'So, if Beverley wants to go ahead,' she said, sounding puzzled, 'why hasn't she phoned me to let me know?'

She was looking at his face now.

'Oh, right,' she said, 'I get it. You disapprove. Hence the visit. Does she know you're here?'

He shook his head.

'She thinks I'm working late at the shop,' he said. 'Look, at the end of the day, I can't stop Beverley agreeing to the surrogacy, but I'm begging you, Naomi, please don't ask her to do this. Have you even the remotest idea what it will do to a woman like Beverley – to give birth and then give up the baby? She adores babies, you know that. When Natalie and Benny were born she used to sit for hours cradling them in her arms, just staring at them. She didn't just love those little mites, she was *in* love with them. If she has to part with a baby, she'll end up in the nut house. I'm warning you, Naomi, don't let her go through with this. It'll finish her off.'

Naomi thought for several moments.

'Finish *her* off, Melvin – or you?' she said coldly. 'I think my sister possesses a damn sight more strength than you think.' She got up and began pacing round the room. 'God knows, she's put up with you long enough. Twenty years you've failed to earn a living, Mel . . . twenty years. In all that time she's scrimped and saved,

145

gone without and stuck by you. You may call that weakness, but I don't.'

She was facing him now.

'Be honest, Melvin. You're not bothered about what effect this will have on Beverley's mind and emotions. We may not have seen each other for five years, but I've known you a long time, Mel, and you can't fool me. You coming here tonight isn't about Beverley's emotions. It's about yours.'

'That's utter crap, and you know it. It's Beverley I'm worried about.'

'I don't think so. Look, I can understand you might find it hard knowing Beverley's carrying another man's child. A lot of men would feel the same . . .'

'Hard?' he said with a grimace. 'That's a bloody understatement. How do you think it feels, knowing your wife's about to become a tart and have a bloke's baby – for money?'

It was his turn to stand up now. He walked over to the French windows and stood with his back to her.

'Oh, stop being so bloody melodramatic, Mel,' she said with a half-laugh. 'I'm sure Beverley's told you over and over again there's no sex involved . . . But it's not simply jealousy we're talking about here, is it? Somehow I get the feeling there's more. I haven't forgotten Beverley telling me what a proud man you are. You can't abide the thought of her being the one to sort out your finances, can you? To be the one who rescues the pair of you. That must hurt, Mel. That must really hurt.'

He made no effort to move.

'It's funny, Naomi,' he said as he finally turned to

face her, 'I always credited you with having hidden shallows rather than hidden depths.'

'So I'm right, then?'

'Maybe,' he shrugged.

'Get over it, Mel, for Chrissake. I'm offering you a straw to clutch at. It's a final chance for you to get off Skid Row. So what if it's Beverley who gets you out of the shit? Who cares. Getting out is what matters. The way I see it, you have no alternative. None at all.'

Melvin said nothing. She was right. He went back to his chair and sat down again.

Naomi watched him close his eyes and squeeze the bridge of his nose. She smiled. She knew she had won. She walked over to the walnut credenza and picked up a bottle of Scotch.

'Drink?' she said, turning towards him.

'No. I'd better get going.'

'Well, I'm having one.'

She poured herself a victory triple.

'Look, if it helps, Mel, I'm suffering too, you know. A few weeks ago I was told I couldn't have children. Do you know how that feels?'

'I can imagine. But a woman like you, with all your money, I mean, couldn't you have sent your personal shopper to Africa or South America and bought a baby?'

Naomi came back with her drink.

'Yes, I suppose I could have adopted. But I wanted Tom to be the father. And as far as choosing a mother goes, genetically speaking, Beverley is the next best thing to me.'

'So, if I agree to go along with this, you've got to promise me something.'

'What?'

'Promise me you're on the level, Naomi, and that there are no schemes or hidden agendas here. If Beverley gets hurt, so help me, I'll . . . I'll . . .' His hands had formed to fists.

'What's the matter?' she said, smiling. 'Don't you believe I'm infertile? I'll give you the number of my gynaecologist if you like . . .'

'No. That's OK. That won't be necessary. Just promise, that's all.'

'I promise,' she said.

He was vaguely aware of her not looking him in the eye.

'Oh, and one other thing. Don't tell her I came to see you. She knows I feel a bit jealous, but she doesn't need to know how I feel about the money. She'll think I'm bloody barking.'

'OK, fine. Whatever . . . I'll walk you to the lift.'

He stood up. They walked in silence as far as the front door.

Suddenly he stopped and gave a nervous half-smile.

'At least you saw sense and put magnolia in the hall,' he said.

'Fromage frais, Mel,' she snarled. 'It's sodding fromage frais.' She opened the front door.

Naomi came back into the flat. Standing with her back against the front door, she looked heavenwards and let out an almighty 'Yesss!' Picking up her Scotch from where she'd left it on the hall table, she went into the bedroom and opened the chest of drawers. From it she removed the battered white envelope which was buried deep beneath a mountain of knickers, tights and bras. Fingers trembling, she pulled out the two letters, read them and kissed them. When she'd finished she took a huge glug of Scotch. Christ, she thought, Beverley got pregnant straight away with Benny and Natalie. So long as Tom didn't lose his nerve and sperm still swam up her sister like salmon returning to their spawning ground, in a few weeks' time Beverley could be expecting.

'And I,' she said softly, as she folded the letters, 'will be on my way to clinching the biggest fucking deal of my entire career.'

She put the letters back in the drawer, threw back her head and drained her glass.

Naomi had just sat down at her desk the next morning when the phone rang. She looked at the caller display. It was Beverley. She rested her hand on the receiver for a few seconds and prayed to God that Melvin hadn't changed his mind and persuaded Beverley not to go ahead with the surrogacy. She picked up the phone.

'Beverley,' she said, doing her best to sound casual, 'hi. So, how are you?'

As she listened she closed her eyes and offered up another quick prayer. A moment later her eyes were wide open.

'Omigod, you will?' she squealed. 'Bev, this is just such amazing news. I just don't know how to thank you. If you were here I'd give you the hugest hug imaginable. I just can't wait to tell Tom. I'm over the moon, Bev. Just over the moon . . .'

Chapter 10

'So, anyway, I rang the company that supplied them, explained to some dozy girl there that they'd gone all speckled – well, not so much speckled as mottled, really – and she puts me on hold. After fifteen minutes sitting listening to a loop of "I Will Survive", I'm thinking, you have to be joking, and I put down the phone.' Rochelle had popped into Beverley's unannounced on the way home from one of her charity 'luncheons'. Now she dipped her spoon into her milky coffee and skimmed off the head which had formed while she'd been recounting her unhappy tale.

'Can you believe it?' she continued, lowering the dripping, head-draped spoon towards her saucer. 'Twelve hundred quid Mitchell had just shelled out and as soon as I have a complaint they don't want to know.' She put down the spoon and picked up her fork. She stuck this into a slice of Beverley's home-made cheese-cake.

'God,' she said with her mouth full, 'I only had lunch a couple of hours ago. I may as well slap this straight on my thighs.'

'What thighs?' Beverley said, biting into a rice cake. 'Look at you. There's nothing of you. You'll just work it off at the gym.'

'No, I've given up the gym,' Rochelle said, still chewing. 'These days I just shop faster. Much more fun . . . So, Mel was OK, then, about you going ahead with the surrogacy?'

'I wouldn't say OK exactly. I mean, yes, he's agreed, though I think he's less than comfortable with the idea. But I think, for him, the money is just too tempting to turn down.'

Rochelle nodded.

'Thing is,' Beverley went on, taking a sip of her hot water and lemon (apparently it acted as an appetite suppressant, but it didn't seem to be working), 'I'm really worried how he'll react if and when I get pregnant.'

'Look, you've said yourself that for him the money's the thing. Believe me, he'll find a way of coping.'

'I hope so.'

'So, Naomi must be thrilled.'

'God, yes. I told her this morning. You should have heard her. She just kept going on and on about how happy she was.'

'Bet she did,' Rochelle mumbled.

Beverley leaned across the table, broke off a tiny corner of Rochelle's cheesecake with her fingers and popped into her mouth.

'So what about the kids and Queenie?' Rochelle asked. 'How have they taken it?'

'Mum doesn't know yet. She's been away for a few

days. Millie, her friend from the day centre, went down with flu and Mum's gone over to look after her. She's due back this afternoon. Funnily enough, once she's got used to the idea, I don't think she'll be a problem. I reckon she'll see it as a way for the three of us to really become a family again.'

'And the kids?' Rochelle prompted.

'They've taken it surprisingly well.' Beverley said. 'I mean, like everybody else, they can't understand why on earth I would want to do it, bearing in mind that Naomi's been such a cow in the past, but once I'd explained how much she'd changed over the last few years, they really warmed to the idea. Natalie got quite carried away, in fact. She's been doing this women's studies course at school and reckons becoming a surrogate is "the ultimate expression of true sisterhood". She even asked me if I'd give a talk about it to the sixth-form girls. I said I didn't see why not, and do you know, from that moment her behaviour really started to improve. I don't think she's been stroppy or moody since. Who'd have thought me agreeing to give a twenty-minute talk to the sixth-form would have brought about such a dramatic change in her? I have to say, Benny went a bit quiet when I told him about the plan. Said he didn't feel right about me giving away his baby brother or sister. But I'm pretty sure he'll come round once he realises the baby isn't going to disappear and we'll all get to visit.

'There is one strange thing he keeps on about, though. He says if it's a boy we should try and persuade Naomi not to have him circumcised. I mean, we're Jewish. Of course Naomi would want her son circumcised.'

'Oh, teenagers get bees in their bonnets,' Rochelle said, with a shrug. There was a brief pause in the conversation.

'Anyway, to get on to important matters,' Rochelle laughed, 'what do you think of my new outfit? Isn't it great? The top's Dolce and Gabbana. Cost Mitchell a fortune.'

Beverley eyed the sheer slate-grey Lycra netting.

'If you really want my opinion,' she said, 'I think it's hideous. You may be thin, Rochelle, but you're not sixteen. For heaven's sake, the whole world can see your bra. And what Jewish woman walks around with a huge sequinned portrait of the Virgin Mary across her front?'

'Don't be so stuffy, Bev,' Rochelle said, laughing. 'It's not meant to be serious. It's just a bit of fun. Look, I got the bag to match.' She held up a tiny black cloth bag. This time the Madonna was hand-painted. Next to her was a smiling baby Jesus. 'I mean, it's not as if I've given up being Jewish or started going to church like Natalie . . .'

The moment the words came out, Rochelle slapped her hand across her mouth like a schoolgirl.

'What?' Beverley had been about to swallow a mouthful of lemon water and it was as much as she could do to stop herself choking. 'What did you say? Natalie's been going to church?' She put down her cup. Incredulous didn't begin to describe the expression on Beverley's face.

'Look, I wasn't going to say anything. Not with all this other stuff going on. You've got enough on your plate just now.'

'Come on. I'm a Jewish mother, for God's sake. I'd shrivel up and die if I didn't have something to worry about. What's she been up to?'

'OK . . . well, Allegra comes home late one night last week and tells me that she and Natalie had gone along to some church hall in Muswell Hill, just round the corner from Natalie's school, for one of those Slap Cosmetics make-over evenings. "Saving Your Face", she said it was called. Leg said Natalie was desperate to go because she wanted to get some tips on how she could make her nose look smaller.'

Beverley raised her eyes heavenwards.

'I tell you, Rochelle, I don't know how long it'll take me to conceive, but I swear the moment I bank that first cheque from Naomi, I'm taking that girl to Harley Street to see a cosmetic surgeon.'

'That may not be necessary,' Rochelle went on. 'I think Natalie may have other things on her mind now . . . So, anyway, they arrive at the church hall only to discover they'd got the date wrong, and some bunch of born-again Christians with a sense of humour had played around with the name and *they* had called their meeting "Facing your Saviour". So, as soon as all the happy-clappy stuff begins, Leg gets up to go. Only Natalie refuses to budge because by this time she's being given the eye by some Leonardo diCaprio lookalike who's sitting the other side of the aisle in a "Men Behaving Godly" T-shirt.' Rochelle paused and then said softly, 'Leg says they're going to the pictures on Saturday night.'

Seeing Beverley's face was now almost drained of

colour, her voice trailed off.

'This is all Melvin's fault,' Beverley said, running her fingers through her hair. She stood up and started to pace round the kitchen. 'If he'd let me send the kids to a Jewish school, this could never have happened. I'm going to lose her, Rochelle. I know it. Six months from now she'll have turned her back on her religion, her culture, her family. This born-again nutcase will force her to convert. Then they'll get married in church. Most of my family will refuse to come to the wedding . . .'

'Bev, calm down and stop being so bloody daft,' Rochelle said, half-irritated, half-amused by Beverley's panic-stricken reaction. 'Listen to me. You are not going to lose Natalie, simply because she's seeing a Christian boy. It's called Jewish rebellion. All the kids do it. They're too scared to take drugs, so they eat bacon and prawns and go out with gentiles. It's a phase, Bev. Believe me, it'll pass.'

Beverley sat down again.

'You think so?'

'Trust me,' Rochelle said, patting the back of Beverley's hand. 'I know how these things work. Look at that wally Allegra went out with last summer, the one who thought he was saving the planet by refusing to drive the car his parents had given him for his eighteenth. The first week she thinks this is oh-so-right-on and she joins Greenpeace. By the second, the Jewish princess in her can't stand slumming it on the night bus and she chucks him.'

Beverley gave a half laugh. 'But at least he was Jewish.'

'Yeah, but you take my general point.'

'I guess,' Beverley said. 'It's funny. There was me thinking Natalie's mood swings had evened out lately because I'd agreed to give this talk to the sixth form, when in fact the real reason she's so happy is because she's found herself a boyfriend.'

'And it would be cruel to get in the way of that happiness,' Rochelle said firmly.

'Yes, I know. I mustn't interfere,' Beverley said with a sigh, as she felt herself coming round to her friend's way of thinking. 'It's just that it feels sort of strange, I suppose. I guess I'd always assumed that when she started going out with boys, they'd be Jewish. But thinking about it, I can't say it's come as the greatest surprise of my life. I mean, she's hardly had the strictest Jewish upbringing. Look at her father. You know how ambivalent Mel is about religion. Whenever anybody asks him what faith he is, he always says he's Jew-ish.'

Rochelle chuckled. 'So, you'll go easy on Natalie?'

'I've got no alternative. If I come down on her like a ton of bricks and forbid her to see this lad, she could do something really daft, like run off with him.' She lifted her cup and drained it.

'S'pose I'd better talk to her. Let her know I'm OK with it.'

Rochelle nodded.

'And if she does decide to convert, I know *the* chic-est little caterer you can hire for the baptism party . . . does these wonderful nibbles – like mini portions of fish and chips in newspaper and tiny little steak and kidney puddings.'

'I'll let you know,' Beverley laughed, picking up the

empty cups and taking them to the sink.

'Oh, by the way,' Rochelle said, 'I keep meaning to ask you . . . ' She reached into her Madonna handbag and pulled out a piece of folded newspaper. 'Have you seen this?' She opened out the paper and began walking over to the sink.

'It's a picture of Naomi and her bloke arriving at the Savoy for the launch of Naomi's cook-in sauce.'

Beverley reached out and took the paper in a rubber-gloved hand.

Facing her was a picture of Naomi in an exquisite black off-the-shoulder cocktail dress. Standing next to her was a tall, thick-set man in his late thirties, she guessed, with collar-length wavy hair and an angular jaw that looked like it had been hewn from marble.

'Gorgeous, isn't he?' Rochelle purred.

'S'pose', Beverley said, rubbing her nose, which had started to itch, with the back of her rubber-gloved hand. 'Naomi did say he was a bit of a dish.'

'A bit of a dish?' Rochelle repeated in astonishment. 'A bit of a dish? Left over lasagne's a bit of a dish. Half a bowl of borscht is a bit of a dish. This man's a full-on blinkin' banquet. Look. Just look at him.'

Beverley looked. There was no getting away from it. Tom Jago was, indeed, a full-on blinkin' banquet.

'Thanks anyway,' said Beverley. 'I suppose it's nice to have a photo of your child's father.' She put the cutting down on top of a pile of red bills.

Sitting at his desk in the tiny office at the back of the shop, Melvin picked up the phone. For what must have been the twentieth time that day, he punched out Vlad the Impala's number.

'Pick up, you ex-commie bastard,' he muttered. 'Pick the fuck up.'

Melvin was more desperate than ever to retrieve his five grand. He still had an overdraft to clear, and, with no guarantee that Beverley would conceive immediately, he could hardly offer Mr McGillicuddy a quarter of a million pounds' worth of collateral on the understanding that it was based on a putative pregnancy.

But in addition, Melvin was still finding it hard to acknowledge his wife as their financial saviour. Having his inability to provide for his family effectively thrust down his throat was causing him profound torment. After meeting Naomi, he had begun to think he could live with it, but now, increasingly, he couldn't. Despite Beverley's protestations that helping her sister was her prime motivation, Melvin was convinced that the money must have played a huge part in her decision to become a surrogate for Naomi. Consequently, he had become fixated with the idea that if he could find some way to make their fortune quickly, even at this late stage, he might yet persuade Beverley to drop the whole ghastly surrogacy idea.

If by some miracle, he thought, Vlad the Impala was still in the country, still had his money and by an even greater miracle was willing to return it, he would put the whole lot on a horse. Mitchell had the occasional flutter. If he didn't know how to find a dead cert, then he would know somebody who did. Of course Melvin knew he would probably lose the lot. Knowing his luck, the horse would develop a politically based aversion to competitive sport five minutes before the off and stage a protest by refusing to leave the box. But what the hell? he thought. His self-esteem, his manhood, his pride were all about to be ripped away from him anyway. Losing the five grand on a horse couldn't possibly make him feel any worse.

The phone continued to ring. He was just about to give up when he heard Vladimir's voice.

'Vladimir – is that you? About bloody time. I've been trying to reach you for days.'

'Ah, Myel-vin,' Vladimir said warmly. 'Good to hear from you, my friend. I was going to call you. I been away from office.'

'I'd worked that much out,' Melvin said sharply. 'So, where have you been?'

'Doing Norwich.'

'I bet you were. The crap wigs scam moves on to East Anglia, then?'

'Sorry, I am not understanding. I am doing Knowledge. Knowledge, Myel-vin. You know. To be cabbie. Every day I am driving round London on my moped – to learn routes. I think maybe I sell business. I make more money driving cab.'

Christ, why had he even bothered phoning? Vladimir had gone bust, hadn't he?

'Thing is, in your country it's such bloody fucking big deal to become cabbie,' Vlad was saying. 'My cousin Viktor – brilliant man, research chemist, you know – he is now driving a cab in New York. Making thousands of dollars. There it's no studying.'

'Well, you see, Vlad, in this country we have this

strange custom. We expect our cabbies to know the way. Bizarre, I know, but there you are. That's Brits for you. Now about the toupees . . .'

'But in America it's simple,' Vlad was continuing. 'If you don't know way, you ask passenger. On-the-job training, Myel-vin. On-the-job training. Much quicker. Much better . . .'

'OK, fine. Whatever. Now, please, let's talk about these bleeding toupees you flogged me.'

'Toupees? You have problem with toupees?'

'Come on, cut the crap, Vlad. They're shedding. I've examined every one you sold me. You've only got to pick them up and the hair starts falling out.'

'Funny,' Vladimir said, 'I had no other complaints, but because it's you, my friend, I take your word. Listen, Myel-vin, it's no problem. I return your money.'

'You will?' Melvin said, utterly gobsmacked.

'Sure I will. I run my business like your Marks and Sparksers. You don't like what you buy. I give you cash refund. Simple. I'll be round in Impala in half an hour with your money.'

'You will?' Melvin said again.

'Of course, my friend. Myel-vin, we've known each other since we were students. You think I would cheat you?'

'No, no. Of course not, Vladimir,' Melvin blustered. 'Thought never crossed my mind.'

'Right then. I'll be with you in a few minutes.' He paused for a couple of beats. 'Unless of course you would like me to let you in on ground floor of amazing new deal.'

'No thanks, Vlad, really. The money will be fine.'

'But hear me out. Just hear me out.'

'Vlad, honestly,' Melvin said, 'I just want the money back. I need it urgently, you see. Personal reasons.'

'You got bad debts? Trouble with loan sharks, maybe? Listen, I get Russian Mafia to put on the scarers, yes?'

'That's frighteners, Vlad. Thanks for the offer, but I'm OK really. It's nothing like that.'

'OK, if you're sure. But listen, my friend, I have way you could turn five thousand into a hundred thousand in a matter of weeks.'

'Oh God, Vlad, no more dodgy deals,' Melvin said with a sigh. 'Just let me have the money. Please.'

'OK, if you're sure.'

'I'm sure,' he said categorically.

'You sure, you're sure? 'Cos I got plenty of people who would kill to get in on this.'

'OK, so what is it this time?'

'Don't mock, Myel-vin. I tell you. I have just pulled off tip-top secret deal.' Vladimir lowered his voice.

'OK, go on,' Melvin said with weary suspicion. 'Let me have it.'

'Well, for Mir – you know, Russian space station – they have just developed this new anti-snoring device . . .'

'Anti-snoring device,' Melvin repeated, barely concealing his contempt. 'For Mir?'

'Ssh, don't say too much. We don't know who might be listening. The Americans are *very* interested in it. Snoring was big problem on space station. Three men sleeping in confined space. At night, they all keep each other awake. But not now. Now they have the cure.'

'The cure,' Melvin repeated, distinctly under-whelmed.

'Myel-vin, believe me. According to my contact Professor Sergei Kalashnikov of Novosibirsk Sleep Research Institute, this incredible invention is about to become big news. And since many years ago we are in Party together, and we have a few little deals then, now I have the world exclusive rights to new device.'

'So if you've got this amazing deal, how come you're doing the Knowledge?'

'Back-up plan, Myel-vin. In Red Army, we always taught must have back-up plan.'

'So, how do they work, these things?' Despite himself, Melvin was becoming interested.

'Nobody knows. It's tip-top secret. All Sergei would tell me is that they fit inside the ear. Sounds crazy, I know. But apparently they are the donkey's bollocks, Myel-vin. Donkey's bollocks.'

'Dog's bollocks.'

'I'm sorry. My English. Anyway, I can do a special deal just for you to say sorry for the toupees and because I don't like to let you down. What do you say?'

'Thanks, Vlad, but I don't think so,' Melvin said, scratching under his chin.

'Listen. You take out huge advertisements in all the top-notch classy papers. You know, the *Economist*, *Newsweek*, the *Exchange and Mart*. "End to snoring guaranteed," you say. "Money back if old lady still kick you out of bed." I tell you, every man in the country will buy one.'

Melvin thought for a minute. He could just feel himself caving in. The anti-snoring devices were, he thought, probably a wiser bet than putting the five grand on a horse. Though with Vlad the Impala's track record of supplying duff merchandise, there couldn't be much in it.

'I must be mad – totally stark staring bloody mad. OK, I'll give you one chance to make amends. I'll buy five grand's worth – *if* you agree to split the advertising cost with me.'

'Done. It's deal, my friend,' Vladimir shot back, sounding, Melvin thought, a tad too eager for comfort.

'I'll be round with a hundred gross in half an hour,' Vladimir went on. 'You won't regret this, Myel-vin, I promise.'

The moment Rochelle left, Beverley stood by the front door, prodded her stomach and grimaced. So much for her sodding diet. Because she'd wanted to give it a chance to work, she'd resisted weighing herself for more than two weeks, but she could hold out no longer. The time had come.

She went to the deep freeze, took out the bathroom scales and put them on the floor. Using her big toe, she kicked the still frosty electronic mechanism underneath the front of the scales and waited for the row of brightly lit zeros to appear. As usual they came to life a little sluggishly, as the mechanism recovered from its polar storage conditions.

After a couple of seconds she took a deep breath and looked. Nine stone eleven. Nine stone bloody eleven.

Naked she'd be nearer nine eight. Yes! Joy shot through Beverley like squid ink through water. The diet, combined with Naomi having walked back into her life and promptly turned it upside down, was clearly causing the pounds to drop off. She patted her stomach. It seemed quite flat all of a sudden. What could have possessed her to think she'd put on weight?

Beverley picked up the scales and virtually skipped back to the deep freeze.

'Beverley, what on earth are you doing?'

She swung round to see her mother coming into the kitchen.

'Oh, hi, Mum. You startled me. I wasn't expecting you back till this evening . . . What do you mean, what am I doing?'

'The scales. Darling, you're putting a pair of bathroom scales in the deep freeze.'

'I am? Oh, God. So I am.' She had to come up with an explanation fast. 'I . . . er . . . I just made a cheesecake – that's it – and I was about to freeze half of it. Must have picked up the scales by mistake.'

'Beverley, tell me, how could you have thought the scales were cheesecake?'

'I didn't *think* they were cheesecake,' Beverley said defensively. 'I've got a lot on my mind just now and I made a mistake, that's all.'

She came over to the breakfast bar with the scales and sat down.

'So, Millie's better, is she?'

'Much. She'll be back at the day centre next week.'

'Great.'

'That's how mine started, you know, Bev – with bouts of confusion.'

Queenie checked there was water in the kettle and switched it on.

'Sorry?' Beverley said. 'That's how your what started?'

'You know.' Queenie paused and pointed to her lower abdomen.

'The change of life.' Rather than say the words aloud, Queenie mouthed them.

'I tell you, Bev, you want to get to the doctor and get some hormones inside you fast. You'll be shoplifting next, if you're not careful.'

'Mum,' Beverley said, doing her best to stay calm, 'I happen to know that the average age women start the menopause in this country is fifty-one. I am forty-two. That means I still have nine years to go. What is more, I still get through a pack of Tampax Super every month and I have yet to use a tube of KY jelly. And since we're on the subject of my fertility, there's something I have to tell you. Look, leave the tea and come and sit in the living room.'

Beverley got up from her stool.

'Omigod, you're not . . .?' Queenie squealed.

'No, not exactly.' Beverley began walking to the door.

'How do you mean, not exactly?' Queenie said, trotting after her. 'Either you are or you aren't. A person can't have a *bit* of pregnancy, like they have a *bit* of indigestion.'

Once Beverley had started to explain about the surrogacy, Queenie went silent. For the two or three minutes it took Beverley to tell the story and explain how the children and Melvin had taken it, her mother said not a word. Finally, Beverley sat back in her chair and waited.

'I tell you, Bev,' Queenie said, smiling and gripping her daughter's hand, 'Naomi doesn't deserve to have you for a sister. Not after the way she's treated you. Let's hope you're right and she has changed. I have to say that when I spoke to her the other day she sounded happier than I'd heard her in years. So, now my other daughter's about to make me a grandma too. I can hardly believe it. Maybe now we can start being a family again.'

Beverley nodded slowly.

'But, sweetheart, have you thought it through? When the time comes, will you really be able to give up this child? After all, he or she will be your baby.'

'Mum, I think about little else. But yes . . . I think I will.'

Queenie looked at Beverley and smiled.

'She's lucky, Naomi,' she said with a sigh. 'So lucky. She'll have her career *and* her baby.'

'I know. That's the way most women do it these days. They want both.'

'I always wanted both, you know,' Queenie said with a trace of bitterness in her voice. 'Before I met your father, I had dreams of running my own business – a gown shop, I thought. You know, something really posh. Then Daddy and I got married and he wouldn't let me. My father even offered to lend me the money to set me up. But Lionel put his foot down. No wife of his was going out to work. And that was that. So I stayed at home and had babies.'

So she'd been right all along, Beverley thought. Queenie had been mad rather than bad, and her father was partly to blame.

'Mum, you must have felt so trapped.'

Queenie shrugged.

'Don't get me wrong,' she said, pulling a scrunched-up bit of tissue out of her cardigan pocket and wiping her eyes. 'It wasn't that I didn't want you. I did. I loved you both, but I just wanted something for me as well. There was all this frustration and resentment burning inside me. After Naomi was born, I think I went a bit loopy with it all . . . People didn't go to see psychiatrists back then either. I am sorry, you know. About how I neglected you. All these years I've tried not to think about it. Can't face the guilt, I suppose. Bev, can you forgive me?'

By now there were tears streaming down Queenie's face. Every time she mopped them up, more came.

Beverley never thought she'd hear her mother say those words. Whenever she'd tried to bring up the subject of her and Naomi's childhood in the past, Queenie had always refused to discuss it. Realising just how brave she was being now, and how much emotional pain confronting the past was causing her, Beverley got up, sat herself on the sofa next to her mother and hugged her.

'Ssh, Mum, it's OK,' she said, blubbing too. ''Course I forgive you. Let it go now. It's all in the past. You don't need to say any more. I think I understand how it must have been. But will you do me one favour, Mum?'

'What, darling?' Queenie sniffed.

'Will you tell Naomi what you've told me? I think she needs to know.'

Queenie nodded.

While Beverley was in the kitchen making tea, Queenie remembered she'd invited Naomi and Tom for Christmas Day. She would speak to her then. And come to think of it, she must mention inviting them to Beverley. Some time.

Chapter 11

Having finished his regular early-morning Lettice-inspired wank, Benny lay on his back waiting to get his breath back. For no reason in particular, he turned his head towards the bedside table. Something had changed, but he couldn't for the life of him work out what. His alarm clock was precisely where it had been ten minutes ago when it went off. His copy of *Popcorn* was lying open and face down, next to it. Then he realised that his glass of water, which had been on the table all night, had been replaced by his ancient Sonic the Hedgehog mug, full of hot steaming tea. Beside the mug lay a couple of digestive biscuits.

Humiliation didn't come close to describing Benny Littlestone's emotions as he heard his mother plodding down the stairs.

Beverley put her son's empty glass in the sink, sat herself down at the breakfast bar and continued reading the wonkily printed instructions.

'On a waxing moon place two acorns, an orris root, a tablespoon of goat's rue and two tablespoons of hyssop oil in a cauldron and heat gently . . .' Beverley snorted as she imagined going into Brent Cross Waitrose and asking where she would find the goat's rue.

She had barely taken her eyes off the instructions since tearing them from their brown envelope a few minutes ago. They'd come through the letterbox just as she was passing the front door with Benny's morning tea. (Until recently, she would make tea for the entire family, but Benny was the only one who drank it. Everybody else would let it go cold and leave it.)

For the second time in just over a fortnight, a letter had arrived which again was clearly not a bill. As before, she had been unable to resist opening it immediately. In the time it had taken Beverley to go up to Benny's room, fail to notice him masturbating, put the mug of tea on his bedside table and go back downstairs to the living room, she had read two of the half-dozen printed sheets.

'Look, don't laugh,' Naomi had said a couple of afternoons ago when they met at Brown's, to discuss when and where the first insemination should take place. 'Fallopia Trebetherick specialises in boosting women's fertility. Di, Demi, Fergie, the Grimaldi women – they all called her in when they wanted to get pregnant. She flies all over the world.'

'On her broomstick, I presume,' Beverley said, only half joking.

'No, usually by private jet. Look, Fallopia's a wonderfully successful healer and natural therapist . . . OK, I admit it, she's into a bit of magic.'

'So I'm right, she *is* a witch then.' By now Beverley's voice had developed a distinctly nervous edge.

'All right, all right, she is a witch, but an exceedingly fashionable one.'

'Who happens to have this amazing knack of getting buns in covens.'

'Funneee . . . Look, Bev, Fallopia Trebetherick doesn't come cheap, but I think we should use her. I mean, you're forty-two now and you may not find it so easy to get pregnant. Look, I know I should have discussed it with you first, but I rang her yesterday. Anyway, she said if we wanted to turn the insemination into a full-scale pagan ceremony she'd be happy to preside.'

'And of course you said thanks, but no thanks,' Beverley said.

'Not as such . . . Look, she said because it's me she'll do it for half her normal fee. You have no idea, this is the most amazing coup, Bev. I mean, Fallopia is always booked up for months ahead. Says she's got some tart out of *EastEnders* pencilled in that night, but she'll put her off. Anyway, I though a bit of incense and meditation might relax us all – you know, get us into the right spiritual mood. I mean, what harm can it do?'

'Oh, not a lot, I suppose,' Beverley said casually. 'So long as we're not bothered about me ending up spread-eagled naked and dead on top of some tombstone in Highgate Cemetery.'

'Oh, come on, Bev. You're over-reacting. Look, witch-craft, or Wicca as Fallopia prefers to call it, has nothing to do with devils and demons and pervy satanic rites –

it's all about worshipping nature and using herbal remedies and a bit of magic to help people. Just see it as a form of complementary therapy – a bit like acupuncture.'

'So where's she from, this Trebetherick woman – Cornwall?'

'No, Cricklewood. The pops always refer to her as the Cricklewood Crone.'

'Great,' Beverley said, imagining some bent, warty woman with no teeth, and filthy matted hair, wearing a necklace of dried bat's intestines round her neck. 'So in no time she'll have me howling at the moon with a dead toad and a head of garlic shoved up inside me? I tell you, Naomi, I'll be a Wicca basket case by the time I get pregnant.'

'Now you're being daft. Look, I've told you, the royals use her . . .'

'And I take it Tom's OK about ejaculating into a jar while this woman stands over him chanting and sprinkling him with newt droppings?' Beverley asked.

'Fallopia has assured me the whole thing will be perfectly respectable and dignified. I haven't actually mentioned it to Tom yet, but I'm sure once she's explained everything to him, he won't have a problem with it. He knows how much becoming a mother means to me. I know he'll do anything I ask him . . . Meanwhile, Fallopia said she'd send you the instructions. And there are some crystals coming too. If you keep them in your pocket, they'll help balance your chakras. Please say yes, Bev, please. It really would mean such a lot to me.'

Beverley said nothing for a few moments.

'You're bonkers,' she chuckled eventually. 'You do know that, don't you? Totally bonkers.'

Naomi grinned.

'So you'll do it then?'

'OK, but on the strict understanding that if we get a whiff of anything remotely pervy, we leg it. Understood?'

'Understood.'

Just before they left Brown's, Naomi reached across the sofa they'd been sharing and hugged her sister.

'I still can't believe you've agreed to carry my baby for me, Bev,' she said, leaning her head on Beverley's shoulder. 'Every time I think about it, I have to pinch myself. You will never know how grateful I am and how happy you've made me. Never. Thanks, Bev. Thank you so much.'

Beverley patted her sister's back and pulled away gently from her embrace.

'It's OK, my pleasure,' she said, smiling and wiping a tear from Naomi's cheek.

Back in her kitchen, Beverley was reading the last page of Fallopia's instructions. Shaking her head and chuckling, she got the pages together, tore them in half and half again, went over to the swing bin and threw them and the crystals in it. She'd never needed bits of old plant or crystals to get pregnant in the past and doubted very much she needed them now.

There was one thing she *did* need now, and that was confirmation that Fallopia Trebetherick wasn't completely barmy. Despite Naomi's, not to mention

Rochelle's, assurances that there was nothing remotely sinister or demonic about the woman and that alternative-therapy-wise she was the most fashionable thing since ginseng, Beverley wanted to make certain for herself. She went back to the bin and pulled out the torn-up instruction sheets. Fallopia's address and telephone number had been printed at the top of the covering letter. Having located the relevant piece of paper, she took it with her to the phone.

She picked up the receiver and hesitated as she tried to decide if half eight was too early to phone. Even though it was a weekday, she thought it would be more polite to wait until it was something to nine. At eight thirty-five precisely, she picked up the phone again.

When the voice at the other end answered with a curt 'Yup,' Beverley was convinced she'd dialled some military establishment by mistake. She was just about to apologise and put the phone down when the voice demanded to know who was calling. Feeling too intimidated to refuse, Beverley announced herself.

'Ah, yes . . . Littlestone, B., Mrs,' the voice boomed down the phone, instantly causing Beverley to move the receiver several inches away from her ear. 'Got you down for a Ritual Seeding, on the ninth of the eleventh, at seventeen hundred hours.'

'I'm sorry,' Beverley said, her confusion and terror growing by the second, 'I wanted to speak to Fallopia, Fallopia Trebetherick.'

'She speaks,' the woman barked impatiently.

'What . . . sorry . . . you are Fallopia?'

'Good God,' the woman muttered, 'I've got a right

whisky alpha lima lima yankee here.'

'Fraid I'm not quite with you . . .'

'You could have fooled me.'

Beverley heard Fallopia tut.

'Now then,' she said, 'let's start again. *You* are Beverley Littlestone. *I* am Fallopia Trebetherick. Now what can I do for you?'

It took Fallopia less than five minutes to deliver her clipped, succinct summary of what the Ritual Seeding ceremony would involve.

'It's done with complete decorum,' she said finally. 'All I do is a bit of ceremonial during which I raise the cone of magic and call upon the goddess to put your ovaries and uterus on red alert. The rest you do in a private room while I carry on chanting outside.'

Having decided the woman was batty, but probably harmless, Beverley's curiosity about Fallopia's distinctly unwitchlike manner began to get the better of her. She had expected if not a cackling hag with warts on her nose, a dotty, merry soul. Fallopia, however, seemed to resemble the hockey mistress from hell. Finally Beverley plucked up the courage to ask about her background.

It came as no surprise to Beverley to discover the woman had spent twenty years as a flight lieutenant in the RAF.

'Stationed down in Cornwall, at RAF St Mawgan,' she explained when Beverley asked her how she became a witch. 'Fell out of a Sea King on a rescue, and me coccyx went for a burton. Kept giving me gyp on and off for months. Went straight to the MO, of course. He could do bugger all. Ruddy shower, doctors, if you ask me. Finally things got so bad that they invalided me out. Then one day I took a drive to Totnes, and while I was having a nose around, I happened to notice a postcard in a newsagent's window placed by one of these alternative healer types. Thought I might as well give it a go. She sorted me out with a few herbal remedies in a matter of days. Turned out she also practised the old religion. Of course, I told her it was a load of old codswallop, but she insisted I went along and met the members of her coven. Nothing like I expected. Jolly decent bunch. Very down to earth. Very soon, my healer friend took me under her wing and became my mentor – taught me everything I know about healing and magic. Then after she died on me, I discovered I had a bit of a gift when it came to helping women conceive, and the rest you know.'

They were saying cheerio when Beverley realised she hadn't asked Fallopia where she was planning to hold the ceremony. Fallopia insisted on doing it outdoors.

'Much better ch'i – that's energy flow to you – than you get inside. Forget anywhere public. Someone might spot me and your sister together and tip off one of the papers. Before you know it, Bob's your whatnot and we spend the next six months repelling a whole load of tabloid flak. Your back garden will do.'

The moment she put the phone down, Beverley realised their back garden would be out of the question. Although she would have to let Melvin know when the insemination was happening, she couldn't bear the thought of it taking place at their house. It would be desperately hurtful to Melvin – a bit like having an affair and using their bed. What was more, if he found out that a witch was popping round beforehand to perform a quick pre-insemination spell over her nether regions, he'd have every right to think she and Naomi had gone off their mutual chumps.

Beverley's thoughts were interrupted by the front door slamming. Suspecting Natalie's moods were in full swing once again and that she'd left for school in another of her strops, she went into the living room, pulled back the net curtains and looked out of the window. Disappearing into the distance, his school bag slung over his shoulder, was Benny. In all the four years he'd been at secondary school, he'd never left without kissing her goodbye. For the life of her she couldn't think what she'd done to offend him.

She walked back into the kitchen, her thoughts returning to the conversation with Fallopia, and the garden question. It took her no more than a few seconds to come up with the answer. Mitchell and Rochelle were off to Aruba the week after next, the day before the insemination. She would ask to borrow their house and garden.

Once again she picked up the phone.

'No problem,' Rochelle said groggily. It was now well after nine, but Beverley had clearly woken her up. 'I'll leave you the keys. Can't believe I'm going to miss meeting Fallopia Trebetherick and the gorgeous Tom.

You'll get to meet him before the insemination though, won't you?'

'Probably not. Fallopia can only do the ninth and he's in Newcastle filming until the eighth. Goes against my better judgement, but I guess I'm just going to have to take Naomi's word for it that he's a wonderful man and that he will make an equally wonderful father.'

'Oh, I've no doubt he will. Naomi may be a lot of things, but she's not stupid. I'm sure she'll have made a wise choice in Tom. Stop worrying.'

But she couldn't help it. She was starting to worry about so much lately.

For a start there was Melvin. He was clearly still having trouble coming to terms with the surrogacy plan. He was permanently tense and preoccupied. She was also aware that he wasn't sleeping. What was more, although she had nothing to go on other than a gut feeling, she couldn't help thinking he was planning or hatching something behind her back, but every time she put it to him that he was keeping something from her, he denied it. Last night he'd actually woken her with his tossing and turning. Each time she'd rolled over to his side of the bed, put her arms round his middle and begged him to talk to her.

'Look, Mel, I know you're finding this thing hard to deal with, but we have to keep talking. Please don't shut me out. You seem to be hurting so much and it just makes me feel more and more guilty.'

'I'll be fine. Honest,' he said without turning over. 'I just need time to come to terms with it, that's all.

There's nothing going on. Honest.'

'Turn over and say that.'

He turned to face her.

'I promise I'm not planning anything,' he said, knowing full well that the advertisements for the Russian snoring devices – part two of his grand strategy to scupper the surrogacy deal – would start appearing in newspapers and magazines from next week.

'Now go to sleep.'

He kissed her briefly on the lips.

As they lay side by side in the dark, Melvin's thoughts turned to Rebecca Fludd, *shikseh* goddess and bagel mogul. These days he found himself fantasising even more than usual about what might have been. The moment he fell asleep he began to dream. He was standing on the deck of a cruise liner. At the same time this was also the Nottingham University students' union bar. He was surrounded by a large group of male students, wearing shirts with long pointy collars and Kevin Keegan haircuts. They were all drinking pints of Shipstone's bitter. Through the crowd, he could see Rebecca. She was playing deck quoits with bagels. Suddenly she turned towards him and smiled. The people disappeared as if by magic. Rebecca dropped her bagels and they began running towards each other in slow motion. They were laughing. Their arms were outstretched. She was wearing a dress made of flowing sheer cotton. He could see her breasts bobbing up and down as she ran barefoot along the wooden deck. Finally he reached her. His heart pounding fit to burst, he put his arms round her, pulled her towards him and kissed her slowly and passionately on the mouth. It was a few seconds later, as they pulled apart, that he realised to his horror that Rebecca had sprouted a droopy moustache and tinted glasses. He had been tonguing Vlad the Impala.

Beverley, still in worry mode, was thinking about Natalie's new boyfriend. Melvin had decided it was wonderful news that Natalie was seeing a Christian boy – the more religious the better in his opinion (Melvin never lost an opportunity to stick two fingers up at his dead father, who had been orthodox as well as autocratic). Beverley, on the other hand, was continuing to have serious doubts about the relationship.

As she drifted off to sleep, she could see the boy standing in front of her. In her mind's eye he wasn't merely Christian, but a wild-eyed, wiry-haired zealot and missionary who looked like he belonged to some eccentric American Christian sect. He would force Natalie to convert, marry her and then drag her off to live among his people in the wilds of Pennsylvania.

A minute later she was dreaming properly. It was ten years from now and she was walking down Golders Green Road with a dozen Amish grandchildren in tow.

Chapter 12

'Queen of Shadows, Queen of Light,' Fallopia chanted loudly, her voice taking on a theatrical tremble, 'Isis, Brighid, lady bright, Hathor of the darksome night, swell my magic power tonight.'

Fallopia had broken off from her task of sweeping away evil spirits from the magic circle and was standing stock still in the November darkness, her arms and her broomstick raised heavenwards.

'Do you mind telling me what this woman is on?' Beverley whispered to Naomi.

'God knows, but isn't it magical?' Naomi enthused, still unable to believe her luck at having poached Fallopia from the *EastEnders* tart.

'If you like,' Beverley replied.

'If you ask me,' she continued, pulling up her coat collar and adjusting the chaplet of cow horns perched uncomfortably on her head, 'the woman's a newt's eye short of a curse.'

Despite her military gait and ramrod posture, Fallopia had clearly shrunk since her days in the RAF. She couldn't have been more than five foot three. She was also fat, with enormous breasts. As she moved, these swung back and forth, apparently untethered, beneath her white robe, which was tied with dressing gown cord at what passed for her waist.

After consecrating the ground by sprinkling it with salt water taken from her cauldron, she knelt down and, with some difficulty because the breeze kept blowing out her matches, began lighting the white candles which formed the perimeter of the magic circle. She then announced that she was ready to proceed with the ceremony.

'But what about Tom?' Naomi asked anxiously. 'It's only just gone half five. He's probably stuck in traffic. Can't we just hang on for a bit?'

'Sorry, no can do,' Fallopia barked. 'I'm due at Highgrove at nine. HRH has got another bull with brewer's droop. If Mr Jago chooses to be late on parade I'm afraid that's his problem. But worry not, Beverley's fertility is our main concern and it is her we must concentrate upon. Now then, let us be silent while I call up the cone of magic.'

'I can't imagine where he's got to,' Naomi whispered while Fallopia began making a sign of a pentagram in the air. 'He promised me faithfully he would leave the office at four. I tell you, if he's playing silly buggers and is about to let me down, I'll bloody kill him.'

Beverley had to confess she felt relieved at the thought of Tom not turning up. It wasn't that she didn't want the insemination to go ahead. She did, but she found the idea of meeting Tom for the first time under these bizarre circumstances embarrassing in the extreme.

They returned their attention to Fallopia. She was now prancing and gambolling, Isadora Duncan-style, round the magic circle, a tree branch wand in one hand, a couple of smoking joss sticks in the other. Furthermore, she was doing it completely naked.

Backlit by the candles, Fallopia, with her bubble perm and dimpled, cellulite-filled limbs, looked like an outsize wood nymph, Beverley thought. But what struck predominantly was the sight of her breasts swaying back and forth across the enormous belly like two animated, fleshy ciabattas.

'Oh my God,' Beverley giggled, 'I wondered what she meant when she said she performed these seeding ceremonies "sky clad".'

She turned to Naomi for affirmation, only to find her sister gazing, apparently enchanted by the ludicrous spectacle.

'I think the whole thing's absolutely beautiful,' Naomi gushed. 'It's all so . . . so feminine.'

As Beverley looked at Naomi with a blinking, head-shaking cartoon expression of total disbelief, Fallopia came to a stop and stood a few feet from them, panting heavily. Her breath was white in the bitter night air. She picked up a silver chalice from the melamine camping table which served as an altar and asked Beverley to drink from it. She took a small sip of the cheap, vinegary red wine and winced.

Finally Fallopia asked her to lie down on the grass.

Giving Naomi a plaintive don't-let-this-be-happening-to-me look, Beverley supported the cow horn chaplet with one hand and lay down on the freezing ground.

Looking up, she had an excellent view of Fallopia's massive pubic area, almost an entire neighbourhood, with its sparse, tundra-like bush.

'Mother Goddess,' Fallopia boomed as she and Naomi knelt down and rubbed their hands in a clockwise motion of Beverley's lower abdomen, 'be here with me as I bless this woman's creative womb. May the seed which shall be planted here grow and flourish so that . . .'

A male voice suddenly broke in. 'Sorry, tried ringing the bell,' it said, 'but there was no answer. Thought I'd come round the back. Mr Jago told me to get this over to you urgently.'

The three women looked up to see a young man in a helmet and biker's leathers. He was holding a Jiffy bag.

'Fuck me sideways,' he said slowly as he took in Beverley's chaplet of cow horns and Fallopia's ciabattas. Clearly deciding he had walked in on a scene of crazed Satanic debauchery, he virtually threw the bag at Naomi and then legged it back across the lawn, shouting over his shoulder, 'No need to sign for it, girls.'

Naomi immediately tore into the bag. It contained a Waitrose sundried tomato jar, minus the tomatoes and with a small amount of white fluid at the bottom. A note was Sellotaped to the lid.

Dear Naomi and Beverley, it said. *Sorry, got cold feet about performing with people around. Went home instead. Hope this reaches you in time. Good luck. Tom.*

Chapter 13

While Beverley stood in the bathroom under the luke-warm drizzle which passed for a shower, Melvin padded downstairs letting out his traditional salvo of early-morning farts as he went. This ended, as usual, at the precise moment he reached the hall. He went into the kitchen and opened the fridge. Standing in front of it with the door wide open he began scratching his balls through his pyjamas while he decided what to have for breakfast. While he thought, he began shoving bits of cold roast potato into his mouth.

Most days Melvin didn't bother with breakfast. The thought of incoming hate mail did little for his appetite. But this morning he didn't give a flying fuck. This morning he was starving. Ravenous even. He couldn't remember the last time he'd felt this hungry. He couldn't remember the last time he'd felt this happy.

The joy Melvin was feeling as he took a carton of orange juice and two eggs from the fridge was the same joy he'd been feeling for the last few weeks. It bordered on the ecstatic. Even the knowledge that Beverley, who had undergone her first insemination just over a month ago, could be pregnant had done nothing to quell his jubilation. A practically menopausal woman and a turkey baster would take months to score a hit, he reasoned. Meanwhile Vlad the Impala's in-ear electronic Russian anti-snoring devices were selling like hot blinis.

Every day another twenty or thirty orders arrived at the shop. He now had Alma, his manageress, on full-time packing duties. He had no idea so many men snored, or – judging by the letters which accompanied the orders – that each of them had a despondent, sleep-deprived wife, desperate to find a cure. He'd already sold two hundred at nearly twenty quid a go, that was four grand he'd turned over in as many weeks. If the orders kept coming like this, by Christmas he would have made more than enough to pay the bank their five thousand. After that everything he made would be clear profit. Very soon he would have tens of thousands in the bank. At this rate the rest of their debts would be paid off in no time.

As he poured himself some KwikSave orange juice and knocked back half of it, he imagined the moment he would sit Beverley down, present her with their bank statement and tell her there was no need for her to carry on with this surrogacy nonsense. She would fall into his arms weeping, bless him for rescuing her from the hell of having to give up her baby, and they would go upstairs to make if not perfect, certainly halfway decent love.

He'd lost count of the times he'd rung Vlad to thank him for letting him in on the deal. His old friend was a tsar among men. How he could have doubted him, Melvin had no idea.

He cracked eggs into a cereal bowl and went in search of a frying pan.

'What you looking for?' Beverley said, shuffling into the kitchen in her dressing gown.

'Frying pan.'

'In the cupboard under the oven. Melvin, you appear to be cooking. You never cook.'

He shrugged. Then he bent down, opened the cupboard and pulled out the frying pan.

'Dunno,' he said chirpily. 'I just woke up and fancied some eggs, that's all. Sit down and I'll do you a couple.'

Beverley grimaced.

'Oh, I forgot, you're still on a diet,' he said, putting two slices of bread in the toaster and failing to notice that his wife was looking distinctly green around the gills this morning. She smiled a weak smile.

'Think I'll just have some dry toast,' she said, nodding towards the toaster. 'Couldn't face anything else . . . So, what's got into you, Melvin? I've noticed you've been distinctly more up recently. Do you think you've finally come to terms with this surrogacy business?'

'Not exactly,' he said, maintaining his good humour.

'What, then? C'mon. What is it that's made you so happy these last few weeks?'

'Soon,' he said, grinning and tapping the side of his nose. 'You'll find out very soon. Everything's going to be peachy, Bev. Just peachy.'

'Probably nothing,' Beverley said to Rochelle on the phone as soon as Melvin had left for work. 'Just feel a bit sick, that's all. Probably caught a tummy bug. Yeah, that'll be it. I'm sure it's nothing.'

She couldn't possibly be pregnant, she thought. After all, she was forty-two, she'd substituted a turkey baster for a penis and used sperm which had been ejaculated into a sun-dried tomato jar. What was more, when she'd taken off the lid, she'd noticed bits of dried-up tomato round the rim. There must have been a mingling of sperm and tomato cells. Even if by some miracle she was pregnant, then she would give birth not to a baby, but a giant squawking sun-dried tomato.

'Beverley, if you're so sure it's nothing, why have you woken me at eight o'clock in the morning to have a conversation about it? Personally, I think it's *something*.'

'You do?'

'I do. Let me guess. It's not just the feeling queasy; you're late, aren't you?'

Beverley hesitated.

'A bit,' she said eventually.

'How a bit?'

'Five days, but I reckon it's nothing more than the stomach upset slowing down my cycle.'

'Beverley, you make it sound like one of your fallopian tubes has a puncture. Believe me, your cycle has not merely slowed down, it has reached a complete bloody standstill and the only thing causing it is sperm. I put it to you that this came, if you'll pardon the expression, from one of two people – Melvin, or the gorgeous Tom.'

'I can't be. It's completely impossible. Melvin hasn't laid a finger on me since I told him about the surrogacy deal. Plus the sperm in that jar were probably hours old and swimming belly up by the time I got to them.'

'You reckon,' Rochelle said flatly.

An hour and a half later she was standing on Beverley's doorstep brandishing a Predictor. It would have been sooner, but she'd had to wait for the shops to open.

When the result turned out to be positive, Beverley refused to believe it. She assumed the kit was faulty and sent Rochelle out to get another one. When that result was the same, she made her go to the chemist down the road and buy a different make. This too confirmed that she was pregnant, but Beverley was having none of it. Indeed, even after Rochelle had driven to half the chemists in Finchley and returned with seven more kits, which all delivered the same verdict, Beverley still scoffed. By now she had convinced herself that all the pharmacists in the neighbourhood had been doing business with one of Melvin's dodgy business contacts and had received consignments of faulty pregnancy testing kits which were giving false positives.

'For God's sake, Bev,' Rochelle said, throwing the empty boxes at her, 'you're pregnant.'

'God, I am, aren't I?', she giggled. She felt overwhelming joy for Naomi as well as delight at having managed it so quickly.

'And my mother thought I was menopausal,' she said with a grunt. 'I'll give her bloody menopause.'

Then almost at once her jubilation turned to panic.

'Christ,' she said, leaning back on the sofa and running her fingers through her hair, 'until this moment I thought I could cope with letting my baby go. Suddenly

I'm not so sure. My own flesh and blood. I'm planning to
give up my own flesh and blood? How will I do it,
Rochelle? Please, please tell me.'

Naomi's surprise, delight and sheer schoolgirl excitement at the news when Beverley phoned her at the office
half an hour later was immediately followed by a suggestion that they meet for lunch to celebrate. Beverley
suspected that the only lunch she'd fancy would be a
couple of water biscuits washed down with some fizzy
mineral water, but she thought it would be too mean to
refuse her sister's invitation. They agreed to meet at
Naomi's office.

'Then we'll go round the corner to the River Café,'
she said. 'Funnily enough, any other day and Tom could
have joined us. He's actually at home all week reading
scripts, but when I tried to get him a few minutes ago to
remind him to pick something up for supper, there was
no answer. Then I remembered he had a meeting in
Oxford with Judi Dench. He's trying to persuade her to
play Lady Bracknell.'

Beverley was disappointed. The insemination had
been over a month ago and she still hadn't met Tom.
Several dinner dates had been set for the three of them
(Melvin said he found the thought of meeting Tom too
humiliating for words and wouldn't consider coming),
but on each occasion, Tom had phoned Naomi at the last
minute to say he had to work late and couldn't make it.
Beverley knew Naomi was desperate for her to meet Tom.
She was always saying how she couldn't wait to show him
off. She'd also sounded genuinely disappointed each time

she'd phoned to cancel dinner. Beverley wasn't prone to
feelings of paranoia, but it looked very much as if Tom
Jago was trying to avoid her.

Dressed once again in Rochelle's funeral suit, Beverley
stood next to Plum's vacant desk and dithered. Should
she wait for him to get back from the loo, or wherever,
so that he could show her into Naomi's office? Or should
she go straight in and risk interrupting Naomi, who was
probably in the middle of some important meeting or
other? She waited a few more seconds to give Plum a
chance to return and come to her rescue. When he
didn't, she tiptoed over to Naomi's door and listened.
Nothing. It was odds on that her sister was alone. But
she couldn't be sure. Beverley decided to take a peek
and began to inch open the door.

   'Bloody sodding cunting fuck.'

   Startled by the booming, enraged male voice, Beverley
stood stock still. Poor Naomi. Somebody was clearly
tearing her off a strip and the poor soul was too cowed to
defend herself. Any residual doubts Beverley had about
Naomi having undergone a complete personality change
vanished there and then.

   'Bollocks. Fucking fucking bollocks,' the voice
roared.

   Whoever was setting about Naomi, it definitely wasn't
Plum. If his meek telephone manner was anything to go
by, Plum's emotional repertoire didn't extend beyond
mild hump.

   Good manners told her to close the door. Curiosity,
not to mention concern for her sister's physical well-

being, made her carry on opening it. Finally she poked her head round the door. The room was empty.

Beverley walked towards Naomi's huge desk. From underneath it came more swearing, but gentler, whispered this time.

Beverley crouched down.

'Hello,' she said chirpily to the man's denim behind.

'Oh God, sorry, who's that . . .?'

He immediately tried to turn round. As he did so he lifted his head and cracked it on the underside of the desk.

'Ouch. Oh, shit.'

As the man continued to turn round, rubbing his head, Beverley crawled towards him. In a second or two she had joined him under the desk.

'You OK?' she asked.

'Yes, yes, thanks. I'll be fine. I think my biorhythms must be up the spout today. Plum had just got me a cappuccino, and I was sitting here drinking it, waiting for Naomi to come out of her meeting, when the phone rang. I reached out to take it and the next thing I knew my lap was covered in boiling-hot coffee and the cup and saucer had smashed on to the floor. 'Course, by then the bloody phone'd stopped ringing. When you startled me I'd just started picking up the pieces.'

Beverley looked round. The patch of beechwood strip flooring under the desk was still covered in jagged bits of broken crockery. She could see that most of the coffee had soaked into the front of the man's jeans.

'Listen, if that coffee was as hot as you say it was,' she said, 'you could have some pretty nasty burns down there.'

Her face immediately turned bright red. What was she saying? She had known this man for precisely thirty seconds and her idea of making polite conversation was to start a discussion about his genitals.

'Oh, God . . . I'm so sorry. I didn't mean to . . .'

'OK. I know what you meant. Don't worry, I'll be fine. By the way, I should introduce myself. I'm . . .'

'Tom. Yes, I know. I worked it out. I'm Beverley, Naomi's sister.'

When they'd both got up and Tom had deposited the pieces of broken cup in the bin, he explained that he'd come to Naomi's office because he needed to borrow some cash. Apparently he'd left their flat earlier that morning on his way to Oxford, only to discover when he reached his car that he'd forgotten his keys and wallet. While he was telling his story, Beverley couldn't help noticing that with his tanned freckled face, greyish-blue eyes and thick, collar-length dark blond hair, he was even better-looking in the flesh than he was in the *Standard* photograph.

'Come on, why don't you sit down?' he said. For the first time, she picked up a trace of a northern accent. Manchester or Liverpool, she guessed. Placing a large, firm hand on her shoulder, he led her to Naomi's chair. There were a few spots of coffee on the leather seat, which he wiped away with a clean folded handkerchief.

She sat down and watched him walk round and take the chair on the other side of the desk. Over his coffee-stained jeans, he was wearing a beautifully cut navy woollen jacket and a pale blue open-necked shirt with a button-down collar.

Having sat down, he began dabbing at the stains with his handkerchief.

'Bloody hell,' he said, turning his head towards his watch, 'I am going to be so late for this meeting in Oxford. Christ knows where Naomi has got to.'

As she watched him continue to dab irritably at his jeans, it hit her.

'Oh my God, Naomi hasn't told you about the baby yet, has she?' Beverley said.

Holding the handkerchief in mid air, he sat staring at her. His face was etched with disbelief.

'I found out this morning,' she continued. 'I still need to see a doctor, but I don't think there's any doubt.'

'You have to be kidding,' he said with a nervous laugh. 'What, you mean that jar actually contained . . . you know . . . healthy . . . ?'

He began to colour up.

'Sperm?' Beverley said. 'Apparently so.'

'And you're quite certain?' he said, shoving the handkerchief into his trouser pocket.

She nodded. He said nothing for a few seconds.

'God, this is wonderful,' he said, laughing. 'It's bloody amazing. Who'd have thought? I can't believe it. Christ, I have to go and find Naomi. I'll see if Plum's back. He'll know which office she's in.'

He opened the door leading to Plum's office, but it was empty.

'Bugger,' he said, 'here I am, over the moon because I'm about to become a father, and my other half's done a bunk.'

'I'm sure she won't be long. She's probably been trying to get you at home.'

He nodded.

'God, this feels so weird,' he said, starting to pace round the room. Beverley watched him walk to the window.

'You feel weird?' she said to the back of his head. 'Believe me, this ain't something I do every day.'

'I know. I'm sorry,' he said, coming back to the desk and perching on the corner nearest to her. 'But at least you've had a few hours to get used to the news. I mean, Naomi and I discussed this whole artificial insemination business for months, but it never occurred to me that it would work without involving clinics and doctors. Not only have I made a baby with a woman I have never met until this moment, but I did it by . . . you know . . . into a bloody sundried tomato jar.'

'Don't forget my bit with the turkey baster.'

'Turkey baster?'

'Yeah. Oh, c'mon, Naomi must have told you that's how the actual insemination is done. You know . . . long glass tube with a rubber ball at one end, works like an eye dropper?'

'God knows what you must think of me,' he said after a moment or two.

'How d'you mean?'

'Well, at the very least I could have picked up the phone and said thank you for agreeing to do this for us. I did try, but every time I sat there dialling your number I became so mortified by the thought of my part in the proceedings that I couldn't face speaking to you. Then I chickened out on the night of the seeding ceremony thing, not to mention each time we arranged to have dinner. I can't begin to describe how furious Naomi's been with me.'

'So you have been avoiding me,' she said with a smile. 'I thought so.'

'God,' he said, 'I really am sorry.'

'That's OK. I understand. It can't have been easy for you.'

'Look, now I'm over my embarrassment, we'll all get together soon, I promise.'

'Great,' she said, 'I'll look forward to it.'

Tom apologised for having to rush off. Beverley offered to lend him the fifty quid she had in her purse, but he wouldn't hear of it.

'Thanks, but I'll be fine. I think I just heard Plum come back. He'll tell me which office Naomi's meeting's in.'

She stood up to say goodbye.

'Thanks again . . . for all this. And take care,' he said, reaching out and shaking her hand.

When he'd gone she sat herself back down in Naomi's chair. She liked Tom. He was intelligent, kind and clearly very sensitive. Not to mention ridiculously handsome. Of course she knew virtually nothing about him and she could be way off base, but every instinct told her he would make a wonderful father.

'See, what did I tell you?' Rochelle said when Beverley phoned her after what had turned out to be a very merry and, on Naomi's part at least, boozy lunch. 'I knew you'd have nothing to worry about as far as Tom was concerned. So is he even more gorgeous in the flesh then?'

'Dunno,' she said, feigning disinterest. She wasn't about to admit, even to her best friend, that she'd given her sister's lover a second glance.

'To be honest, I didn't really look,' she said.

'Come on, don't give me that. 'Course you did. So is he?'

'Is he what?'

'Bev, for Chrissake stop playing silly buggers. Is the gorgeous Tom more gorgeous in the flesh?'

Beverley took a deep breath.

'He's very good-looking, yes.'

'God, your sister certainly knows how to pick them.'

'Yeah, that's my sister. She hooks the romantic lead while I have a walk-on part as Madame Ovary.'

'Meeaaaow. Heavens, Bev,' Rochelle said in mock horror, 'do I detect the teeniest hint of sisterly jealousy here?'

'Maybe,' Beverley said thoughtfully. 'I know I shouldn't be jealous. After all, Naomi's infertile and I've got two kids, but somehow I can't help thinking she's having all the fun. Oh God, do I sound really sorry for myself? I don't mean to.'

'Don't be daft. You'd have to be a blind nun during Lent not to be jealous . . . So have you told Melvin about the baby yet?'

'No, I'm still girding my loins.'

Beverley knew Melvin wouldn't be exactly happy when she broke the news – hence the loin-girding – but she hadn't bargained for him being quite so shocked the moment she told him she was pregnant.

'God, I can't believe it,' he said, turning white, and slumping on to a kitchen stool. 'I never thought . . . I mean, you're forty-two. I reckoned England would win the World Cup before it worked . . . So you're definitely up the . . .'

'Please don't, Mel,' she said, mildly irritated. 'I'm up nothing. I'm expecting a baby.'

'Yeah, somebody fucking else's.' By now his face had gone from white to red.

'Mel, I don't understand. You've been happy as Larry for weeks and now you look like your whole world's fallen apart. I knew this would be painful for you, but please try and look on the positive side.'

'The only side I'm positive about,' he said tartly, 'is that you've got this Tom bloke's baby inside you. How could you, Bev? How could you?'

'Hang on. What do you mean, how could I?'

She looked and sounded exasperated.

'Have you forgotten,' she went on, 'that it was a joint decision for me to go ahead with this thing?'

He shrugged and said nothing. She thought he might be about to burst into tears.

'Look, Mel,' she said gently, 'couldn't you stop playing cuckold for five minutes and just try to get real. I have got us out of the financial poo, Mel. I did it. Me . . . who hasn't contributed a penny to this family's finances since before Natalie was born. I was hoping that at some stage you might even say you were proud of me. It's going to be hard for me too. The thought of giving up this child is almost tearing me apart. Come on, please don't make me feel guilty about agreeing to have Naomi's baby. After all, I didn't just do it for her and Tom. I did it for us too.'

He looked at her and gave a weak smile.

'Yeah, I know. I'm sorry,' he said, patting her hand. 'I am grateful and I am proud of you, Bev. Really.'

A few more weeks, a few more sodding weeks selling the snoring devices, he thought, and he could have been the one announcing he'd made the family's fortune. Why the fuck did she have to get pregnant first bloody time? Why did she have to be the one to rescue them?

If it weren't for bad luck, Melvin thought, he'd have no bloody luck at all.

He couldn't bring himself to tell Beverley the truth. That his self-esteem was so low it was virtually giving a minus reading.

'Please try and cheer up, Mel,' Beverley said gently as she put her arms round his shoulders. 'It's like you said, everything's going to be peachy. In a few days' time we'll have the first half of the two hundred and fifty thousand. For the first time in our lives we'll have money in the bank. Doesn't that excite you in any way – 'cos I tell you something, Mel, it sure as hell excites me.'

'Yeah,' he said resignedly, kissing her cheek. ''Course it does, Bev, 'course it does.'

In truth, there was only one thing he found even remotely exciting at that moment. The cash he was coining in from the anti-snoring devices would prevent his worst nightmare coming true. At least he would never have to ask his wife for money.

Despite his determination not to hurt Beverley, he couldn't help it. He started sleeping on the sofa.

Beverley did her best to make light of it and told Queenie and the children what Melvin had told her – that he'd moved out of the bedroom because he'd started having difficulty sleeping and didn't want to keep her awake in her condition with his tossing and turning.

She knew he was lying. Of course she didn't know the whole truth, but she knew enough. Melvin couldn't bear to share her bed because she was carrying Tom's child.

There I was, she thought bitterly to herself one night as she lay alone in bed, Lady bloody Bountiful. I thought I could make everybody happy. I'd give Naomi a child, Melvin and me the chance of some financial security, and get my mother and sister back together. A couple of months down the line and I'm trying to come to terms with giving up my baby while my marriage heads for the rocks. Nice one, Bev. Bloody nice one.

Chapter 14

'Ah, Naomi,' Eric Rowe said, beaming, as they met in the corridor. 'Glad I bumped into you. I was wondering how the live Christmas Eve special was coming along.'

'Fine, Eric,' she said without even a hint of enthusiasm. 'It's coming along fine.'

'Jolly good,' he said, waving his pipe in the air. 'I thought my idea for a celebrity apple-bobbing competition was somewhat inspired, didn't you?'

Naomi's teeth, buttocks and hair clenched simultaneously.

'Oh, absolutely, Eric. We've lined up Lionel Blair, Sharron Davies and Pam Ayres, just as you suggested.'

'And the Seekers? Did you manage to get them out of retirement and persuade them to come on? Back in the sixties, "I'll Never Find Another You" was our song , you know – mine and Audrey's.'

'Oh yes,' she said through a tight-lipped smile. 'Can't say it wasn't a struggle, after all these years, but we dug them out all right.'

'Splendid. Splendid. Audrey will be pleased. And I take it we've still got the family of eight from Shepton

Mallet who can gargle "Gloria in Excelsis Deo"?'

'Indeed we have, Eric. Indeed we have.'

'And the battling grannies idea we discussed a few weeks ago in my office, how's that coming along?'

'Oh, Plum's working on it as we speak,' she lied. (She considered the idea so cosmically, so world-beatingly dull that she hadn't even mentioned the idea to Plum, let alone made any progress with it.)

'Excellent, excellent. Keep up the good work. Now then, cut along, Naomi. I'm sure you've got lots to be getting on with.'

He put his pipe in his mouth and began striding out down the corridor, swinging his arms as he went and whistling 'How Do You Solve A Problem Like Maria?'.

Two minutes later, Naomi was sitting at her desk, stuffing her mouth with cheese and onion Pringles. Celebrity apple-bobbing, the Seekers and sodding garglers – that was what she'd been reduced to. Even if her ratings were down, she knew full well that this bland, vapid crap going out on Christmas Eve wasn't going to improve matters.

What was more, Eric had been right when he said there would be no hope of her finding another job. She'd phoned various contacts at the BBC and Channel 4. They told her what Eric had told her: that due to the Real People Initiative, producers and presenters were being replaced daily by lollipop ladies and school caretakers, that she was very lucky to have a job at all, let alone one paying what it did, and she should hang on to it while she could.

Her only consolation was that Eric had bought her idea to do a six-part docu-soap on a year in the life of a witches' coven, with Fallopia Trebetherick as the star. She would have plenty of time to make it as *Naomi!* was now off the air until the new series began in May.

As she'd expected, he hadn't exactly warmed to the idea initially.

'What?' he'd gasped when she first mooted it. 'A documentary on Satanism? Devil worshippers cavorting round the countryside in their birthday suits, having sexual intercourse willy-nilly? Have I been talking to a brick wall all these weeks, Naomi? Haven't you taken anything I said about good clean family entertainment on board?'

But she'd cracked it – or rather she'd cracked Eric Rowe – in one. She simply asked Fallopia, who was bursting to become a TV star, to come into the office and butter him up. As Naomi had cleverly guessed, the two of them had gelled instantly. Within minutes of being introduced, the pair were chatting about the countryside and Eric was on the phone to Elaine in the canteen ordering tea and slices of cherry Genoa all round. The moment they discovered they'd both been Morris dancers in their youth, he was hers. By the time she left, he was prepared to see witchcraft as just another jolly English eccentricity. And, to his own chortling delight, he'd even invented a name for the series: *Wicca's World*.

'Can't tell you how much I'm looking forward to making our programmes,' Fallopia had enthused to Naomi after she'd seen Eric. 'If all the gossip I've read about you is to be believed, then you and I are going to make the perfect team. Both as bossy as whatnot. Couple of true kindred spirits, I reckon. What star sign are you?'

'Taurus.'

'Huh,' she laughed. 'Blinkin' bull, are you? Might have guessed. You'll have to let me do your chart one day.'

'Oooh. Would you, Fallopia?' Naomi trilled. 'I'd really like that.'

''Course I would. No probs. You must come and have dinner one evening.'

Naomi, who had taken to Fallopia from the outset, was truly warming to her by now. She was starting to realise that underneath her brusque, flinty outer coat there lurked a generous, caring soul – attributes Naomi rarely appreciated or even noticed in other people, but that she found inexplicably appealing in Fallopia. There was no doubt in Naomi's mind that she, too, was looking forward to them spending some time together.

But *Wicca's World* didn't alter the fact that Naomi's Christmas show was going to be unwatchable in the extreme. They'd attract more viewers by showing all the Queen's Christmas broadcasts back to back. She had to do something. If she became associated with this kind of drivel, her reputation really would start to suffer. She bellowed for Plum. He came trotting in with his notebook.

'OK, Plum. Sit down. Sit down. Right, you know those virgins you found who were drugged and raped on the beach?'

He nodded, and stared at her with wide eyes, clearly petrified about what was coming next.

'Well,' she went on, 'keep the virgins, but scrap the beach. I want virgins who were raped – all right, maybe not raped, perhaps that's overdoing it for the time of year, let's say sexually assaulted – at Christmas.' She got up and began pacing.

'Hang on. Hang on, it's coming . . .'

'Righty-ho, Nay-ohmi,' Plum said, pen poised. She could have no idea, but by now his heart was in his Adidas Gazelles.

'OK, I've got it,' she said, clapping her hands. 'Their vicars groped them in church . . . after the midnight carol service. Perhaps they were middle-aged spinsters who sang in the choir. I want tears, Plum. I want hands up cassocks. I want home-made mince pies strewn over vestry floors.'

Plum sat gazing at her, a pathetic look in his eyes. It was several seconds before he plucked up the courage to say what he needed to say.

'But Nay-ohmi,' he said in a virtual whisper, at the same time tugging nervously at his goatee, 'the show goes out on Christmas Eve. That's tomorrow.'

'And your point would be?' Naomi shot back. Plum cleared his throat.

'Well, it's just that it's nearly seven o'clock now. We're doing the show tomorrow afternoon. I'll never come up with the women you want in that time. Please, Naomi, let's just stick with the garglers from Shepton Mallet and the Seekers. Plus you know what Eric thinks about all this sex stuff. He'll have a fit if we do groping vicars on Christmas Eve.'

Not once in the two years Plum had worked for Naomi had he questioned an order. She could feel her cheeks reddening. Her hands were forming into two tight fists. She got out of her chair, walked round to where Plum was sitting and brought her face to within an inch of his.

'Look, you puny, bum-fluff-faced twit,' she bawled, 'it's easy. You've got the Internet, you've got the cuttings library and if you still fail, you've got that agency who'll supply a couple of actors who'll *pretend* they were groped by the vicar. For Christ's sake, a bloody chimp could do it . . .'

'Hello, Naomi.'

She shot round to see Tom standing by the door.

'Tom . . . darling . . .' she gushed. 'Gosh, this is a surprise. I wasn't expecting you.'

'Clearly,' he said quietly, giving her a faint smile. 'I did knock, but you were too busy bellowing.'

'All right, Plum sweetie,' she said, turning back to Plum, her face suddenly beaming. 'Why don't you leave everything for tonight? Do what you can in the morning. I'll see you tomorrow.'

'Really?' Plum said, looking as if he didn't quite believe her. 'You really mean I can go, Nay-ohmi?'

''Course I do, sweetie. What do you think I am, some kind of ogre? After all, it's Christmas. Go home. You deserve it.'

'Right,' he said with an eager smile, 'I will then. Thanks very much, Nay-ohmi.'

He jumped up before she could change her mind,

virtually ran towards the door which connected her office to his and closed it gently behind him.

'Why do you do it?' Tom said quietly, sitting himself down in Naomi's chair. 'Every time I come into this office, I catch you being utterly foul to that poor lad. God knows why he puts up with you.'

'Oh, he knows I don't mean it,' Naomi laughed nervously. 'You know me, Tom. My bark's worse than my bite.'

'Oh, I know you, Naomi, but he doesn't know you like I do. You scare the shit out of him. I'm telling you – ease up, or he'll walk.'

She nodded.

'You're right, darling. I will try.' She walked round the desk to where he was sitting, plonked herself down on his lap and kissed him on the mouth.

'Am I forgiven then?' she said, sounding like a naughty schoolgirl.

He grunted.

'So what brings you here?' she asked.

He explained he'd popped in because they needed to go shopping for gifts to take to Beverley's on Christmas Day.

'If we leave now, we'll just catch the shops before they close. I'd go on my own, but you know what she and Queenie like better than me.'

Naomi didn't say anything for a moment.

'Actually, I'm not coming,' she said casually.

'OK,' he said, his tone breezy and easy-going. 'If you're tied up here, I'll go on my own. Just tell me what to get.'

'No, you misunderstand. I mean I'm not coming to lunch on Christmas Day. Fallopia has suggested we film a typical Wiccan Yule ritual as part of the documentary. Her coven's based in Cornwall. I'm leaving tomorrow – as soon as we've done the Christmas special.'

'You *are* joking?'

'Why would I be joking?'

'I can't believe I'm hearing this,' Tom said, confused rather than angry. 'After all Beverley is doing for us – after all the effort she's making to be friends with you again – and you can't even turn up for Christmas lunch.'

'Look, I know it's a bummer, but it's work and that's it. There's a film crew booked. I have to go.'

'Bollocks. The witches could mock up their Yule ritual on Boxing Day . . . or in February if necessary. You know as well as I do that nobody would be any the wiser. Come on, you know how much your mother's looking forward to seeing you – and meeting me. You said yourself she's been building up to this family reunion for weeks. Naomi, you haven't seen her for years. How can you let her down?'

'She let me down long enough,' Naomi said bitterly. She got up off his lap and walked over to the window.

'Oh, stop it, Naomi,' he said to her back. 'That's all in the past. She's an old lady and she wants to show you how much she loves you. I can't believe you'd rather be with this mad Fallopia creature than making peace with your mother.'

'She's not mad,' Naomi said, turning round to face

him. 'She's very sweet and kind and I happen to find her absolutely fascinating.'

'Clearly,' he said.

'Look, Tom, I don't know why you're getting so worked up about this. It's hardly the crime of the century. I have to work Christmas Day. So what? It happens to loads of people and their partners understand.'

'I agree. And I would too, if I thought you hadn't the option, but you have. You simply don't want to be with your family.'

'That's ridiculous. Of course I do. Christ almighty, Tom – it was my suggestion we went to Beverley's for Christmas lunch . . .'

'Maybe it was. But that was before a better offer came along. I know how you operate, Naomi. You can't see the point of going because there's nothing in it for you. Beverley's done her bit by getting pregnant and now she's no use to you any more. So you do what you do to everybody who outlives their usefulness, you simply cast her aside. Come on, I'm right, aren't I?'

'That's not true,' she protested half-heartedly. 'I'll phone her, from time to time – see how she's doing. Take her out to lunch occasionally.'

'Yeah, until the baby's born. What then?'

'Look, we're different,' she reasoned. 'Come on, Tom, you can see that. She's a housewife, I'm a TV star. We've got nothing in common. We move in different worlds. I mean, after the baby's born she'll get the rest of her money. What more can she want?'

'What?' he gasped. 'You've told me yourself what she

wants. She wants a sister. She's desperate for you all to be a family. For Chrissake, she was even prepared to have the baby for nothing. Everybody does their best to love you, Naomi, but you make it so hard.'

'What's that supposed to mean? I love you, don't I?'

'Naomi, your idea of loving me involves displays of temper that would have Satan yelling fainites . . . plus you eat during sex.'

'Oh, once, that's all,' she said, going on the defensive to hide her embarrassment over the Tidgy Pudd episode. 'When I was tired and absolutely famished . . . Oh, come on, Tom . . .'

She sat herself back down on his lap and began running her fingers along the inside of his trouser belt. 'Everything's going to be so wonderful soon. Don't let's fall out over something so petty as Christmas lunch. In a few months we're going to be a family. It's going to be so exciting. I can't wait. Just think, this time next year we'll have our very own Norland nanny . . . and a baby. I mean, don't get me wrong . . . of course I'm most excited about the baby.'

'Of course,' he said sarcastically. He took hold of her wrist and removed her hand, which by now was a considerable way down his trousers. Naomi's face fell. She got up from his lap.

'I'm going shopping,' he said, glancing down at his watch. 'Fortnum's closes in half an hour.'

Naomi couldn't believe she'd been so stupid. Not only had she let Tom catch her shouting at Plum – again – but she'd completely underestimated how upset he'd be about her not going to Beverley's for Christmas lunch. She knew all she needed to do to make amends was to get on the phone to Fallopia and put her off, but she simply couldn't bring herself to do it. Something was stopping her and it had nothing to do with the film crew being booked and paid for.

Chapter 15

It was the smell of the turkey roasting which had caused Beverley to charge upstairs for the third time that morning, stick her head down the loo and chuck up what little was left of her stomach contents.

The Littlestones didn't exactly celebrate Christmas. They certainly didn't exchange presents or have a tree, but like most non-orthodox Jews, they could see no reason why, when the rest of the world spent a week stuffing its face, they shouldn't join in. What was more, since Beverley was now pregnant and she and Melvin had received and banked Naomi's first cheque for a hundred and twenty-five thousand pounds, she felt sufficiently confident to push the boat out, food wise. To wit the fridge, now groaning with posh cheese, a large piece of six-pounds-fifty-a-pound ball rib, and half of Mitchell Softness's deli.

As Beverley came back downstairs to give Queenie a hand with lunch, her face was still white and clammy from vomiting. What turned it even whiter wasn't the sight or smell of the half-cooked turkey sitting in its roasting tin on the worktop. It was the sight of her mother standing over it holding a thick nine-inch-long glass tube with a large rubber ball at one end. Beverley stared in disbelief and horror as Queenie squeezed the ball, dipped the tube into the meat juices and released the ball again. In an instant the tube had filled. Then before Beverley could stop her, she had squeezed the ball a second time. A moment later the turkey's still pallid breasts were dripping in hot, fatty gravy.

'Mum,' Beverley shouted at Queenie from across the kitchen, 'please put that down.' She charged over to the cutlery drawer and took out a large long-handled spoon. She handed this to her mother and at the same time snatched the turkey baster from her.

'But I don't understand,' Queenie said, looking at her daughter in utter bewilderment. 'They've been selling these on the shopping channel all week. They look so clever. Then I found this one in the cupboard under the basin in the bathroom. God knows what it was doing there. I presumed you'd sent off for it and then mislaid it.'

'Yes, yes . . . I did. Couldn't work out for the life of me where it had got to,' Beverley lied nervously. 'But, you can't possibly use it because . . . because it's broken. Look, it's got a chipped end. Bound to be full of germs.'

She held the turkey baster up for less than half a second before pushing it against the flap of the swing bin and letting it drop inside.

'Can't be helped,' she said. 'Spoon'll do just as well.'

It would have to. Beverley wasn't about to let her mother baste their lunch with the same nine-ninety-nine top-of-the-range – 'luxury', it had said on the pack – turkey baster she'd bought from a posh kitchenware shop in Muswell Hill, and which, only minutes after the seeding ceremony, she'd taken up to Rochelle's bathroom, used to suck Tom Jago's semen from the sundried tomato jar and shoved up inside her. The same turkey baster which afterwards had lain beside her on the floor while she kept her feet raised on a pile of towels, and into whose rubber ball she had gazed adoringly and asked, 'So, tell me. How was it for you?'

Queenie shrugged and continued to baste the turkey with the spoon. She knew when to back off. If Beverley's hormones hadn't been all over the place before she got pregnant, they most certainly were now.

'You look lovely, by the way,' she said, partly to calm her daughter down.

Beverly beamed.

'You don't think the trousers are too tight?' she asked, running her hand over the seat of the stretch black bootlegs Natalie had made her buy from Whistles in Hampstead. Morning sickness was causing the weight to fall off her. She'd taken the scales out of the deep freeze the night before, after everybody had gone to bed, and discovered to her delight that she was down to nine stone three. Queenie shook her head.

'No, darling, they're perfect. Absolutely perfect.' With that her mother gave her a kiss on the forehead.

Beverley couldn't believe how well the two of them were getting on these days. Ever since she'd discovered she was pregnant, Queenie couldn't do enough for her. Nor could the children, come to that. She wasn't sure how long it would last, but for now they were taking it in turns to bring her tea in the morning, and Natalie was even picking her dirty underwear up off her bedroom floor and putting it in the linen basket.

'Now then,' Queenie continued, 'you check the table while I get the turkey back in the oven.'

Beverley headed towards the kitchen door.

'Oh, Mum,' she said, the tension rising in her voice again, 'for God's sake make sure this bloody bird is properly done. The one you cooked last year was so rare I'm amazed we didn't all go down with salmonella. A bit of heart massage and the thing could have climbed off the table.'

Queenie gave an indignant sniff and smiled to show she wasn't really offended. Then, with a small sigh, she lifted up the heavy roasting tin with her oven-gloved hands and turned towards the cooker.

Beverley walked round the long dining room table making imperceptible adjustments to the position of the knives and forks.

As it did every year, the table looked as if it had been set for Friday-night dinner rather than Christmas lunch. Instead of a candle-filled centrepiece overflowing with seasonal greenery, taking pride of place in the middle of Beverley's ancient off-white lace tablecloth was a long, shallow dish of Mrs Elswood vertically sliced sweet and sour cucumbers. Next to this was a cholla (yesterday's, refreshed in the oven – not even Jewish bakers baked on Christmas Day). On each of the eight hors d'oeuvres plates – three or four of which matched – was a mashed-potato-sized scoop of her mother's chopped liver. In a spirit of religious tolerance and comic irony, Queenie had crowned each ball with a tiny sprig of plastic ivy. (Not her first choice of artificial greenery, but Smith's in Brent Cross had run out of everything else.)

'Oh my God,' Beverley said out loud as her eyes went from the bread to the hors d'oeuvres plates and back again, 'it's the bloody cholla and the ivy.'

'Do you like it?' Queenie said, coming into the room with the salt and pepper pots and putting them on the table. 'I thought something a bit festive would make Naomi's chap feel more at home.'

Beverley shot her a shocked look.

'What?' she said, panic rising in her voice as she began counting place settings and discovered there were two extra. How she could have failed to notice this a few minutes ago she couldn't imagine. 'What do you mean, Naomi's chap? Christ, you've invited Naomi and Tom for lunch, haven't you?'

'You know I did,' Queenie said, doing her best to make her voice sound casual and failing miserably. 'I told you ages ago.'

'Mum,' Beverley said, gripping the back of one of the dining chairs so that her knuckles started to go white, 'you most definitely did not tell me anything of the sort. If you had, I would quite simply have got back on the phone to Naomi and put her off.'

'Why would you want to do that?' Queenie said. 'I don't understand. You know how desperate I am to see her and that new man of hers. I was also planning – you know – to have that talk with Naomi . . . to say

219

sorry about everything that happened when you were children.'

'I know, Mum, I know,' Beverley said, gently now. 'But please, just think for five minutes. I am carrying Tom's baby. Did it not occur to you that Melvin might not be particularly thrilled by me having another man's child inside me, and might be even less thrilled about sharing Christmas lunch with that man?' She lowered her voice. 'For God's sake, Mum, why else do you think he's sleeping on the sofa? Did you really believe that nonsense I told you about him having trouble sleeping and not wanting to disturb me?'

'Goodness, Bev, I didn't think.'

Beverley knew exactly what had happened. Her mother wasn't daft. At some stage it must have dawned on her how difficult it would be for Melvin if Naomi and Tom were to come for Christmas. But her emotions had blinded her common sense. She'd decided to keep quiet about having invited them until it was too late for Beverley to do anything about it.

She looked at her mother and shook her head.

'It's OK. Don't worry, Mum, I'll sort it with Melvin,' she said with a sigh. 'God alone knows how, though.'

It took her ages to convince Melvin the invitation had been Queenie's doing and not hers. Even then he said there was no way he could sit at the same table as Tom Jago.

'Please, please, Mel,' she said, panicking, as it was well after twelve and Naomi and Tom were due in an hour. 'I know this is a bloody mess, but don't go creating atmospheres this late in the day. If you bugger off now, Mum will start feeling guilty, and the kids'll demand to know what's going on and get upset. Naomi and Tom will be embarrassed – after all it's not their fault – and I'll be left trying to dish up and calm everybody down.'

She had to burst into tears before he took pity on her.

'OK,' he said, 'I'll come and I'll be civil, but don't expect me to greet him like a long-lost bloody brother, that's all.'

'Fine, Mel, fine,' she said with a sniff. 'Civility is all I ask.'

Five minutes later the phone went. It was Naomi, sounding dreadful, saying she'd got flu and wouldn't be coming.

'I've lost my voice,' she rasped. 'Plus I've got a temperature of over a hundred. Tom's given me Lemsip and now I'm in bed with Vick on my chest.'

'So it's not all bad news then,' Beverley joked lamely, but it was lost on Naomi.

'Tom's still coming, though. I insisted. I know Mum's desperate to meet him.'

As she told her sister how much they would miss her, Beverley couldn't help wishing for Melvin's sake that it was Tom who had flu and not Naomi.

'I'll make it up to you, Bev,' Naomi said finally, her voice barely audible down the phone. 'We'll have lunch again as soon as I'm better. And tell Mum I'll be in touch soon. Promise.'

Had Naomi not cautiously dialled 141 before making the call, Beverley would have been able to discover that it came not from her flat in Holland Park, but from Cornwall.

Tom arrived bearing Belgian chocolates for Queenie, a bottle of Van Cleef and Arpels for Beverley and a couple of bottles of vintage champagne which he handed to Melvin. To Beverley's surprise, Melvin accepted the gift with extremely good grace and shook Tom's hand. The handshake was lukewarm on Melvin's part, but Beverley was the only one to notice.

'I got HMV vouchers for the kids,' Tom said after Melvin had disappeared to put the champagne in the fridge. 'Hope that's OK.'

'Oh, you are kind,' she gushed. 'But you didn't need to bring anything, really. I'm sure the kids'll be delighted.' She took the rest of his parcels and led him into the living room. She couldn't help taking in his blue denim shirt and beige Dockers and thinking how sexy he looked.

'So how was Naomi when you left?'

'Naomi?' he said, taken aback. 'Fine as far as I know. Why?'

'Fine? But I thought she had flu. A few minutes ago she rang to say she was in bed with Vick on her chest.'

'Oh, oh, right,' he said, suddenly realising that Naomi had chosen to lie rather than explain her preference for work over Christmas lunch with her family. He was surprised that she hadn't bothered to warn him about the excuse she had decided to give. 'Sorry, I was confused for a minute. Yes, she's pretty rough really. Bloody awful, in fact.'

'Poor soul,' Beverley said.

Tom grunted.

'If you say so,' he mumbled under his breath.

'You OK?' Beverley said, vaguely aware of the mumble. 'You seem a bit distracted.'

'No, I'm fine,' he said. 'Really.'

So it was that apart from the four Littlestones and Queenie, there sat around Beverley's cholla-and-ivy bedecked dining table on Christmas Day Rochelle and Mitchell Softness (who had been invited back in November and who were minus Allegra on account of her having gone to stay with cousins in Miami), and Tom Jago.

To Beverley's amazement and continued delight, Melvin rose to the occasion and continued to make polite if stilted conversation with Tom about such emotionally neutral topics as computers and GM foods. Rochelle sat the other side of Tom, barely able to contain her excitement. This was due in part to her having downed two glasses of buck's fizz before lunch.

'He's gorgeous, absolutely gorgeous,' she'd mouth to Beverley when she thought Tom wasn't looking.

When she wasn't drooling over Tom, she was bickering with Mitchell.

'Rochelle, I've lost my reading glasses,' he said, just as Rochelle was telling Tom how she'd always wanted to be an actress but her mother had put a stop to her ambition by forcing her to do a Pitman's shorthand-typing course.

'I can't find them anywhere,' he went on. 'Maybe you put them in your bag.'

'They're your glasses, Mitchell,' she said, clearly irritated that her husband had interrupted her in mid flirt. 'Why should they be in my bag? Anyway, what's the problem? Surely you don't need glasses to find your way from your soup bowl to your mouth . . . Don't let Mitchell have too much chicken soup, Bev – it gives him heartburn.'

'Rochelle, please . . . give me a break. It's Christmas. Just for once in my life let me eat something I enjoy.'

'OK, go ahead. See if I care. But you know as well as I do that if you eat too much neither of us will get a wink of sleep tonight. You'll be pacing round the bedroom for hours on end, clutching your chest, convinced you're having a heart attack. I don't know why we don't just offer the emergency doctor the spare room.'

'Great idea. Then you could redecorate. Any excuse to spend money.'

'What's that supposed to mean? I can manage on a budget.'

'Whose, Japan's?'

Everybody laughed. All except Rochelle, who, having heard Mitchell crack this joke umpteen times, simply raised her eyes heavenwards.

Usually Beverley could have relied on Melvin to lead the conversation over lunch, while she dashed back and forth into the kitchen, but despite his best efforts he wasn't on top form. Fortunately, Mitchell was. (The more engrossed Rochelle became with Tom, the less she nagged and the happier Mitchell became.)

For the next couple of hours, while Rochelle continued to knock back far more wine than she was used to and flirt outrageously with Tom, Mitchell banged on about the euro. Occasionally he broke off to point out to his wife that if she leaned any further in Tom's direction, her breasts would be in his broccoli, but she ignored him.

'So you don't think thirty-five's too late to think about starting an acting career?' she purred.

'No, no, not at all,' he said brightly. 'If you're serious, go for it.'

Beverley nearly choked on a roast potato. Rochelle would be forty-six next birthday. She shot Tom a glance which she hoped said 'Sorry about my friend – are you coping?' He smiled back to indicate that he was.

Like his mother, Benny was happy to let Mitchell take centre stage. Not that he gave a toss. Mitchell talking bollocks or his father talking bollocks – it was all the same to him. All he wanted was to be left alone to fantasise about Lettice. Although he hadn't pulled her as such, she was still giving him the occasional hair flick and sexy smile. All that was getting him down was his lack of progress foreskin-reclamation-wise. There didn't seem to be the remotest possibility of his developing even a soupçon of foreskin in the near future. Although he had eventually plucked up the courage to go to the angling supplies shop in Palmers Green, and was now hanging heavy fishing weights from the thirty-two-millimetre rubber washer, the shaft of his penis, apart from being red and sore most of the time, looked much the same as it always had.

Natalie, too, was spending much of her time these days living inside her head. She was in love as well. Whereas Benny's was unrequited, Natalie's was very much reciprocated. Duncan Newbegin, the Leonardo diCaprio lookalike she'd met at the born-again Christian church service, never stopped telling her how much he adored her. Of course, being a committed Christian he refused to sleep with her. But she was in no doubt that he wanted her. During their closed-mouth kisses, she could always feel a higher power rising from beneath his Bible Belt.

She had to admit her mother had been brilliant about her going out with a Christian boy. 'If he makes you happy, Natalie,' she'd said as she hugged her, 'then I won't stand in your way and nor will your father.'

The problem was, her relationship with Duncan had become a tad more complicated than she'd bargained for. Despite her mother's liberal attitude towards her seeing a Christian boy, she wasn't sure Beverley would be quite so open-minded if she discovered her latest bit of news.

Duncan, beautiful, sweet-natured Duncan Newbegin, who swore it was her long hair and huge brown eyes he'd noticed long before her nose, talked to her endlessly on the phone about how he had found Jesus and begged her to come to another service with him. After weeks of gentle persuasion she went along to his parents' church in Barnet.

In the beginning, she went because she was petrified that Duncan would dump her if she didn't. Now she was hooked. Despite her best efforts to fight it, the happy-clappiness of it all, the warmth and vitality of the services, had drawn her in and touched her soul. Moreover, through Duncan she was making new friends who, unlike her supposed mates at school, clearly didn't give a damn about her nose. For the first time in her teenage life, nobody was making Concorde jokes. As her self-esteem grew, her desperate need for a nose job began to fade.

Now, after months of secret church-going, Bible witness classes and revivalist meetings, Natalie had made a momentous decision; a decision which would change her life.

As she made circles in her gravy with the end of her knife, she fingered the silver crucifix hidden under her thick-ribbed polo neck.

Melvin was vaguely aware of Mitchell usurping his role as host, but didn't particularly mind. Having run out of small talk with Tom, he began staring at the sideboard – or, more accurately, at one particular Christmas card sitting on the sideboard. The Littlestones, being Jewish, received a mere handful of cards each year. There was always the one from Alma, and a few from the children's non-Jewish school friends, plus a huge card from Rebecca and Brad Fludd-Weintraub.

Although Melvin and Rebecca hadn't seen each other in two decades, she'd steadfastly refused to lose touch and sent a Christmas card every year. On Melvin's say-so, he and Beverley never returned the gesture. This was because Melvin knew it would lead to Rebecca insisting the four of them got together at some West End restaurant the next time she and Brad were over from New York. That meant buying suitable clothes and being in a position – although he knew Rebecca would never accept – to pick up the tab.

Getting together with Rebecca would also have forced Melvin to come quite literally face to face with his entrepreneurial failure. It was bad enough seeing Rebecca on TV every five minutes and being reminded of what might have been. A real live meeting would, he had no doubts, obliterate what little remained of his self-esteem.

The theme of Rebecca's large embossed Christmas cards was always the same – the Fludd-Weintraub summer vacation. Each year, beautifully mounted on the front, was what looked at first like a casual holiday snap. Only on second or third glance did it become clear, and even then only to somebody who possessed an artistic eye (which Melvin liked to think he did), that the photograph was of a standard more often associated with *Vogue* or the *National Geographic* and was about as casual and spontaneous as a royal garden party.

It seemed to Melvin that there was hardly a beach or ski-slope in the world on which the tanned, smug (so he'd decided) Fludd-Weintraubs hadn't frolicked and cavorted. Clearly they agreed, because last year's card had presented them at their most exotic location yet – the Amazon basin. In the background were tents and a huge camp fire on which some animal was being spit-roasted. In the foreground was Rebecca, looking as exquisite and slender as ever in combats. Brad was standing next to her in white trousers and matching open-neck shirt. Each of them had an arm round a ferocious-looking spear-brandishing tribesman smeared from head to toe in thick warpaint, his bottom lip stretched by a wooden implant to grotesque saucer-like proportions.

In the bottom right-hand corner, the Fludd-Weintraub children, their laughing faces also covered in paint, were apparently trying to teach a third tribesman how to play soccer.

Last year Rebecca had included her traditional five-page family newsletter. This was divided into twelve monthly headings. It contained an exhaustive account of the remodelling of the Fludd-Weintraub residence in Montauk, an inventory of Rebecca's transatlantic comings and goings, not to mention a record of the children's academic and sporting achievements, as well as their orthodontic ups and downs.

This year, however, the card couldn't have been more different. It looked expensive, but was clearly shop-bought. There was also no newsletter. Underneath the 'Happy Holidays' greeting was Rebecca's signature. Below this she'd added a postscript: 'Militant. Thinking of you, as always. Much love, Becca.'

Rebecca had never included a personal message in the newsletter or Christmas card. Nor did she sign them in person. Why had she started now? It had occurred to Melvin that maybe the business was in trouble. That would account for the cheaper card and the absence of the printed signature. But it was unlikely. Even if Tower of Bagel had gone bust – which he doubted, because the financial pages would have been full of it – Rebecca still had an enormous personal fortune. Even in the direst of commercial circumstances, she was never going to be hard up.

And what did the 'thinking of you, as always' bit mean? Was it even remotely possible that she thought about him as much as he thought about her? That she'd never stopped thinking of him? The idea was absurd. Nevertheless it was one Melvin hadn't been able to get out of his mind.

To make sure Beverley didn't start reading as much into the message as he had, he'd smudged the 'Militant' bit with a wet finger in the hope that she would imagine it said, at least, 'Melvin'. When this merely made it look ridiculous, he poured coffee over the bottom of the card, hoping Beverley would believe it was accidental. In the event, she didn't even notice it.

As Beverley offered round seconds of the flaky turkey (due to her salmonella anxiety, she'd insisted on giving it an extra hour in the oven), Mitchell was discussing health. In particular, *his* health. When he'd finished delivering a tube-by-orifice account of his recent barium enema, Rochelle took up the theme and began telling the story of a friend of hers who had recently been diagnosed with melanoma.

'Ideal for worktops,' Queenie butted in, shaking a huge dollop of cranberry sauce on to her plate. 'Irene down the road just had her units covered in kingfisher-blue melanoma. Looks lovely with the yellow wall tiles.'

Queenie had no idea why everybody was laughing, but aware that she suddenly held centre stage, she reached across the table, grabbed Tom's sleeve and seized her moment. It was what she'd been building up to for weeks. One of the reason she'd so desperately wanted Tom and Naomi to come for lunch was because she'd promised her day centre buddies, Lenny and Millie, that she would tell Naomi all about the scandal. 'Media coverage,' she'd said. 'That's what we need. Leave it to me.'

Queenie had been on her feet since six and her hip was playing her up. She was also upset about Naomi not being there. Not only had her hopes of a reunion been dashed – albeit temporarily, she hoped – but now she would have to depend on Tom to relay the day centre story to Naomi. All this, combined with the two glasses of champagne she had knocked back, had exhausted her. As a result, her account of how Martin, the new catering manager at the day centre, and Lorraine, 'the head one', were serving up inedible food and stealing money, came out in a long, unfocused ramble. This included detailed accounts of what food was served at various friends' grandchildren's weddings, who wore what, who managed to offend whom and who should have been sitting at the top table but wasn't.

'So,' Tom said eventually, 'how long has all this been going on?'

'How long is a piece of cake? I mean, the food started to deteriorate a couple of months ago. The thing is, it's got even worse since then. Now they're making us pay what they call a condiment charge. In other words, every lunchtime we have to hand over ten pence for our salt and pepper. Two bob. Can you believe the bloody liberty of it? Two bob for a bit of salt. Then there's the money we all laid out for a coach trip to Brighton. That never happened, and now Lorraine's refusing to refund us. Say it's something to do with the Common Market, and she's only allowed to pay us back in euros. I tell you, Tom, we're helpless old people and they're fleecing us, the pair of them.'

'Mum, why on earth didn't you tell me about this?' Beverley asked. 'If I'd known about the cancelled trip and the money going missing, I'd have gone straight to the police.'

'We discussed it, but we – that's me, Lenny and Millie – thought it would be better to gather up more evidence on the QT and then pass the story on to Naomi. "Day centre supervisor and her lover conning senior citizens." I thought it would make a good article for her programme. Plus I've read in the papers about how Naomi uses hidden cameras and microphones to catch crooks in the act. That's just what we need – evidence on film that they're stealing from us. So, Tom, d'you think Naomi might be interested?'

'Quite possibly,' he said. 'Funnily enough, she's been going on for weeks about this new controller at Channel 6 wanting more stories involving the elderly. Apparently he's been putting quite a bit of pressure on her to come up with something. Of course, I can't say for sure, but this might just fit the bill. I'll speak to her when I get home.'

'Promise?'

'Promise.'

Queenie beamed. Her instinct that the day centre

scandal would make a great story for Naomi's show had been right. She couldn't wait to tell Lenny.

Beverley turned up the radio. Singing along to 'Away in a Manger', she sat herself down in front of the turkey carcass and began tearing off bits of leftover meat which she dropped into a Tupperware. Natalie and Melvin had done the washing-up (Melvin saw it as an excuse not to have to make conversation with Tom) and were now in the living room with everybody else, watching *The Great Escape*.

'Here you are, Mum. Dad and Nat forgot these. Where do you want them?'

She looked up to see Benny coming into the kitchen carrying a pile of dessert plates, their spoons stacked neatly on top.

'Oh, thanks, sweetheart,' she said. Natalie had washed up, Benny was putting chairs away and gathering up missed plates. Her children's you're-pregnant-now-Mum-let-us-do-that behaviour was clearly not a fleeting thing.

'Just put them anywhere you can find room,' she told Benny, waving a greasy hand.

He put the plates down and turned to go.

'Come here,' she said.

He went over to her.

'Now bend down.'

He bent.

She planted a huge kiss on his cheek.

'Thanks, Benny . . . for being so nice lately. I really appreciate it, you know.'

'My plesh,' he said, beaming.

'Mum,' he said after a moment or two.

'What, love?'

'This baby . . . I mean, I know you're supposed to be having it for Naomi and everything, and I know she's paid us stacks of dosh, but isn't there some way we could keep it? I mean, couldn't you tell her you've been thinking and that you've changed your mind? Me and Nat were talking last night in her room, and although we both think what you're doing is absolutely amazing, we couldn't help thinking how great it would be to have a baby around. I could take it to West Ham.'

'Yeah, there's nothing a baby likes better than spending a Saturday afternoon standing in the North Bank yelling, "Ginola is a tosser!" '

He laughed.

'No, but you know what I mean. It would be fun to have a baby in the family.'

'I know, Benny, I know,' she said kindly. 'We will have a baby in the family, only he or she won't happen to live with us. We'll all get to visit. When it gets bigger, it can come to stay. I'm sure Naomi will be only too grateful for the break. Benny, please cheer up or you'll have me blubbing into the cold turkey. I mean, I've got to give birth to this little mite and then give it up. Think how that feels.'

'I can imagine. Sorry,' he said.

'It's OK, darling. Come on, I've just given you and your sister five hundred quid each to spend on anything you want. The sales start tomorrow. Why don't you go to Dixons or PC World and see how quickly you can blow it? Take your dad. He'd like that.'

'No, he wouldn't,' Benny said in a sullen tone. 'He's so miserable lately. What's his problem? I mean, we've got all this money now. Surely he should be happy?'

'He will be, Benny,' she soothed. 'I think the surrogacy idea has thrown him a bit, that's all.' She paused. Benny was sixteen. He deserved a proper explanation. So did Natalie. She would have to speak to her too.

'It's just that he thought he could handle the idea of me carrying a child that wasn't his, but now he's not so sure.'

Benny nodded.

'You mean, to him it feels like you've been sleeping with somebody else?'

Now she was embarrassed. She had no wish to discuss the intimate details of her marriage with her sixteen-year-old son.

'Yes,' she said quietly, looking down into the container of turkey.

'But he will come round?'

'Just give him time.' She gave her son a half-smile.

'I hope you're right,' he said thoughtfully, heading towards the door.

'So do I,' she whispered as he disappeared. 'So do I.'

'Beverley, thanks for a lovely lunch, but I really have to go.'

Startled, she looked up. Tom was coming into the kitchen, his jacket over his arm.

'I'm filming in Lyme Regis on the twenty-seventh – we're doing a new *French Lieutenant's Woman* – and I have to leave at the crack tomorrow morning. That way

I'll get there in time to give the location the once-over while it's still light.'

'Oh, it's a shame you have to go,' she said. 'We didn't have much time for a chat.'

She stood up, walked to the sink and squirted washing-up liquid on to her greasy hands.

'I know. I'm sorry,' he said. 'We've only met twice and each time I've had to shoot off. But I'd like to make it up to you, if you'll let me. Before she passed out in front of the telly, Rochelle mentioned you've got your first scan the week after next. I was wondering . . . that is, if you wouldn't mind . . . whether I could come with you? I'd really like to be there. It would be nice if one of us came – and I'm pretty sure Naomi's busy right through January, making some documentary or other.'

Beverley looked at him in utter astonishment.

'Unless of course you were thinking of taking somebody else,' he said.

She shook her head and reached for a towel.

'No,' she said, starting to dry her hands, 'I was planning to go alone.'

'So, would it be OK if I came along, then?'

'Sure.' She was feeling awkward all of a sudden and she wasn't sure why. She was also aware that her heart was going like the clappers. 'It'll be nice to have some company.'

'Great,' he said, pulling on his jacket. 'See you in a couple of weeks, then.'

He bent down and gave her a peck on both cheeks. She detected the faintest hint of expensive aftershave.

'OK, but don't worry if you change your mind,' she said. 'I know how busy you are.'

'Don't worry, I'll be there,' he smiled. Then he disappeared out of the door.

Chapter 16

There were a couple of elongated farting sounds as the middle-aged woman radiographer squirted cold gel on to Beverley's belly.

'Right then,' she said chirpily, angling the monitor so that all three of them would have a decent view, 'as soon as your husband gets back we'll take a look at how baby's coming along.'

The moment Beverley had climbed on to the couch, Tom had realised he needed an urgent pee and dashed to the loo.

'Gosh,' the radiographer had chuckled the moment he left the room, 'I feel quite flushed. I know I shouldn't be saying this, but your husband is dead good-looking. Liam Neeson came in once when Natasha Richardson was pregnant and I remember thinking I wouldn't kick him out of bed in a hurry, but just between you, me and the gatepost, he's got nothing on Mr Littlestone. And he's so attentive. He obviously thinks the world of you. I tell you, Mrs Littlestone, take my advice and hang on to him. You don't get many like that to the pound.'

'Probably not,' Beverley said, smiling. She couldn't be bothered to explain about the surrogacy and how she and Tom weren't married. It would have taken too long.

'I'm sorry Mr Pettifer isn't here,' the radiographer went on, referring to Beverley's obstetrician, whom she'd seen for the first time the previous week and who was costing Naomi an arm and several legs, 'but he had to dash over to the Portland to do an emergency Caesarean. He promised to pop along if he finished in time, just to double-check everything's OK.'

'OK, that's fine,' Beverley said, doing her best to sound cheerful when deep down she felt distinctly lack-lustre. She'd been dreading this moment for days. Having a scan meant seeing and confronting the living, breathing proof of her pregnancy. It meant she would be forced to look at the baby, her baby – the baby she was planning to give up.

She was lying on the couch, her hands under her head, doing her best to convince herself that she was about to undergo some minor medical procedure completely unconnected with pregnancy, when Tom reappeared. She could see the nervous excitement on his face.

'Oh, you're back. Brilliant,' the radiographer said, gaping at Tom, her turkey neck colouring up.

It was only as she squeezed hard on the bottle of gel she was still holding and a good deal of it shot out of the spout and dribbled down the sides that the woman came back to earth.

'Right,' she said, reaching for a tissue and wiping the bottle, 'if you sit yourself down next to your wife, we can start.'

'Wife?' Tom mouthed to Beverley.

Beverley shrugged.

As Tom sat down, the radiographer began running the hand scanner over Beverley's stomach. Past experience had taught her that because she was only nine or ten weeks into her pregnancy, the pictures on the monitor would be incomprehensible to an untrained eye. They would look more like underwater sonar images than anything remotely human. Past experience had also taught her that the moment she so much as glanced at the screen, her heart would go out to the tiny scrap growing inside her.

'Come on, Mrs Littlestone, take a look. You're missing the main feature,' the radiographer said. 'I know there's not a great deal to look at, but if you hang on I'll see if I can locate the heart and you'll be able to see it beating.'

As Beverley continued to stare at the wall, she felt the scanner glide across her tummy in smooth circular motions. Occasionally a button clicked as the radiographer changed the image on the screen.

Tom glanced down at her, his face etched with concern. She could feel him looking at her, but she refused to make eye contact.

'It's OK,' he whispered. 'You don't have to look.'

Gently, he pulled her hand from behind her head and held it in his. She could feel tears streaking her face. At that moment she would have sold her soul to the devil if it meant she could keep her baby.

'Oooh, look. There you are,' the radiographer piped up merrily, her finger hovering next to the screen.

'That's it . . . that faint black blob just there. You can just about see it beating. And very healthy it looks too. Have you got it, Mr Littlestone?'

'Yes,' Tom said excitedly, 'I can see it. Wow, that is truly amazing. I can hardly believe it. That's my child's heart pumping away.'

He turned to look at Beverley, who was still crying.

'I don't know whether this is the right time to say this,' he said, grinning, and patting her tummy playfully, 'but my mum's always had this mass of natural tight blonde curls. I mean, with her hair and your Jewish looks, we could have Harpo Marx in there.'

Beverley immediately burst out laughing. Then she wiped her face and turned her head towards the monitor. In the murkiness, among the shades of grey, she found it, the faint rapid flicker of her baby's heart.

Twenty minutes later, Mr Pettifer having eventually turned up, looked at her over his pince-nez and confirmed the baby was developing 'Splendidly, Mrs Littlestone, absolutely splendidly,' Beverley and Tom were standing in Harley Street saying their goodbyes.

'I'm sorry it was such a strain for you in there,' he said. 'It didn't occur to me how difficult it would be for you to see the baby. Will you be OK?'

'Yeah, I'll be fine,' Beverley said, doing her level best to sound upbeat. 'I'm off to John Lewis to spend some more of Naomi's money. I plan to drown my sorrows in a vacuum cleaner and one of those giant American fridges with an ice dispenser.'

He smiled.

'Look, I can see you're not fine. Your eyes are all puffy from crying. Come on, let's go and get a cup of coffee and talk for a bit.'

'No, really. The walk to John Lewis will do me good. You get back to work.'

She smiled a weak smile. Then he took off his large black shoulder bag and stood it on the pavement. The next moment he was giving her a big, friendly bear hug.

'I'm sorry you've got to go through all this,' he whispered.

Taken aback by this sudden show of affection from her sister's boyfriend, she stood rigid and tense in his arms. He simply carried on holding her. Slowly she felt herself relax against him. Then, suddenly realising just how much she was enjoying him holding her, she pulled away. Despite the bitter cold, her cheeks were burning.

'Come on,' she said firmly, 'you have to get back and I have a date with a vacuum cleaner.'

'Sorry,' he said, sensing her embarrassment. 'I didn't mean to make you feel uncomfortable. You just looked like you could do with a cuddle, that's all.'

'I know. And thanks. I appreciate it. But I'm feeling much better, honest.' She reached up and gave him a quick peck on the cheek.

'Bye, Tom,' she said. Then she turned away and began walking briskly down Harley Street.

As she continued walking towards Cavendish Square, drops of freezing January rain started falling on her face. She tightened the belt on her new three-quarter-length black PVC coat (another Natalie-inspired purchase), pulled up the collar and cursed herself for having come out without a brolly. For the best part of a minute, she managed to keep her mind occupied with vacuum cleaners. Should she buy a cylinder model or an upright? An upright was easier to manoeuvre, but the wisdom according to Rochelle was that a cylinder picked up better. Then again, what did she know, the au pair did all her hoovering. Rochelle said she'd never use a vacuum cleaner until they invented one you could sit down in.

Despite her best efforts, she soon found herself replaying the moment during the scan when Tom had reached out and taken her hand. This threw her for a moment, but almost at once her mind was back on track. Did she want a model that used bags or one where the dirt went straight into the machine? She suspected old-fashioned bags would be less messy. Even when she remembered the way he'd looked at her just now when he realised how upset she was, her mind went back to crevice tools almost at once. It was only when she relived the moment of the hug and remembered how gloriously sexy it had felt to be held by Tom Jago that she gave in.

She fancied him. She fancied him something rotten. It wasn't simply his good looks which had caused her entrails to loop the loop as she'd stood there in his arms. It was more. He was kind. He was gentle. He made her laugh. He was also extraordinarily perceptive. It had taken all her emotional strength to refuse to have coffee with him. If she was honest, she'd felt drawn towards him from the moment they met under the desk in Naomi's office. She was desperate to get to know him.

She felt far too unsettled to go shopping. Instead she went straight home.

Try as she might, she couldn't get Tom out of her mind. For the next couple of days she went round in a virtual trance. This was partly due to the extreme tiredness she always experienced in early pregnancy. But for the most part it was thanks to her mind being full of thoughts involving Tom Jago tying her naked to a bed, massaging her with exotic oils and slowly, oh so slowly, bringing her to the most seismic of orgasms. Her concentration on mundane matters lapsed to such an extent that moments after imagining herself going down on Tom, she phoned a posh West End hairdresser (recommended by Rochelle) to make an appointment and asked the receptionist how much they charged for a cut and blow job. Then, a few hours later, when the milkman knocked at the door to be paid and remarked on how tired she was looking, she'd smiled vacantly and announced, 'Do you know, I'm so exhausted these days, I can barely keep my legs open.'

Along with the lust, she was, of course, overwhelmed by feelings of guilt. What sort of woman had warped, depraved thoughts about being licked out by her sister's boyfriend? For Christ's sake, Naomi and Tom adored each other. They were about to have a baby – the one she'd agreed to carry for them. To have the hots for Tom was unforgivable. She wondered how long it would take God to process the retribution paperwork. And would He go easy on her, sentencing-wise, if she asked for all her other offences to be taken into consideration? After all, in the last three months she'd agreed to make a baby with a man who wasn't her husband and give it away in return for money, and in so doing had caused her husband no end of misery. If there were such a thing as reincarnation, she thought, God would send her back as athlete's foot.

Her attempts to get the better of her feelings for Tom weren't helped by him phoning her three days after the scan. As soon as she heard his voice her insides turned to instant liquid mush.

'I just wanted to check you were OK after the other day,' he said, his tone distinctly awkward. She suspected he was still embarrassed about the hugging incident.

'Oh, that's sweet of you,' she said brightly. 'I'm fine now.'

'Great.'

'Yeah.'

There was an awkward pause.

'So,' he said eventually, 'did you get what you wanted in John Lewis?'

'No. I was feeling so tired that I decided to go straight home.'

'I can imagine. It had been quite a morning.'

'Yeah.'

She was trying to keep her replies as short as possible because she wanted to get him off the phone. Talking to Tom was throwing her distinctly off balance.

'Oh, I nearly forgot why I called,' he said. 'I mentioned Queenie's story to Naomi. She seemed pretty keen. Said to tell your mother she'll be in touch as soon as she gets back from Cornwall . . . I take it Naomi's told you all about this series she's making with mad Fallopia?'

'Oh yes,' Beverley laughed, 'in detail. Several times. OK, Tom, that's great. I'll tell Mum. She'll be over the moon.'

There was another pause.

'Beverley?'

'Yes?'

'Look, I was wondering . . . I mean, say no if you feel uncomfortable with the idea, but I was thinking that maybe it would help you if the two of us sat down and talked about this whole surrogacy thing. Perhaps I could explain to you just how much it means to me and how much Naomi and I appreciate what you're doing. Might make you feel a bit better about it all . . .'

His voice trailed off.

'Look, Tom,' she said firmly, 'that's a really kind thought and I can't tell you how much I appreciate it, but I know the two of you are grateful . . . and despite the other day, I really am coping extremely well. Plus, if I feel a bit low, I've always got Rochelle.'

'Of course,' Tom said. 'I forgot.' He sounded disappointed – as if he'd truly wanted to see her again.

'Bye then,' he said.

'Yeah. See you. Love to Nay.'

Beverley put the phone down. Was it even remotely possible, she thought to herself, that he had feelings for her which went beyond indebtedness and affection?

'What?' she said out loud. 'Mr Superstar Film Director has feelings for a forty-two-year-old Finchley housewife. Yeah, right.'

Nevertheless she couldn't stop her thoughts turning to Tom handcuffing her ankles to a table and taking her from behind. Then she started to feel guilty all over again.

Chapter 17

Four weeks later, Beverley was back in Harley Street.

She closed the door of Mr Pettifer's consulting room and went into the reception to make her next antenatal appointment.

'All right, Mrs Littlestone,' the receptionist smiled, 'we'll see you in another month then.'

Beverley returned the smile, slipped her diary back in her handbag and walked into the hall. She was standing doing up her coat when the front door opened and Tom walked in.

'Good Lord,' she said, startled. He looked breathless – as if he'd been running. 'What on earth are you doing here? God, there's nothing wrong, is there? Is Naomi OK?'

'Yes, yes, fine,' he said, trying to catch his breath. 'Nothing's wrong. I was running because I thought I'd missed you.'

'What is it, then? Why are you here?'

He held his hand out in front of him while he took another couple of breaths.

'I know when we spoke after the scan you said you

were coping fine with the whole surrogacy thing and that you and I didn't need to talk, but I've been really worried about you.'

'You have?' she said, reddening. Having not seen or heard from him for a while, she'd just about recovered her emotional equilibrium. Now she was starting to get the hots for him all over again.

'Look, it's nearly lunchtime,' he said. 'It's freezing out. How do you fancy a bowl of pasta?'

Beverley's pregnancy sickness had in the last couple of days started to give way to constant hunger. A bowl of pasta? She could have downed a bucket of the stuff. Nevertheless she had to refuse. Lunch with Tom was a mad idea. It was crazy. If they said goodbye now, she might well escape with a minimal amount of churned emotion. She opened her mouth, expecting 'No' to emerge.

'OK,' she found herself saying brightly. 'Why not?'

'Brilliant,' he said, grinning. 'I know this great place round the back of the BBC.'

As they sat in the cab (Tom insisted, even though it was only a ten-minute walk), Beverley asked him how he'd known about her appointment with Mr Pettifer.

'Resorted to subterfuge, I'm afraid,' he said, pretending to look guilty. 'I phoned masquerading as your husband and told Pettifer's secretary that you'd mislaid your diary and didn't know when your next appointment was.'

He was clearly desperate to see her, Beverley thought. But why? Could she possibly have been right? Did he have feelings for her? The hell he did. Gorgeous sophisticates like Tom Jago did not fall for dowdy suburbanites

like her. Not that she looked remotely dowdy these days
– thanks to Rochelle and Natalie – but Beverley found it
hard to see herself as anything other than a frumpy
forty-something housewife. No, she said to herself, Tom
Jago was simply a very caring, compassionate man.
Naomi was a very lucky woman.

The restaurant was packed with a mixture of BBC grey
suits and pairs of Home Counties women up in town for
the sales. As they ploughed through great steaming
plates of spaghetti Napolitana, Beverley's guilt about
having lunch with Tom forced her to keep directing the
conversation towards Naomi. She talked about how
much she'd missed her sister during the five years they
didn't speak.

'When she rang back in October, I couldn't believe
how much she'd changed. She's so much more easy-
going than she used to be. I mean, she's an absolute
pussycat now compared to how she once was.'

'Oh, really?' Tom said, raising his eyebrows.

'God, yes. And I can see how much being in therapy
has helped her.'

Tom virtually choked on his spaghetti.

'You OK?'

'Yeah, I'm fine,' he spluttered. 'Bit of tomato went
down the wrong way, that's all.'

After a few seconds he stopped coughing.

'You know, it's going to be wonderful,' she said
brightly, 'after the baby's born and we're one big family
again. I can't wait.'

Tom reached out and forced her to put down her fork.

'Come on,' he said gently, holding her in his grey-blue eyes, 'that's not quite how it feels for you, is it? Has it got any easier, knowing you have to part with the baby?'

She said nothing for a moment or two. In the end she could see no point in lying.

'No,' she said softly. 'No, it hasn't.'

He put his hand on top of hers and kept it there for a few moments.

Beverley decided to change the subject. This was getting far too heavy, too intimate for comfort. 'So,' she said, desperate to steer the conversation back to safety, 'tell me a bit about you.'

'Nothing much to tell. All pretty boring really.'

He told her he'd been brought up in Middleton, just outside of Manchester. His father was retired but used to run his own printing business. His mother was a housewife. He'd been married briefly to a girl he met when he was a student at Sheffield.

'Brothers and sisters?'

He shook his head.

'So what are they like, your mum and dad?'

'Mum's a hygiene and housework fanatic. You know the kind of thing – washes her rubbish before she takes it out, and puts newspaper under the cuckoo clock.'

'She doesn't,' Beverley said, laughing.

'No, you're right, she doesn't, but you get the picture. Drives my dad mad. Not that he's any less strange. Hates all foreigners. Always going on about how the Asians should be repatriated. Yet at the same time he loves animals and babies and every Saturday he stands in the local shopping precinct collecting money for the blind and disabled. I suppose you'd call him a Nazi with a small N.'

She found this hysterical.

'God, do you know, I haven't laughed this much in ages. Everything's been a bit heavy at home since I agreed to have the baby.'

He took her hand again. This time Beverley didn't pull away.

They sat chatting, laughing and drinking coffee for the next couple of hours. When Beverley finally looked at her watch it was gone three and they were the only ones left in the place.

'Lord, I'd better get going,' she said. 'I'm meeting an old schoolfriend for tea at the Churchill at four. Then we're going to the pictures. But it's been great seeing you. I'm glad we had this talk. You really cheered me up.'

She stood and picked up her coat from the back of the chair.

'I've really enjoyed your company too,' he said, getting up and towering over her.

By now he was standing directly in front of her, his hands on her shoulders. They stood in awkward silence for a moment or two, gazing at each other. She watched Tom bring his hand towards her face. He was going to touch her. She felt her heart begin to race. Once again she began to consider the possibility that he might have feelings for her which went beyond affection and indebtedness. She felt his fingers on her fringe. He flicked some hair out of her eyes. She couldn't remember the last time she'd felt so desperate to be kissed. Slowly she started to bring her face closer to his. He was wearing the same expensive aftershave he'd been wearing at Christmas.

It seemed to take a few seconds for her to realise what was happening. Or to be more precise, what wasn't happening. She was suddenly aware of his entire body going rigid. Then his hand left her face at lightning speed. He planted two pecks on her cheeks. Humiliation hit Beverley like a blow from a wrecker's ball. She just about managed a choked 'Bye. And thanks again' before making a dash for the door.

After the warmth of the restaurant, the bitter cold almost took her breath away. She stood in the doorway putting on her gloves. A few seconds later she began making her way, virtually at a trot, towards Oxford Street. How could she have been so dim-witted? she thought. How could she have misread the signs, have mistaken affection for desire? The long looks over lunch, the flirting, the fingers on her fringe just now were nothing more than gestures of fondness. Tom and Naomi adored each other. Why couldn't she get that into her thick head? By now mascara tears were streaking her face.

'Beverley. Beverley. Hang on.'

She shot round to see Tom, breathless once again, running to catch her up. Quickly she wiped her eyes with the back of her hand and stood waiting for him.

'I couldn't let you go like that,' he said.

'Like what?' she said, pretending to have no idea what he was talking about.

'Stop it,' he said softly. 'You know as well as I do

what's been going between us – ever since we went for the scan.'

'There's nothing,' she said in a choked voice. 'Nothing's been going on.'

'Well, I think there is and now I'm going to prove it.'

He put a leather-gloved hand to her chin and turned her face gently towards his. For a moment or two they simply looked at each other. Tom wiped away a brown streak of mascara from Beverley's cheek. Then he bent down and kissed her on the mouth.

'You've no idea how much I've been wanting to do that,' he said afterwards.

'Then why didn't you – back in the restaurant?'

'Guilt, I suppose. You've got a husband – even though I know you're not happy. I'm not blind. At Christmas, you and Melvin hardly said a word to one another. I'm right, aren't I?'

'It's a long story, Tom. But let's just say things between me and Mel have never been hot in the bedroom department. And since I got pregnant with your baby, it hasn't exactly improved.'

'I guessed it was something like that. Beverley, I can't help it. I'm crazy about you.'

'You are?' she said, almost in a whisper, hardly daring to believe him.

He nodded.

'But what about Naomi? I thought the pair of you were mad about each other.'

'Mad with her, more like. Oh, come on, Beverley . . . she's your sister, you know her better than anyone. It's taken me over a year to realise that the only person

Naomi loves is herself. When we got together everybody warned me about her. They said she was manipulative, had an evil temper and walked all over people to get what she wanted. Of course, I was in love and couldn't see it. All I saw was this beautiful, exciting woman with fire in her belly, and I wanted to tame her.'

'But she loves you. I know she does.'

Tom put his arm through hers and they carried on walking.

'She doesn't, Beverley. I know that now. Naomi is the best actress I've ever met. Christ, you want to see how she fakes it in bed. She's brilliant.'

'Tom, please,' Beverley said, putting up her hand. 'Spare me the details.'

'Sorry, but it's true. She pretends to fancy me, but I know she doesn't. I suspect she never has. I don't know why she stays with me. I get the feeling she sat down one day, made a list of my good points – you know, presentable, reasonably rounded vowels, good job, that kind of thing – and decided I would make excellent husband material. She feels she *ought* to be with me. I'm not sure she particularly wants to.'

'You've got her all wrong,' Beverley began protesting anxiously. 'She's changed. Five years ago she was all the things you describe. But since she's been in therapy . . .'

'Naomi seeing a shrink? Yeah, right. Twice-a-week group therapy with the boys from Hamas. Come on, Beverley, don't you think I'd know about it if she were in bloody therapy? She's not. Never has been. She's the same old Naomi. She lied to you to get what she wanted.'

Beverley stopped in her tracks, her face etched with disbelief.

'No, you're wrong. I know you're wrong.'

'Beverley, listen to me. I've told you, she's a wonderful actress. She's had you fooled. Christ, she had me fooled and I live with her.'

They walked on. Beverley said nothing for a minute or so while she tried to take in what Tom had told her.

'I thought she wanted to be friends. Instead she's just treating me the way she always has. Rochelle and Mel were right. They said people like her never change.'

'The thing is,' Tom said, 'she treats everybody like dirt. She doesn't think about it. I swear it's a reflex action. God knows what goes on in that brain of hers.'

'I suppose I should feel sorry for her really. The thing is, apart from the five years we didn't speak, I've never done anything else except make excuses for Naomi. How much longer is she going to keep doing this?'

Beverley didn't wait for an answer. Instead she stopped in her tracks.

'But she is definitely infertile, right?' There was more than a hint of panic in her voice. 'Please don't tell me she lied about that as well,' she said.

'No, that part's true,' he said. 'I spoke to her gynaecologist on the phone a couple of times.'

He pulled her gently towards him.

'Come home with me,' he whispered. 'Now. Please.'

'Tom, we're not starring in some Old Testament story. You can't finish with one sister and then take up with the other.'

'I thought the first sister had to die before . . .'

'Tom, stop it,' she said, smiling despite herself. 'You know what I mean. Look, you and Naomi are about to have a baby together – the one I have growing inside me. You have responsibilities. You can't simply ditch her because she's giving you a hard time. You have to get your relationship sorted.'

'It's not like that and you know it, Beverley. You know there's something powerful going on between us. I felt it the first time I saw you under that desk, when you couldn't take your eyes off my crotch. Do you remember how tongue-tied you were? You were just so, so sexy.'

She looked down in embarrassment.

'Why don't you phone your friend and put her off? Then come back with me. I've still got my flat in Battersea. I sometimes use it as an office. In fact I'm staying there at the moment while Naomi's away . . .'

He pulled her towards him and began kissing her face and neck.

'Look,' she began. She was trying to sound adamant, but the lust rising inside her was causing her to fail miserably. 'If I . . . er . . . if I agree, it would be on the understanding that . . . what happens between us is nothing more than a fling. We have to make a pact that this will not develop into anything heavy. You need a break from Naomi. I, well . . .'

'OK,' he said between kisses, 'I agree. Whatever you say. A fling. Nothing more.'

She paused for a beat, maybe two, in order to feel the guilt rising inside her. Whatever Naomi had done to her, she didn't deserve this. Melvin certainly didn't deserve it.

'OK. Let me borrow your mobile,' she said.

★ ★ ★

The moment they stepped into the empty lift and the doors closed he held her face in both of his hands and began kissing her on the lips, his tongue coming deep into her mouth.

'You are so beautiful,' he said when they finally pulled apart. 'And I love this coat. Makes you look like a French whore.'

'I take it that's a compliment?'

'C'mon, you know how sexy you are. Melvin must have told you a thousand times.'

'Not since the Bay City Rollers were at number one.'

'Well, take my word for it,' he said, laughing. 'I work with beautiful actresses all the time and half of them aren't a patch on you. You've got the most gorgeous face, Beverley. You'd look great on the box.'

'Oh, Mr Jago,' she simpered, doing her best Marilyn Monroe impersonation and at the same time batting her eyelashes, 'could you get me into the movies?'

'Stop taking the piss,' he chuckled and kissed her a second time.

She didn't believe the bit about her being beautiful for a minute. It was only when she put her hand under his open coat and traced the outline of his erection that she thought perhaps she would take his word for it after all.

He began undressing her even before he'd closed the front door. The moment her soaking-wet coat, jacket and shoulder bag fell to the floor he was pulling her silk shirt out of her trousers. Moments later the tiny buttons were undone and the shirt had slipped from her shoulders.

She could feel herself start to shake. She knew she wasn't cold. The place was roasting. It took her a couple of moments to realise she was trembling because she was frightened. Apart from a couple of fumbling teenage flings, she'd only ever had sex with Melvin. Their lovemaking had become so tediously lacklustre and suburban that Melvin's foreplay was more like one-and-a-half-play. What was more, he rarely seemed bothered about her taking time to turn him on. It must have been a decade since she'd given him a blow job. She was certain she was about to get it all wrong. She'd be all teeth. Within seconds she'd be giving Tom an accidental Lorena Bobbit and they'd end up dashing to casualty with the top of his penis packed in ice in a plastic bag. She felt as if she were about to sit her A level in strumpeting and hadn't done any revision.

Then, as she noticed him gazing down at her breasts, she realised there was something vaguely humiliating and yet hugely sexy about standing in front of him half naked while he was still fully dressed. In an instant, her fear was overtaken by desire. It occurred to her that the sexual energy she was feeling at that moment could have powered a small town for a month.

He clearly perceived her delight. Apart from taking off his damp coat, he made no other moves to undress himself. When she reached for his jacket, he gently pulled her hand away.

'No,' he whispered, slipping his keys into his jacket pocket, 'you first. Come with me.'

His arm round her waist, he kicked the front door closed with his foot and led her along a short, curved passageway, one side of which was made of greenish glass bricks.

What greeted her as she rounded the glass bend took her breath away almost as much as Tom. When she'd asked him on their way over in the cab about where he lived and what his place was like, he'd said little more than that it was a New York-style loft which he'd bought just before he met Naomi and that she hated it.

'My God, this is truly beautiful. And vast,' she exclaimed, calculating that the room had to be at least fifty feet long. 'And it's so light,' she went on, eyeing the floor-to-ceiling windows which went the entire length of one wall.

'Yeah, only problem is, the people on the other side of the building can see right in.'

While he pulled down the white roller blinds and turned on table lamps, she gazed at the huge abstract canvases hanging on the white walls, took in the twisted, misshapen sculptures, the fifties-style sofas and chairs covered in apple greens and purples.

'If you're that interested, I'll give you the guided tour later,' he said, coming back to her. He slid her bra strap down on to her arm and began kissing her shoulder. His hands went to her trouser belt. For a few seconds she continued to take in the modern wood floor, the kitchen units a few feet away with their aluminium doors and beechwood worktops. For a while, as her head turned excitedly from one exquisitely designed gadget to the next, she was like a patient determined to fight the anaesthetic.

Her last faintly whispered words, having noticed how

many of Tom's kitchen appliances seemed to be made of metal, were: 'I see you've got everything including the kitchen zinc.' Then she succumbed. Not to anaesthetic, but to indescribable pleasure. Tom had undone her trouser zip and was stroking her through her pants.

'Come on,' he said gently, pulling away. 'Take the trousers off.' Wondering how much longer she was going to be able to stay upright, she slipped off her shoes. It was only then that she remembered she was wearing hideous flesh-coloured pop socks. The image of her standing there in front of him naked except for the socks was too gruesome for words. As she pulled down her trousers she managed to tuck a thumb under one sock band and then the other, yanking them off as she went.

'OK, now the bra,' he said, smiling. He watched as she reached behind her and unhooked it. She'd been waiting for this moment. Even though she was only weeks into the pregnancy, she'd already gone up to a thirty-four double D. She took off the cream lace bra and thanked the Lord she'd treated herself to posh new underwear the week before. (She couldn't have stood the humiliation of letting Tom see her in her slack grey jobs with the perished sides and lost underwires which only a skilled mechanic could have retrieved from the innards of her washing machine.)

Her huge breasts flopped on to her front.

'Wow,' he said appreciatively. He circled one enormous brown areola with his forefinger before leaning down and covering her nipple with his mouth. She closed her eyes while he licked and sucked and then ran his tongue over the rest of her breast. After a minute or so he moved on to the other one.

Finally, clearly sensing that her legs were about to buckle under her, he took her hand again and led her to the low bed at the far end of the room. Above the cast-iron headboard was a huge oil painting of a plate of bacon, sausages, eggs and black pudding. Bizarrely in the circumstances, it briefly occurred to her that although she had illicitly tasted pork once, she had never in her life eaten so much as a crumb of black pudding. Now she was about to make love to a man who not only had, but had hung a portrait of one above his bed. Most surprising of all, she found this obvious familiarity with the epitome, the embodiment, of non-kosher food yet another of the myriad turn-ons about Tom Jago.

She turned to face him and this time he allowed her to take off his jacket. She let it fall to the floor. While his hands went to his shirt buttons, her nerves having well and truly vanished now, she undid his belt and unzipped his fly. She pulled his trousers down to his knees and for a moment simply stared at the outline of his erection under his boxers. As she ran her hands over it, he dug his fingers into her shoulders and sighed. Finally she tugged the shorts down.

'I had a feeling that being so tall you'd be above average in other departments,' she said, grinning. She knelt down and licked the tip of his penis very lightly with her tongue. She watched his stomach muscles quiver. Enjoying the power she had over him, she did it again. His entire body shuddered. Stroking his balls, she began trailing her tongue the entire length of his erection. Finally she covered it with her mouth and began moving back and forth over the shaft. From time to time she would let him slip out on purpose. Then he would cry out in frustration and she would go back to feather-light touches with her tongue.

'God, you're good. Really good,' he said, trying to catch his breath.

'Yeah, well, you know, I've been around,' she said, looking up briefly. Then she took him in her mouth again.

'No, stop,' he gasped eventually. 'I haven't finished with you yet. Climb on the bed and lie face down.'

She looked at him and didn't move. He knew. She had no idea how, but he did. He knew damned well she hadn't been around. What was more, he knew or had guessed accurately that she and Melvin had only ever made love with him on top of her. For the first time in her life, for the first bloody time, she was about to experience something quite different. She could feel the blood rushing through her ears.

She watched him while he walked over to a chest of drawers, took out a small bottle and unscrewed the top. The next moment she felt drops of oil falling on the backs of her legs. There was a powerful smell of lavender and what she thought she recognised as jasmine.

With slow, firm strokes, he began massaging her calves and thighs. The ache between her legs was now excruciating. If he didn't touch her, some dial on her was going to slam, cartoon-style, into the red danger zone and a siren start going whoop whoop whoop. After a couple of minutes he turned her over and began rubbing oil into one of her breasts. The other hand went to her belly button and down over her pants towards her pubic bone.

'Please,' she begged, 'please.'

'Ssh,' he whispered. 'What's your rush?'

The next moment his finger, still outside her pants, was thrusting repeatedly into her. She could feel the roughness of the lace inside her and let out a gentle sigh.

Finally he made her lift up her bottom and pulled off her pants. Barely conscious now, she let her legs fall open.

But instead of doing what she wanted, he turned her over once again. As she knelt on all fours, he placed a couple of pillows under her stomach.

She felt more oil. Lots this time, dripping down her buttocks. He began sliding his hands over her bottom. The next thing she knew, he was running his fingers towards her swollen, aching clitoris. The moment he touched her, she cried out in delight. He rubbed her, flicked and teased her, varying the pressure all the time. Just as she was on the point of coming, he moved away from her and drew himself on to his knees. He spread open her labia and pushed himself into her. She thought she would come within seconds, but he teased her clitoris, keeping her going until he was ready to come. Finally the thrusting stopped and he rested his head on her back. Her orgasm, powerful and blissful as it was, reminded her nevertheless of Melvin's decrepit Passat and the way its engine overran when the timing was out.

'I know this sounds daft,' she said afterwards as she lay wrapped in his arms, 'but until this moment I think I've always felt like a virgin. Now I've got this sudden urge to tell the entire world that at the age of forty-two I finally lost it. Maybe I should throw a coming-in party.'

'Maybe,' he said, laughing. He began trailing his finger from her navel to her pubes, 'You know, Bev, I promise we'll make up for lost time.'

'Really?' she said, looking up at him. 'OK, then let's do it again. Now.'

She let out an exceedingly theatrical moan.

'Hang on,' he chuckled. 'What are you doing? I haven't touched you yet.'

'I know,' she giggled, 'but I couldn't wait, so I started without you.'

While Beverley and Tom devoured each other, Melvin shovelled fridge-cold bolognese sauce into his mouth.

Beverley had left him a note reminding him she was spending the evening at the pictures and that Queenie and the children had gone to see *My Fair Lady* at the kids' school. She also told him to heat up the bolognese sauce and pour it on the fresh M&S spaghetti she'd left in the fridge, but he was tired and miserable and couldn't be bothered. Instead he'd taken the Tupperware full of sauce from the fridge, along with a bottle of Budvar. Then he'd gone into the living room and plonked himself down on the sofa, the TV remote at his side.

As he ate the cold sauce, complete with solid globules of pale orange, tomato-dyed fat, he took the occasional swig of beer and channel-surfed. The best he could come up with was a documentary on the Serengeti or an ITV quiz show. He plumped for the quiz show.

'So, Donna from Billericay – you're going for answer number three,' the quiz master gushed. 'And remember, ladies and gentlemen, if she gets it right, our Donna will be taking a state-of-the-art deep-fat fryer home to Billericay tonight. So, Donna, you say a Pavlovian response is one which comes about as a result of craving for meringue . . .'

Melvin grimaced and stabbed the remote again.

'And just before we end this edition of *Watchdog*,' Anne Robinson was saying, 'a quick word of warning to all you snorers out there . . .' He'd been about to hit the remote again and go in search of football on Sky, but the word 'snorers' had caught his attention.

'People have been e-mailing us all week,' Anne Robinson continued, 'to complain about some electronic snoring devices – reputedly developed for Mir, the Russian space station. And if you believe that you'll believe anything. Anyway these are they . . .' She held up two five-pence-coin-sized pieces of white plastic. Melvin leaned forward on the sofa, holding a forkful of bolognese sauce in mid air. Fucking shitting bollocks, they were his, the ones Vladimir had sold him.

'According to the advertisements which have been cropping up in all the national newspapers over the last few weeks, you put *this* in your ear – yes, you did hear correctly, your ear – and hey presto, it'll stop you snoring. The manufacturers don't explain exactly how. Funny, that. Well, it seems there are hundreds of gullible punters out there who've shelled out twenty pounds for these things which, according to the ads, are "guaranteed to put an end to snoring". Right, let's give one a try.'

Melvin's heart went from canter to gallop as he watched her place one of the anti-snoring devices in her ear.

'Well,' Anne Robinson said, grinning broadly, 'I have to say that the only thing this will put an end to is a decent night's sleep. You see, the moment you put the thing in your ear, you discover that what you've in fact bought is a miniature radio and, lo and behold, you start picking up – wait for it – Radio 5 Live. I kid you not. Right now, even inside the studio here, which our engineers say is pretty well shielded from radio transmissions, I'm getting full live commentary on Nottingham Forest versus Birmingham City, loud and clear. And Forest are one down already . . .'

Melvin lowered his fork and stuck it into what remained of the bolognese sauce. Then he picked up the Tupperware and his beer bottle and placed them both on the coffee table in front of him. He didn't scream. He didn't cry. He didn't punch sofa cushions. He didn't start ripping at his clothes. He stared with his mouth open.

Above all, he was just puzzled. He'd been selling Vlad the Impala's in-ear anti-snoring gadgets for a month without a single complaint. OK, his own desperation and wishful thinking had prevented him testing the devices himself. It was quite possible that if they simply didn't work very well, customers wouldn't have bothered to demand refunds. But surely if they were useless and also picked up Radio sodding 5, there'd have been a riot?

Then, his lips moving, he repeated to himself what Anne Robinson had said: '*People have been e-mailing us all week.*' All *week*! It was the latest bunch, the last case he'd opened, that he'd been selling for the past ten days. These were the ones which were faulty, and which, by utterly horrific bad fortune, *Watchdog* had got wind of. Melvin had thought they were a slightly different shade of white when he saw them. They must have been a different design, and thanks to the incompetent, useless Russian cretins making them, they were going to be his final nemesis.

Even a congenitally unrealistic man such as Melvin knew what would happen now. Once they'd been on *Watchdog*, the game was totally up. It would be no use squealing that they were a dud consignment. He would never sell another, and half the OK ones would probably come back if they hadn't effected a total cure. By a stroke of atrocious, definitively, exquisitely Melvin-esque luck, the game was up.

There was now no hope of his clearing his overdraft under his own steam, unless Vladimir turned out to be the most honourable Russian businessman ever born and refunded him for all the soon-to-be returned devices.

As for Melvin making his fortune from Russian space technology, fat chance. Of course, he wouldn't now go bust because Beverley's surrogacy money would come to the rescue. As she'd paid it into their joint bank account, he wouldn't need to ask her for the money or even discuss it. All he had to do was make one phone call to the bank and ask for it to be transferred into the business account. But to Melvin it still felt like a hand-out. The humiliation would be too much to bear.

He reached into his back pocket and pulled our Rebecca's crumpled Christmas card. He still had fantasies about her carrying a torch for him and couldn't bring himself to throw it away. He sat gazing at the 'thinking of you, as always' part of her message – as he had done umpteen times since Christmas. Then he wished to God – as he had done umpteen times during his adult life – that he'd gone into business with her instead of walking away.

'Just think what I could have had,' he whispered to himself as a single tear started rolling down his face. 'And what have I got? Bugger fucking all. Here lies Melvin Littlestone, the fifth Beatle of the bagel business. Rest In Torment.'

Chapter 18

Once again, Queenie took her powder compact out of her handbag and dabbed at the non-existent shine on her nose and chin.

'Bev, are you sure I look OK?' she asked anxiously, snapping her compact shut.

'Mum, how many more times?' Beverley said, starting to get fed up. 'If you put any more powder on your face you'll start to look like Marcel Marceau in drag. Believe me, you look fine.'

Queenie and Beverley were standing by the front door, looking out for Lenny's car. Naomi had been as good as her word. She'd phoned Queenie a couple of nights ago to arrange their long-awaited reunion, which was going to double up as a meeting to discuss the day centre scandal. Queenie asked if she could bring Lenny, since he was her co-conspirator. Naomi said the more the merrier and suggested the three of them met at the Dorchester for coffee. If she was honest, Queenie had been hoping her daughter would suggest lunch or dinner. After all, they hadn't seen each other for six years and they had so much to say and catch up on. But so desperate was she to see Naomi and tell her about the scandal that she buried her disappointment, said coffee would be lovely and that she couldn't wait.

'Look, it's you Naomi wants to see,' Beverley went on, still doing her best to reassure her mother, 'not your clothes.'

'I dunno. Maybe I should go upstairs and put on something a bit more dressy.'

'Mum – enough,' Beverley said, finally putting her foot down. 'You've already changed three times this morning.'

At that moment there were several loud beeps from a car horn.

'Right,' Beverley said, 'that's Lenny. Now then, off you go. And have a wonderful time. Give Naomi my love.' She kissed her mother on the cheek.

'You sure these trousers aren't a bit past it?'

'Mum, just get outa here.'

But Queenie was already halfway down the garden path. Beverley closed the door and stood with her back resting on it, praying that her mother's reunion with Naomi would live up to her expectations. After a few moments she went upstairs to run a bath.

'Oh my God, you didn't?'

'I did,' Beverley said, colouring up. The portable to her ear, she scooped up a handful of bubbles and deposited a tiny fizzy mound on each of her nipples. She'd waited a week to tell Rochelle about having slept with Tom. Somehow, sharing the news, even with her best friend, felt like she was betraying Mel even more than she had already. Then, just as she was about to get in the bath a couple of minutes ago, she realised she couldn't keep it to herself any longer.

'Oh my God. You and the gorgeous Tom. Of course I knew you would. Oh my God.'

'How? And stop saying "oh my God" all the time. Makes you sound about fourteen. So come on – how did you know?'

She flicked the foam off her nipples and watched a few tiny bubbles float up into the air.

'Well, of course nobody else noticed, but I saw the way he looked at you during Christmas lunch . . . out of the corner of his eye when he knew you weren't watching. I could see he fancied the pants off you. And now they're off. Oh, God, please tell me you were wearing new ones and not those vast flesh-coloured jobs I usually see hanging on your washing line. I mean, a couple of tent pegs and you could camp out in them.'

'Yes,' she said, raising her eyes heavenwards, 'I had on new ones.'

'So,' Rochelle said, 'is this serious or . . . um, just a flash in the pants?'

'Ha, blinkin' ha,' Beverley said, sitting up in the bath and turning on the hot tap. 'We're doing our best to keep it light. You know – passionate, but casual.'

'Blimey. Bit of a contradiction in terms, if you ask me. And you think you can keep it like that?'

'We've got no choice,' she said, swishing hot water round the bath. 'You know as well as I do we can't afford to get serious. We've both got partners. I've promised to give Naomi this baby. There's just too much at stake.'

'So you're not about to leave Mel, then?'

'Look, I won't say I haven't fantasised about it over the last few days. But you want to see the state he's in just now, Rochelle. He's so depressed. I feel awful even thinking about leaving him.'

She turned off the tap. As she began soaping herself, she explained that for the past week Melvin had barely spoken to her. Or to the children, come to that. She told Rochelle that when he wasn't at work he would shuffle round the house in his old slippers and dressing gown, or sit slumped in front of the TV for hours on end. Although he was still showering, he hadn't shaved in days and he only put on clean clothes if she left them out for him.

'It did occur to me that somehow he'd found out about Tom, but knowing how jealous he's become lately, I reckon he wouldn't hesitate to confront me if he thought I was cheating on him.'

She told Rochelle how she'd begged and pleaded with Melvin to tell her what was worrying him, but he always refused to.

'He's clearly never going to come to terms with me becoming a surrogate. I know that now. But I've got this gut feeling there's more to his depression than that. I think it's got something to do with money. I mean, when I brought up the subject of these toupees he started selling a few months ago and asked how they were doing, his face turned almost purple with fury. Couldn't tell you why. Even if they bombed, we've got plenty of money to pay off the bank. I don't get it. Our financial situation couldn't be better, and yet he's going round the house looking like his world's come to an end. Anyway, I've decided there's no point in forcing the issue. He'll tell me when he's ready.'

The conversation skipped a couple of beats.

'You know something, Bev – you've changed.'

'I have?' Beverley said, slightly taken aback. She put the soap back on the soap dish. 'How?'

'Well, for a start you're putting yourself first for once in your life. You're also playing the bad girl for a change. I mean, if I'd turned to you a few months ago and said you were about to start shagging your sister's lover, you'd've had a fit.'

'I know. The thing is – and God forgive me for saying it – I think I'm enjoying being bad. All my life I've had to consider other people – Naomi, my kids, my mum. Now I've realised I just want some fun . . . God, you think I'm being really wicked, don't you, having an affair – particularly with Mel in this state?'

'It may not be the wisest thing you've ever done, Bev. You're certainly putting your marriage and your relationship with Benny and Natalie at risk. But wicked. . . ? No, I don't think you're being wicked. Believe me, I could see it coming. You and Mel have lived through some crappy times. It would have been different if there had been some passion there to fall back on, but there never was. If it hadn't been Tom, it would have been somebody else.'

'But I'm cheating on my seriously depressed husband with my sister's lover, for Chrissake. And he's Catholic.

That's it. God'll probably send down an eleventh plague just for me.'

'No, he won't, Bev,' Rochelle laughed. 'Listen, of all the people I know, you are the kindest, the most caring and the most loving. If there is a God up there, believe me, He knows that too. Don't worry. You'll get off with a dose of thrush. Maybe hairy nipples, if He really wants to make an example of you.'

Beverley smiled.

'Thanks, Rochelle. Hearing that means a lot to me. Honest.' She paused. 'By the way,' she said, picking up the soap again and running it over her armpit, 'Naomi was never in therapy.'

Rochelle hooted so loud, Beverley had to move the phone six inches away from her ear.

'Now there's a surprise. Lying cow. I told you she'd never change. Mel told you the same, but would you listen . . .?'

'All right, Rochelle, I get the point.'

'God, I bet you're livid. Tell you what, she's still in Cornwall, isn't she? Let's drive down there now, garrotte her with her Prada belt and ram a giant piskey up her.'

'Don't think it didn't occur to me,' Beverley laughed. 'I'm still furious with her. I just don't know why she had to lie. Anyway, I've decided to let it go for the time being. I mean, I'm sleeping with her bloke. I don't think this would be the right time to claim the moral high ground, do you?'

'Maybe not. But she *is* infertile, right?'

'That's what I asked Tom. He seems pretty sure she is.'

Rochelle grunted.

'Watch her, Bev. I tell you, she's bloody devious. My breast implants are more honest than she is.'

'Yeah. You're right. I need to have it out with her. But not yet. I just can't, not while I'm seeing Tom.'

'I know . . . Listen, Bev, I know you said you'd keep this affair casual, but it may not be that easy. Don't let it run too long without making a decision about you and Mel.'

'It won't come to that, Rochelle,' she said firmly. 'Believe me, I've got this thing completely under control.'

'OK, Bev. If you say so,' Rochelle said gently. 'Listen, I gotta run. I'm due at David Lloyd at ten.'

'I thought you'd given up the gym.'

'I did. Then I heard about this cute new trainer they've got working there. I tell you, Bev, I took one look and hired him on the spot. He's called Dartford. Six six if he's an inch. Makes Mr T look like Eddie Izzard.'

Still laughing, Beverley reached over the side of the bath and let the phone drop on to the mat. Then, grabbing both metal handles, she eased herself into a sitting position and started to climb out. She was convinced the new tub was at least a foot narrower than it had been in the shop. This was particularly bad news because in just over three months from now she would have morphed – as she inevitably did in late pregnancy – into Lard Woman. Even if she smeared her bum with butter, she would never get out of a bath as narrow as this. She winced as she pictured a scene involving six hulking firemen smashing the side of the bath with axes while she lay there on her back and helpless, like some giant stranded aquatic beetle.

As she stood making foam-capped puddles on the new ceramic floor tiles, she realised that, despite her worries about Melvin and her ongoing guilt about the affair, she was feeling distinctly chirpy. The last twenty years with Melvin had been bloody tough. She'd never really considered just how tough until now. Now, after the endless financial struggle, and the lying-back and thinking of Artex, she wanted some fun. Even if it did mean being more than just a bit wicked. Rochelle was right. She had changed.

What Beverley failed to acknowledge, however, was that Tom Jago had started to mean far more to her than mere fun.

Still dripping, she stood looking at herself in the full-length mirror and smiled. In almost four months she'd put on no weight at all. Turning to the side she detected a hint of a bump, but she was months off a huge swollen belly. It would be ages before the baby moving inside would feel like a family of ferrets hell-bent on escape.

Her breasts, on the other hand, had, even in the week since she'd slept with Tom, gone up at least one more cup size. Her spirits sank for a moment as she remembered the hideous thirty-eight F mammary hoists she'd ended up wearing at the end of her last two pregnancies. Yet she had to admit that big tits were the best part of being pregnant. She could have done without them being smothered in a network of blue veins to rival a map of the Mississippi Delta, but on the whole she thought they looked pretty excellent.

She took a bath towel off the heated rail and began drying herself. She'd arranged to meet Tom at his flat in a couple of hours. Although they'd spoken on the phone every day – often for hours at a time – they hadn't been able to see each other since they'd made love. Beverley could only get away during the day when everybody was out of the house and she wasn't required to make excuses. Tom, of course, was still tied up all day filming *The French Lieutenant's Woman*. (The good news was that the shoot had now moved from Lyme Regis to London.) In the end their mutual horniness had become so intolerable that Tom decided to do something he'd never done before. He would throw a sicky so that he and Beverley could spend the day together.

'Tom, you can't possibly do that,' she'd said, utterly horrified. 'You can't not turn up. You'll be letting down the crew and the actors.'

'Don't care,' he said simply. 'I have to see you.'

As she sat on the bed blow-drying her hair, replaying his words in her head, Beverley felt overwhelmingly sexy. Melvin had never said anything like that to her, even when they first started going out.

She finished her hair, spent ages putting on her make-up and then went to the wardrobe. At the back was a black bin liner full of her old clothes waiting to be taken to the Oxfam shop. Hidden halfway down was another tiny bag. Inside this was a brand-new and exceedingly expensive black lace suspender belt and black stockings. She'd been shopping in Fenwick's in Brent Cross the day before and wandered into the lingerie department. For some reason, the suspender belt had caught her eye. She'd walked over to the rail and begun fingering the lace. Melvin always said there was nothing he found more offputting than women in tarty underwear. It was then that she remembered Tom saying how much he liked her trenchcoat because it made her look like a French whore. He clearly had a thing about tarty clothes. That decided it. She took the suspender belt off the rail, marched straight up to the counter and bought it and the stockings. The moment she got home, she secreted them in the Oxfam bag. Although she was unaware that her husband occasionally went rifling through her underwear drawer searching for signs of her infidelity (as irony would have it, he hadn't done this for months), she had no wish to rouse his suspicions.

Beverley pulled on the suspender belt and stockings, went back to the bathroom and looked at herself in the mirror. As a forty-two-year-old Jewish mother, she knew very little about the contents of porn magazines, but even she knew enough for the phrase 'readers' wives' to spring instantly to mind. She began to panic. She didn't look like mutton dressed as lamb. She would have paid money to look like mutton. If she added a whip and a pair of thigh boots she could have passed for some seedy middle-aged dominatrix who dispensed discipline from her semi in Bexleyheath.

She was about to pull the whole thing off and get dressed, but something stopped her. She looked at herself again. It wasn't that she looked old. She didn't. People kept telling her how great she looked since her make-over. She knew damned well that in the right light she could easily pass for thirty-five. Her make-up was just right. Heavy enough to give the desired effect, but not so heavy that if it fell off it would kill the cat. Her crimson nails, which had taken her nearly an hour to get right, were now perfect. And even she had to admit that her hair (newly bobbed and streaked, this time by Rochelle's West End hairdresser) looked dead trendy.

She carried on looking. After a moment or two she got it. It was simple. She needed heels.

She went into the bedroom and fetched the black satin stilettos she'd bought years ago (with some help from Queenie) for a family wedding. She slipped them on in front of the mirror. Her legs suddenly looked like they'd gained six inches, not to mention two rather slim, sexy feet. She thrust out her tits, put one foot up on the loo seat and moistened her scarlet lips with her tongue.

'Hi,' she purred, pouting at her reflection. 'The name's Bondage. Beverley Bondage.'

It was then, the strumpet effect complete and her body image higher than it had been since she was a teenager, that the idea occurred to her. She immediately started to giggle. It was absurd. She didn't care. Then again, maybe she did dare. No she didn't. A woman of her age – a pregnant woman of her age. Suppose she got run over? Or arrested? Although why on earth she should get run over or arrested driving to Tom's, she had no idea. She dithered for another minute or so.

'Oh, stop being such a wuss all your life,' she said

eventually. 'Just bloody do it. It's a bit of fun. He'll love it.'

She went to the wardrobe, took out her black PVC trenchcoat and put it on over the suspender belt and stockings. Quickly, before she had time to change her mind, she did up the buttons, tied the belt and ran downstairs. She collected her handbag and keys and walked briskly down the path.

Knowing Beverley had a date with Tom, and knowing Melvin needed the Passat to get to work, Rochelle had lent Beverley her 4x4.

'That's really sweet of you, but I can easily get a cab,' Beverley had said when she mooted the idea.

'Why waste money? Mitchell's in the Algarve for a few days playing golf. It's no problem. I'll drive the XJS.'

'Well, if you're sure.'

'Sure I'm sure.'

As she climbed into the Jeep and turned on the ignition, Beverley giggled with childlike excitement. This was the flashiest vehicle she'd ever driven. As she pulled away – to her surprise relatively smoothly – she felt like a cross between a Jewish princess and a high-class whore. And she had to admit she was loving every second.

After ten minutes or so, having got the measure of the four-litre automatic, she started to relax. As she pulled up at traffic lights on the Finchley Road, she began hunting around under the dashboard for cassettes. Rochelle's collection appeared to begin and end with Barbra Streisand's Greatest Hits. Grimacing, she shoved it into the tape player. First she started humming along. Then she began mouthing the words. In the end she was so busy belting out 'The Way We Were' that she was starting to lose concentration on her driving.

She was slowing down as she approached another red light when she realised she was being pulled over by a policeman. She stopped, wound down her window and looked on utterly terrified as the huge burly officer came striding towards her in his black boots and motorbike helmet. Suppose he suspected her of something other than a traffic offence and insisted on searching her? Even if he didn't think she was a drug pusher or car thief, maybe he would still want to search her. Just for fun. Beverley's heart was beating so fast she thought it might stop at any moment. She almost hoped it would. Death was infinitely preferable to the excruciating humiliation she was about to experience. Finally he reached her. He poked his head through the window.

'Now then, madam,' he said sarcastically, 'do you have a bus hidden somewhere about your person?'

'My bust?' she blurted, pulling the trenchcoat tight across her front. 'With the greatest of respect, Officer, I can't quite see what my bust has got to do with you.' Any second she thought he was going to insist she get out of the car, bend over the bonnet and spread 'em.

'No, madam,' he said patiently. 'I'm enquiring as to whether you think you are driving a bus – a passenger vehicle. In case you hadn't noticed, you are in a bus lane.'

'A bus lane,' she exclaimed, laughing with relief. 'Oh God, is that all? A blinkin' bus lane.'

'I'm glad you find it so funny, madam,' the policeman said solemnly.

'Oh, no,' she blustered. 'I'm sorry, Officer. No. I don't find it funny at all. I realise it's very, very serious. Very serious indeed.'

'Are you taking the mickey, madam, because if you are . . .'

'Oh God, no,' she said, starting to gabble nervously. The adrenaline rush had clearly affected her brain and turned her into a gibbering idiot. 'I'm sorry about going into the bus lane, I truly am. I just wasn't concentrating. Women's trouble. You know how it is. Bloating, loss of concentration, irritability. Last month was much worse. I broke into the Cadbury factory and murdered my husband and six kids.'

'You did what? I'm sorry . . .?'

'Not really. Just trying to lighten the atmosphere with a bit of PMT humour, that's all. So you won't be wanting to search me or anything?'

'Is there a reason I should want to search you?'

'No, no, Officer.' She swallowed hard. 'Absolutely none, I assure you.'

'Right then. You will wait here with me for three minutes in order to lose the advantage you gained by your illegal use of the bus lane. Then you may carry on.'

'I can? God, that's great. I mean, I'll stay for five minutes if you like. Ten even. Or twelve. How about twelve? Then you can really make an example of me.'

'It's all right, madam. Three will do nicely.'

Queenie's desperate hope of a tender and emotional reunion with her daughter was shattered the moment they came face to face in the hotel lounge. Although

Naomi had no trouble feigning fondness towards Beverley, she found it impossible to do the same with her mother. While Queenie stood before her, beaming, her arms wide open to receive her long-lost daughter, Naomi responded by giving her a weak smile and a perfunctory peck on both cheeks. She then shook hands with Lenny, whom she addressed as Kenny, before turning back to her mother.

'My God, Mum,' she hissed, eyeing Queenie's navy nylon slacks, lilac padded coat and multicoloured knitted beret, 'nothing bloody changes, does it? I mean, couldn't you have made *some* kind of effort, just for once? I mean, this is a five-star hotel. I tell you, if you make matters worse by asking the waiter for "a nice schmaltz herring bagel", I'm outa here, story or no story.'

As they sat down Queenie did her best to put on a brave face. But Lenny could see she was upset and he gave her a couple of affectionate and supportive pats on the knee.

What Queenie didn't know – and it was probably best she didn't – was that Naomi had finally arranged to see her not because she was desperate to be reunited with her mother, but because she hoped against hope that the day centre story might save her career. She'd never needed her career quite as much as she needed it now. Her master plan, the details of which were still in the envelope hidden in her underwear drawer, depended entirely on her continued media fame. If she lost her job, stopped being the nation's most loved talk-show host, the deal would be off. And she could kiss goodbye to a fortune.

Despite Plum's warnings, Naomi had insisted on including in the *Naomi!* Christmas special the virgins – all fakes Plum had reluctantly hired from an agency – who claimed to have been groped by vicars. When he found out, the usually avuncular Eric Rowe had been beside himself with fury. So outraged was he that he had called her on her mobile on Christmas Day.

'I want you to know,' he shouted down the phone, 'that you have ruined Christmas for Audrey and me. That broadcast was nothing short of gratuitous, prurient filth. Audrey had the chairwoman of the local WI on the phone complaining at eleven o'clock last night. I will not have it, Naomi. This flagrant disregard of my wishes will not continue. It is only because this is the season of goodwill that I am prepared to give you one last chance. But it is on the strict understanding that you fall in with the station's new, wholesome image. Now do you hear me?'

'Yes, Eric,' she mumbled, 'loud and clear.'

'Very well. You will continue with *Wicca's World* as planned. On top of that you have four weeks to find and film a battling grannies story. Do I make myself clear?'

'Crystal, Eric.'

'Any deviation from my instructions and you will be given your marching orders, my girl. By way of punishment your parking space in the staff car park will from immediate effect be moved to the far end. What is more, Ee-laine in the canteen informs me that your tea and cherry Genoa chitties are still not in order. This is utterly unacceptable and I will be issuing you with a formal company warning to this effect.'

With not even a sniff of a new job in the offing, Naomi finally realised she had no option but to submit to Eric's demands.

If it hadn't been for Fallopia's endless compassion and support, Naomi would have been feeling truly distraught. During the Christmas filming in Cornwall the two women had begun to develop a strong friendship. Since they'd returned to London, Naomi had been to Fallopia's house for dinner a few times. She'd gone again a couple of nights ago. Standing in the pleasingly shambolic stripped-pine kitchen putting together a green salad while Fallopia chopped olives and anchovies for the puttanesca spaghetti sauce, she'd poured her heart out about Eric Rowe's plodding provincial ideas, the ever-increasing pressure he was applying to her to put them into action – and the disastrous effect both were having on her career.

Fallopia had put down her spoon, come over to Naomi and hugged her.

'To be honest, I thought he was a navigator short of a squadron as soon as I got talking to him,' she said with a wicked laugh. 'Only pretended to like him because both of us were so damned desperate get this bloomin' series off the ground. Come on, don't let the bastard get you down. Things will pick up. Just see if they don't.'

As the Cricklewood Crone continued to hold her and pat her back gently, Naomi couldn't help noticing how comforting she found both Fallopia's physical presence and her sympathy. People tended not to hug Naomi, on the whole. Tom did occasionally, but it never felt quite like this. Before letting her go, Fallopia kissed Naomi briefly on the cheek. They exchanged a glance which lasted a fraction of a second longer than either might have expected it to. What passed between them in those few moments, Naomi found oddly confusing. Later she couldn't get the incident out of her mind. Neither could she forget the way Fallopia had blushed, cleared her throat, and darted back to the pasta sauce.

'Right, let's see if Tom's given me all the facts,' Naomi barked, getting out her notebook and at the same time ordering Jamaican Blue Mountain and biscuits for three with no reference to her mother or Lenny. 'You say Lorraine and this Posner character have been palming you off with substandard food, stealing cash and taking money for days out which never happen?'

'Yes, but there's more. That's not the half of it,' Queenie said, her upset suddenly turning to excitement. 'Quick, put this down in your book. They've started stealing people's watches and jewellery while they're snoozing.'

'This is quite good, actually, Mum, very much the kind of story Channel 6 has been looking for lately. It's a shame there's been no violence or abuse . . . or sudden deaths. I mean, that would be the dream ticket. Still, I suppose you can't have everything . . . But surely somebody's gone down with the trots?'

'Now you mention it,' Queenie said, 'a couple of people were complaining of stomach cramps last week.'

'Ah-ha, that's more like it,' Naomi said, beaming.

'Now we're getting somewhere.'

Mass outbreak of E coli, she scribbled into her note-book.

'Now then, while I'm getting my team to check this lot out, it's essential everybody at the day centre carries on as normal and does nothing. I'll need a couple of weeks to decide exactly how and when I'm going to approach these jokers. What I don't want is some old biddy buggering everything up by going to the police or the papers. Of course, the vital thing is not to spread panic among the old people. You lot can bring sandwiches to the day centre if you want, but on no account must you stop the rest of them from eating. This Lorraine and Posner pair will instantly smell a rat and scarper before you can say salmonella.'

'Right, Naomi,' Queenie said eagerly. 'Whatever you say.'

'Look, I've got to dash,' Naomi said, standing up and putting her notebook in her bag. 'I've got a meeting in Cricklewood in an hour. But I'll be in touch. Promise.'

'OK,' Queenie said, looking more than a little crestfallen that her daughter was having to rush off. 'It's been lovely to see you, darling. But Naomi, please do your old mother a favour. Try and put on some weight. In that black suit you look like a stick of liquorice.'

As he sat in the greasy spoon, staring into his mug of tea, Melvin's nonentity crisis was about to enter its final, not to say decisive phase.

He'd set off for work at eight, got to the end of the

road and decided he couldn't face it. Going to the shop meant confronting his failure. He'd done it for two decades. Now he'd simply had enough. What was more, the moment he opened the door, he would be greeted by a sea of furious letters demanding cash refunds on the snoring devices. Instead he'd taken himself off to the caff just off Muswell Hill Broadway, and spent the morning drinking mugs of tea. Every so often he would pick up his mobile in a vain attempt to reach Vlad the Impala. Once again he'd been trying to phone him for days, and as usual all he got was the answer machine. Melvin didn't know why he was bothering. This time the bastard had clearly done a bunk. 'Doing the Knowledge, my arse,' Melvin muttered. 'Yeah, him and the Queen Mother.'

He stabbed the off button on his mobile. How could he have been such a fool? Instead of getting wiser as he'd got older, he'd simply learned new ways to be stupid. He took a sip of tea. For a minute or two he pondered driving to Beachy Head and throwing himself off. But he couldn't do it. First he was a coward. Second the Passat, which they were still driving because they hadn't got round to buying a new car, wouldn't survive a long journey, since it was now steadfastly refusing to go any higher than third gear.

He finished his mug of tea and thought about ordering another. Realising he was already speeding from the caffeine, he decided not to. He looked at his watch. It was nearly lunchtime, but he wasn't even slightly hungry. He decided to spend the rest of the day in the library, reading the papers. It was warm and maybe he could take

some comfort from swapping hard-luck stories with all
the other down-and-outs.

Melvin never made it to the library. Instead, having
paid his bill and peed out the half-dozen mugs of tea into
the caff's squalid loo, he got back into the Passat and
started to drive aimlessly. Although he didn't know it,
his depression had taken a sudden and extremely serious turn for the worse.

After half an hour, he ended up heading east on the
North Circular. This was his route to work. He didn't
want to go to work, he knew that. But for some perverted reason his subconscious mind was taking him
somewhere else, to a place where he would be forced to
confront yet another of his failures.

After fifteen minutes he was aware of passing the
North Middlesex hospital on his right. At the same time
he was struck by the wretched realisation that he was no
more than a few minutes now from F.R. Shadbolt, the
renowned wood veneering factory in Chingford.

He had made his daily treks from Finchley to
Buckhurst Hill for the best part of twenty years, and
for as long as he could remember there had been a
huge sign on the front of the Shadbolt factory
announcing 'Veneer of the Week'. Melvin had always
assumed it was some kind of wacky sales gimmick. But
not one which made any sense to him.

'They're mad,' he'd mutter to himself each morning
as he drove by. 'Totally mad. Some chipboard-brained
marketing executive seriously expects people to see the
sign, turn to their husband and say, "Blast. We bought
eggs, we bought bread, we bought cheese, but d'you

know what we forgot? The veneer. Let's pull in. What do you fancy this week, Ash or Peruvian Walnut?" '

In those early weeks, Melvin's attitude towards F.R. Shadbolt and their sign went from irritation to amusement and ended in a fascination bordering on obsession. Every Friday night, knowing that the factory had changed the sign during the day, he would head home in the Passat and endeavour, between Buckhurst Hill and Chingford, to guess the veneer of the week.

In all the years he had been playing 'Name that Veneer' he had never got it right. Not once.

'Yew, Yew, Yew,' he would urge as he sat gripping the wheel at a pre-Shadbolt traffic light. A moment later he would get an overwhelming sense that he should change tack and go for European Cherry or Honduras Cedar.

Melvin would change his mind five or ten times before reaching the factory. Without fail, the correct answer was one he'd rejected.

It wasn't long before he began to see his perpetual failure at Shadboltism as a metaphor for his general incompetence and uselessness.

As he approached the Shadbolt factory this afternoon, he could feel adrenaline starting to fill his body. He was overcome with the mad desire to make one last-ditch attempt to guess the Veneer of the Week. Maybe, just fucking maybe, God would let him get it right for once. If he did, he would take it as a sign that he wasn't a feeble, impotent loser and that he was capable of getting better and making a success of his life. If he got it wrong he would throw himself off the factory roof.

As he sped past MFI he realised he had a matter of seconds to make his decision.

'Pine, Pine, Pine,' he screamed breathlessly. 'No, Eucalyptus. No, Myrtle Burr. Coromandel. Wenge. Ash. No, Scots Fir . . . That's it, Scots Fir. Come on. Come on . . . it has to be Scots Fir.'

The last thing he remembered was looking up at the white letters and seeing the words 'Rose Zebrano'.

Chapter 19

Beverley stood in front of Tom's front door, her hand
hovering nervously over the bell. As she took a few deep,
calming breaths, she ran over her plan. She would ring
the bell, wait until she heard footsteps approaching and
then let the coat drop to the floor. The moment he swung
the door open, he would be greeted by her standing in
front of him wearing nothing but the black lace suspender belt and stockings.

But suppose he took one look and hated it? Suppose
he really did think she looked like a reader's wife, or a
seedy dominatrix from Bexleyheath? What then? She
took another deep breath while she thought. In that case
she would simply smile, bend down (from the knees, not
the waist, because then her tits would go pendulous and
start swaying), pick up her coat and walk out of his life
for ever. At no stage would she let him see she was upset
or embarrassed. Then she would cry all the way home
and allow herself five or six hundred years to live down
the humiliation.

Finally she pressed the bell. After a few seconds she
heard footsteps. She glanced round quickly to check

nobody was coming up or down the stairs or out of any of the other flats. Then she dropped the coat, formed her lips into a sexy pout and assumed her best temptress pose with her forearm draped sexily behind her head.

The next moment the door was wide open. Beverley let out a horrified gasp.

'Oh, Mr J,' the tiny elderly woman in the teacosy hat called out, turning her head, 'I think your lady friend's here.'

Beverley said nothing. She didn't need to. Her head-to-toe blush said it all. In a flash she'd retrieved the coat from the floor, put it on and was busy doing up the buttons.

'Don't mind me, my darlin'. I'm unshockable,' the woman laughed. She motioned Beverley towards her and lowered her voice. 'You have to be, if you've been married for forty years to a man with a goitre the size of a cauliflower on the side of his 'ead. Ta-ta. Tell Mr J I'm off now and that I'll give 'im a thorough seeing-to when I come in again on Friday.'

'OK,' Beverley said, offering the woman an embarrassed smile. 'I'll tell him.'

She went in and closed the door behind her.

'Oh good, Lily let you in,' Tom said, coming towards her in jeans, bare feet and wet hair. He'd clearly just got out of the shower. 'She's lovely, isn't she? Been cleaning for me for donkey's years. She's too old for it really, but I haven't got the heart to . . . Beverley, you OK? You look slightly red in the face. You're not coming down with anything, are you?'

'No. No. I'm fine. Really,' she said uneasily. 'It's . . .

er . . . well, I had this stupid plan to surprise you. And it sort of backfired.'

'Sounds ominous. Let me take your coat and then you can tell me all about it.'

'No. Don't,' she exclaimed, pulling the coat tight round her. He immediately took two steps back.

'OK, sorry,' he said, raising his hands in mock surrender. 'Beverley, do you mind telling me what is going on?'

She lowered her head and blurted it out. She thought he would burst out laughing, but he didn't.

'God, I've made such a twit of myself,' she said finally.

'No, you haven't. I promise.'

He held out his hand. She put her bag down on the floor and let him lead her into the huge living area. The blinds were already down. The table lamps were on and every surface was smothered in lighted candles.

'Gosh, this is so pretty,' she remarked.

'Come here,' he said softly, ignoring the comment.

Her face still burning with embarrassment, she stood in front of him. Very slowly, he began unbuttoning her coat. She closed her eyes because she couldn't face seeing his disgusted expression. He opened the coat.

'Oh my God,' he said slowly, pulling it off her shoulders.

'There,' she said, her eyes still closed, 'you think I look ridiculous, don't you?' By now she was close to tears.

'Why don't you just have a feel of how ridiculous I think you look,' Tom said. She opened her eyes and placed her hand on the front of his jeans. He was rock hard.

'This is amazing,' he said. 'You look so absolutely beautiful. I just love this suspender belt thing.' He ran his hand over the black lace. Then he took one of her nipples in his mouth and began sucking and nipping it. She could feel herself getting more and more wet.

'God, you look like such a tart,' he said eventually. 'I can't believe you did this for me.'

As his tongue came deep in her mouth, he forced his hand between her legs. A moment later his fingers were deep inside her. The delight was so intense, she thought her legs were about to give way.

'Come with me,' he said.

He took her hand, picked up a small purple cushion and led her to a glass table. He slid the turquoise Apple Mac along it to make more room. Then he put the cushion down on the table.

He kissed her again very slowly.

'Now, bend over,' he said.

She did as he told her.

The next moment he had undone his flies.

'Spread your legs,' he whispered in between licking the back of her neck.

She stood astride in the black satin heels.

For a few moments he rubbed her wet into her buttocks. Then, clearly unable to wait any longer, he pushed himself inside her. It was sudden and without warning. The sensation was somewhere between ecstasy and pain and she couldn't stop herself from crying out. But he didn't ease up. He carried on pushing and thrusting and separating her buttocks. Occasionally he brushed her clitoris with the lightest, most teasing of touches, but she was aware that he was taking his turn first this time to show her how much the outfit had turned him on – and she was adoring it.

After he came copiously in her, he pulled her up, turned her towards him and kissed her.

'Jeez, I feel a bit dizzy,' she said.

'Ill dizzy or sexy dizzy?'

'No, sexy dizzy.'

'Good. Come on, I'll carry you to bed.'

She laughed as he scooped her up in his arms and carried her over to the bed, kissing her all the way.

As he let her down, her head sank into the huge feather pillow.

'You know you really are very, very beautiful.'

'You mean that?'

He pulled off his jeans and tee-shirt. As his pants came off his huge erection sprang out in front of him.

'Once again, you have your answer,' he said.

He sat on the edge of the bed, leaned across and kissed her. The deep, tender kiss seemed to go on for minutes. Afterwards he lay down beside her, swept her hair off her face and began licking the inside of her ear. She giggled and begged him to stop because the pleasure was unbearable. He smiled, nipped her earlobe one last time and eased himself gently on top of her. They kissed again. This time it was urgent and frantic. She wrapped her arms and legs tight round him as if she never wanted to let him go.

'Please,' she managed to gasp eventually, 'please, make me come.'

'Soon,' Tom whispered.

Without taking his eyes off hers, he began stroking her stomach. Little by little his hand moved towards her bush. Suddenly she felt his finger tips trailing over her labia. As the ecstasy took over, she pushed her pelvis up towards his hand.

'Please,' she whimpered again.

'Sssh.'

She watched his face form a grin. Gently, gently he opened her legs a little wider. She could feel her milky liquid trickling down her inner thighs. He massaged it slowly into her skin. From time to time he allowed his hand to brush the opening to her labia. He carried on with his tantalising rubbing and occasional brushing for a minute. Maybe two. Only then did he finally part her. A moment later she could feel his finger gliding over her clitoris. She let out a series of little cries.

'God, you are so wet,' he said.

But she barely heard him. By now he was flicking her lightly with his fingers and tongue.

'Come on. Your legs are still tense. Relax. Let me do the work.'

She let her legs flop open on to the bed.

'That's better.'

He carried on whispering into her ear, gently urging her to let go and float away. After a while she felt as if she was slipping into some kind of light hypnotic state. She'd read about this in books, but never once imagined it could happen to her. As she began to lose touch with reality, she realised she was completely and utterly out of control. If she was going to come, then Tom would control when, not her. Although her eyes were shut, she could sense him watching her facial expressions. His touches on her clitoris were painfully, frustratingly light. But there was nothing she could do about it. There was no point pleading. He would allow her to come when he was ready. Her breathing became heavier and heavier. Suddenly the pressure changed. His flicking became heavier. Now he wasn't simply flicking, he was rubbing. She could feel his fingertip making large circles. As her head sank further into the pillow and her bottom relaxed onto the bed, she felt the first tremor inside her. This was followed by another and another. Her orgasm seemed to go on for minutes. Every time she thought it was over, she felt another spasm deep inside her and her entire body would shudder. When it finally ended and she lay on the bed limp and exhausted, he kissed her.

'It's not your tongue I want in my mouth,' she said eventually.

'OK,' he said, moving his body so that his knees ended up straddling her face.

She licked the tip of his penis with her tongue and he threw his head back with delight. Finally she parted her lips and took him deep in her mouth. He thrust inside her, crying out with pleasure. When he came she swallowed every drop.

'So, sperm's kosher then, is it?' he said, grinning, as they lay wrapped round each other. 'What does it count as, fish?'

'Dunno,' she chuckled, as she pulled gently on his chest hairs. 'Never really been an issue up to now. I've only tried the guaranteed kosher sort.'

'So what you did just then could really get you into trouble with him upstairs?'

'Absolutely. I mean, this time next week I'll probably be seeking political asylum in Sodom and Gomorrah.'

He laughed and began kissing her breasts, while she massaged his head tenderly.

'Tom,' she said, 'speaking of fish. I don't know whether it was that hors d'oeuvres just now, or all this exercise, or just being pregnant, but I'm absolutely starving. You'll never guess what I could really murder.'

He thought for a moment. 'I know, black pudding sarnies,' he said. 'The perfect main course to follow a starter of non-kosher sperm.'

'You're really serious about this trip to Sodom and Gomorrah, aren't you?' She giggled. 'No, I'm not sure black pudding sandwiches are *quite* what I had in mind.'

'What then?' he said, looking up from kissing her left breast. 'Oh God, this isn't going to be some ridiculous pregnancy thing, is it, like anthracite and chips?'

'No,' she laughed. 'Salad cream and beetroot sandwiches.'

'Right,' he said slowly. 'I'm fine on the bread part. Salad cream and beetroot might be a bit of a problem. Just gimme five minutes to nip to the Mace on the corner.'

She protested, but he insisted on going. She watched him pull on a sweatshirt and his jeans over his bare backside. A couple of minutes later he was gone, but not before he'd forced her legs apart and spent a while flicking her with his tongue.

★ ★ ★

He stood spreading slices of beetroot onto Hovis while she dipped her finger into the salad cream bottle and licked greedily.

'Beverley,' he said, looking up.

'Yeah,' she said, noticing the way he never shortened her name. She liked that.

'There's something you ought to know. I'm pretty sure Naomi is seeing somebody else.'

'What?' she gasped. 'Say that again.' Beverley dropped on to one of the stainless steel kitchen chairs and wiped her finger on the baggy shirt he'd given her to wear.

'It's true,' he said, rinsing his beetrooty hands under the tap. 'I'm convinced she's got a bloke down in Cornwall. The film thing's just an excuse. Anyway, half the time she's down there and she hasn't even got a crew with her. I checked with Plum. It's now March and she hasn't been home for more than three nights at a stretch. Then if she does come back, she doesn't spend any time at home. I hardly go to her flat these days. Most nights I stay here. She claims she's having meetings with Fallopia at her house in Cricklewood, but I'm sure she's seeing somebody.'

'Why didn't you say anything about this last week?'

'I wasn't sure then, but I've spoken to her a couple of times since then on the phone. She sounds so cold. So distant. Something's definitely up.'

She looked at him quizzically.

'You don't seem particularly upset that she might be seeing somebody else.'

He shrugged.

'Maybe I'm not. I told you what it's felt like living with Naomi. I am going to finish it, you know.'

'No, Tom,' she shot back. 'You can't do that. Please. Please. You have to stop her going off with this bloke and you have to get her back. For heaven's sake, the pair of you are about to become parents.'

He went over to where she was sitting, knelt beside the chair and began running his finger along the inside of her thigh.

'Beverley, you have to understand,' he said gently, 'one way or another, Naomi and I are finished. I know it's crap timing . . .'

'Crap?' she retorted, 'It's bloody disastrous. Have you given even a moment's thought to this baby and what's going to happen to the poor little mite?'

'Beverley, of course I have. I keep thinking about the baby . . . but I'm also aware of what's happening to me. Beverley, I'm falling in love with you.'

She immediately turned away and started gazing down at the floor. She didn't want to hear this. He put his hand gently under her chin and brought her face back towards him.

'And you love me, too, don't you?' he said softly. 'Sit there and tell me you don't.'

She said nothing.

'Oh, God,' she said with a half laugh, 'here was me only a matter of hours ago convinced I could keep this thing casual, that you were my bit of fun on the side. Talk about a self-deluding twit . . .'

'So you do love me, then?'

She took a deep breath and looked into his eyes.

'Yes, Tom. I love you. I'm mad about you.'

He pulled her on to her feet, held her tight in his arms and almost kissed the life out of her.

'Look,' he said afterwards, as he stood gently pushing her hair behind her ears, 'I want to spend the rest of my life with you. I want us to bring up this baby together. Please, Beverley. Will you just think about it.'

'What? Leave Mel?'

He nodded.

'Tom, don't think I haven't fantasised about being with you, 'cos I have. But I can't, not while Mel's so miserable. He really needs me right now. And I have to think about my kids too. By leaving their father, I'd be breaking up the family. They'd be devastated. I'm not sure they'd ever forgive me.'

'Of course they would. They'd be angry at first, but they're almost adults. Kids their age understand that relationships break down. What you're forgetting in all this is that you have needs too. You've spent twenty years in this mediocre marriage. Perhaps now is the time to get out. And what about Melvin, don't you think perhaps he needs a second chance too?'

'Maybe. Never really looked at it that way.'

'Well, perhaps you should start. Please, Beverley. Don't turn your back on us.'

She took a deep breath.

'Tom, I do love you and I will think about it. But you must promise not to put pressure on me. Mel's not well. I have to be there for him. Maybe when he's back on his feet . . .'

'OK. I understand.'

At that moment Beverley's new mobile rang from inside her bag.

'I'd better get it,' she said. 'Could be one of the kids in trouble.' She ran off to the hall. By the time she came back into the kitchen, her face was ashen and she was shaking.

'What the hell is it?' Tom said, helping her to a chair.

'That was my mum,' she said, struggling to stay calm. 'It's Mel. He's in hospital.'

'Christ, what's happened? Did he have an accident? Is he ill? What?'

'No, from what I can make out, he's fine physically. Apparently he burst into some factory somewhere on the North Circular and went berserk. He kept demanding to be shown the way up to their roof because he wanted to commit suicide by jumping off it. When they tried to get rid of him he turned violent. Apparently the blokes there managed to restrain him until the police arrived. As soon as they got there they carted him off to a bin.' She paused for a moment as the panic started to rise inside her.

'Tom, they're planning to section him under the Mental Health Act. That means he might have to stay there for months . . . years, even.'

Chapter 20

One Saturday morning three weeks later, Melvin sat on his bed at the Friary, waiting to go into his therapy session. It was thanks to Beverley that he'd been admitted to the exclusive private clinic in Richmond. Desperate that Melvin should have only the best psychiatric care and aware that the hospital fees wouldn't be a problem, she'd arranged for Melvin's immediate transfer to the Friary from the seedy NHS hospital in Chingford where he had been taken from the roof of the F.R. Shadbolt factory.

As he sat, his thumb and forefinger continued to faff around just inside his left nostril. Although he'd plucked six nose hairs so far, he had to his intense irritation yet to locate the well-spring of this latest bout of nasal itching. By now his eyes were watering so much that the article he was reading in the *Daily Mail* Week-End section on Dame Kiri Te Kanawa's passion for collecting commemorative porcelain thimbles had become nothing more than a blur. As he put the newspaper down beside him on the bed and plucked for a seventh time, he heard loud voices coming from the room next door. His neighbour, a multiple personality named Val, Bernard and Cilla, was bickering among her selves about whether to go for a pub lunch before or after shopping for loose covers.

The worst part about being in a nut house, Melvin had decided – even a private, not to say fashionable one like this, where the names of the resident druggies and piss artists read like the membership list at the Soho House – was the noise. When the obsessive-compulsives weren't bawling over whose turn it was to Domestos the loos or clean the ashtrays in the day room, the sexual compulsives were hitting on the passive dependants and the manic depressives were playing the video of Princess Di's funeral at full volume. The only place he could find peace and quiet was in the upstairs lounge among the catatonic schizophrenics.

Melvin's psychotherapist at the Friary, whom he saw for an hour each day, was called Wim. He was a humourless but unendingly compassionate Belgian – in his early sixties, Melvin guessed – who wore a wiry Salvador Dali moustache, the kind of arty, funny-shaped glasses beloved of Europeans, and a brocade fez thing with a tassel. Melvin strongly suspected that one day as he sat sharing his misery with Wim, a door would open, Monty Python-style, in the man's fore-head, and through it would shoot a giant, hissing and whistling steam train.

Although his sartorial style gave the impression that he was in far greater need of therapy than his patients, Wim had in three weeks brought about a conspicuous improvement in Melvin's state of mind. Slowly his self-esteem was re-emerging.

Wim had finally made Melvin accept what Beverley had been telling him for years: that the pharmacy had failed not because he was intrinsically stupid or lacked ability, or because God had it in for him, but because his obsessive need to get back at his father had got in the way of his business sense.

'You know, Melvin, in Belgium we have an old saying to describe what you did,' Wim said, smiling and twisting one end of his waxed moustache. 'You buried your waffle to spite your stomach.'

Beverley visited most days. Melvin always looked forward to seeing her. She arrived with newspapers and magazines, and foil containers of Queenie's home-made strudel. Food was the last thing he needed, but he didn't have the heart to tell her. Firstly, he had no appetite. The weight had fallen off him since he'd been at the Friary. Secondly, what little hospital food he'd tasted had been superb. He wasn't alone in this view. In a recent survey of the world's most sought-after psychiatric hospitals, *Tatler* had bestowed upon the Friary's chef the coveted Golden Straitjacket Award.

Apart from bringing food he didn't need, Beverley sat and held his hand, told him how much better he was looking and put him back in touch with the real world by telling him about the kids, the revision Benny should have been doing for his GCSEs and wasn't, and the jungle-effect wallpaper Rochelle was trying to persuade her to buy for the hall.

It wasn't until he started to get better and slowly emerge from his psychotic miasma that he noticed his wife had developed a new and intensely irritating habit. She'd started to gabble. She arrived, sat on the bed, yammered uncontrollably for an hour or so, barely letting him get a word in, and then left. He also noticed she was avoiding making eye contact with him. He began to perceive in her a distance, a remoteness which he couldn't explain. When he tried to discuss it, she bridled and told him he was imagining things. Melvin was certain there was something she wanted to tell him but couldn't. On the few occasions he'd caught her off guard and looked into her eyes, he almost got the sense that he'd lost her.

'Physically she's still here, but I know that in her mind she's somewhere else,' he'd said to Wim. 'Who could blame her? Twenty years she put up with varying degrees of my madness. She was only doing what she thought best for me and the kids when she agreed to have her sister's baby, but my ego just couldn't cope.'

He paused for a few moments.

'The odd thing,' he went on eventually, 'is that although I feel sad at the thought of losing her, I don't feel devastated – not like I thought I would.'

He explained about the years of going through her underwear drawer looking for signs of her infidelity. Wim didn't say anything for a few moments.

'So, Melvin . . . tell me, who is it you really love?'

'What on earth makes you think there's anybody else?' Melvin said, taken aback by Wim's insight.

'I don't know,' Wim said slowly. 'It's a feeling I get from you sometimes – a sense of bereavement, almost.'

★ ★ ★

From then on, Melvin spent each session talking about Rebecca and asking how it was possible for him to be in love with a woman he hadn't seen for over twenty years.

A week ago he'd taken Rebecca's now battered and stained Christmas card from his wallet and explained how he hadn't been able to throw it away. He unfolded it and passed it to Wim.

'That's the first time in twenty years she's included a hand-written message,' he said excitedly, leaning forward in his chair. 'Take a close look, you can still just about read it.'

'Melvin, I really don't think this is a very useful exercise. The fact that you have kept this card is simply more evidence of your obsessive nature.'

'Please, Wim,' Melvin said, virtually pleading, 'indulge me. Just for a moment. Go on, take a look at it.'

Sighing, Wim pushed his comedy spectacles on to his forehead and read the message.

'You see,' Melvin said, warming to his theme, like a detective, 'it says "Militant". She called me that because when she knew me I was twenty and a Marxist. You're the shrink. What do you make of that? I mean, don't you think it's a bit bloody familiar after twenty years?'

'Melvin, Melvin,' Wim said slowly, his tone verging on exasperated, 'you said yourself, it was what she called you. What should she write – "Dear Mr Littlestone"? Come on . . .'

'OK, OK,' he shot back. 'So maybe I got that wrong,

311

but what about the "thinking of you" bit? I had no idea she thought about me. Clearly I still mean something to her. And what do you make of "always"? That was the clincher for me. It means she must have been thinking about me all this time and never dared say anything because we were both married. Come on, Wim, you have to admit, it's a bloody strange thing to say. I mean . . .'

'Melvin. Stop,' Wim said, raising his voice slightly and pushing the glasses back on to the end of his nose. 'Just stop and listen to me.'

Melvin knew what was coming. Embarrassed by his naive stupidity, he lowered his head and refused to meet Wim's eyes.

'After all these years,' his shrink said gently, 'you are in love with a bittersweet memory. Nothing more. She is unattainable. You told me yourself. She's married. She has children. She lives thousands of miles away. Not only that, she is now rich and famous. Wanting what we can't have can drive us crazy. Let her go, Melvin. Don't let another obsession take you over. This one could destroy you.'

The shrink held out the Christmas card towards his patient. Melvin didn't move. Neither did Wim. They remained locked in this mental stand-off for a few seconds. For Melvin, taking the card back meant acknowledging that Wim was right.

In the end Melvin leaned forward, snatched it from Wim's fingers and folded it in half, along the ancient fold. As he shoved it in his trouser pocket he could feel tears stinging his eyes.

As Beverley flip-flopped into the bedroom in her slippers, she took her watch out of her dressing gown pocket. It wasn't yet twelve. She'd told Melvin she'd get to the Friary at about four. She had ages. It would take no more than forty-five minutes to drive to the bin. Bin, strange how such an alarming word has eased its way into the family vocabulary. After three weeks it had become as mundane and familiar as 'socks' or 'Ready Brek'. She supposed it would have been the same with carcinoma or persistent vegetative state. Even the children, who had been devastated when they were told their father was in a psychiatric clinic, had, now they knew he was on the mend, stopped lolling aimlessly about the place and started going out with their friends again.

Beverley decided to lie down for a couple of hours. Not only did she have time to kill, but for once the house was empty. More to the point it was silent. There was no Benny demanding cinema and Burger King money and no Natalie standing wailing in her bedroom because each of the fifty-six outfits she'd just tried on, and which were scattered all over the bedroom floor, made her look gross.

Natalie had gone shopping. Benny, who had bought a guitar last week, had gone to his first lesson, and Queenie had gone to Brent Cross with her friend Millie from the day centre to catch a sale at Smith's and bulk-buy condolence cards ('Listen, at our age it makes sense.').

Beverley was particularly glad to see the back of her mother for a few hours. Ever since her reunion with

Naomi, Queenie had been wandering round the house looking like a wet weekend in Frinton. Beverley knew the occasion hadn't lived up to her mother's fantasy.

'Oh, it was fine. Very nice,' Queenie had said afterwards, doing her best not to let her disappointment show. Then, a few days ago, Queenie's sombre mood had suddenly changed, but not for the better. When it dawned on her that Naomi hadn't been in touch about the day centre story, she started to fret. If Beverley had been asked once for her opinion as to why Naomi hadn't phoned, she'd been asked fifty times.

'I mean, she promised to call,' Queenie had said yet again last night, on her way up to bed. ' "Just give me a couple of weeks", she said. It's been three now and still no word. What do you think I should do?'

'Mum,' Beverley said, on the verge of exasperation, 'I keep on telling you. She's a busy woman. Two weeks was just a figure she plucked out of the air. Listen, if she promised to phone, she'll phone. You have to be patient.'

'Do you think maybe I should phone her? Or would that look too much like nagging?'

'I tell you what,' Beverley said finally, 'give it another couple of weeks and then phone. Then it will have been well over a month since you met. I don't think she'd see that as nagging.'

'OK, Bev. If you think that's the best bet, I'll wait.'

Queenie had carried on upstairs.

Lying on the bed next to Beverley was the latest edition of *Marie Claire*. Having finished with it, Natalie had left it when she came in to say she was going clothes shopping with Allegra.

'You know I'll always love you, Mum,' she'd whispered, bending down to kiss her mother, who was still fast asleep.

Without opening her eyes, Beverley had kissed the air and mumbled, 'Yeah, love you too, sweetheart. Don't forget your keys.'

It was only now, flicking through the magazine, that her daughter's exact words hit her. Natalie often told Beverley she loved her, particularly when they were making up after a row or when Beverley gave her money, but it was always a casual 'Love ya, Mum.' Beverley had never known her add the 'I'll always' bit. There was, she thought, something oddly ominous about it. In the end, assuming it was nothing more than Natalie showing daughterly affection and concern for her lone, pregnant mother, she shrugged and went back to the magazine. But she couldn't concentrate. She tossed it on to the floor.

Beverley didn't know it was possible to feel such guilt. In the three weeks Melvin had been in the Friary, hardly a night had gone by when she didn't lie in bed and promise herself she would finish it with Tom. After all, Melvin's breakdown was her fault. Through Wim, with Melvin's permission, she now knew all about Vlad the Impala, the shedding toupees and the unfortunate business of the anti-snoring devices. More to the point, she knew Mel had been driven to make these dodgy deals because he saw them as a last-ditch attempt to prove himself as a provider.

'Of course, when the scams failed and at the same time you became the family's financial saviour,' Wim had explained on their first meeting in his office at the Friary, 'he saw himself not simply as a failure. By usurping his role as provider so spectacularly, you had virtually emasculated him. But I must emphasise this, Mrs Littlestone – it wasn't your fault. Please, please don't punish yourself over this. You became a surrogate for your sister for the best of intentions. You simply weren't to know Melvin would react in the way he did.'

Naturally, she hadn't stopped punishing herself. There were even times, when her feelings of self-loathing were particularly acute, that she saw Mel's breakdown as her punishment for allowing herself to even think about leaving him for Tom.

Most of the time, though, she was merely furious with herself for having been so insensitive, for her lack of perception and tact. She knew Melvin's self-esteem had been at rock bottom and all she'd succeeded in doing was rubbing his nose in his failure.

As she saw it, the very least she owed Melvin was to finish it with Tom. But guilty as she felt, loathe herself as she did over it, she couldn't bring herself to do it. Several nights a week they would meet, go out for dinner, and almost at once Tom would tell her he loved her. Then he would start fantasising about their future together with the baby, and despite herself, Beverley would join in. Very occasionally, Tom would take time off work and they would drive to Putney and take walks along the river. One day they decided to play tourists. They took an open-top bus ride, went to the Tower of

London and ended up late that afternoon at St Paul's Cathedral. They climbed the stairs to the Whispering Gallery and spent ages messing around with the bizarre acoustics and murmuring silly messages from one side of the vast dome to the other. Still giggling like a pair of teenagers, they went downstairs to the café in the crypt and had tea and scones.

Most of the time, however, they went to bed and spent hours having the kind of sex that left Beverley reeling and walking on air for days afterwards.

Even when she'd thought they'd finished making love they rarely had. She remembered how, two days ago, she'd been standing in the kitchen eating another of her beetroot and salad cream sandwiches while he was buttering himself some toast, when he suddenly put down his knife, turned to her with a mischievous smile on his lips and said sorry, but he just had to have her one more time before she went home. He took hold of her shoulders and pinned her against one of the tall kitchen cupboards. As he kissed her he undid the buttons of the shirt he'd given her to wear and began biting and sucking her nipples. Then he pulled the crotch of her pants to one side and shoved two fingers hard inside her.

'Tom,' she cried out, her mouth full of bread and beetroot, 'at least let me put down the blinkin' sandwich.'

Laughing, he took it from her and threw it down on the worktop. A moment later he had undone his fly buttons. She watched his erection spring out of his jeans. Then, gripping her buttocks, he thrust himself into her over and over again.

He came quickly, leaving her gasping with frustration.

'Come over here,' he said softly, pulling her to the wooden peninsula unit standing in the middle of the kitchen. Directly underneath was a shelf. On it there lay a row of large cook's knives.

'Christ, what are you going to do?' she gasped.

'Don't be daft,' he laughed. 'Go on, climb up and lie down.'

Giving him a quizzical look, she laid herself down. The unit was almost the same length as her body.

'Now then,' he said, 'shuffle towards the end.' He pulled off her pants and told her to open her legs.

She let them flop open, and he stood between them and began running his tongue over her clitoris. Her gasps turned to loud grunts as he subtly altered the pressure, and went from light, fleeting, tantalising licks to firmer, longer caresses. She was on the point of orgasm when he moved away. She begged him to come back, but he didn't. She was vaguely aware of him picking up a tall silver object from the worktop.

She cried out like a wild animal as she felt the cold, smooth metal make contact with the opening to her vagina.

'What you have to realise,' he said, 'is that I haven't so much got designs *on* you, as *in* you.'

Slowly, bit by bit, he eased into her the rounded end of the Alessi lemon squeezer.

If there were two or three days in a row when she couldn't get to see him, Beverley sat on her bed and wrote him long, long letters telling him how much she loved him and was missing him and about all the wondrously disgusting things she wanted him to do to her.

'I know I've got to end it,' she'd said to Rochelle on the phone the day before, 'but I love him . . . and the sex is just so utterly indescribable . . .'

'Don't, Bev, please. You'll only me feel worse. Me and Mitchell did it last night and I'm still suffering from post-coital depression.'

They both giggled.

'Look,' Rochelle went on, 'if you're sure you really do love Tom, maybe you should start thinking about leaving Mel. It would be cruel to stay with him under false pretences. He's not a fool. He's soon going to see how miserable you are and realise something's up. That you don't really want to be with him. Chances are it'll end eventually anyway.'

'Possibly, but I just haven't got it in me to desert him. He needs somebody to come home to. Somebody to love him and look after him. I owe him, Rochelle. If I hadn't agreed to take Naomi's money, he'd still be OK. Then there's Naomi. I promised her and Tom this child and look what I've done to her. She and Tom would still be happy if it weren't for me.'

'The hell they would,' Rochelle shot back. 'Now you're just being ridiculous. Only the Prince of Darkness could be happy with that woman.'

'Well, at least I have to give them a chance to patch up their relationship. I must end it with Tom. And soon. The longer I leave it, the harder it will be.'

Beverley was replaying those last words in her mind and wiping away the tears when the phone rang.

She carried on wiping for a few more seconds. Then she turned towards the bedside table and picked up the receiver.

'Hello,' she sniffed.

'Is that Beverley? Beverley Littlestone?' It was a woman. She sounded extremely nervous.

'Who is this?' Beverley asked curtly. She never gave her name to strangers – even harmless-sounding ones.

'Look, you don't know me,' the voice went on. 'My name's Mo. Mo Newbegin.'

The woman's voice went up at the end of each statement, as if she were in some doubt about her own identity.

'Oh, right,' Beverley said, her voice immediately friendly. 'Duncan's mother.'

'Yes. I'm Duncan's mum. For my sins.' She gave an uneasy giggle.

'Goodness, this is so embarrassing,' Beverley said. 'I feel awful about never having met Duncan. I keep asking Natalie to invite him over, but she always finds an excuse. I'm convinced she thinks I haven't come to terms with the religion thing and that I'm going to cause a scene, but . . .'

'Look,' Mo broke in, 'that's sort of what I wanted to talk about. You see, I've got Natalie here. I'm afraid she's in a bit of a state and she asked me to call you.'

Beverley froze with terror.

'Oh my God. What's happened? Is she all right?'

'Don't worry. She's absolutely fine physically. She's just a bit upset. Well, very upset really.'

'But how come she's with you? She told me she was going shopping with her friend Allegra.'

'I think that may have been a little white lie. She's actually been here for the last couple of hours. Look, I don't quite know how to put this, but she's asked to stay with us for a while.'

'How d'you mean?' Beverley said, sounding confused. 'What – overnight?'

'No,' Mo said gently, 'for a bit longer actually. It's just that under the circumstances, Natalie thought it best if she came to *live* with us. Just for a while. To give the two of you some space . . . until you get used to the idea.'

'Live with you? What idea?' Beverley exclaimed. 'Sorry, Mo, I'm losing the plot here. Why on earth would my daughter want to come and live with your family?'

'She's been trying to tell you about it since Christmas, when it was first planned, but she kept getting cold feet. I know how hard it's been for her, what with you being of the Jewish persuasion . . .'

'Nobody persuaded us, Mo,' Beverley shot back, her hackles not so much raised as standing to attention. 'You make it sound like we worship some kind of ethereal double-glazing salesman.'

'Oh, sorry. No, I didn't mean it like that. Please don't think we're anti-Jewish. We've got nothing against the Jews. No, not at all. And we don't think you tortured and murdered our Lord at all. Well, not you personally. And we even like Vanessa . . . well, tell a lie – my husband Clive can't stand her actually. Every time she comes on he calls her "that kosher pig", 'scuse my French. I mean no offence.'

'None taken, I'm sure,' Beverley said curtly. 'Look,

Mo, I don't mean to be rude, but do you mind telling me what the bloody hell, 'scuse my English, you are on about?'

'Well, it's Natalie . . .'

'Oh, for pity's sake,' she barked, sounding exactly like Naomi all of a sudden, 'will you please spit it out?'

'You see . . . well . . . Oh, Lord, where do I start? OK. You see, a couple of times a year we hold a special service at church where everybody stands up and gives their personal testimony about how they came to be born again. Take me, for example, five years ago I became a neo-virgin. My hymen grew back overnight. It was a miracle, an absolute miracle . . .'

'Mo, I sense a distinct lack of spitting,' Beverley growled.

'Well, you see, the next service is at the end of the month and it . . . it always ends with half a dozen people being . . . Look, the fact of the matter is . . .' She took a deep breath.

'Natalie is going to be baptised a month next Sunday.'

Melvin got back from his therapy session, during which Wim had once again made it clear, in the most gentle of terms, that he should forget Rebecca. But suppose, he cogitated, just *suppose*, Wim was wrong. It wasn't impossible. He was only human. What was more, the man wore a fez. Wonderfully helpful as Wim had been, surely that fact alone had to cast a shadow over his credibility. How many times had Melvin walked down the street, seen a man wearing a Salvador Dali moustache and a brocade fez and remarked to himself: 'Ah, there goes a sensible, rational human being'? How could he sit back and let this bloke, who looked like he'd been dispatched to the Friary by surrealist central casting, tell him how to run his life?

He sat himself down on the edge of the bed. Without thinking, he yanked open the drawer in the bedside cabinet and took out his wallet. Somewhere among his long-ago-cancelled credit cards and photographs of Benny and Natalie as babies was a scrap of paper. On it was Rebecca's home telephone number in New York. All her printed Christmas messages had included her number. Two or three years ago he'd written it down and kept it hidden in his wallet ever since. At the time he had no idea why he'd done it. Back then, although he had feelings for her, he certainly had no desire to meet her. He'd been far too ashamed of his business failure for that.

He looked at the paper. He still felt ashamed and humiliated, but not as badly as he had back then.

He looked at his watch. Three thirty. Ten thirty, New York time. He picked up the phone from the top of the bedside cabinet and placed it on the bed next to him. Then he lifted the receiver. Giving no thought to the fact that the Friary charged the same extortionate rates for phone calls as most hotels, or the likelihood of his wife walking in at any moment, he dialled Rebecca's number.

Long ring, long gap. He could feel his heart starting to race. Suppose Wim was right. Maybe 'Thinking of you, as always' meant nothing. Perhaps she was just being polite. She couldn't think of anything else to say, so she wrote that.

It's what you say, he thought. It was like being on holiday and giving your address to the Dullard-Borings from Widnes who'd latched on to you for the entire fortnight. You insist they look you up when they're in the neighbourhood. You don't mean it. You're just being polite and at the same time hoping the fuck they don't get out of Widnes much.

Long ring, long gap. What if Brad answered? What was he supposed to say – 'Hello there, you don't know me, but I'm one of your wife's old boyfriends and I'm simply phoning to say I that in twenty years I've never stopped loving her'? He was on the point of putting the phone down.

Long ring . . .

'Fludd-Weintraub residence.' Sing-song voice. Not even a hint of Yorkshire. Puerto Rican at a guess. Clearly the maid.

Melvin swallowed hard.

'Er, oh, hello. Would it be possible to speak to Mrs Fludd-Weintraub?'

'May I ask who's calling?'

'Could you just say it's Militant.'

'Pardon me? Is that Millie Tan?'

'No, that's Militant.'

'Mr Milligan?'

'No, it's Militant. You know as in belligerent, combative, aggressive.'

'Sorree?'

'Mi-li-tant. That's M for mother, I for India, L for Lima . . .'

But before he could finish, Val, Bernard and Cilla,

who'd been quiet for the last few minutes, suddenly started going at it again at full volume. It appeared that Val and Cilla were arguing in favour of a cup of decaf, while Bernard was complaining that the caffeine gave him palpitations.

'Shut the fuck up down there, you cunting bunch of psychotic bastards,' Melvin yelled. 'I can't hear myself think.'

'Meesis Weintraub,' the maid shouted, 'you come queek. I think I got some wacko crazy man on the phone . . .'

'No, no, I didn't mean you. Sorry,' Melvin blustered. 'It's just some people next door making a noise. Look, tell Mrs Fludd-Weintraub it's Mr Littlestone. I'm an old friend.'

'OK,' the maid said, 'I tell her.'

There was a pause.

'Meesis Weintraub,' he heard her calling, 'shall I hang up? Wacko crazy person now say he Old Fred Flintstone.'

When Beverley arrived at the Friary just after four, bearing half of Marks and Spencer's fruit department, her husband seemed noticeably distracted. Even when she broke the news of Natalie's forthcoming conversion to Christianity, all he did was smile vaguely and say, 'That'll be nice.'

Several times she waved her hand in front of his face and said jokily, 'Beverley to Mel. Come in, Mel.' He immediately came back to earth, but was gone again a few seconds later. She hoped to God he wasn't taking a turn for the worse.

Chapter 21

At the same time as trying to pluck up the courage to get Tom out of her life, Beverley had spent the last two weeks trying desperately to get her daughter back in it. Every time she rang the Newbegins, Natalie steadfastly refused to come to the phone. Beverley had stopped trying to discuss the situation with Melvin because the bit of his brain which dealt with concentration still wasn't functioning. She assumed his vagueness and inability to focus on everyday issues was due to his having reached a particularly painful stage in his psychotherapy. Although Wim assured Beverley he was on the mend, he made it clear that Melvin hadn't quite got to the point where he could start taking on parental responsibilities again.

Beverley turned to Rochelle, who told her (as did Queenie and Tom) that Natalie would get in touch when she was ready and that she should back off and give her the space she clearly needed. But when Natalie was still refusing to speak to her after two weeks, Beverley could bear it no longer and decided to take action.

She phoned Mo, determined to brook no objection to

327

her plan or even let the poor woman get a word in edgeways.

'Please don't get me wrong,' she said firmly. 'I'm very grateful to you for taking her in, but I am Natalie's mother and I need to find out why she feels she can't talk to me any more. I must insist on seeing her. I'll be round in a few minutes and I'd be grateful if you didn't tell her I'm coming because it might frighten her off.'

Mo Newbegin opened the front door of the small Victorian house.

'Ah, Beverley.' She smiled uneasily. 'Do come in.' Beverley stepped into the hall.

Mo gave every appearance of having just emerged from a Sketchley bag. Her calf-length floral skirt contained not so much as a hint of a crease. Her brilliant white pie-crust-collar blouse looked like it probably moonlighted in soap powder commercials and her flat green T-bar sandals were so highly polished that if Beverley had bent down only slightly she would undoubtedly have seen Mo's freshly ironed knickers reflected in the leather. The woman was clearly in the prim of life. Even her straight chin-length bob looked like it had been cut with the aid of a set square.

'I wonder,' Mo said, giving a nervous giggle, 'if I could ask you to take off your shoes. Only we've just put down brand-new twist pile. You know what it's like with beige. Shows every mark.'

No, Beverley thought – this woman's hymen hadn't grown back just the once. A neatness fanatic like her would have trained it to grow back each time she had sex. Not that she'd have done it more than once – to make Duncan. The mere thought of a damp patch probably caused her to hyperventilate. Beverley couldn't help thinking that Mo Newbegin gave a whole new meaning to the phrase 'immaculate conception'.

'Oh, no, that's fine,' Beverley said, kicking off her scruffy trainers.

'Come through,' Mo said, leading Beverley down the plastic carpet protector. The smell of baking bread wafted in from the kitchen.

'Oooh, what a wonderful smell,' Beverley said by way of making polite conversation.

'Yes,' Mo said smugly, leading Beverley into the excruciatingly neat John Lewis living room. 'I bake all my own bread and cakes and we grow all our own veg. There's almost nothing shop-bought in this house. Oh no. I even make the church communion wafers.'

'Goodness,' Beverley said, feigning admiration and at the same time noticing that there was no TV or stereo in the room, only two bookcases lined with religious books.

Mo showed Beverley to the floral sofa. She hovered over the seat cushion for a moment or two until she was satisfied Mo wasn't about to slide a newspaper under her bum.

'I do hope you don't think Duncan influenced Natalie's decision to be baptised,' Mo said, squatting on the edge of an armchair. 'I mean, we brought him up to respect all religions. And I do so admire you Jews. I mean, you're all so shrewd businesswise, aren't you? I know it's wrong to make generalisations. I mean, you personally – you're probably not shrewd at all. Probably quite the opposite, in fact. Not that you're stupid, I don't mean that. Goodness, no. But it doesn't matter what business empire you think of, you can be sure there'll be a Jew at the helm. Aren't I right, Beverley?'

'Well, I'm not sure that's quite the case,' Beverley said, doing her level best not to get up and throttle the woman.

'I mean, take Harrods, for example,' Mo said, warming to her theme now. 'There's that little Al Fayed chappy.'

'Actually, Mohammed Al Fayed isn't strictly Jewish, Mo.'

'You sure?'

'Absolutely.'

'Oh. Well, he certainly looks it. Anyway, you take my general point.'

'Oh yes, Mo. I take it. I take it exactly.'

'Right. Well, you'll be wanting to speak to Natalie. She's upstairs in her room. Duncan's doing his homework. I've been very strict about them spending at least some time apart. Why don't you pop up and see her?'

Beverley went upstairs, walked the couple of paces to the box room at the far end of the landing and knocked on the door.

'C'min,' Natalie said casually.

'Hi, Nat,' Beverley said softly. Her daughter was curled up on the bed reading a magazine. Beverley made her jump.

'Mum,' Natalie gasped. 'What are you doing here?' She put the magazine down on the bed and sat up against the headboard.

'I've come to talk to you,' Beverley said, sitting herself down on the edge of the bed. It was all she could do to stop herself scooping her daughter up in her arms and cradling her like a baby, but she knew that would only irritate and antagonise her.

'I've been really worried about you, Nat. Couldn't you have at least telephoned me?'

Natalie shrugged defensively and began scraping at her nail polish.

'I just don't understand,' Beverley said gently, 'why you didn't tell me about this baptism thing. I had no idea you were even going to church.'

'Look, Mum, I'm really sorry,' Natalie said, her face suddenly bathed in guilt, 'I know it was wrong of me, but I just thought you'd be furious if I mentioned it. Then when I came here, the longer I didn't speak to you the harder it got to pick up the phone. I mean, you've always been more religious than Dad.'

'But what did you think I'd do? I can't believe you see me as some kind of bigot who'd throw you out of the house and tell you never to darken my door again.'

'No, not quite. But I reckoned it would really upset you and what with the baby coming and Dad in the bin, I didn't want to put you under any more strain.'

'And you thought I'd see you leaving home in the middle of your A levels as the strain-free option?'

Natalie shrugged.

'Listen to me,' Beverley said, stroking her daughter's hair. 'You're nearly eighteen, almost an adult. I know you think you'll be on the verge of the menopause before I'm prepared to cut the umbilical cord, but that's not true. Honest. Whatever religion you want to be is OK with me and your dad.'

How she was getting the words out she had no idea. Her dreams about Amish grandchildren had become more frequent and even more disturbing of late. Instead of steering a dozen of them down Golders Green Road, she saw herself at the head of a marching, hymn-singing battalion of the little mites. As she sat on the bed smiling her understanding, liberal parent smile she cursed the Jews for not having nunneries. At least then she could have arranged for Natalie to be banished to one until she abandoned all this baptism nonsense.

'I mean,' Beverley went on, 'I may not be entirely comfortable with you being baptised a Christian, but I refuse to let a quick dunk in a tank of water come between me and my daughter.'

'See, there you go, making fun,' Natalie snapped, pushing her mother's hand away from her hair. 'It's not just a quick dunk in water. It really means something to me. I've found Jesus. I've found Jesus, Mum. Last night Duncan and I went to church and we were all singing and clapping like mad and God was just so . . . so totally out there. I mean, He just blew our minds.'

'Yeah, well in my day it was LSD,' Beverley said. 'But I guess it's much the same. Look, Natalie, I really do understand what it feels like to be passionate about something. We all go through it at some stage. Usually it's in teenage . . .' She paused and her voice softened. 'Sometimes it doesn't happen until much later. But if Christianity is what you want right now, then go for it.'

'You really mean that?' Natalie said, looking up at her mother.

''Course I do. Listen – me, Dad, Benny, Grandma, we'll all come to the baptism. We'll throw a party afterwards. Rochelle's already got a caterer in mind. I've got a great idea for the centrepiece on the top table. How's about Jesus on the cross, carved out of chopped liver?'

'See. You say one thing,' Natalie shot back furiously, 'but deep down you just can't take me seriously, can you?'

She turned to face the wall.

'Sorry,' Beverley said. 'Bad joke. I was just trying to lighten the atmosphere, that's all.'

Natalie grunted, but refused to turn round.

'Listen, whatever you want to do,' Beverley said to her back, 'I'll support you. Just come home. I've missed you. God help me, I've even missed the trail of mess you leave about the place. Come on, turn round and give me a hug.'

Natalie didn't move.

'Please,' Beverley pleaded.

A second later Natalie had turned round and thrown her arms round her mother.

'Mum, I'm sorry,' she blubbed. 'I shouldn't have run off like that. I'm really, truly sorry.'

They sat holding each other and crying for a moment or two.

'Right,' Beverley said, wiping her tears and her daughter's, 'do you think you're ready to come home?'

Natalie nodded.

★ ★ ★

After they'd said their thank-yous to Mo and Natalie had spent ages kissing Duncan goodbye, Beverley and Natalie walked down the Newbegins' garden path arm-in-arm.

'Natalie,' Beverley said thoughtfully, 'I know this is a funny question, but does Mo own a washing machine?'

'No, refuses to have one. Insists on doing it all by hand. Even the sheets. I tell you, there's nothing in that house – no telly, no sound system, no central heating. At night it was totally freezing in there. His parents are so tight. Lord knows how Duncan puts up with it.'

Beverley nodded, and continued to ponder.

'And Duncan,' she said casually, 'he's never said anything about whisking you off to the wilds of Pennsylvania one day, has he? I mean, the word "Amish" has never cropped up in conversation?'

'Amish,' Natalie repeated, shaking her head. 'Never heard of it. Why?'

'Oh, no reason,' Beverley said. 'I had this weird dream a few months ago, and it's just a bit of a coincidence, that's all . . . No, forget I mentioned it. I'm sure you're right and the Newbegins are just a bit careful with their money.'

Chapter 22

'Ah, the Cricklewood Crone, I presume,' Tom said brightly, extending his hand. 'I recognise you from your pictures in the newspapers. Tom Jago. How do you do?'

Bearing in mind the circumstances, he could hardly believe he was being quite so gung-ho. A few hours later, over a large Scotch, he would put it down to shock.

Fallopia Trebetherick had only ever been at a loss for words twice in her life: the time she had a general anaesthetic, and now.

Ignoring Tom's outstretched hand, a naked Fallopia simply gave a yelp like a stuck pig and leapt off Naomi's four-poster. She spent a few moments scrambling around wildly for her clothes. Then she bounded, her ciabattas swaying as she went towards the bedroom door. Tom couldn't help noticing how her tomato-red face clashed with her nipples, which looked like two elongated raspberries.

Naomi, apparently unperturbed that Tom had just discovered her *in flagrante* with Fallopia Trebetherick, pulled the duvet up under her armpits and smiled at him.

'Tom,' she said, colouring up, 'you must stop surprising me like this. What are you doing here?'

'Apparently discovering my girlfriend's a lesbian,' he said with faux chirpiness. It was the nearest he'd ever seen to Naomi being grievously humiliated, and yet such was the woman's towering self-esteem that she didn't appear a great deal more embarrassed or flustered than when he'd found her bellowing at Plum before Christmas.

He bent down to the floor and picked up an off-white bra with gargantuan cups. 'So, when did all this happen?'

He grimaced and threw the bra on the bed.

'I can't imagine you're that interested, but I think I was attracted to Fallopia from the moment I first saw her at the seeding ceremony back in November. Look, Tom, this had nothing to do with you personally. If I'm honest, I think at some level I'd always known I didn't fancy men, but you know . . .'

'Actually, no, I don't.'

'Well, I couldn't bring myself to do anything about it – until I met Pia.'

'Pia?'

'That's my pet name for her. Fallopia's such a mouthful.'

'Yes, I can see,' he said with a smirk.

'Stop it, Tom. You can say what you like about me, but I won't have a word said against her. She's helped me come to terms with my sexuality. If it hadn't been for her, I would never have found the courage to come out. For years I was so bloody confused. I couldn't understand why my relationships with men never lived up to my expectations. Now I do. Suddenly a light has been switched on in my brain. For the first time in my life I am in touch with the real me. I feel utterly liberated and very, very happy. What's more Pia is the only person I've ever met who really cares about me and understands that deep down I'm as soft and vulnerable as everybody else.'

'Yeah, about as soft and vulnerable as a Scud missile,' he said.

'Whatever, but no man has ever cared for me like she does.'

'Only because no man, other than the Dalai Lama on a good day, could put up with you.'

'Look, all I know is that Pia's the best thing that's ever happened to me and I absolutely adore her.'

'Well,' he said, 'I had come here to end our relationship, but you've done it for me, really. I don't think there's much left to say, do you?'

She said nothing for a moment.

'Tom?'

'What?'

'I'm sorry that you had to find out like this. I was going to write you a note.'

'How thoughtful,' he said with a sarcastic laugh. 'Over a year we've been together, we were about to become parents, and you thought you'd write me a note. Blimey, when will you finally stop treating people like the shit on your shoe? Look, give me a few minutes to put my clothes in a bag and I'll be off. I'll collect my books and stuff another time.'

'OK,' she said, pulling on a black silk kimono. 'I'll leave you to it . . . Oh, by the way . . . about the baby. I still want it, you know.'

'Really. Well, we'll see about that,' he said quietly.

'Don't fight me on this, Tom,' she retorted, tightly knotting the kimono belt. 'You know that one way or another, legal or otherwise, I always get what I want.'

He thought about whether or not to tell her about his relationship with Beverley and that she was thinking of leaving Melvin so that they could be together. He decided against it. He would give Beverley that pleasure. She might quite enjoy it.

'Well, maybe that's about to change,' he said.

'Don't flatter yourself,' she snapped as she walked to the bedroom door.

For some reason Tom opened Naomi's underwear drawer instead of his own. Sticking out of the untidy pile of lace pants was a battered white envelope. Vaguely curious as to why Naomi should be hiding correspondence in her underwear drawer, he picked it up and took out two letters. As he started reading, his face turned to thunder.

'The evil, two-faced, scheming fucking cow,' he muttered when he'd finished reading. Then, as fast as he could, he put the letters back in the envelope and shoved it into his jeans pocket. At that moment he could have happily murdered Naomi. His instinct was to march into the living room and confront her there and then. He certainly had every right. What stopped him was the feeling that Beverley's right to beat Naomi to a pulp was even greater than his own.

★ ★ ★

He phoned Beverley just after eight the next morning, sounding, she thought, highly agitated. He explained he had something majorly important to tell her and asked her to come to the flat that evening. Beverley assumed he was about to break the news that Naomi had ditched her boyfriend, that the two of them had made up and that his relationship with her was over. Although she knew that hearing the words would leave her devastated and grief-stricken, her one consolation was that this way he was at least saving her from the misery of having to end it herself.

The moment she arrived at the flat that evening and he started to tell her about his visit to Naomi's the night before, she began biting the inside of her mouth as she prepared herself for the worst. When he finally broke the news about Naomi being a lesbian, all she could do was sit staring at him in utter gobsmacked astonishment. She couldn't have been less prepared if she'd tried.

'A woman,' Beverley repeated finally. Her shock was such that her voice was devoid of emotion. 'She was in bed with a woman?'

'Yep.'

'That's absurd. Naomi – my sister, the pretty one – a lesbian. You're mad.'

'Beverley. Please, I know what I saw.'

'But it could have been completely innocent,' she said in desperation. She started to gabble. 'I mean, maybe you were mistaken and they weren't actually *in* bed. Perhaps they were bouncing *on* the bed in pyjamas and huge fluffy slippers and playing the *Grease* soundtrack at full blast.'

'I think I'd have noticed,' Tom said calmly. 'Beverley, grown women do not have sleepovers. Not the sort you mean, anyway. They were naked, for God's sake.'

'Maybe they got hot?'

'Not that kind of hot.'

'This is absurd. There has to be some kind of rational explanation. My sister may be a lot of things, but she's not gay.'

'I promise you she is. She's positively frolicsome.'

Beverley shook her head, still not quite able to take it in.

'So,' Tom said, 'aren't you going to ask me who she was in bed with?'

'OK, who?'

'Fallopia Trebetherick.'

'What?'

He nodded.

'But she's ugly,' Beverley said, doubly shocked now.

'Tell me about it,' he said. 'She's got these huge wobbly bits. And these nipples, I mean, you cannot imagine . . .'

''Fraid I can,' she said. 'I've seen them . . . But what on earth does Naomi see in her? Clearly the attraction isn't physical.'

'Dunno. Once Fallopia had gone we talked for a bit. Naomi clearly worships her. I think she sees her as some kind of mother figure.'

Beverley finished her coffee.

'Tom, this really is taking some believing, I tell you.'

He didn't say anything for a few moments.

'Look,' he said, his voice suddenly dropping and becoming much more serious, 'when I went round to the flat last night, I didn't just find out about Naomi being gay. I discovered some other stuff too. And it's not pleasant.'

He paused.

'OK,' Beverley said, forcing a smile, 'don't leave me hanging. Tell me. What is it?'

He got up from the sofa and went over to the dining room table. Then he picked up the two letters he'd stolen the night before.

'When I was packing my things, I opened her underwear drawer instead of mine by mistake and I found these.'

He handed her the letters and sat back down beside her.

The first was from Naomi's gynaecologist. It was dated over a year ago. Beverley read the single paragraph in a few seconds. A shiver shot down her back.

'What?' she gasped, sitting bolt upright on the edge of the sofa. 'My God, there was never anything the matter with her. No blocked tubes. Her eggs were fine. I don't believe this . . . But I thought you said you spoke to her doctor and he confirmed she was infertile.'

'I did,' he said, 'but only on the phone. I realise now that the whole thing was a set-up. He was probably just some actor she'd paid to pretend he was her gynaecologist.'

'But I don't understand. Why did she lie?'

He passed her the second piece of paper. It was from the cook-in sauce company. Their request was couched in the most discreet and diplomatic of terms, but the bottom line appeared to be that because they were anticipating huge sales of Pure Gold sauces, they wanted her to endorse another of their products. In short, they were offering Naomi a million pounds to have a baby and put her name to their new range of organic baby foods.

'Even with all her money,' Tom went on, 'she wasn't about to pass up an offer like that. My guess is that at first she toyed with the idea of getting pregnant herself. Being in her late thirties, she even went as far as seeing a gynaecologist, who, as we now know, gave her the go-ahead. I can only assume she then decided it would have put her career in jeopardy.'

'In what way?'

'She knows how much they always hated her at Channel 6 even before this Rowe character turned up, and that her bosses might well have seen it as a brilliant excuse to get rid of her. They'd have called her in, told her quite simply that a pregnant presenter didn't suit the channel's image and chucked her out on her ear.'

'But that doesn't make sense. Can you imagine what a field day the papers would have had with a story like that? "Sacked For Being Pregnant . . . Naomi Gold Shares Her Agony with the Nation." I mean, Channel 6 would come across as complete bastards. Not only that, but by selling her story she'd stand to make even more money than the cook-in sauce people were offering her.'

'Possibly. But how long do you think it would have been before somebody at the TV company tipped off the papers about the real reason they wanted to give her the boot? From then on there would have been posses of reporters camped outside the Channel 6 building just waiting for the likes of Plum to blab about her being the bitch boss from hell. Once a couple of quotes like that made the papers, the entire nation would have turned against her. Her career, not to mention the cook-in sauce deal, would have been finished. Naomi's no fool. She would have seen all this coming. In the end it was much less risky to make out she was infertile and ask you to carry her child.'

'But she could have adopted a child – from China or South America. Why involve you and me?'

'Simple. Genes. She knew what she'd be getting.'

Beverley began looking over the letters again. 'I can't believe that even she could have done this,' she said, still sounding more stunned than angry. 'She lied about everything. About her fertility, about being in therapy, about wanting us to be a family again. She simply manipulated all of us so that she could make money. I mean, what were you to her? Simply a sperm donor?'

'Probably,' he said coldly.

Slowly the rage began to bubble up inside her.

'Do you know, in my entire life I don't think I have every really hated anybody. I mean, there were times when I was growing up when I came pretty close to it with Mum, but it never felt like this. Tom, I actually think I'm starting to hate her. After everything I've done for her over the years, I don't think I'll ever be able to forgive her for hurting me like this.' She burst into tears. 'Christ, I actually put Mel in the bin to give her this child.'

Tom put his arms round her, but she pulled away. She

stood up and began pacing round the room, clenching and unclenching her fists. 'Suddenly I feel like I want to kill her. That wretched, evil, lying . . .'

'Beverley, calm down,' Tom said, getting up and taking her hand. 'It's bad for the baby. Now come and sit back down.'

She sat.

'Look,' he said gently, 'you've got yourself so worked up that you're missing the big picture here. Just think about it for a minute. After what Naomi has done to us, you have no reason to feel beholden to her. Now you can keep the baby.'

She blinked at him.

'Blimey,' she said, starting to laugh. In an instant she became almost intoxicated with delight.

'You're right. God, I can keep my baby. I don't have to give it up. It's mine. It belongs to me. It will stay with me for ever . . .'

'And me,' he said excitedly. 'It's not just yours to keep. It's ours. We can bring it up together. It's what we wanted. I'm not saying you have to stop being angry with Naomi, but if it hadn't been for her and all her Machiavellian scheming, we would never have met. Beverley, we can start thinking about our future together.'

Once again he reached out and took her hand.

'You're forgetting Melvin in all this,' she said quietly.

'But we agreed. You're going to leave him.'

'No, we agreed I'd *think* about leaving him. And I have. I can't do it, Tom. I just can't.'

'What?' he said, sounding shocked and exasperated.

'I don't believe I'm hearing this. It never occurred to me that you'd actually choose this clapped-out marriage of yours over what we've got.'

'Tom,' she said, gripping his hand, 'what you don't understand is that I still love Mel. I admit I don't love him with the passion I feel for you. But it's a warm, comfortable love, a deep, deep affection that spans twenty years. I'm not prepared to turn my back on that. Especially not when he needs me.'

'But what about the baby?'

She shrugged.

'When Mel's strong enough, I'll tell him everything. Then I suppose I'll have to throw myself on his mercy and hope he'll accept the baby into the family. I think that after I've explained what Naomi did to me, he'll come round.'

'Oh, fucking excellent,' he shot back with bitter sarcasm. 'Suddenly you've got it all worked out. And I get to see the baby for a couple of hours each Sunday, I suppose?'

'Tom, I'm so, so sorry,' she said, tears rushing down her cheeks. 'I really do love you. I always will.'

She stood up to go.

'Beverley, if you love me, please, please don't do this,' he said, blocking her way and taking her by the shoulders.

'I really have no choice,' she said, sobbing as she pulled away. He took hold of her again and once again she struggled free. On her way to the front door she picked up her coat and handbag, which were lying on an armchair.

He stood watching her, willing her to change her mind and come running into his arms. But she didn't even look back.

Beverley was crying so much that she could barely see to drive. She didn't know what was causing her more agony, the thought of living to ninety and having to spend the next forty-eight years without Tom, or Naomi's betrayal. As she drove home through the centre of London, one moment she was feeling the searing loneliness of a life without Tom, the next she was rehearsing her blazing showdown with Naomi. After five or ten minutes, when the obscene epithets were truly rolling, Beverley felt an overpowering need to lob them at Naomi sooner rather than later. When she got to Hyde Park Corner, instead of heading north up the Edgware Road, she suddenly turned left, down Bayswater Road, towards Holland Park.

It was nearly midnight when she reached Naomi's flat. Although she knew the address, she'd never been there before and she kept getting confused and lost and having to refer to the A to Z which she could rarely make head or tail of even when she wasn't bursting into tears every five minutes. She buzzed the entryphone three times before a bleary-voiced Naomi answered.

'Nay, it's me, Bev. Let me in. I want to talk to you.'

'Bev, do you know what time it is?'

'I don't give a flying fuck what time it is. Let me in or I swear I'll make enough noise to wake up the entire neighbourhood.'

The electronic door mechanism clicked instantly.

★ ★ ★

Naomi stood at the front door in her black kimono. Her face was red and creased with sleep.

'Bev, do you mind telling me what the bloody hell this is all about?' she said, stepping back to let her sister into the hall.

'So, Naomi,' Beverley said sarcastically, ignoring the question, 'all alone tonight. No Fallopia?'

'Oh, so that's it. You've been talking to Tom. Look, Bev . . .'

'Yes, I have been talking to Tom, but the reason I'm here has nothing to do with you and Fallopia. Believe it or not, I don't give a monkey's about your sexuality. You can shag wildebeest for all I care. I'm here because of these.'

Beverley reached into her handbag and took out the letters. She held them out towards her sister.

'Where did you get these?' Naomi said, snatching them.

'Tom,' Beverley replied simply.

'I see,' Naomi said with a smile that was half snarl. 'The two of you seem to be getting rather cosy all of a sudden.'

Beverley decided to let the remark go for the moment. She followed Naomi into the living room.

'Nice,' Beverley said sarcastically, trailing a finger over one of the gilt angels. 'I see you went for a period look. Pretty bloody heavy one if you ask me.' (That would pay Naomi back, Beverley thought, for the time she'd suggested that Mr Kipling had decorated her sister's through lounge.)

347

Beverley sat herself down in one of the hard Regency chairs and waited for Naomi to return to the subject of the letters.

'OK, so what do you want me to say?' Naomi began defensively, plonking herself down in a chair opposite Beverley. 'That I'm sorry?'

'That might be a start.'

'OK, I'm sorry I lied. There, satisfied?'

'Don't be so bloody stupid,' Beverley snapped. 'Of course I'm not.'

'Suit yourself,' Naomi shrugged. She went over to the credenza and poured herself a Scotch.

'Naomi, have you any idea what you've put me through over the last few months? My husband's in a nut house as a result of me agreeing to have your baby. I have spent most of my adult life trying to understand and make allowances for you. Ever since we were children, I've looked out for you. I have cared for you, loved you and forgiven your wickedness time and time again. In all those years you have done nothing but belittle and demean me. I allowed you back into my life after five years because I was stupid enough to believe you've changed. Now I find out it was all just one huge lie. You haven't changed at all. In fact, you've got a thousand times worse. I tell you, Naomi, looking at you now, I'm convinced Lucrezia Borgia is alive and well and living in Holland Park.'

'Impressive speech, Bev,' Naomi said with quiet sarcasm. She picked up her Scotch and returned to her chair. 'Since when could you string more than two sentences together at a time without tying yourself up in knots and forgetting where to put the verb?'

'Since I discovered,' Beverley said simply, 'what a treacherous, deceitful, double-dealing cow you are. People do their best to love you, Naomi, but all you do is take that love and destroy it. Your head needs sorting. For Christ's sake, get yourself a shrink. No. Correction. Make that a lobotomy.'

'Well, we all know what made me the way I am, don't we?' Naomi shot back.

'Naomi, plenty of people have shit childhoods. It doesn't give them the right as adults to take their anger out on the rest of the world.'

Naomi took a huge slug of Scotch.

'Oh, stop deluding yourself, Bev. You're not such a bloody saint. The fact is that you stood to make a quarter of a million quid just as you and Mel were about to go down the bloody Swannee. It was just as much a business deal for you as it was for me. So what if you didn't know all the details? I bloody rescued the pair of you, if the truth be known.'

'How can you even suggest I agreed to have your baby simply for the money?' Beverley cried, banging the arms of her chair. 'Just because you've never done anything in your life that wasn't motivated by greed or self-interest, you think the rest of us function the same way. You really are a toxic tart, aren't you? When you die they won't bury you, they'll have to dump your body in the middle of the Atlantic in a lead box.'

By now Beverley could hardly believe what was coming out of her mouth. In the past, whenever she'd got into a confrontation with Naomi she'd simply dissolved into tears. Suddenly all that had changed. For the first time in her life she'd found the courage to stand up to her sister and bring her to heel.

'Well,' Naomi said, ignoring the insult, 'since we're on the subject of greed and self-interest, I think we should talk money. I assume you'll want to keep the baby now. So I'm sure you won't mind returning the hundred and twenty-five grand I gave you.'

Beverley had been expecting this and had come well prepared.

'All right, Naomi, you can have it back,' she said slowly. 'But seeing as I've spent most of the money, I'll have to find some way to raise it. Now then, how could I do that, I wonder? Oooh, oooh, I know . . . how's about I go to the *News of the World* and sell them this whole sordid story?'

'You wouldn't,' Naomi gasped.

'Just watch me.' Of course in reality Beverley wouldn't have dreamed of doing such a thing, but by now she just couldn't resist watching Naomi squirm.

'All right. All right,' Naomi snapped. 'You keep the bloody money. But when the baby's born don't even think of asking me for another penny. That money is all you'll ever get from me . . .'

'Apart from your . . .' Beverley was about to say 'boyfriend', but stopped herself. Furious as she was with her sister, she simply couldn't bring herself to be that vindictive.

Just then the phone rang.

'Christ, it's the middle of the bloody night,' Naomi hissed. 'Who the bloody hell is this?' She stretched across to the Regency side table and picked up the receiver.

'Ah, Tom,' she said acidly. 'The well-known film director and thief. Beverley's already here. Let me put you on speakerphone and we can make a party of it.'

'I thought she might be,' Tom said, sounding like he'd been hitting the booze since Beverley left. 'Just for the record – in case Beverley hasn't got round to mentioning it yet – I think you should know that for the last few blissful weeks she and I have been carrying on a mad, passionate affair.'

'What? Don't be so ridiculous, Tom,' Naomi snapped. 'You're drunk. You and Beverley, I've never heard anything so absurd.'

'OK, ask her.'

Naomi turned to Beverley, who, despite her resolve of a few seconds ago, couldn't help smiling a smug smile.

'Good God,' Naomi exclaimed, looking for the wicked queen when the mirror announces that Snow White is the fairest of them all. 'You and Beverley? How could you possibly fancy Bev?' By now she had started to gabble uncontrollably. 'I mean, she's a housewife. From Finchley. She lives in a semi with a through lounge. She's completely without sophistication. She shops in Principles. For Chrissake, the woman owns *fish knives and forks*. Tom, I know we're not together now because I've finally faced up to my sexuality. But you know as well as I do how much you always fancied me.'

'Naomi,' he said acidly, 'I fancy you about as much as I fancy a barium enema. Get this straight. She may have decided to go back to Mel, but it doesn't alter the fact that I loved Beverley. I loved her like I have never loved anybody in my life. She was the sweetest, the kindest, the most beautiful, sexy woman I have ever met. And for your information, virtually all we did over the last few weeks was make love in my flat. And let me tell you, she is hot. She was the best I've ever had, Naomi. That Finchley housewife makes love like a fucking tiger . . .'

'Stop it, Stop it,' Naomi screamed, hanging up. 'I don't have to listen to this. I didn't come here to be made fun of and humiliated. It's me he fancies. Me. It was always me. I'm not sticking round to hear any more of this. I'm off.'

To Beverley's utter astonishment, not to say profound amusement, Naomi stormed out of the room, tightening her kimono belt as she went. Then she flung open the front door and slammed it behind her.

Beverley sat in the Regency chair and waited. What must have been half a minute went by before she heard a tentative tapping on the door and the letter box flapping. She went to the door, bent down and looked through the slot. Naomi's huge tear-filled brown eyes were blinking back at her.

'I forgot, I live here,' she sniffed. 'Bev, will you let me in, please?'

Chapter 23

Beverley got home just after two in the morning. The confusion brought on by extreme tiredness cause her to spend several seconds trying to open the front door with her ignition key.

She stepped into the hall and took off her coat. As she hung it over the banister post, she glanced at the answer machine on the table. One message. Convinced that it could only be one of Benny's mates, she almost didn't bother playing it. Then it occurred to her that it might be Wim phoning to say Melvin had taken a turn for the worse. She flicked the switch and waited for the tape to rewind.

'Hello? Did the beep go yet? Queenie, it's Millie. I got your message. So, where are you? Maybe you're having an early night. Hang on . . . hang on, I got a piece of salt beef stuck between my teeth . . . OK . . . that's better. I mean, you're telling me it's a breakthrough. Miracle more like. I couldn't believe it when Lenny phoned and told me what you found when you searched Lorraine's office. Bloomin' smart move to think of getting her keys copied. All that stuff you found. It's truly amazing. Now

353

then, don't worry about a thing. Tomorrow's all sorted. Between us Lenny and I have rung round all the members of the action committee and everybody knows what time to be there. I tell you, Queenie, this is so exciting. I feel like a kid again. I can't wait. We're gonna get 'em, Queenie, we're gonna get 'em.'

A perplexed expression on her face, Beverley let the message rewind and then played it for a second time.

'Oh my God,' she gasped, 'they think they're Bonnie and flaming Clyde.' At that moment she was in no doubt that as far as her mother was concerned, the combination of the words 'Holloway', 'six', 'months' and 'in' were about to become as familiar a part of family vocabulary as 'bin'.

Suddenly it all made sense. Naomi still hadn't contacted her mother about the day centre story, despite Queenie having now left umpteen messages on her work and home answer machines. The old people had obviously got fed up with waiting and had decided to take the law into their own hands. Clearly, the upshot had been that Queenie and Lenny had broken into the day centre in order to recover the stolen loot. What Millie didn't make clear when she said 'action committee' was precisely what action they were planning. Whatever they had in mind, it was plainly due to happen in a few hours' time.

She couldn't wake her mother now – even to accuse her of breaking and entering and masterminding some lunatic geriatric uprising. Besides, she'd experienced quite enough confrontation for one day. She would get up early and give Queenie the third, fourth and fifth degree before she was even out of bed.

She trudged slowly up the stairs. Lying in bed a few minutes later, her thoughts inevitably turned back to Tom – about how much she loved him and whether it was even remotely possible to ever get over an affair which had been as passionate as theirs. Then she began thinking about Naomi. Try as she might, she couldn't go on hating her. The woman was clearly barking. Furthermore, Tom was right. As a direct result of Naomi's wickedness, the baby was now hers to keep. She sank into the pillows and wept tears of sheer bloody relief.

She was woken just after six by an urgent need to pee.

Beverley stood washing her hands in the bathroom and looked at herself in the mirror. In an effort to make herself look less like a bloated bloodhound, she splashed her face with cold water. Her eyes closed, she began groping for the towel which, unless somebody had forgotten to put it back, lived on the metal hook next to the basin.

'Here.'

Beverley jumped at the unexpected sound of her son's voice.

'Blimey,' he said, squinting, 'you made me jump.'

She reached out, took the towel from him and began patting her face.

'Sorry,' he said, 'but the door was open.'

'I know.' She never locked the bathroom door these days in case she suddenly felt faint in the bath or shower and needed to be rescued.

'So, what are you doing up this early – got an essay to finish before school?'

'No, I couldn't sleep,' he said. 'I've been tossing and turning all night. Mum, I'm really worried about Dad.'

'Why? Wim said he's definitely on the mend. They're even talking about letting him out soon.'

'I know, but it's just something that happened yesterday evening when I went to see him.'

'What?' she said, suddenly concerned. She draped the towel over the bath. 'Come and sit on the bed and tell me what happened.'

He followed her back to her bedroom. Beverley got under the duvet and Benny sat next to her on the edge of the bed.

'OK, go on,' she said.

'Well,' he said, 'I took him a pile of magazines I found on your dressing table.'

She nodded.

'He seemed really pleased that I'd remembered,' Benny went on. 'Apparently you'd forgotten them twice. Anyway, as he took the magazines from me, a letter fell out from between a couple of them. Dad picked it up and started reading it. I couldn't see who it was from.'

'A letter?' she said with a shrug. 'Can't think what that could be.'

'Well, anyway, he read it and then when he'd finished he just sat staring at it for ages. Then he started roaring with laughter. He wouldn't stop. But it wasn't happy laughter – you know, like somebody had just told him a brilliant joke. It was this mad, demonic, like, cackling. I tell you, Mum, something in that letter really upset him. He pulled it away every time I tried to get a look. Mum, think. Have you got any idea what it was?'

'No,' she shot back, defensively. 'Absolutely none.'

By now Beverley had turned white and was starting to shake. She knew exactly what the letter was. It was a love letter she'd started writing to Tom weeks ago, but never got round to finishing. Careless idiot that she was, she must have left it out on her dressing table.

'So, go on. Did he say anything?' she said, doing her best to sound calm.

'Nothing. He just carried on laughing for about ten minutes or so. In the end, there were tears streaming down his face. Then he got this mad attack of hiccoughs. I didn't know what to do. I was really scared. In the end one of the nurses heard him and gave him a glass of water and a pill to calm him down. I tell you, Mum, Wim's got it all wrong. I reckon that letter was just some circular or something and he's started having mad delusions. God knows what he thought he was reading. I mean, if it was genuinely something serious, you'd know about it. I reckon he'll be hearing voices next. Honestly, Mum, Dad's much more ill than any of us could have imagined.'

Beverley sat staring into space. The unimaginable had happened. Melvin had found out about her affair with Tom, weeks before he was in any fit mental state to cope with the news. With his history of depression, God only knew what he might do now. She was feeling sick and her hands had started to tremble.

'Mum, you OK?'

'Yes, sweetheart, I'm fine,' she said, running her fingers through her hair. 'Just a bit concerned about your dad, that's all. Look, after what you've told me I

357

think I'd better get over to the Friary right away. Now then, I don't want you to worry. I'm sure this will turn out to be nothing more than a minor setback. Promise me you and Natalie will go to school as normal?'

He nodded, but was clearly terrified.

'OK,' she said brightly, planting a kiss on his forehead. 'Now disappear. I need to get dressed.'

Twenty minutes later, all thoughts shelved of whatever nonsense Queenie was involved in, she was driving round the North Circular in the heavy Monday-morning traffic towards the bin.

The Friary's electronic glass doors slid open in front of her. Beverley dashed across the empty reception area and headed for the stairs.

'Mrs Littlestone. Please. Wait,' a voice shouted from behind her. Beverley turned round to see Jean, one of the nice lady receptionists, slam down the phone and come waddling towards her on fat ankles.

'Oh, Mrs Littlestone, thank heavens you're here,' she said as she reached Beverley, her breathlessness bordering on asthmatic wheeze. 'We've been trying to get you at home for the last hour, but your line's been permanently engaged. And your mobile's switched off.'

Beverley stared at Jean for a few moments, taking in the woman's anguished face.

'Oh my God, I'm too late, aren't I?' Beverley's voice was trembling.

Jean stared down at the floor, clearly unable to speak.

'Melvin's gone, hasn't he?'

'I'm afraid he has, Mrs Littlestone,' Jean said gently

as she looked up. 'I am most terribly sorry. There was absolutely nothing we could do.'

'Please, do you think I could sit down?' Beverley said, feeling sick and fearing her legs were about to give way.

'Of course. Of course,' Jean said, taking Beverley's arm and leading her to one of the sofas by the main door.

'Thing is, he couldn't have picked a worse time if he'd tried,' she continued as Beverley sat down. 'All the staff were busy doing the breakfasts. Then there was an emergency. One of the paranoid schizophrenics thought he could hear his poached egg and an Earl Grey tea bag hatching a plot to assassinate Prince Andrew. It took five male nurses to calm him down. There was egg yolk everywhere by the time they'd finished.'

'So Melvin was upstairs . . . all alone?' A single tear rolled down Beverley's cheek.

'Yes. I'm sorry. By the time we got to his room it was too late.'

'Was there a lot of mess? I mean, how did he . . .?'

'Mess? No, he didn't leave any mess. Such a tidy man, Mr Littlestone. Never gave the cleaners a moment's trouble.'

'So, how had he, you know . . . done it? What did he use? His belt? Had he been storing sleeping pills?'

'Oh no, nothing like that,' Jean explained, looking a little puzzled. 'He used women's clothing. A rather nice navy two-piece, actually, with cream trim on the pockets and lapels. Wouldn't have minded it myself. Can't imagine it doing anything for Mr Littlestone.'

'What, Melvin killed himself with women's clothing? I'm sorry, maybe it's the shock, but I don't . . .'

'Killed himself?' Jean said in astonishment. 'Mrs Littlestone, Mr Littlestone isn't dead. Good Lord, no. He *escaped*.'

'Escaped?' she repeated.

'Yes, about two hours ago. There's this woman in the room next to him – you know the one. Thinks she's three people. Total basket case. Needs putting away if you ask me. Anyway, it seems Melvin went into her room while she was asleep, stole some of her clothes, make-up and a headscarf. Then he swans out of the door in drag, without anybody noticing. The staff searched the building and the grounds and then called the police . . . They'll find him, Mrs Littlestone, I just know it. Now you sit there and I'll fetch you a nice cup of tea.'

She sat. After a few moments Wim appeared. She'd spoken to him several times over the last six weeks, so was quite used to the fez, comedy spectacles and moustache ensemble. As he lowered himself on to the sofa, he confessed to being utterly perplexed by Melvin's behaviour. 'During last night's group therapy session he seemed more upbeat than I have seen him in weeks. In fact, I was thinking seriously about letting him go home next week. Now I can only assume that this outward display of contentment was masking some deep-seated inner turmoil.'

'Wim, tell me honestly, do you think he could be suicidal?'

Wim twirled the end of his moustache.

'Let's just wait for the police to find him,' he said, avoiding her question and patting her on the knee.

But she couldn't wait; wait for the police to walk in a few hours later to tell her they'd found Melvin swinging by the neck from a tree.

She was convinced he was still planning to kill himself. Why he had first gone to all the trouble of escaping dressed as a woman, she had no idea. Nor did she care. All that mattered to her was finding him.

She ran back to the car and decided to head for Richmond Park.

She'd been driving for a couple of minutes before she remembered that her mobile was still switched off. It was on the passenger seat inside her shoulder bag. She reached inside with one hand, pulled out the phone and stabbed the on button. It rang almost immediately.

'Mrs Littlestone?'

'Yes,' she said, not recognising the male voice.

'You don't know me. My name's Phil Capstick, sergeant. Finchley police.'

'Police?' she repeated, her voice trembling. 'Oh my God, you haven't found Melvin already, have you?'

'I'm sorry, Mrs Littlestone – not with you. Who is Melvin – a missing moggy?'

'No he bloomin' well isn't,' she shot back at the bemused sergeant. 'Melvin's my husband and he's just gone missing from the Friary psychiatric hospital in Richmond.'

She gave him a brief, tearful account.

'South-west London's rather off my patch, I'm afraid,' he said when she'd finished. 'But I'm sure the Richmond boys will pick him up. He can't have got far with no transport and no money. And I'm sure if

361

they've been briefed properly, and know he could be suicidal, they'll be keeping a special watch on all the parks. Look, Mrs Littlestone, I realise you are under a great deal of stress and I don't want to add to it, but it's your mother, you see. One of my PCs has just radioed into the station to say she appears to be leading some kind of mutiny down at an old people's day centre in Temple Fortune . . . One of the helpers there gave me your number and I thought you ought to know.'

'Christ,' Beverley exclaimed, remembering Millie's cryptic message on the answer machine. 'So what exactly is going on?'

'Mrs Littlestone, your mother is on the day centre roof and refusing to come down. The roof is large and flat, but they're old folk, and we're frightened one of them could miss their footing and . . .'

At that moment Sergeant Capstick's voice began to crack up.

'Hello? Sergeant Capstick, speak to me.'

Nothing.

Beverley looked at the mobile, which was showing the 'no service' message.

'Shit,' she muttered, throwing it down on to the passenger seat.

Beverley had never felt so emotionally torn in her life. On the one hand, there was Melvin, missing and suicidal; on the other was her mother, who any moment could slip and fall off the day centre roof.

She drove through the gates of Richmond Park and decided she would go twice round the park and then, assuming she hadn't found Melvin – or, God forbid, his corpse – head back to north London. She couldn't bear not knowing what was happening to her mother. It also occurred to her that Melvin might have had some money on him after all and could be on his way home.

Just her luck. The eastbound traffic along the North Circular was the heaviest she'd ever seen it. In the two hours it took her to reach Temple Fortune, she kept trying to call the Friary and Sergeant Capstick, until her phone battery gave out.

Beverley pulled into the day centre car park. It was packed. She assumed most of the cars belonged to the old people's relatives. There were also two ambulances.

She climbed out of the car and looked up at the roof. Queenie was standing close to the edge, holding one side of a giant white banner which was billowing in the breeze. Lenny was holding the other end. Emblazoned across it in huge black felt-tipped letters were the words: 'Greys Embrace Violence and Unrest in search of Legality and Truth'.

'GEVULT,' she exclaimed, looking at the even huge first letters of each word. It was clearly the name of the old people's action committee.

Their friend Millie was holding half of another sheet, which read in untidy upper-and lower-case letters: 'Posner must fry – in bacon fat.'

Behind them, another twenty or thirty elderly men and women, many stooped over walking frames, were waving smaller 'Grey Pride' banners or standing chatting in groups. It was only when she looked closely that she realised there wasn't a woolly hat, a pair of polyester slacks or a long cardigan in sight. Each person was wearing a bright red track suit and a baseball cap. She could just about make out 'GEVULT' written in gold across their sweatshirts.

'Mum,' Beverley screamed, having seen her mother take another step closer to the roof's edge, 'for Chrissake come down.'

At that point Beverley heard a man's voice behind her. She turned round to see a uniformed policeman.

'I don't think she can hear you from this far away,' he said. 'You're Mrs Littlestone, I take it.'

She nodded.

'Sergeant Capstick,' he said. He was about fifty, she supposed, with a kindly community copper air about him.

'Perhaps you'd like to come with me and I can explain exactly what's been going on.'

Once they were sitting down in Lorraine's office, Sergeant Capstick told her that a couple of hours ago one of the old boys had come down from the roof and handed him a letter signed by all the protesters.

'To cut a long story short, it seems the old folk managed to remove several packets of out-of-date meat from the day centre deep freeze which they handed over to the public health people. They also managed to uncover a large quantity of stolen watches and items of jewellery. These items are now down at the station. Most of them were wrapped in plastic and hidden in sacks of flour or tins of instant coffee. It must have taken hours of painstaking searching to find this lot. How they pulled it off – right under Lorraine's nose – I've no idea. I tell you, Mrs Littlestone, if I didn't know better, I'd swear they broke in.'

He chuckled.

'There's an image to conjure with.' She leaned back in her chair and laughed far too loudly. 'OAPs in stocking masks and balaclavas. I don't think so.' She would bloody kill her mother if and when she got hold of her.

'I have to say,' Sergeant Capstick continued, failing to notice that Beverley's face had suddenly turned scarlet, 'their initiative has been quite remarkable. They also hid a tape recorder in this office, in the hope that the pair would incriminate themselves. And they did. Their recording equipment was pretty sophisticated, I have to admit, but bearing in mind this was only a ninety-minute tape, their luck was beyond extraordinary.' He waved the cassette in the air.

'What I have here is these Lorraine and Posner characters on tape, laughing and joking with each other about serving up rotten food and the fact that they were stealing money and jewellery.'

'But I don't understand,' Beverley broke in. 'If they handed you the letter, the booty and the tape, why are they still demonstrating?'

'I spoke to the chap who gave me the letter and asked him the same thing. It seems they don't trust the police to act quickly. They say we won't take them seriously because they're old and that by the time the DPP decides whether or not to prosecute, Lorraine and Posner will be long gone, and most of them will be pushing up daisies.'

'So you haven't found the pair of them, then?'

''Fraid not. I can only assume they smelled a rat. Neither of them turned up for work this morning. But I'm sure we'll find them. The CID boys did some checking on the Police National Computer and it turns out they're actually known to us. Seems they've spent the last ten years working with the elderly in various parts of the country. Several complaints have been made against them – usually accusing them of theft – but we've never been able to pin anything on them until now.'

'So what do you want me to do?' Beverley said. 'Why have you brought me in here and not taken me to the canteen with the other relatives?'

'Well, you see, your mum is one of the ringleaders. If she decides to come down, the others will follow. We think you can persuade her. They've already said they'll talk to you – or to your sister. Apparently she's a journalist?'

Beverley nodded.

'OK,' she said, 'I'll give you my sister's number. Perhaps you could phone her. It's a bit complicated, but we're not actually on speaking terms at the moment. You know what families are like.'

'Fine . . . Look, what we want you or her to do is convince them we will take their complaint seriously and that we will act. I hope you don't mind heights, Mrs Littlestone.'

While Beverley was being briefed by Sergeant Capstick, Naomi was being given her marching orders by Eric

Rowe. In the last ten minutes, his voice had assumed the tone of a rather benevolent hanging judge.

'So you see,' he continued gravely, 'my senior colleagues and I have decided that *Naomi!* is in dire need of an image change. Presenter-wise, we see somebody a little more fresh-faced.'

'I can do fresh-faced,' she leapt in, her enthusiasm nothing short of desperate. 'I'll book a laser treatment tomorrow. Add some khaki combats and a cropped T-shirt, in forty-eight hours, I can look eighteen.'

'No, Naomi, you misunderstand me,' Eric said, drawing gently on his pipe. 'When we say "fresh-faced" we don't necessarily mean youthful, we mean more, er . . . wholesome. The general consensus of opinion is that we would like an earth-mother type to present this show. I myself, personally – along with my wife Audrey and her WI pals – see this person as a placid, heavily pregnant lady, her ample, milk-engorged breasts swaying under her floral smock. It's Channel 6's view that it would be quite mould-breaking to have the first pregnant daytime show presenter.'

'Bollocks,' she retorted.

He winced.

'This has nothing to do with you wanting a change of image,' she said furiously, standing up and leaning over his desk so that she was only inches from his face. 'This is just a ploy to get rid of me.'

He drew on his pipe again.

'I'll be honest, Naomi,' he said, leaning back in his chair. 'We were heading for an image change anyway, but I admit that your flagrant disregard of our commitment to decent family entertainment made it happen sooner rather than later. What finally put the tin lid on it was your constant refusal to produce this battling grannies story.'

'But I've been working on it,' she said, her tone pleading now. 'You know I have. I've got this stonking old bats' story that's almost ready to go. It's just that *Wicca's World* has been taking up so much of my time.'

Of course this was a lie. Although her enthusiasm for the *Wicca's World* series was considerable, the only thing which had been taking up all her time over the last few months was her love affair with Fallopia.

'I'm afraid it's too late for excuses, my dear. You have been given numerous chances to make a fresh start here at Channel 6. But you have simply refused to knuckle down and toe the line. Now you've finally shot your bolt and it's time for a parting of the ways. I'm afraid we shall not be renewing your contract in May. As a gesture of goodwill, however, we are prepared to let you finish making *Wicca's World*.'

She slumped into her chair. Not only had she failed to pull off the million-pound cook-in sauce deal, but there wasn't even the remotest chance of her finding a new job while the media continued to be gripped by the Real People Initiative frenzy. Eric Rowe wasn't simply ending her contract, he was putting an end to her entire career. It was over, finished, kaput. The sudden realisation cut through her as surely as any knife.

'Please, Eric. Please don't do this to me,' she sobbed. 'I'll do anything you want. If it's sponsored London-to-Brighton supermarket trolley races, you shall have them. Stories about petrol prices and noise from ghetto-blasters: I'll get Plum on the case right now. From now on I'll hand in all my cherry Genoa chitties, I promise. But please, please don't sack me. I'm begging you, Eric. I need this job. All my life all I've ever wanted is to be rich and successful. You can't simply destroy me like this. You just can't.'

'As I said, Naomi, you had your chances, but you blew them. Now, if you'll excuse me, I have another meeting to get to.' He stood up to go.

Before Naomi could stop herself she had ingested her pride in one go, leapt out of her chair and was sitting on the floor, gripping Eric Rowe by his leg.

'Please, Eric,' she begged, hysterical now. 'Just give me one more chance. I promise I won't let you down.'

'I'm sorry,' he said. He did his best to pull her off his leg, but she refused to budge. Even as he dragged himself to his office door she was still holding on for grim death.

'Please, Eric. Please. I think I'm going to be sick.'

They continued like this, her pleading and pretending to retch, him struggling to get her off him, for several yards down the corridor. It was only when two Channel 6 security guards happen to pass by and see the commotion that she was finally dragged off.

'Plum, Bacon Bastard. Now,' she yelled as she stormed into her office. Having sat in the Ladies' for twenty minutes, her panic and desperation had subsided. In their place had come wild fury with Eric, her sister, Tom, Tony Blair and the RPI, the cook-in sauce people – everybody except herself.

It was a moment before she realised that Plum was sitting with his feet up on her desk, coughing his heart out as he tried to smoke a huge Cuban cigar.

'What the fuck is going on?' she roared. 'Get your bloody feet off my desk. Put that thing out and go to the canteen.'

'Sorry, Nay-ohmi,' he spluttered, spraying her with gobbets of cigar-infused spittle. 'No can do.'

She stopped in her tracks.

'Oh, I get it,' she snapped. 'You've heard about me being fired, haven't you, and this is some kind of celebration. No doubt the moment I'm out of the door, the corridors will be one long conga line.'

'Well, it is a celebration, Nay-ohmi, but it's not about you getting the sack . . . it's more that I've been promoted, really. Eric says that because you've worked me so hard over the years – you know, getting me to find all those groped virgins and whatnot – that I deserve a reward. When they find a new presenter to replace you, I'm going to be her producer. He also said I could take over your office with immediate effect. I think that means now, doesn't it, Nay-ohmi?'

She let out a high-pitched squawk, picked up a container full of biros from the desk and threw them at the door.

Plum didn't move. His feet still on the desk, he said, 'Tell you what, Nay-ohmi, I could really murder a Bacon Bastard too.'

'Oh, really?' she said sarcastically.

'Yeah, but don't put any mustard on mine. I prefer brown sauce. Preferably HP. Now then, I like it spread on the bread, not the bacon. Goes nice and soggy that way. Oh, and with it I'd like a large English Breakfast tea. Bring me lemon and milk and then I can choose how I want it. And perhaps I'll have a packet of prawn cocktail Monster Munch and a couple of mint Wagon Wheels for later.'

At that moment the phone rang.

'Take that, would you, Nay-ohmi, there's a dear?' he said imperiously, waving his cigar in the air.

Naomi stormed over to the phone and snatched the receiver.

'Naomi Gold,' she barked. There was silence for a second while the caller identified and explained himself.

'Sorry, Sergeant Catsick . . . oh, all right then, Capstick . . . You'll have to run that by me again. My mother's where?'

Beverley had spent an hour trying to persuade her mother and her cronies to come off the roof, but they made it clear that they would only come down when the media – preferably in the shape of Naomi and a film crew – turned up. In the end Beverley realised there was nothing for it but to stand there and prepare for a long wait. It could take hours, Beverley thought, for Naomi to gather up a crew and fight through the traffic.

Finally, just after one, the door which led to the staircase burst open. Standing in the doorway, swaying and gripping the handle for support, was Naomi.

When she finally put one Bruno Magli in front of the other she didn't so much walk as lurch on to the roof. Beverley assumed her sister was suffering an acute attack of height-induced dizziness as she watched her take a few wobbly steps on her four-inch heels. She'd moved less than a yard before she lost her balance completely, tripped over a handbag somebody had left lying on the asphalt and fell flat on her face. Beverley dashed over to help her.

''S OK,' Naomi shouted to Beverley, as she pulled herself up into a sitting position and let out two loud hiccoughs. 'Stay where you are. I didn't feel a thing.'

Reaching into her shoulder bag, she pulled out a half-bottle of Absolut, unscrewed the top and brought it to her lips. She was wearing the same red suit she'd had on the day they had lunch at the Morgue, only now the front was covered in dirt from the roof. Her black tights had a huge hole in one knee.

'You're pissed,' Beverley said, stating the gobsmackingly obvious.

'You're not wrong, Bev. You're not wrong,' Naomi slurred. 'But at least I'm not an unlisted dress size.' She prodded Beverley's barely visible bump through her long denim shirt and roared with drunken laughter.

'In case you'd forgotten, I'm five months pregnant,' Beverley said acidly.

'Oh yeah . . . so you are, Bev. So you are.' Once again Naomi put the vodka bottle to her lips and threw back her head.

''Course,' she said, shaking a finger at her sister, 'up the spout's what you have to be these days if you want to get up the ladder.'

Beverley looked down. Naomi was weeping snail trails of black mascara.

'What are you going on about?' Beverley said, her tone a mixture of weariness and impatience.

'I reckoned I was being so bloody clever,' Naomi said, waving the Absolut bottle in the air, 'persuading you to get pregnant instead of me. I thought if I got up the duff, Channel 6 would refuse to renew my contract. And guess what . . .'

'What?'

'The fucking bastards *still* refused to renew it.' She gave a loud, bitter laugh. 'An' jew know why, Bev, jew know why? I'll tell you fucking why . . .' She paused to hiccough. 'They refused to renew my contract because . . . get this . . . because I *wasn't* pregnant. Talk about fucking irony.' She took another swig of vodka and laughed again.

'Don't be absurd,' Beverley said. 'Nobody gets the sack for not being pregnant.'

'Oh yes they do . . . when that pointless, feeble-minded yokel Eric Rowe decides pregnant presenters are the way forward because of the wholesome image they project. Can you believe it? The whole bloody country adores me . . . but that's not good enough for that sheep-shagging bumpkin.'

Beverley was in the middle of processing this not inconsiderable weight of information when she heard banging, crashing and shouting coming from the door-way.

'OK . . . let go . . . I've got it.' A young lad in a baggy T-shirt and flares standing just outside the door was bent over a huge stainless-steel box which he was dragging towards himself.

'Right,' he shouted down the stairs. 'Now the mike.'

A moment later he had taken hold of a long pole with a large fluffy microphone on the end. As he laid it gently on the floor by the box, three more people appeared. Two of them were men. One had a Sony Betacam TV camera on one shoulder. The other was carrying a Nagra tape recorder. A woman in combats and trainers was carrying a clipboard and a mobile phone. Strung round her neck was a stopwatch.

'Film crew, great,' Beverley said. 'Once you've got the old people's story they'll come down off the roof. So how long do you reckon it'll take to set up and get going?'

No answer.

Beverley looked down. Naomi was lying on the roof floor as if it were a bed, her legs drawn up to her chest, clutching the Absolut bottle. Her eyes were closed. Beverley tapped her cheeks.

'For Christ's sake, wake up, Naomi. You've got a bloody report to do.'

'I'm finished, Bev. Finished,' she mumbled, almost incoherent now.

Beverley sat herself on the ground and cradled her sister's head.

'No you're not,' she soothed. 'No you're not.'

Lying there sobbing, an overgrown foetus in grubby Armani, Naomi had never looked so sad and pathetic. Beverley couldn't help feeling sorry for her.

'Oh, God . . . I thought this was going to happen. She was already pretty slaughtered when we got in the car.'

Beverley looked up. The woman with the clipboard,

whom Beverley took to be Naomi's producer, was standing beside her. She held out her hand and helped Beverley to her feet.

'The day centre story's been hanging over for ages,' the producer went on, 'but Naomi never got round to doing it – even though she knew Eric was insisting on her coming up with a story about the elderly. I think she ignored it partly to spite him. Anyway, when she found out what was going on here, she rounded us up in a last-ditch attempt to do the story, win Eric over and save her career.'

They both looked down at Naomi, who had started to snore loudly.

'Some hopes,' Beverley said.

At Beverley's suggestion, the producer, whose name was Harmony, phoned Fallopia and asked her to come and fetch Naomi. She'd just come off the phone and was in the middle of telling the crew not to bother unpacking their equipment when she noticed the GEVULT members standing at the edge of the roof.

'What do we want?' Lenny was shouting through a megaphone.

'The bastards out,' the old people roared.

'When do we want it?'

'Now. Now. Now.'

Harmony broke into a broad smile.

'Wow. Look at those codgers go,' she chuckled. 'This story is far too good to give up on. I mean, even if there isn't going to be another series of *Naomi!*, I'm sure I could sell it somewhere else at Channel 6.'

'So where's Naomi?'

Harmony and Beverley turned round to see Queenie, who had spotted the film crew and come limping over, bursting with excitement.

'Has she gone off to do her hair and make-up?'

As the final word left her mouth she saw Naomi lying on the ground.

'My God, what's happened?' she said, her voice full of panic. 'Is she ill? Somebody should get a doctor. For heaven's sake, shout down to one of the ambulancemen.'

'Mum, don't panic,' Beverley said. 'She'll be OK. She's been drinking. She's passed out, that's all.'

'Drunk?' Queenie exclaimed. 'Why?'

'Don't worry, Mum, I'll explain later.'

'So who's going to cover the story?' Queenie said anxiously. 'What about our publicity?' She looked as if she were about to burst into tears.

Harmony, on the other hand, was staring at Beverley's stomach.

'Can I help you?' Beverley inquired.

'Oh, sorry. Now I'm really embarrassed. It's just that I was trying to work out if you were pregnant . . .'

'Or fat?'

Harmony went red and nodded.

'It's OK,' Beverley said. 'I'm pregnant – just not very, that's all.'

'God, that's great,' Harmony said. 'Look, this may sound daft . . .'

'What?' Beverley asked.

'Well, I was just thinking that since this is such a brilliant story, since your mother and her friends are so desperate for the publicity and since you are pregnant and therefore fulfil all Eric Rowe's criteria for a presenter, why don't you try your hand at doing the interviews? It would take no more than five minutes. You just vox-pop the old folk, ask them what's been going on at the day centre and what they're trying to achieve by protesting, finish with a short piece to camera and Bob's your . . .'

'Me? Interviewing? Yeah, right,' Beverley laughed dismissively.

'No. I mean it,' Harmony said. 'Look, nobody at Channel 6 even knows we're here doing the story. If you make a hash of it, there's no harm done. Go on. Have a go.'

'Ooh, Bev . . . why don't you?' Queenie urged. 'Look, what have you got to lose? And think, if you pull it off you'll be getting us the publicity we need, and saving my reputation.'

'Don't be daft,' Beverley laughed. 'It's an absurd suggestion. I couldn't possibly get up in front of a camera. Naomi never stops telling me how inarticulate I am. I'll go all to pieces. It's out of the question . . .'

'If you do it,' Queenie said, 'we'll come down. I promise.'

Beverley stood considering her mother's proposal.

'You would? You'd persuade everybody to leave the roof?'

'Yep.'

Beverley contemplated for a few more seconds.

'No, it's crazy,' she said finally. Her tone was adamant. 'I can't do it. I'll clam up. I won't be able to put one sentence in front of another. I'll be useless. Naomi's the egomaniac, not me. And look at what I'm wearing – baggy trousers and a bloke's denim shirt. My hair's all over the place. I can't do it . . .'

Harmony bent down over one of the metal equipment boxes and took out a can of hairspray and a huge make-up bag.

'Please?' she pleaded.

Five minutes later, her hair brushed and heavily lacquered, to say nothing of Queenie's quilted coat shoved up inside her denim shirt to make her pregnancy look more obvious, Beverley stood blinking in front of the camera, the blood pounding in her ears.

Chapter 24

'. . . And so we come to the end of a story which I think you will all agree is quite remarkable. These elderly rebels, this proud band of Grey Panthers standing beside me today, have, over the last seven months, fought a ferocious, passionate and above all top-secret battle. It required courage, fortitude and grim determination. As we have heard, there were times when the struggle became almost too much to bear. There were days when they felt cowed and disheartened. But the word "defeat" had no place in their vocabulary. Theirs was a cause which had to be fought for and won. Let GEVULT be an inspiration to us all. This is Beverley Littlestone for Channel 6, at the Sidney and Bessie Hamburger Jewish Day Centre in Temple Fortune, north London.'

'And cut,' the producer shouted.

At the cameraman lowered the Betacam and the sound man took off his headphones and nodded enthusiastically, the old people burst into spontaneous applause. Beverley stood in front of them, still shaking with nerves.

'Beverley . . . my Beverley,' Queenie cried, coming up to hug her daughter. 'I can't believe it. I never knew you had it in you. You're a star, darling. An absolute star.' Beverley looked at her mother. Queenie had tears in her eyes.

'She's right, Beverley,' Harmony said, putting her stopwatch back in her pocket. 'That was an incredibly professional piece to camera. You'll have the whole country weeping buckets when this goes out.'

Beverley looked at her, stunned.

'You mean I was actually good?' she said. 'You're not just saying that to be polite?'

'Believe me, Beverley, you were great. Your interviews with the old people were superb. You were gentle with them, but you still managed to get the facts. It's hard to believe you've never done any television. I tell you, I can't wait for Eric to see this.'

'You think he'll be pleased, then?'

'Pleased? Believe me, he'll be knocked out. You're pregnant, articulate and pretty – everything he's looking for in a new presenter. If I were you I'd stay close to the phone for the next couple of days.'

While Harmony and the crew started packing up, Beverley walked to the far end of the roof. Her board of lacquered hair flapping in the wind, she stood gazing out across the rooftops, blushing with pride. So, the useless, inarticulate fat matzo pudding wasn't so useless after all. Of course Tom had been telling her for ages that all that stood between her and a successful career was confidence, but she'd always laughed at him. He loved her. Or did before she dumped him. What else would he say? But Harmony didn't even know her. She had no agenda, no reason to flatter her. Beverley smiled. She realised how, over the last weeks and months, her self-esteem and confidence had grown. It had begun when she made the decision to have the affair with Tom and culminated in her finally being able to stand up to Naomi. Although she was too modest to admit it to anybody else, deep down she wasn't surprised she'd found the courage to perform in front of the cameras.

Standing there on the roof, she suddenly began toying with the idea of having some kind of professional future. Not in telly. She laughed. That was absurd. She may have performed well in front of the camera for a first-timer, but she was nothing like as talented as Naomi and never would be. Eric Rowe would see that in a flash. No, to consider for one minute that she was about to be offered a job as a television presenter was laughable. But it wasn't laughable to think that in a year or so she might start a masters degree, or go back to teaching. She'd only taught for a few months. She'd given up when Natalie was born. Or, maybe now that she'd suddenly found her voice, perhaps she might even read for the bar. For a few brief moments, she was able to suppress her gnawing anxiety about Melvin and think about herself – about how far she'd come and where she was heading.

Queenie and the rest of the demonstrators went down first, followed by the film crew. Beverley stood watching from the roof as the old people came out of the building and were immediately mobbed by their relatives. A reporter from the *Evening Standard*, as well as a pair from GLR and 5 Live, were doing their best to push their way to the front of the scrum. She and Naomi, who by now had pretty much sobered up, came down last.

When they reached the ground floor, Fallopia was standing at the bottom of the stairs, her breasts forming an enormous continental shelf under her baggy rainbow sweater. Naomi fell into her arms, sobbing.

'He sacked me,' she cried into Fallopia's shoulder. 'That bastard sacked me.'

'I know, I know,' Fallopia soothed with the stomach-churning tenderness of the lovesick. Her feelings for Naomi had clearly caused her to go soft. 'Don't worry,' she went on, 'Pia's here. I'll have you home in two shakes, Pookie-Wookie.'

'Pookie-Wookie?' Beverley repeated under her breath, barely able to stifle her giggles.

She looked at her sister while Fallopia comforted her. The red suit was filthy and ruined. Her hair was all over the place. Her white face was streaked with mascara. She looked wretched, drained and exhausted. Anybody who knew her could see at a glance that the fire which had once roared inside Naomi Gold's belly had finally been extinguished. After a few moments she lifted her head from Fallopia's shoulder and turned towards Beverley.

'Bev,' she said almost in a whisper.

'What, Nay?' Beverley said tenderly.

Naomi sniffed.

'A big part of me did genuinely want that baby, you know. Pia will tell you – there's this blinkin' great cupboard back at my flat filled with teddies and baby clothes. Every night I used to go to bed reading Penelope Leach. I know all about colic and what to do when their pooh goes a bit green.'

Beverley smiled.

'I'm a mess, Bev. I know that now. Please don't hate me.'

'I don't hate you.' Beverley walked over to her sister and put her arms round her. 'None of us do.'

'You mean that?' Naomi blubbed, returning the hug.

Beverley held her tighter and patted her on the back.

'Yes, I mean it.'

They carried on holding each other for a few minutes. By this time even Fallopia had tears in her eyes.

'I promise I'll look after her, Beverley,' she said. 'Girl Guide's honour and all that.'

'I'm sure you will,' Beverley said, letting go of her sister. 'So, Nay, what are your plans now?'

Naomi sniffed.

'Well, for a start I think it's time to get my head sorted.'

'That's the ticket, Pookie,' Fallopia said heartily, giving Naomi a quick squeeze. 'Find yerself a trick cyclist, chin up, chest out. We'll soon have you back on your feet.'

Naomi and Fallopia gazed adoringly at one another for a few seconds.

'Maybe I'll book into Melvin's place for a few days,' Naomi said. 'God knows how you managed to get him in there, Bev. I always understood the Friary was strictly A-list.'

'A few days?' Beverley repeated in astonishment, stoically ignoring her sister's barb. She was thinking more in terms of months, after which she imagined Naomi still needing to visit the Friary as an outpatient for several decades.

'Yes. I mean I'm not bonkers. Not like Mel. I've just been working in a high-stress career for far too long and I need a bit of a rest, that's all. God, I wonder who'll be in my group therapy? Imagine the kind of names you get to share your angst with. Then I have to think about what clothes to pack. I'd guess it's pretty informal during the day and smart casual at dinner.'

Beverley smiled and shook her head. A huge part of her couldn't help feeling relieved that Eric Rowe hadn't succeeded in knocking all the stuffing out of her sister.

'Look, Pookie,' Fallopia said, interrupting Naomi, who seemed to have lost herself in her reverie on mental institution chic. 'Perhaps now would be the time to give Beverley our other bit of news. You know . . .'

'Oh, God, yes. I nearly forgot.'

She blushed like an awkward schoolgirl and turned back to Beverley.

'The two of us are planning to get married. I mean, it won't be a proper wedding like you understand it. We thought perhaps a Wiccan ceremony in Cornwall. Both of us would really love you to be there. You would come, wouldn't you?'

''Course,' Beverley said beaming. 'We'll all come.'

Fallopia grinned with delight and hoiked up her bosom.

'And I'd be more than happy to take you out to

choose something to wear,' Naomi gushed. 'I mean it won't be easy, 'cos you're bound to be pretty porky still, after having the baby.'

Beverley didn't get a chance to reply. At that moment Queenie came over, half-trotting half-limping.

'Sorry, blinkin' reporters. Couldn't get away. Nay, darling, you OK now?'

'Yes, I'm fine.' Naomi took a deep breath. 'Look, Mum, I've treated you so badly. I know you'll find it hard to forgive me . . . but you know how we've never really sat down and talked about the past? Well, I was wondering whether maybe, if you had the time and you weren't too tired, you could come over to the flat now and the two of us could sit down and have a . . .'

'Lead the way,' Queenie said, beaming. Naomi's words weren't merely music to her ears – it was as if Mantovani and his entire orchestra had just turned up.

'The only thing is,' Naomi explained, 'I've got guests coming for dinner, so you can't stay long. The caterer's due around five. Maybe you could give her a hand in the kitchen before you go. You know, bash lemon grass stems, do the kumquats, shell the quails' eggs, that sort of thing.'

'There's a lot I need to say to you too,' Queenie went on, failing to register that her daughter's attempt at reconciliation largely involved pressing her into domestic service. 'A lot I have to say sorry for and explain. Tell you what, I'll make you my special pancakes like I did when the two of you were little.'

'What?' Naomi and Beverley gasped in gobsmacked unison.

'Mum,' Beverley said, 'You never made us pancakes

in your life. The only person who made us pancakes was old Mrs Woodcock next door, who used to take pity on us when you disappeared for hours on end.'

'Oh well, I knew somebody must have made them,' Queenie shrugged. 'Now then, let's go.' With that, she put her arm through Naomi's. Then she smiled at Fallopia, who appeared to be bemused but not untaken with this little old Jewish lady, and took hold of her arm too. The three women said their tearful goodbyes and headed towards the door.

'So, Fallopia,' Queenie said, 'Beverley tells me you're a lesbian. How *are* things in Beirut these days?'

Beverley hadn't had the heart to put the dampers on Queenie's happiness by telling her about Melvin. She would phone her at Naomi's later, when she had some news – whatever that turned out to be.

She waited in the canteen while Sergeant Capstick put in another call to the Richmond police. Her anxiety was mounting by the minute. After all the excitement and elation of the last couple of hours, she suddenly felt sick. He was dead, she knew it. It was her fault. She should have carried on driving round the park. Instead she'd abandoned him. Left him to his leafy gallows.

She wandered over to the canteen window. As she stood watching the cars queuing to get out of the car park, she noticed a rather anxious-looking woman hovering a few yards from the front of the building. She was wearing a navy suit, trainers and a headscarf. Her face had a definite trace of five o'clock shadow.

'Melvin,' yelped Beverley as she raced to the door.

★ ★ ★

It took him a minute to calm her down. The second she reached him she hugged the life out of him. She followed this with a breathless, tear-laden stream of half-sentences about how she'd thought he was dead and that it was all her fault he wanted to kill himself.

'I'll never forgive myself. Never. You have to believe me, Tom means nothing to me. I've already finished it. I know we can start again, Mel, I just know it. We'll go away. Just the two of us. That's it, we'll find some sun . . .'

'Beverley,' he said gently, gripping her upper arms, 'look at me. Read my lips. I am not suicidal and I never have been. I know you love Tom. I was angry, very briefly, after I found the letter, but not any more. You must believe me. And I'm not running away so much as running *to* something – or, to be more exact, someone.'

'*Someone?*' she sniffed, wiping her eyes and dripping nose on her sleeve. 'I don't understand. What someone?'

'Rebecca? . . . I'm just so shocked,' she said to Melvin. They'd been sitting in the coffee shop over the road from the day centre for well over an hour, and in all that time, her incredulity had failed to abate. She picked up her chocolate eclair – her third – and bit off the end.

'I mean, it's been twenty years,' she went on. 'I thought you hated her.'

'I think I did for a while,' he said, scratching his head under the silk headscarf. 'When she first made it big. Do you think it's possible to love and hate somebody at the same time?' He drained his coffee cup.

'S'pose,' she shrugged. 'You want another coffee?'

He nodded. Beverley turned in her seat and caught the eye of the girl standing behind the refrigerated counter full of cakes.

'You angry with me, Bev?' he said, reaching across the Formica table and taking her hand.

'Bit, I guess,' she replied with a weak smile. 'I mean, you're jetting off to Rebecca and I walked out on Tom to save our marriage. I mean, it's a bit bleeding ironic.'

'Does he love you?' Melvin said.

'He did. Before I dumped him.'

'Then he'll forgive you and take you back. After all, that's his baby you've got in there.'

'I hope you're right. Mel, I treated him so badly.'

She looked up. The waitress was standing in front of them, ogling Melvin. She'd been staring at him from the moment they walked in an hour ago.

'Two more cappuccinos, please,' Beverley said. The girl carried on gawping. Her eyes were fixed on Melvin's bosom.

Beverley tugged at the girl's apron.

'Two more cappuccinos, please,' she repeated.

'Oh, right,' the girl said, still staring at Melvin. It was a full ten seconds before she turned back to the counter.

'Your left tit's disappeared,' Beverley said with a giggle when the waitress had gone.

He felt under the navy jacket, located the bundle of socks, which had somehow ended up in the small of his back, and turning in his seat, so that he had his back to the counter, manoeuvred it into his bra. Beverley sat watching him, and try as she might, she couldn't stop herself giggling.

'And you forgot to shave your legs,' she said. 'Blokes find that a big turn-off.' She popped the last piece of eclair into her mouth.

'So,' she went on, 'does Rebecca feel the same way about you?'

He shrugged.

'Maybe. When I phoned her, I got the feeling she was genuinely pleased to hear from me. She also said that not a day had gone by when she didn't think about me or wonder how I was doing. Apparently when Brad finally walked out on her a few months ago – he'd been screwing around for years – she said she had this desperate urge to phone me, but she didn't because she didn't want you to find out and get suspicious.'

Beverley nodded.

'So what made you decide to escape from the Friary?'

'Simple. She invited me to come and stay. She also said she'd spent the last twenty years feeling guilty that I'd never seen a penny from Tower of Bagel – after all, it was my idea.'

'So, what – she's gonna start offering you money?'

'Maybe, we'll see. But anyway, as far as I knew, Wim had no plans to release me, so I phoned Vladimir.'

'Vladimir?' she said incredulously. 'What, the bloke who did you out of the five grand?'

'Yeah. In the end he came up trumps. Having dropped out of sight for ages, he finally contacted me at the Friary. Alma told him I was there. Said he was terribly sorry about the anti-snoring devices, that there had been some production difficulties at the plant in Irkutsk and that he'd refunded the five grand directly into my bank account.'

'Blimey. There's a turn-up. So he helped you get out of the hospital?'

'Yeah, I told him the whole Rebecca story. Turns out he's a bit of a romantic on the quiet . . . got dead excited, in fact. He said if I could get out of the building he'd wait for me on the main road. We drove around for a bit, trying to work out where would be safe to go, and then we heard about the day centre on the GLR news . . .'

The waitress arrived with the cappuccinos. As she set them on the table, she was almost doubled up with giggles. They ignored her.

'I need to see her, Bev. I have to find out if there's even a remote possibility of us recapturing what we once had.'

'So when are you off?' she asked, picking up a spoonful of cappuccino froth and putting it in her mouth.

He looked at her for a few moments before answering.

'Tonight. Ten o'clock.'

She put down her spoon and nodded slowly.

'Tonight? But what about the kids? We've got so much explaining to do.'

'They'll be here in ten minutes. I sent Vlad to pick them up from school. It's OK. Don't panic. I know they don't know him. I phoned the school first to explain.'

'God knows what I'm going to tell the police.'

'You don't have to say a word,' he said. 'I'll phone Wim in a few days.'

'What about the business?'

'I thought you had enough on your plate, so I phoned Mitchell and asked him if he'd mind handling the sale. He agreed. Plus he's lent me some money to tide me over. I'm skint since I paid off the overdraft. I hope you don't mind, but I felt more comfortable asking him than you.'

'No, that's OK.'

Suddenly there was a desperate sadness in her eyes.

'Wassup?' he said gently.

'Oh, I don't know,' she sighed. 'I'm worried about how the kids are going to cope with all this. Don't forget Benny's got his exams in a few weeks.'

'And Natalie's got her baptism,' he chuckled.

'Oh, God, don't remind me.' She took a mouthful of coffee. 'Plus I suppose I'm just sad about us,' she said.

'What? That we didn't make it?'

'Yeah . . . that we didn't make it.' She gave a half smile.

He stood up and walked round to where she was sitting. Then he pulled her up out of her seat and held her to him.

'I'll always care about you, you know,' he said.

'Yeah, me too,' she said, tears tumbling down her face. 'Me too.'

He took a ten-pound note out of his wallet and placed it under the stainless-steel sugar bowl. His arm round Beverley's shoulders, they walked to the door. Neither noticed his right tit falling out from underneath his blouse, leaving a trail of socks across the coffee shop floor. Odd socks.

★ ★ ★

They walked back to the day centre car park. It was obvious even from a distance that Vlad was there because the Impala was. As they got closer, they could see Vladimir standing smoking a cigarette next to the ancient white monster with its years-out-of-date New York plates.

'Ah, Myel-vin, my friend, and this must be Beverley. You must not worry. You will soon find new husband. You are very beautiful woman. Here, let me show you. I have photograph of my unmarried brother in Tomsk.' He pulled his wallet out of his back pocket and started searching through it. 'His name is Ivan. Back in Russia he was concert pianist. To tell the truth, he wasn't that good. In fact he was pretty bad . . . so bad the newspapers called him Ivan the Terrible. Good joke, no, Myel-vin? Now he is television repair man. When he began he wasn't so great at that either, but he's getting better. Last year he only blew up three TVs . . .'

Beverley smiled politely.

'Another time, eh, Vlad,' Melvin said. 'We really need to talk to the children now.'

'Sure, Myel-vin. Sure. They're in Impala. I stay outside while you have big family chest-to-chest.'

Beverley and Melvin climbed into the front of the Impala.

'Oh my God,' the children cried as one when they saw Melvin.

'Dad? Is that you?' Natalie gasped, bursting into fits of giggles.

The explaining seemed to go on for ever. First came the story of Melvin's escape in drag. Then Melvin decided to go right back to the beginning and tell the saga of his student relationship with Rebecca and the setting-up of Tower of Bagel. Finally he explained how he thought he was still in love with Rebecca and Beverley told them about her relationship with Tom.

'Oh my God,' Natalie said. 'So you're splitting up?'

Beverley and Melvin exchanged anxious glances and then nodded.

Natalie immediately burst into noisy sobs and Benny started biting his bottom lip to stop the tears.

'Dad is going to New York,' Beverley said gently, 'to see if he and Rebecca can make a go of it, and I need to find out if Tom will still have me.'

'But that means he'll come to live with us,' Benny said. 'Fuck that. I'm not having some strange bloke barging in thinking he can order me about . . .'

'Benny, calm down and listen,' Melvin said, reaching into the back seat of the Impala to hug him. 'I'll always be your dad. Tom will never take my place in that sense. He's a kind, intelligent man, Benny. He wouldn't want to. And I'll phone every day. Promise. And as soon as I'm settled, the pair of you can come to New York and stay.'

Two hours later they were still sitting in the steamed-up Impala while Vladimir carried on smoking and – Melvin couldn't help noticing out of the corner of his eye – intently studying a London A–Z as he waited patiently outside. So his friend really was doing the taxi driver's Knowledge.

Finally, after more tears, hugs and the anticipated adolescent recriminations, the family climbed out of the car and said their final and emotion-charged goodbyes to Melvin. The plan was that Beverley would drive the children home in the Passat and Vladimir would follow in the Impala with Melvin, who was still sectioned and technically a fugitive, hidden under blankets on the back seat. There, Vladimir would collect Melvin's passport and some proper clothes and take him on to Heathrow.

Beverley and the children walked across the car park. Still sobbing quietly, Natalie went on ahead. Benny took his mother's arm.

'If Tom doesn't want to be with you, Mum, me and Nat'll look after you. You know that, don't you?'

''Course I do, sweetheart,' she said, reaching up to plant a kiss on her son's cheek. They'd walked no more than a couple of paces when Beverley heard the soft tinkling of small metallic objects landing on asphalt. Benny stopped dead in his tracks and went instantly red.

'What are they?' Beverley said casually, spotting three of the five fishing weights which had, unknown to her, extracted themselves from the thirty-two-millimetre washer round Benny's penis and fallen down his trouser leg.

'Don't ask me,' he blustered, at the same time gathering up the fishing weights. 'Look like ball bearings. Never seen 'em before.'

'But Benny,' she said, looking puzzled, 'maybe it's my

imagination, but it looked to me like they fell down your trouser leg.'

'Did they?' His red cheeks were now almost purple. He said nothing for a few seconds while he tried to work out what to do next.

'Oh yeah,' he said finally, 'I remember now. I picked them up the other day while we were doing metalwork at school. Must be a hole in my pocket.'

'Oh, right,' she said as she took his arm again and they carried on walking.

It was several days later, when her mind was clearer, that Beverley finally remembered that Benny hadn't done metalwork at school since the third year.

When they got home, it was Benny, still smarting with humiliation, who checked the answer machine in the hall while his mother and Natalie searched the house for Melvin's passport. Thirty seconds later, he came away from the phone. 'Blimey,' he whispered, sitting down with a thump on the bottom stair.

Lettice Allard's message had been a rambling one. She was phoning to inform him of an article which had appeared in that day's *Guardian* Women on male circumcision. It explained, as she gushingly precis-ed it, that far from being seen as a primitive mutilation, male circumcision was now regarded as a major aid to women's health, cervical cancer-wise. Therefore a circumcised knob was becoming an exceedingly cool thing for a man to possess – which was why several of the more politically OK film stars and rock musicians were queuing up for the chop.

'So, anyway,' she had concluded, 'I've kept it for you, so give me a call, and we can, like, share our thoughts on the whole thing, yeah?'

It was all Benny could do to stop himself calling Lettice there and then, but he didn't want to appear too desperate to speak to her. Was he in with a chance after all he had been through, culminating in today's cosmic embarrassment in front of his mother? Or was he reading too much into Lettice's words and seemingly suggestive tone? Whichever way he looked at it, there was one central fact: Lettice Allard, who had never phoned him in her life, had rung up to discuss not merely knobs in general, but his in particular.

He dashed upstairs and proceeded to empty his collection of Homebase washers and spare fishing weights from their hiding place in his ancient piggy bank. Then he opened his window, threw the lot into the bushes below and stuck a single finger up at them in a symbolic gesture of victory.

Beverley kept trying Tom's number until well after eleven, but only got the answer machine.

'Tom, it's me,' she said desperately, every time it clicked on. 'If you're there, please pick up. I must speak to you.'

When he didn't come to the phone, she decided he'd either stopped loving her and never wanted to see her again as long as he lived, or he was genuinely out or away. She hoped and prayed it was the latter.

In the end, just after midnight, she could fight her exhaustion no longer and fell into a deep sleep in which she dreamt about giving birth to triplets fathered by Ivan the Terrible.

She woke just after ten. Even if Tom had come home last night, she reasoned, he would have left by now. She rang his production company in Soho. Bronte, his PA, who Beverley had spoken to several times, said he was filming in London all week. Apparently *The French Lieutenant's Woman* was finished and he was working on a BT commercial. For the next couple of days he was shooting outdoors, in the piazza in front of St Paul's Cathedral.

She spotted the bright lights and white umbrellas from hundreds of yards away. When Beverley arrived on the set, feeling sick with nerves and certain Tom was about to send her packing, he was nowhere to be seen. One of the young runners told her they were taking a break and that Tom had said he was going for a walk.

'How does he seem?' Beverley asked the lad anxiously.

'Tom? Christ . . . Been in a stress all morning. You only have to look at him in the wrong tone of voice and he loses it. Some tart giving him a hard time, I reckon.'

'Probably,' she said, nodding. 'You've no idea where he went, have you?'

'Nah . . . but last time I saw him he was walking towards the cathedral.'

He was inside, she knew he was. He would have remembered the afternoon they sat in the Whispering Gallery, her on one side, him on the other, sending daft messages to each other. He'd gone there to get maudlin. She could feel it.

By now it had started to drizzle. In a few seconds this turned to great sheets of pelting rain. By the time she reached the cathedral steps her freshly blow-dried hair was plastered to her head and dripping water on to her PVC trenchcoat.

A few minutes later, she was climbing the wooden spiral staircase which led to the Whispering Gallery. She thanked the Lord she was only five months pregnant and that it was an easy, gentle climb. She couldn't help noticing how few tourists there were. From time to time, a pair of blubbery American rears would overtake her, but that was about it. Maybe the others had decided to stay on their coaches until the rain stopped.

By now she was beginning to shiver – partly because she was cold and wet and partly because her anxiety about Tom rejecting her was now verging on full-scale panic.

After a couple of minutes she could feel herself starting to feel sick. She stopped, gripped the handrail and took several slow, deep breaths.

'You all right, my dear?'

Beverley turned round to see a concerned-looking sixty-something woman in sensible shoes and a long plastic mac. Behind her were a dozen or so more macs, with leather shoulder bags and Sureshots. Beverley decided they were on an outing from some Women's Institute in the Home Counties.

'Oh, yes, fine,' she said. 'I'm pregnant, that's all. Felt a bit faint.'

'Look, maybe you should sit down and put your head between your knees,' the woman said. 'Or perhaps you need some fresh air. I'll come back down with you if you like.'

'That's really sweet of you,' Beverley smiled, 'but I'll be fine in a minute. Honest.'

'All right. If you're sure,' the woman said reluctantly.

Beverley nodded and the Women's Institute party carried on climbing. Each of the women smiled at her as they passed.

Finally Beverley reached the doorway to the Whispering Gallery. She hovered outside for the best part of a minute. Then she stepped on to the narrow stone walkway which formed the huge circular gallery. The WI ladies were already there, giggling like schoolgirls as they tried to speak to one another from one side to the other. When they saw Beverley, they waved.

Because the place was virtually empty, she spotted Tom immediately. He was on the opposite side, leaning on the wrought-iron railing and staring down into the well of the cathedral. She started to walk towards him. His mind was clearly miles away and he didn't see her coming.

'Hi,' she said softly, tapping him on the shoulder.

His head spun round towards her. There were black shadows under his eyes. He clearly hadn't shaved since she walked out on him.

'Beverley?' There was a question in his voice, as if he doubted his eyes.

'I was when I last looked,' she said, laughing nervously.

'No, I mean, what are you doing here?' he said. 'Are you OK? There's nothing wrong with the baby, is there?'

She shook her head, but no words would come. She leaned on the railing and began looking down.

'How far to the bottom, do you think?' she said eventually.

'Beverley,' he said quietly, ignoring the question, 'please tell me. Why have you come here? What's going on?'

She bit her bottom lip and suggested they sat down. They moved back to the stone bench which ran round the gallery. Then, in a voice that never went above a soft murmur, she blurted out everything that had happened over the last few days.

'So,' she said finally, 'I was just wondering . . . well, more hoping, really . . . if . . . if you would take me back. You know, if we could be together, like you said, and bring up the baby.'

'What?' he gasped softly.

'Right,' she said, 'it's OK. You don't have to say any more. I can understand you wouldn't want me back after the way I treated you. It was unforgivable. I'll go.'

She started to get up, but Tom grabbed her arm and pulled her back down.

'Beverley,' he said, putting his hand under her chin and moving her face towards his, 'of course I want you back. How could I not want you back? I love you, you dope.'

'You do?' she said, looking up at him and blinking.

'Oh yes,' he said, running his hand over her wet hair. As he took her in his arms and kissed her she could feel her relief segue into almighty, entrail-melting lust.

'I just want you to know,' he said when they'd finally

finished, 'that I'm crazy about you, Beverley. I love you and worship you. You are the most important person in my life and I will do anything and everything to make you happy. Beverley, I want to marry you, bring up this child we made and grow old with you. Just promise me you'll never, ever leave me again.'

'I promise,' she whispered, and he started kissing her again.

Beverley heard it first, the unmistakable sound of people clapping. It was tentative and muted, the kind of polite applause which might follow a piano recital held for a select few in a grand drawing room. It seemed to be coming from the other side of the gallery.

'Oh my God,' she said, pulling away from Tom. She turned her head and saw the group of beaming Women's Institute ladies clapping, waving handkerchiefs and giving them the thumbs-up.

Tom looked at the women and then back at Beverley. He was completely bemused. His long blinks of myopic confusion made him look like a contestant in the International Mr Totally Bewildered Competition.

'Sorry, Beverley,' he said, blinking again, 'am I missing something here?'

'Tom, it's the Whispering bloody Gallery,' she said, laughing.

'You mean those women over there . . . they actually . . .?'

His humiliation was such that it rendered him incapable of adding the words 'heard everything'. Instead he touched his ear.

She nodded.

He turned scarlet. Then, almost immediately, he started to grin.

'Oh, sod it,' he chuckled. 'Who cares? Come here, let's give 'em a real thrill.'

He threw the ladies a quick smile and a wave. Then he pulled Beverley towards him again. Very quietly, and in great detail, he began telling her about all the filthy things he was planning to do to her the moment he got her home.

Postscript

Hi-ya! Magazine, October.

RECENTLY VOTED THE NATION'S MOST POPULAR TV PRESENTER, BEVERLEY LITTLESTONE AND HER DIRECTOR PARTNER TOM JAGO OPEN THE DOORS TO THEIR UNPRETENTIOUS FINCHLEY HOME AND INVITE US TO HELP THEM CELEBRATE THE BIRTH OF THEIR BEAUTIFUL DAUGHTER ROSIE . . .

Beverley Littlestone, currently attracting audiences of over five million to her emotion-packed daytime talk show *Beverley!* introduced the newest addition to her family last week when some hundred couples attended a buffet catered by the ebullient super-chef, Gordon Ramsay.

Little Rosie, who was born at London's Portland Hospital two months ago weighing in at a bonny eight pounds three ounces, looked almost edible in Baby Kenzo – 'A present from her godmother, Rochelle,' Beverley was quick to point out. 'I would never buy a baby anything so extravagant.'

Svelte and stunning in an off-the-shoulder black evening dress by Princess Diana's favourite designer, Caroline Walker, Beverley rarely left Tom's side all evening. Although both have been through difficult times in the past, the pair seemed blissfully happy as they took turns holding Rosie and mingled with an eclectic mix of celebrities from the worlds of TV and showbusiness. Chief among these was Lord Lloyd Webber and Beverley's younger sister Naomi Gold. She shocked the nation back in April by announcing her departure from television to 'pursue other interests'.

Naomi and her partner, the world-renowned occultist Fallopia Trebetherick, now divide their time between their witchcraft supplies shop in Cornwall and their £5 million retreat in Tuscany, which once belonged to Mussolini. At the glittering star-studded launch of the Venice Beach, California, branch of their shop last week, the couple, who seem besotted, were still laughing off press reports that Naomi had been sacked by Channel 6.

Naomi and Fallopia will tie the knot at Hallowe'en with a traditional Wiccan wedding ceremony in Tintagel.

The highlight of the evening came when Tom paid fulsome and affectionate tributes to Beverley and his new daughter, whom he described as 'the two most important people in my life'. Then, standing up amid rapturous applause, Beverley made a short speech, during which she saluted four more members of her family.

First to receive lavish praise for her determination and courage was her daughter Natalie, who recently abandoned Judaism and was baptised at a moving ceremony at All Saints, Barnet. A dazzling eighteen-year-old beauty with a list of showbusiness names queuing to romance her, she only had eyes for her long-standing boyfriend, and fellow Christian, Duncan Newbegin.

The second person to be honoured was Beverley's son, Benny, who is now studying for A levels having gained six A stars and three As in his GCSE exams. Benny attended the bash with his gorgeous and cerebral girlfriend, Lettice Allard, on his arm.

The final, and no less heartfelt, toasts went to Naomi and her bride-to-be – and to Beverley's mother Queenie, who is also about to be married. Queenie recently announced her engagement to Leonard Shupak. The couple met at the Sidney and Bessie Hamburger Jewish Day Centre which they both attend. They are planning a spring wedding and are currently flat-hunting in Cliftonville.

Queenie spent much of the evening encouraging people to buy tickets for a quiz night to be held in December in aid of the Finchley and District Mothers of Jewish Lesbians Support Group.

Sadly, Beverley's estranged husband Melvin, with whom she maintains a warm relationship, was unable to attend the bash owing to work commitments.

He is reported to be romancing New York bagel billionaire Rebecca Fludd, who recently separated from her husband Brad. Sources close to the couple, who were sweethearts when they were at university in Nottingham twenty years ago, before Melvin left to pursue his career in the pharmaceutical industry, say the pair are inseparable and plan to marry. The same sources report that Melvin has accepted a position on the board of Tower of Bagel, which would put him at around number fifty on America's list of richest people.

After dinner, Lord Lloyd Webber led guests into the marquee, enchantingly lit with thousands of fairy lights, where he took up his position at the piano to accompany Mr Shupak as he sang 'Always'.

Tom and Beverley then opened the dancing.

Rosie Meadows regrets . . .

Catherine Alliott

Well, what could I say? If he was smitten then I could be too, and I sank back into the whole cosy relationship with a monumental sigh of relief. I didn't have to try too hard, didn't have to be too witty, too amusing, too beautiful . . . It was like landing on a feather mattress after all those years of being Out There.

Three years down the line, however, Rosie's beginning to think that 'cosy' isn't all it's cracked up to be. Bridge parties have never really been her thing, and it would be nice to feel beautiful just once in a while. Enough is enough. It's time to get her life back.

'Alliott's *joie de vivre* is irresistible' *Daily Mail*

'Hilarious and full of surprises' *Daily Telegraph*

'A joy . . . you're in for a treat' *Express*

0 7472 5786 8

HEADLINE

Head Over Heels

Jill Mansell

Jessie has kept the identity of her son Oliver's father a secret for years. She's stunned when she discovers that the man in question, actor Toby Gillespie, has just moved in next door. The truth's about to come out.

One glance at Oliver, and a little mental arithmetic, and Toby has the situation sussed. Meeting the son he never knew he had is the shock of a lifetime. It's a shock, too, for Toby's wife, the beautiful Deborah, though she seems to take it in her stride.

Would Deborah be so relaxed if she knew just how close Toby wants to get to the mother of his firstborn? As the attraction between them flares up again, Jessie just can't see her way to a happy ending. But no one is quite what they seem, and there are more surprises to come . . .

'A light-hearted and likeable tale' *Prima*

'Fast, furious and fabulous fun, to read it is to devour it' *Company*

'Slick, sexy, funny stories' *Telegraph*

'A riotous romp' *Prima*

0 7472 5736 1

HEADLINE

If you enjoyed this book here is a selection of other bestselling titles from Headline